WHAT

No doubt abou̲ ̲ ̲ ̲ ̲ ̲ ̲ ̲ ̲ ̲ ̲ ̲ ̲e̲n̲am,
Marchioness of Rayne̲ ̲ ̲ ̲ ̲o̲n̲e̲ whole day, drove him to
distraction. Oblivious to his man's needs, ignorant of
her own—and yet almost completely uninhibited—she
was any bridegroom's dream.

Henry's nightmare. He rose. "We'll settle this in the
morning."

In daylight, in public.

· She let out a snort of disapproval and headed for his
dressing closet.

He blocked her way, her breasts level with his ribs.
"You can't sleep there." *He* would. *She* should have
the bed.

"There you go again," she said triumphantly.

He must have looked puzzled. He was. He wanted
her closer. He needed her very far away. "What?"

"You're trying to make me do things I don't want to
do."

Irritation ripped him. Of course he was. It was his
castle. He was its lord.

"No, my lady, *this* would be making you do things
you don't want," he said, and pulled her body into his,
lowered his head and claimed her mouth.

THE MAD
MARQUIS

FIONA CARR

LEISURE BOOKS NEW YORK CITY

A LEISURE BOOK®

April 2003

Published by

Dorchester Publishing Co., Inc.
276 Fifth Avenue
New York, NY 10001

ISBN 0-8439-5186-9

Visit us on the web at www.dorchesterpub.com.

In tribute to Sir Winston, Cherie Noire, and Just a Gossip, my teachers and my friends.

With grateful thanks to Sabrina Jefferies, Virginia Kantra, Nancy Northcott and Alicia Rasley.

THE MAD
MARQUIS

Chapter One

From every quarter have I heard exclamations against masculine women, but where are they to be found?
—Mary Wollstonecraft, *Vindication of the Rights of Woman*

Frills and fripperies! Lady Julia Westfall tapped an impatient foot on her father's dance floor. She would have exchanged it all—the bejeweled guests, the fancy dress, the throng of happy tenants—for her beloved stableyard. For muck and clatter and the sweet smell of a hot horse. For large, mute friends who accepted her as she was.

The first wave of company had passed through the receiving line at her family's end-of-summer ball. Her stepmother fussed Julia's silver hairpin into place.

She felt like a plowhorse decked out in ribbons for a fair.

"She's already beautiful, Letitia," said her father, the earl of Wraxham, from his wheeled chair.

"Wishing won't make a nag a winner, Papa," Julia protested.

"We have no nags in Wraxham's stables," he said testily.

Her heart sank. He'd missed the point again. His health declining, he couldn't even decide what to do with his prize horses. *Her* prize horses, if only he would settle them on her. Them, and a competence.

He patted her hand with his bony one. "Your legs are young and light. I'd like to see you dance."

She fingered the heavy lace that chafed her neck. "I have the manners of a donkey, and I'm clumsy as a newborn foal."

He ignored her. "And you must meet with Lord Rayne, my dear."

"Rayne!" Her fiercest competitor on the hunt field and the turf. Her handsomest, too, hard as she tried denying his appeal. Her stomach clenched. "Our Fleur beat his Chance fair and square last week. Did he complain?"

"Not yet, my dear." But his gaze slid away. "Even so, it does concern the horses . . . more or less—"

"Our ball's not the place to bargain over horses, Wraxham," the countess said.

Julia disagreed. Horse trading beat dancing any day. "Which horse, Papa?"

Her father weakly waved a hand. "Well, as to that . . . You must ask Lord Rayne."

"Rayne covets all your horses," she said. And could afford them. The thought stopped her in her tracks. The horses were her life, her reason for being. Breeding, raising, training them was all she did. All she knew. All she was good at.

Her father couldn't sell them off to Rayne. Could he?

"Just hear him this once, my dear," the ailing earl insisted, then closed his eyes on the crowd and on her.

Julia stalked off in search of Rayne, clutching her lemonade. Though champagne by the beaker would suit her better now. She frowned, scanning the great hall for Rayne's tall, lean figure. If he thought to buy up her last five years' work, he had another think coming.

Under a thousand glittering candles, he was nowhere to be seen. Not sitting on the damask chairs that lined the walls. Not lounging by the gilded tables piled high with food and drink. Not moving amongst the band of revelers who danced a vigorous gavotte.

Half a circuit round the room, and no Lord Rayne anywhere.

How very unlike him, she thought.

Her neighbor, Henry Pelham, marquis of Rayne, earl of Seabright, Baron Meeth, was never late for anything.

The Mad Marquis

What to do? She glanced back and saw Rayne standing by her father, chatting. Like the crack shot he was, Rayne drew a bead on her and strode across the room. He sported full fancy dress—his usual snowy white cravat, but a stark black evening coat and skin-tight satin breeches she rarely saw him in.

A damn good thing, she thought, tamping back unwelcome admiration.

She couldn't help assessing him like an equine offering at auction. His ground-covering stride promised speed. His easy carriage boded well for balance over fences. Broad shoulders and a deep chest signaled stamina and heart. The muscles of his iron-hard legs bunched with each nearing stride, bunched and lengthened, and . . . Oh! . . . his private attributes . . .

If Rayne had been a stallion, she'd have bid her last guinea to install him in her breeding shed.

"Lady Julia." Rayne bowed correctly. But he looked rushed. Up close, his ash-brown, short-cropped hair was ruffled and disordered. Disarming.

She pasted on a smile to mask her wandering thoughts. His gray eyes narrowed. "Something amuses you?"

She was blunt by nature, but not that blunt. Her stepmother, when clearheaded, had drilled her on propriety. "It's just that you're rarely late, my lord," she improvised.

A quick tic in his eyelid showed . . . annoyance? Uncertainty? Surely not. He jerked his waistcoat into place, recovering his elegance in an instant.

"Not too late, I hope, my lady, to request the pleasure of a dance."

Flabbergasted, she almost spilled her lemonade. "My style of dancing is not worth your trouble, my lord."

"You are worth my trouble," Rayne said gallantly.

Julia focused on the floor, flummoxed as a schoolgirl by his unexpected notice.

"Lady Julia," Rayne commanded quietly, his fingertips lifting her chin. "Surely the woman I've seen astride a horse can dance." Then he claimed her gaze, deliberate and determined, as before a race.

She shivered, thinking how hard he rode. She'd beaten him in races but couldn't hope to match him here. She'd seen him dance with his late wife, that confection of French womanhood and feminine accomplishments. Julia was all arms and legs and large, un-trained feet.

"They're striking up a waltz," he continued, as the string quartet applied its bows.

"Not the waltz!"

Inescapably his fingers touched her elbow and turned her toward the dance.

"My lemonade, my lord," she objected.

He freed it from her clutch, set it on the nearest console, and steered her toward the dancers. In front of everyone, she balked, suddenly as confused as a green horse under a new rider. A confi-dent rider, with gentle, inspiring hands.

"Truly, Henry, I can't dance," she said desperately. She hadn't used his given name since she'd come out and he'd been elevated to mar-quis.

He didn't even blink at her forwardness. "Come," he said. "All you have to do is follow." His right hand placed her aimless one on his shoulder, then settled at the small of her back.

Her stomach did a little somersault, like a tumble over fences, and she looked up, slightly shocked. His free hand clasped her other one.

"Quite simple," he assured her, and led off gracefully.

She missed her first step. "Quite hopeless."

A corner of his well-shaped mouth fought a smile. "I give green fillies every chance, my lady."

Then he swirled her onto the polished marble, murmuring a cas-cade of simple, clear directions even a dolt could understand. But not necessarily execute. Her legs were long and stupid, and her spine went stiff with self-consciousness. But her partner's eyes were keen and his hand stayed warm and insistent at her back.

Oh, if she could find his rhythm, it would be exhilarating.

She sucked in an uneasy breath and caught a potent mix of soap and starch and brandy.

He whirled her about, a beat behind the music until they made it halfway round the floor. The room grew hotter. Grew smaller and more crowded, with dangerous feet and trailing shawls and elbows everywhere. Hazardous knees, Henry Pelham's knees, which she bumped against and cracked into and almost tangled with. Another turn, and she trod upon his toes.

The Mad Marquis

She cringed.

He grimaced, then commanded softly, "Follow, follow me."

"You know I'm better on a horse," she said crossly, mortified for him to see her utter lack of feminine graces.

"Think of floating over fences then," he persisted, his voice low beneath the violins that pulsed the rhythm of their steps. One, two, three. *One,* two, three. "Think of soft hands, soft mouths."

Oh, lord. He meant a rider's hands, a horse's mouth. But she felt his hands on her, coaxing and secure. She saw his mouth, dipped and bowed, yet firm.

She lost the little rhythm she had found, and slammed into his chest. He caught her up against him. Up against his hips. Up against his privates.

Which—from all she knew of barnyard mating—seemed interested in her. She was flattered until common sense clicked in. Men, like stallions, she reminded herself firmly, were always primed to service any filly in the breeding shed.

In a moment, he set her at a careful distance and spun her about. "Couples talk while dancing, Lady Julia. Think of things to talk about."

"You think I can talk, and not get tangled up?"

"I think you had better," he said grimly.

Perhaps he was right. Though she didn't understand why she should lead the conversation. He was the one who'd come on business. Still, his grace and strength and skill distracted her from dancing. But she racked her brain for anything to shield her from his manliness. Anything at all.

Ah. She cleared her throat. "You were uncharacteristically late, my lord."

He grasped her gambit like a drowning man. "Late? Quite right. Athena foaled, the first by Hazard."

"It's past the season for foaling," she said, trying to sound casual, concentrating on where to place her feet. The mare and her new foal had lost the benefits of summer pasture. It was not the way Julia ran her breeding operation.

One, two, three.

"Athena was old and would not catch," Rayne said more easily. "And the sire's quite young."

"But they're from separate lines." *One,* two, three. His ploy was working.

"Precisely. And the new foal has their every virtue," he said, confident, almost proud.

"Bah! It'll have no speed. You should try line breeding."

"Newfangled nonsense, and no subject for a lady," he said, flatly rejecting her female counsel.

She did not take counsel either. "I never asked to be a lady. If I had my wishes, I had rather be a horse."

He looked down his aristocratic nose, disapproving, his stern black coat and crisp cravat disturbingly close.

"I'm sure your father prefers you to be a lady."

She stumbled, caught herself. "He instructs my stepmother to dress me as one. To no avail, as you can see."

"You might try," Rayne urged.

Odd for him to press for that, she thought. Especially with her shrouded to the throat in tulle and lace, and putting on her best manners. Yes, putting them on. He liked women who were born to them. A quick image of his late and ultra-feminine wife reared up to mock her.

"I am trying," she bit off. "And look at the result."

Distracted by a swell of misery, she crushed his foot. He missed a step, and she stopped cold in the middle of the marble hall, thoroughly put out with her own clumsiness . . . and his insistence that she dance.

"I'm hopeless, my lord! If I cripple you, you'll never race again!"

"We have to talk," he insisted, his voice low and important.

Finally. Horse trading. On this topic, she could hold her own. "Very well then, talk."

He hesitated just a moment. "The library is no doubt free."

She frowned, confused. "We can haggle anywhere."

He frowned in confusion too. "I have permission, Julia."

"Permission?" she asked, feeling suddenly off course. "Permission for what?"

"Our talk," he said, embarrassment crimping his full mouth.

Henry Pelham, neck or nothing 'chaser, ferocious after foxes . . . embarrassed? Over trading horses?

Puzzled, she let him escort her down the hall as her father wished. At the library, Rayne stopped and held the door as courtly as the imaginary lover in her girlish dreams. But she was a girl no longer. And Rayne would never be her lover. She mustered her self-possession and marched in.

For Julia Westfall took her fences no matter what lay on the other side.

Even the loss of all her horses.

"Shall I close it?" he went on considerately. "Or shall we leave a decorous crack?"

"Close it! I'm of age, my lord, as you well know," she said crossly. Twenty-three and counting. Effectively on the shelf. She crossed the room, plopped into a deeply upholstered chair, and sighed. "No one gives a rip about my reputation."

"I might," he said, shutting the door and coming up to her with his quiet, athletic stride.

She felt a sudden need to protect herself from him. "I thought you minded only when my horses beat you."

"That, too," he said reasonably, then frowned at the gaping hearth. With quick, irritated movements, he built a precise pile of faggots, lit kindling off a candle, and blew the whole into a friendly blaze. It gave her much the same view of his strong back and muscled buttocks as when he thundered past her in a race. But they were not now thundering across the downs ahead of a pack of half-drunk county squires and swells.

They were all alone. Unhorsed. Inside. Behind closed doors.

A strange and frankly thrilling sensation fluttered in her stomach. She had almost mastered it when he gave her an assessing gaze.

It thoroughly unnerved her. "So . . . which horse—or should I say, horses—is it?" she stammered.

He made an impatient gesture, then cleared his throat. "Lady Julia. I, ahem, this isn't about your horses. It's about us."

Warning prickled down her neck. "What about us?"

Beneath his light outdoorsman's tan, Henry Pelham flushed. "It's about a match."

"A race?" It wouldn't be their first. But why bring it up tonight?

"Not a race," he amended awkwardly. "A marriage."

"Marriage!" Her heart thumped in her throat. Lightning in the dead of winter would not have surprised her more. "You can't mean you and me."

He nodded, recovering his poise.

Fiona Carr

For one brief moment, she imagined her ungainly self married to this once-upon-a-time object of her fourteen-year-old heart's desire. Her twenty-three-year-old's most secret, unattainable dream. The man was devastatingly handsome, fearless over fences, ruthlessly controlled at any other time. Could he be hers?

Her thoughts galloped wildly into fantasy. But she hugged her filmy shawl around her shoulders and stood up to him. "If this is a proposal, my lord, it lacks all sentiment and charm."

"I have spoken to your father, Lady Julia."

"He did not speak to me." She hoped she didn't sound as stricken as she felt. Her father's deception stung like a branch across her face. But he hadn't consulted her about the horses' future. Why consult her about her own?

Just pass her off to Henry Pelham like chattel. Which, as a woman and a daughter, she was. With no more rights than one of her precious equine friends.

"I have given the notion my most grave, most rational consideration," Rayne went on evenly. "I will do well by you, and you . . . suit me."

"Do well by me? Suit you?" It all sounded so cold-blooded. Anger rose through her hurt and shock. Anger enough to ditch propriety and challenge his confidence. "We're oil and water, fire and ice. Opposites!"

"Complementary, I'd like to think," he said, still calm, still in control.

"Hardly a compliment to me. Really, my lord!" If he'd been a horse, she'd have cuffed him. He wasn't. She couldn't.

"My apology, Lady Julia. I did not mean to mince words with you," he said formally. "You're the most forthright person I know."

She crossed her arms and glared at him. "Yes, and you hate it."

Chapter Two

In the union of the sexes, both pursue one common object, but
not in the same manner. . . . The one should be active and
strong, the other passive and weak; it is necessary that one
should have both the power and the will, and that the other
should make little resistance.
— Rousseau's *Emilius,* from Wollstonecraft's *Vindication of the
Rights of Women*

Taken aback by Julia's intensity, Henry Pelham gentled his voice. "In
this instance I am grateful for your honesty."

She tilted her head distrustfully. "Thank you, my lord. I think."

He studied his prospective bride's handsome face and saw gleaming health and radiant energy. Energy enough to run his household
and manage his baffling daughter. Julia had no flimsy femininity, no
girlish guile. Surely just the facts would bring her round. "I propose
a union between us. Not of the heart, for we both know our hearts
are not involved."

Her high, wide brow furrowed. "So why would you want me?"

Blunt, but refreshing. He owed her truth for that partial truth, at
least. "Because you're young and strong and healthy."

9

"I might as well be a horse!" Her green eyes darkened with sudden understanding, quick offense. "You're marrying me to get the horses."

Bugger all! Wraxham had implied she'd jump at the chance to follow her horses to Pelham Castle. Evidently not. What had looked like a brilliant solution in the bright light of day was awkward.

Damned awkward, given Julia's quick assumption. Encouraged by her father, he'd made the rational choice. "No," he said frankly. "Not for them alone. But they will be your marriage settlement."

"Which makes them yours," she argued.

"True, but better mine than sold to strangers."

Her face pinched with betrayal. "Father wouldn't do that."

Henry didn't know what Wraxham might do, but he hated to see Julia building castles in the air. "He could."

She frowned in defiance. "I eat, sleep, breathe, live those horses. They're my life."

Her weakness was his opportunity. "Then marry me, and secure them."

"Have you ever seen a happy marriage, my lord? I have not."

He had imagined one. Once, when he was younger and naive. "Marriage is an accommodation to family and society. Moreover, it is women's lot."

"Not according to Mrs. Wollstonecraft," she said with conviction.

That free-thinking virago? Henry almost recoiled. He diverted Julia with the cold, hard facts. "Your father's dying, my lady. And you'll be left here under your brother. I don't suppose Mrs. Wollstonecraft approves of dependent spinster sisters."

"Of course not . . ." Julia began.

"You could move in with the dowager countess," he pointed out. But the mere suggestion felt a little cruel. Rumor had it Julia's opium-loving stepmother was moody and exacting.

Julia shuddered.

"Or you could befriend your brother's wife."

Julia winced. "I don't see how."

Henry almost softened when he saw her confidence fade. For once, she looked feminine, biddable, everything he intended to avoid. But he'd come on a mission. Much as he wanted the horses and needed a marchioness, his daughter simply had to have a mother. An energetic young woman of good family and healthy turn of mind . . . a counterbalance to his dotty great aunt and daft uncle.

"I hear Cordrey cannot keep a governess for your nephews. I've no doubt you have the spirit. There are how many—five?"

"Six. Six hellions," she admitted. "But this is beside the point. My father could have settled my future easily enough. I asked him to give me the horses and a competence. He promised to consider it."

Henry took a poker to the fire, the air heavy with the disappointing news. Wraxham's secrecy did not make Henry look good either. "He appears to have thought better of it."

"And worse of me." Tight-lipped, Julia put her fist to her mouth as if to stifle . . . a sob?

Henry had the oddest feeling he should offer comfort, he, who had taken it away. But she looked as if a touch would make things worse. So he merely stood. Reason, sweet reason, should settle her down. "Loving papas don't thrust their daughters out into the world alone, Julia, no matter how strong and capable they are."

"It doesn't feel like love."

Love was not his best subject, especially not after his own father's remote, neglectful rule. "Your father's mind seemed quite made up to me. My mind is, too."

Mutiny darkened her fine green eyes.

"Oh, bugger all, Julia. It's your most practical option."

"Exactly how many horses am I worth?"

Damnation. Wraxham had put him in a spot. He'd put himself in a spot. "It wasn't like that," he said firmly.

"How many?" Then she sighed heavily. "The brood mares, surely?"

She was yielding. Henry nodded, careful not to show relief. "Absolutely."

"The colts and fillies?"

"The promising ones," he assured her, imagining how badly she needed to know.

"The racing stock?"

"The prime goers, yes. The heavy hunters, cobs, and carriage horses stay."

She frowned, recovering her spirit. "What about my pony, Fidget?"

"You can't have them all, Julia."

"Fidget babysits the weanlings."

11

"Don't expect your father to strip your brother clean. Cordrey will have the title to uphold and an estate to pay for."

Her chin lifted stubbornly. "Fidget was my pony."

Henry relented. It was hardly sporting for her brother, father, and bridegroom to have the upper hand in everything. "I'll get you the pony, then."

"You will? Thank you for that." She looked surprised, even pleased, but only for a moment. "Did you discuss Meteor?" she asked anxiously. The stallion was Wraxham's prize stud, the linchpin in his breeding program.

"Top of the list. He comes with you."

"You mean I come with him," she corrected.

Henry would not take the bait. "I've never seen you missish."

Her eyes flashed, but she was too proud to pitch a fit. "Then, my lord—so I won't seem missish—perhaps you'd better explain exactly what you want of me."

He rested an elbow on the marble mantle. "I want you to be my wife, the marchioness of Rayne," he said, deliberately bland while his insides churned. So much was riding on his offer. An offer that would make for better lives for all concerned—aging aunt, troubled daughter, fractious bride. But Julia was challenging him on every point. She wasn't ladylike. She wasn't feminine.

And he wasn't supposed to admire her for it.

Julia seethed. How could the man stand there, handsome, lean and rational, when her nerves were raw and her pride trampled?

"What exactly are my duties?" she asked as calmly she could.

"They will be the usual for a wife in your new station," he said mildly. "Command of the castle, public functions, private charities. Hostess for country weekends and the odd county ball. You needn't worry—"

But she did. She was a domestic disaster. "I mean my duties with the horses."

"Naturally, you will ride to hounds. And you may visit the stables whenever you see fit," he added.

"*Visit* the stables? I spend my life there." Defiance surged through her, and hurt. For a moment she had truly wanted to marry him, but not if he denied her everything.

He had the gall to smile. "Not anymore, my dear. It was a handsome sacrifice, Julia, while your father was ailing and needed your assistance there. My marchioness need not be my stable hand."

"I have *never* been a stable hand," she said with quick wrath. "I run the stables here, as you know, and I do it extremely well. To say nothing of the fact that I love my work. Why would I give that up to marry you?"

"I could buy the lot outright and leave you here," he pointed out.

"What's to stop you?" she asked bluntly.

One of his carefully placed logs toppled, and a shower of sparks crackled in the hearth. "Meteor's not for sale. Some nonsense about . . ." He lifted his hands in a gesture of defeat. "Bloody hell, Julia. Your father thinks you're the only one can manage him."

"I am the only one."

Rayne scowled, unbelieving. "He won't let him go without you."

"He shouldn't let any of them go without me."

Rayne's left eye ticked. "My stable, Lady Julia, is second to none."

"Your stable perhaps. But not your racing record. That's why you came to me."

"After your father proposed it, yes. It seemed a reasonable offer. Mind you, any other way, you lose them all. And I lose, too. So . . ." He recouped losses, elegance, control. "Lady Julia, will you marry me?"

Julia fingered her useless shawl. Marriage was far from the independence she had pushed for. And yet even though it hurt that he didn't want her as a woman . . . marriage to Rayne was not the worst of the courses that lay before her. As he made clear, he was her best prospect. With him, she could escape her stepmother's capricious rule and stand free of her brother's burgeoning brood.

In their place, Rayne offered a family she could manage—an aunt, an uncle, and a pretty little girl. The best of all, her horses would be crossed with Rayne's! She'd have great fat mares in foal. And her colts and fillies—her children, really—would be winning on the flat and over fences.

The heady feeling of successes yet to come almost stole her breath. "Julia," he prodded.

"I'm thinking about it. Seriously thinking about it."

"So we're agreed." He wasn't even asking.

She cast off the shawl. "If we can come to terms. I supervise the breeding, foaling, and the training."

A corner of his mouth turned down with displeasure. "A woman in charge? I think not."

She glared at him. No way would she abandon her horses to new stalls, strange grooms, unfamiliar paddocks, and Henry Pelham's rigid training. "My father entrusted me with the entire operation— selecting mares for breeding, overseeing foaling season, backing the green colts and fillies—"

"And racing, Lady Julia? Did he knowingly let you run wild?"

"He sent me to the races."

"You gave him full reports," Rayne said dryly.

Hours' worth, sitting at his bedside, night after night, his only evening's entertainment. Her brothers had long since fled the strictures of the earldom and the caprices of their father's second wife. "Every flat race, hedge, and timber."

"You gave him a true report of the races you, yourself, have ridden?" Rayne prodded.

"Oh, those. Jem Guthrie was injured."

"You could have hired jockeys."

She could have. She didn't. "None who ride as well as I."

Rayne pushed away from the fireplace, forbidding in his aristocratic bearing. "My marchioness cannot race horses," he said flatly.

"You allowed the hunt, my lord."

"Naturally. But racing is dangerous. And for a marchioness, downright eccentric."

"Surely, there's room for an eccentric marchioness at Pelham Castle."

Irritation flicked across his face, a fissure in his iron control. "No, madam. Another scintilla of peculiarity in my eccentric household, and it would tilt into the sea."

"Horsefeathers." His gravity was almost laughable; his concern was not. "Your aunt manages your castle and wears old-fashioned dresses. And your uncle is an expert on exotic animals."

Rayne gave her a look of utter disbelief. "My aunt is positively dotty, and Uncle Bertie's obsession with his menagerie worsens by the day."

She did laugh then, uneasily. "You hardly recommend your household, my lord."

His sharp cheekbones flushed. "I counted on the reputation of my stables to recommend me, and . . ." For an amazing instant, he looked vulnerable.

"And . . . ?"

"Your compassion. My daughter needs a mother's guiding hand."

Her heart twisted painfully. He wanted her for his horses and for his little girl. For anyone but who she was.

She'd bite her tongue off before admitting just how much that hurt. "I'm better with fillies, my lord."

"Isabeau is not a horse," he said tautly. "She's a confused, lonely little girl."

"Surely a bracing draft of salt sea air—"

"She's too delicate for that. She needs a woman's touch, a mother's care."

Julia felt his gaze assessing her in her figured silk, lace up to her throat, useless slippers on her great large feet. As if the person he saw, tricked out in feminine finery tonight, could be that woman, that mother. *Oh Henry,* she thought miserably, *these are only clothes, and not my choice.* She stood in best for jockeys, not for mothers.

"Perhaps she needs a father's love," Julia suggested.

A muscle in his jaw rippled. "She has that, Julia, never doubt it," he said grimly. "But like you, she lost her mother far too young. I'm counting on you to help her, understand her."

How? When she didn't understand herself? Julia hadn't felt so exposed since she last fell into a stream, horses and riders vaulting over her, leaving her behind, wet and cold and feeling stupid. "I know nothing of girls."

His brow knotted. "Not to belabor the obvious, but you were one. And so should sympathize."

"I do." In a general sort of way, she thought glumly. It was hard to say whether her girlhood had been so painful because she'd been a hoyden or because she'd lost her mother. And it was folly to hope that her stepmother's example taught her how to meet the needs of a little girl. "But with children, my lord, truly, I go all fumble fingers. I lack a mother's . . . instinct."

Unexpectedly, his expression softened, and his voice too. "Do you not wish for children?"

Mutely, she shook her head. She was not prepared to make such an intimate disclosure tonight. But the man proposed to marry her, and so deserved the truth. She'd never wanted children. If he retracted his offer, and with it, her future with her horses, so be it.

She owed him that.

"Why would I wish to prove myself a wretched failure?"

His gray gaze warmed, and a kind smile crinkled the crow's feet at the corners of his eyes. "Lady Julia, you never failed at anything you set your mind to in your life."

It might be a compliment, but given what he asked, she was not flattered. "I couldn't handle the horses as well as any children we might have."

He smiled with evident relief. "Then there you are. No children."

"You don't want them either?"

His gaze shuttered. "Don't want them, cannot have them."

Henry Pelham couldn't have children? She looked up and down his fit, rangy body in disbelief. He was so obviously . . . male, so obviously . . . potent. "You have a daughter. Can you not now . . . ?"

Her suitor blanched again. "Of course I can," he bit off. "But adding to my family would be rash."

"Rash to have an heir?"

"Precisely. Rash. Ill-advised. Irresponsible to perpetuate the family madness. Particularly when there is a saner branch to pass the line onto."

Julia sank into the deeply upholstered leather chair, perplexed. Time out of mind, the Raynes' and Wraxhams' property lines had marched along together. Her family was known for ploddingly dull accomplishments, plows and politics, but Rayne's for admitted eccentricity—a mad inventor, half a dozen zealous scholars of obscure knowledge, antiquarians fixated on silver plate, ancient coins, and odd bones. That lopsided castle was evidence, too, she supposed, of something amiss about its builders, and rumor had it that the late marquis's death was not an accident.

Even so . . . "The family has hidden its madness rather well, I think."

"Not from me," he said, a dark hint of self-censure in his voice.

"Surely, you don't think yourself mad!" she burst out.

He clasped his hands behind his back. "I have myself well under control, thank you very much."

"Indeed you do, my lord," she hastened to assure him. "I've never seen the slightest sign of anything mad about you. Why, you're the fiercest competitor in five counties. You never stand down from a challenge. You fear no danger. You're obsessed with winning."

"You've just painted me as an outright fanatic," he said harshly.

"Rubbish! If you're mad, I'm mad, too."

16

"All the more reason for us to have no children, Julia," he said, in his authoritative way. "My cousin, Erskine, *archdeacon* cousin Erskine, will restore the line to sanity."

She was shocked. Henry meant to have no children? She didn't want them either. And yet . . . now that he'd actually offered marriage—Lord Rayne himself, of all impossible imaginings!—not having children didn't sit right with her. She smoothed her skirts and marshaled her thoughts. Children meant pregnancy—and no riding. Pregnancy meant months of confinement stranded on a sofa—and no riding. Childbirth followed, and weeks of healing—and no riding—then months of nursing, and a lifetime of responsibility, self-sacrifice, and demands.

Because if she did have children, she would never abandon them to the loneliness she'd endured under her stepmother's fickle care.

She looked up. He was watching her intently, his iron-gray eyes penetrating her very thoughts.

"No children, my lord. I quite agree," she said evenly, but with the subtle, sinking feeling of something dreadfully amiss.

Again he took the poker to the fire. "And so, no marital relations," he said, almost casually.

Her body went hot and cold, and her breath hung in her chest. She didn't want that either, did she? She didn't want children, so she couldn't want to do the one thing that made them, could she? But it hurt. Once, in a girlish way, she'd thrown her heart after Henry Pelham. With effort, she'd reined it back. She could do so again. But this casual, calculated rejection hurt like a tumble onto rocks in a stone-strewn field.

"No children, no . . . marital relations. Why marry at all?" she asked.

"For Isabeau, for Meteor."

Just as she suspected. Not for her, herself. Evidently she repelled him. Probably she always had, she thought, her heart wilting with rejection. She forced herself to stand and face him. "Providing a mother for your daughter is no reason to wed a woman you hold in obvious contempt."

He rose too fast and hit the marble mantel. Wincing, he said roughly, "I never held you in contempt, Julia. Or I would not ask you to be my bride."

Filling with old pain, she gathered herself up. "I know they call

17

me Horse-face." As a girl, Julia Horatia Westfall's brothers had dubbed her Horse-face. The grooms had too, behind her back, but could not keep it secret. Nor could the men she'd raced and beaten.

Rayne rolled his eyes. "I never called you that. This is not about that."

"I would not want to bed a tall, mannish, horse-faced woman either," Julia said, her voice trembling.

"You just said you don't want children," he reminded her firmly. But he did not contradict her portrait of herself, she noticed, her heart sinking in the mire of her brief, dashed hopes.

"There are . . . preventatives, are there not? Nothing to stop you but an aversion to me." Even as she spoke, she wondered why lovemaking, and with Henry Pelham, suddenly seemed the most important thing in the world to her.

"Prophylactic measures, as they're called, don't work," he said harshly.

To cover up some hurt? "You mean Isabeau—"

"—was an accident," he finished for her, a fierce glint in his eyes. "If you ever breathe a word of this to her . . ."

"I would never!"

"Isabeau is precious."

"Whereas I am not. Face it, my lord. You want the horses, not me. Once you get them, I will be in your way," she said, careful not to show how much it hurt.

Suddenly Henry Pelham's large strong hands clasped her shoulders, gently cupping them. "Trust me, Julia. I've admired you since you were a little girl haranguing Squire Purvis about starving his hounds. But if you want children, you had better tell me now, and I'll cry off. Because on this one point, I will stand firm. I will not risk an heir, for the future of the marquisate. A gamble, whether you or any other woman is my bride, I must not hazard."

Henry Pelham had never been a liar. His hands steadied her, and his eyes held her gaze. She pushed back disappointment. "As long as that is clear between us."

"Few couples share the marriage bed for long, Julia. For our class, marriages are conveniences, and friendly tolerance a worthy goal."

She preferred his reassuring clasp. "We've always been friends."

"Yes, for a very long time," he said quietly.

"Nevertheless, you're marrying me to get the horses."

18

He pressed his lips in consternation, then said, "If it weren't for my daughter's needs and your father's bloody horses, I wouldn't marry anyone at all. But once he proposed it . . . I thought you're the only woman I might come to terms with."

Was there a buried compliment in what he said? If so, it seemed a risk to trust it. "The only woman desperate enough."

"The only woman practical enough."

"As proposals go, my lord, yours lacks passion."

"Because this marriage is not about passion," he said through gritted teeth.

Then why did his warm hands still hold her? She looked down to the left and then the right, observing them. His blunt-tipped nails were filed and clean where hers were stained and jagged. His beautiful hands were shapely, sinewy, strong.

He stripped them away from her, but a glance showed turmoil in his eyes. Was he backing down? Could he feel desire?

She felt a little desperate. She felt a little bold. But she was not without resources. She crossed her arms below her breasts, plumping them up beneath the revealing lace that veiled her chest and throat.

His nostrils flared, and she felt an unaccustomed surge of power. *Not so indifferent after all, my lord, and not so controlled.* She shifted toward him slightly.

"Julia . . ." he warned.

But she had him thinking. *Feeling.* She tilted her head and pursed her lips to provoke him further. "I've never been kissed. Why should I marry a man who won't even kiss me?"

With a sigh of annoyance, he bent his head and gave her cheek a cool, dutiful peck.

"My brothers have kissed me, my lord," she said scornfully. And she'd seen how differently her brothers kissed their young misses and coquettes. Rayne's kiss wasn't even close to that.

He scowled severely. "Kisses are—"

"—no part of the business arrangement, I know," she finished for him. Then she launched herself into Henry Pelham's arms, glad for once in her life to be as big as a man and really good at staying just one step ahead of large, unruly stallions.

Because she caught him off guard.

He struggled for balance, his arms embracing her, his stance compromised by her weight and his surprise. An instant before he gained control, she planted her mouth on his.

His lips were surprisingly full, unexpectedly warm, and entirely uncooperative.

She pulled away, an inch or two, and opened her eyes. He was glaring at her, maybe just a little shocked. That was better. Now, for a challenge a betting man like Henry never could resist.

"If I were a man, I bet I'd do better."

She saw that angry tic in the corner of his eye.

"But you're not a man, my lady, are you? You're a hot little filly playing with fire."

A big step up from Horse-face Westfall, she thought, so pleased she almost lost her edge. Almost. "I'm not burned yet."

A muscle in his strong jaw tensed.

"I'm going to regret this," he said roughly, his warm breath moist with brandy and forbidden knowledge. Then he inclined his head toward hers and engaged her mouth with his.

Tenderness, Julia mused dreamily, long moments later as the kiss continued. She hadn't expected tenderness from Henry Pelham. Or such a depth of concentration. She hadn't counted on being subsumed by his heat. She never would have guessed his kiss could turn her knees to pudding.

Or that kisses could go on this long.

And on and on. Exploring, testing. Angling his mouth against her. Nibbling her lower lip. He groaned with something very much like pleasure, a sound she knew well from the breeding shed.

Henry, she was thinking. *Henry. How could you give this up?*

How could she?

Out of nowhere, unwanted and unasked, she heard her own high sigh.

He pulled back abruptly. "Satisfied now?" he rasped.

No. Her mouth felt swollen, her blood raced, and her stomach had dipped and soared as if she'd just cleared the most fearsome obstacle of the 'chase. She wanted more—more time, more heat, more of his consuming tenderness, more of his fierce control.

But not tonight, not in her father's house, hot on the heels of her suitor's too-cold, too-practical proposal.

"That will do for a start," she said tartly, hiding her sharp hurt, her quick panic. If Henry Pelham ever wanted more, she would surrender in an instant. If he demanded less—she realized for the first time since her girlhood crush—he could break her heart.

He eased away from her and, with both fists, jerked down on his vest to straighten it. She watched, amazed to glimpse the bulge of an obvious erection, startled to detect a tremor as his fingers buttoned his waistcoat. Did he want her? Did he not? Then she lifted her gaze to his face and found a vulnerable regard he'd never ever let her see. He wanted her. If he just would allow it.

In seconds, he masked it ruthlessly. "Don't push me, Julia," he said harshly. "I cannot guarantee control."

She didn't want him controlled. She wanted him as rattled as she was. But she wanted the right to her life—her horses—more. The right to escape the petty tyrannies of her childhood home. The right to be the woman she could best be.

She blinked at him, feeling a perfect fool for throwing herself at him, for being turned away. "So we're agreed," she said stubbornly.

He clasped his hands behind his back, donning formality like armor. "Count yourself well kissed, Lady Julia Westfall, and count yourself betrothed."

And he stalked out of the library, leaving her to the little fire he'd built and the unexpected tumult of her heart.

Chapter Three

While girls are yet young, they're in a capacity to study agree-
able gesture, a pleasing modulation of voice, an easy carriage
and behaviour; as well as to take the advantage of gracefully
adapting their looks and attitudes to time, place, and occasion.
—Rousseau's *Emilius,* refuted in Wollstonecraft's *Vindication*

Nine o'clock sharp. But nothing else about his wedding day was
going as he'd planned, Henry fumed. He galloped Hazard up the
avenue to Wraxham Hall in a whipping wind. The sky was gray and
ominous, and he held little hope that the weather would improve.
He'd wanted something simple, something quick.

Archdeacon Erskine Pelham, cousin, family adviser, and friend,
concurred. So much so that he'd come down from London to assist
in the formalities and help keep everyone in line. Their joint effort
was failing miserably.

For the massive black and gilt family carriage, pulled out for state
occasions, rumbled along behind Henry.

Aunt Augusta had insisted.

Uncle Bertie would settle for no less.

Isabeau had burst into tears. For all Henry knew, she'd cried the entire eleven furlongs from Pelham Castle to Wraxham's ancient limestone chapel where he would marry Julia today. Isabeau didn't want to go for a carriage ride on such a dreadful, dreary day. She didn't want a new dress, not even one with ice-blue ribbons that circled her waist and trailed to the ground and matched her weepy eyes.

And she especially didn't want a new mother.

He should have introduced her to Julia first, he admitted reluctantly. He'd had a month, during which time he'd limited seeing Julia to two strained visits. On the first he'd given her her engagement present, his mother's and grandmother's and great-grandmother's in perpetuity, an ornate diamond necklace with a giant sapphire cabochon dangling from its coils.

Dressed for the occasion, Julia had tried it on. It nestled cozily—seductively—on the lace that barely veiled the tempting mounds of her breasts.

He'd fled, resolving to avoid temptation. The innocent ardor of her kiss had already cost him sleep. He'd returned only yesterday to organize moving the horses to Pelham Castle. To his relief and disappointment, she'd worn an everyday riding habit, severely tailored and buttoned halfway up her throat. Which boded well for their promised celibacy, if ill for his composure. Her habit's snug fit to her horsewoman's curves was a good bit more alluring than he'd ever allowed himself to notice when she was just his fiercest competition.

The carriage rounded the avenue, its wheels throwing up fine gravel as it pulled up in front of Wraxham House. The golden stones of its Palladian façade glistened in the damp. Cousin Erskine followed well behind in the light trap that carried him round London on his clerical duties.

Henry reined in his mount, handed it to a waiting groom, and watched the carriage lumber to a halt. He should see to his family, but cousin Erskine was already moving to help them out.

Julia's relations lined the steps of her ancestral home: the earl, frail in his wheeled chair, and the countess in black lace. Lionel Westfall, Viscount Cordrey, heir apparent and Henry's brother-in-law to be, had assembled his pinch-faced spouse and stair-step brood of half a dozen boys, the youngest in leading strings. Cordrey walked down the steps to Henry.

"Rayne," he said, as affable as a man married to a witch could be. "Neighborly of you to take in our troublesome sister."

Henry tensed, then recalled his boyhood friend's ironic nature. "Doubtless the horses will compensate," he replied in kind.

Cordrey laughed, but Henry anxiously moved to take his motley band in hand. Uncle Bertie, tall and gaunt, unfolded himself from the carriage first, his dapper gray parrot on his shoulder. Henry clamped down on an urge to wring its neck. Exactly what he did not need—Raj, cursing in Hindi, over the wedding vows. Henry had all but ordered his daft uncle to leave the blasted beast at home, but the pair were inseparable.

"Don't worry, Henry. Where there's a spot of trouble, Raj always oils the wheels," Uncle Bertie had said sunnily, doubtless already planning to sneak the bird into the carriage.

In moments, Bertie was helping Great Aunt Augusta master her voluminous, old-fashioned skirts. Pressing toward the narrow door, she shrieked when skirts and crinolines billowed up behind her. They filled the cab and threatened to dislodge her precarious powdered wig. Raj screeched and flapped his wings, and Isabeau squealed. Aunt Augusta twisted round to silence her, and her skirts ballooned out the door.

Chaos and madness, his family's stock in trade. Grimly, Henry watched the familiar spectacle. Not even cousin Erskine, sane to the diamonds of his clerical rings, was immune. He'd struggled into the carriage to assist the family out of it. Henry had a momentarily amusing image of the elegant, black-frocked archdeacon under siege from Aunt Augusta's skirts.

"Careful, Aunt!" Uncle Bertie yelped, but his squawking bird kept him from lending a hand.

"Careful yourself, Albert, and watch out for your niece!" Aunt Augusta poked her powdered curls out the door and cried, "Henry! Henry! Your daughter needs you! On the other side!"

Clucking like one of his menagerie hens, Uncle Bertie set about extricating his aunt and her skirts from the carriage's cramped cab and through its narrow door. Leaving his elders to their usual harum-scarum ways, Henry hurried to the near side door, arms up to his daughter. *"Voila, ma petite,"* he said, deploying her mother's French with a cheer he did not feel.

Isabeau shrank into the coach's velvet shadows. Top hat askew,

Erskine left her to Henry, as he followed their aunt out the other side.

Isabeau's voice was reedy with distress. "Will you still be my pappa if you marry?"

His heart squeezed. She needed another mother, not a fear of losing him. "*Toujours, mignon.* Always," he reassured her.

Footsteps crunched behind him. Cordrey, he thought, come to lend a hand he did not need.

Misery ravaged Isabeau's pale face. "But will you still *love* me?"

He mounted a step and reached into the shadows for her hand. It was wet and cold. "More than ever," he said earnestly. "More than anyone."

She scooted reluctantly across the seat, blue eyes widening as she peeked over his shoulder. "Is that *her?*"

It had to be Julia—he knew before he looked. What other woman in the county would flaunt tradition and show herself before her wedding? Worse yet, now, with Isabeau in tears and his family at its bedlamite best.

"*Sans dout, cherie,*" he managed to say evenly, fighting rising aggravation. "But let's get you out of here."

Backing out with his delicate burden in his arms, Henry found the pebbled ground with one foot, then the other. Braced, he took his daughter's slender body in his arms, out of the carriage and down.

He turned to see Julia, outrageously still in her riding habit on her wedding day. Had she missed the part about becoming his marchioness? Evidently.

Windblown, rumpled, she smiled past him at his daughter. "You must be Isabeau," she said in the comforting tone he knew she used with panicky colts. "I'm very pleased to meet you."

Isabeau's chin jutted out. "I don't want another mother."

"Isabeau!" he admonished her. What had Aunt Augusta told her?

"Well, she's not my mother!"

Julia smiled harder, as determined as if she was at a race. He'd always admired her fortitude.

"Of course I'm not, dear," she said. "But this afternoon, after your father marries me, I'll be your new stepmother."

Isabeau's kneecap dug into his ribs. "Stepmothers are wicked."

"Isabeau, enough of that!" he scolded, steaming, certain now Uncle Bertie had been telling tales again.

"Problems, nephew?" Mobcap askew and bell-like skirts abobbing, his great aunt peered around the towering rear wheel of the carriage.

"None at all," he smoothly covered up. Why make matters worse on his wedding day? "Will you take Isabeau?"

Augusta Pelham put out her hand, and he passed Isabeau to her great-great-aunt. He'd deal with his daughter's fears after he greeted his bride.

Uncle Bertie bowed gallantly and took Augusta's elbow. "Ladies," he intoned, "this way." Lip protruding, Isabeau cast her father a baleful glance. With Raj clinging to his shoulder, a laughing Albert escorted his charges up the stairs to meet and greet the in-laws and astound prospective nephews with new tales.

Henry was not laughing. A prickling sensation heated up between his shoulders. Julia's glare. He pivoted. She was frothing at the bit.

"Really, my lord, abandoning your daughter," she tossed over her shoulder, crunching across the gravel driveway toward the granite stairs.

Henry grabbed her hand and pulled her back behind the carriage, counterattack his only option. "I'm giving my attention to my wife."

"Not wife yet, my lord."

He let his gaze travel down the neat fit of her habit. "Yes, your riding habit shows how enthusiastic you are about your wedding."

"How I dress is not the point. Your daughter would prefer me dead," she hissed, angry enough to upbraid him, though apparently unwilling to shout it to the world. "I should have met her sooner, not today. I would have come to her if you had given me the slightest encouragement to do so. Instead, she sees me as a perfect stranger. An interloper."

"The woman I choose to be my wife is not an interloper."

"Isabeau thinks so. She was practically in tears!"

For his timid daughter, tears constituted a revolt. But if Julia saw them sympathetically, he would not protest. "She'll come around. Girls are flexible."

"When did you first tell her? Yesterday?"

He hadn't the foggiest notion. For all of Aunt Augusta's deficiencies with the child, she had a better handle on her, so he'd left it up to her. But he didn't want his contentious bride thinking he didn't care about his daughter. Not when they would say their marriage vows in, oh, about two hours.

"Better a day than a month of misery. She's easily upset."

"I'm the one upset. Isabeau is confused."

"Naturally," he said. "She's a little girl."

But Julia had the bit between her teeth. "You should have assured her I will be a good stepmother."

He hadn't. He should have. He hadn't even thought to. "You'll have years to prove yourself to her. This was my decision."

"About as sound a decision as racing a horse without warming him up. It's a recipe for injury."

He tamped down a hot retort. "I'm sure you'll succeed."

"No thanks to you. I can hardly believe you sprang this on her yesterday. She must think I'm nothing more to you than the odd horse picked up at an auction."

Despite her censure, Julia sounded hurt. "Isabeau can see you're not a horse." Then it struck him she'd overheard him tell Isabeau he loved her. Good God, Julia couldn't be jealous. Couldn't be hoping he would fall in love.

"About what I said," he began, ignoring a burst of laughter from the families on the stairs.

She gave him a blank look. "What you said?"

"That I love Isabeau more than anyone."

Julia recovered everything—height, dignity, boldness. "I should hope so. And I should hope that you would show it. But if you expect me to be any kind of mother to that little girl, you should be a proper father."

He clamped down on the rage that shot through him. "I've clothed, fed, and provided for her in every possible way. Protected her, coddled her. If you think I'm going to change my ways just because I'm marrying you today, you can walk right up those stairs to Wraxham House and kiss your horses goodbye."

She bridled, then dipped her head, yielding.

"Just so we understand each other," he said. "What's mine is mine—my daughter, my horses, and you if you choose to go through with this. And I take care of everyone always."

She gave the oddest, stiff, consenting curtsy he had ever seen. He took it for concession. With every appearance of composure and conciliation he could muster, he led her across the gravel, up the stairs, and handed her to her family's keeping.

Start as you mean to go on, Henry reminded himself an hour later. It had been his old horse master's ruling principle, and he had made it his. *Firmness, consistency, and clear commands.* If Dubois's methods worked for fractious fillies, they'd have to do for a headstrong bride.

Still, as Julia's relations assembled in Wraxham's tiny limestone chapel, Henry worriedly paced the rector's narrow robing room. Where was his family? He'd lost track of them, except for Erskine, who'd come to his side to witness the signing of the papers. That was relieving, in a day when nothing else was.

Since dropping his family off under Wraxham's stony portico, he'd been closeted with the earl, negotiating for the blasted pony, which he'd almost forgotten to add to the marriage settlement. The earl wanted it for his grandsons. But promises were promises. Especially to a man's new bride. In the end Henry had won out and signed the final papers, grateful the ailing earl had plied him with a fine, aged whiskey.

It helped him push back second thoughts, thoughts Erskine had seconded last night over port. "Women want children, old man," he'd said, slipping out of his worldly wise and witty London character, and donning the cloak of earnest family advisor. "All women. Why else d'you think the wife has presented me with a quiverful of the little arrows? Enough to impoverish a country parson. And send me scrambling for advancement."

"Not Julia. The horses are her children. She made that plain enough."

"What if she likes . . ." his chiseled Pelham features had flushed ". . . ahem, marital relations."

"She doesn't," Henry had said hastily. That was more than he meant to say, even to Erskine. And besides, it wasn't true. Wedding nerves shot all to hell. He cleared his throat. "I mean, she won't. We agreed to a marriage of convenience."

"Some women do . . . ahem . . . *like* it, no matter what they say beforehand," Erskine said with delicate pastoral concern. He not only held the family sanity, he was its exemplar of tact.

"Then it's up to me to hold the course."

Erskine had clasped his shoulder warmly. "All best, then, old man."

He might as well have said, *I hope you know what you're doing.*

Did he, Henry asked himself now, in the rector's robing room.

Why the devil had he settled on Julia? A woman with a temper, with ideas, with too much appeal. But also, he reminded himself, with a caring heart and healthy energy and no romantic notions. Unless he remembered that extraordinary kiss. That aberration of a kiss. Once wed, they would settle into a proper, dispassionate partnership with him in charge, his daughter in good hands, and Wraxham's horses in his stable. All in all, he should be pleased.

Angry whispers spiked through the heavy drapery.

"I say, Julia. It's not the done thing." It was Cordrey, his hushed voice no doubt ricocheting off the chapel walls for all to hear.

Henry stiffened.

"I'll see my husband when and where I please," Julia whispered vehemently.

Had he thought her proper? Dispassionate? She was a willful wench. Best to take her in hand now. "I'll see her," he murmured. He lifted back the curtain.

"She's all yours," Cordrey said with disgust, releasing his sister's arm and retreating to his family.

Julia swept into the rector's cramped quarters, flushed and out of breath. This was the hoyden he'd long known, far from his ideal. Indelicate, unfeminine.

Safe from his ravaging desire.

And yet a creamy white confection of a wedding dress streamed around her. She clutched a bright bouquet of orange and scarlet early autumn flowers in white kid gloves. Her transformation took his breath away. He gawked, then ordered himself not to look so hungrily.

But one of those female things with flowers crowned her burnished auburn hair. A gathering of lace framed her perfect throat, softening her strong jaw and gentling her masculine features. Tiers of ornate, leafy fabric skimmed a figure he'd found too boyish. Today it was entrancing. Somehow all that foam was harnessed by a silken cord that crisscrossed her young but womanly breasts.

So firm pressed to his chest that night. Desire coiled through his loins. *Firmness . . .*

No, he needed firmness of another kind. He gave her a corrective bow.

"My lady," he said sternly but too quietly for their audience to hear. "We marry momentarily. It's time to put off childish things."

Her eyes blazed. "Let me tell you something about childish things. I just tried speaking to your daughter in the hall. She shrank from me. She was worse than by the carriage. Why, she's—"

"—delicate, as I told you," he broke in, hoping to slow her down. "Like her mother. And confused. It's against her nature to be as bold as you."

"As bold as me? She's timid as a mouse. She was trembling at the sight of me. I am not a witch."

No, she was not. She was a delectable young woman, even as she rushed headlong to challenge him. "Clearly, Julia, she was not prepared to see you romping through a large, strange house."

She drew herself up. "I do not romp in my father's house."

He doubted that. She romped through barns and stable yards and over downs and ditches. He'd seen her. Watched her. All her life. He savagely repressed amusement, and a wildly inappropriate impulse to indulge his willful, wayward bride. *Clear commands,* he reminded himself, clearly needed to keep Julia in line.

"And you will not romp through mine," he ordered.

She snorted, a not altogether unladylike snort, but an expression greatly at odds with her fetching matrimonial attire. "Isabeau was with her aunt." Julia's eyes narrowed as understanding dawned. "I'll bet you always give her to her aunt. Not only does Isabeau not want me, she doesn't even need me." A hitch in Julia's confident voice betrayed her hurt, but he had no time to solace her today.

"Her great-great aunt's too old and addled to manage her day in and day out."

"A governess could."

Something cracked in him. "I won't have my daughter raised by servants."

"That's not what I heard. I heard you've been through troops of nurses."

He drew a warning breath. "I don't have to explain myself to you."

Recovering, she smiled, almost triumphant. "Naturally, my lord. I would not explain myself to someone I had purchased underhand either."

The Mad Marquis

"A low blow, Julia. Our agreement is mutual and aboveboard."

"As you say, my lord." Beneath tiers of tulle and lace, her shoulders squared. "So, she has been raised by servants, and the occasional attention of her aging aunt."

"Of necessity. Her mother was too frail to care for her. While she lived, Isabeau had to tiptoe around her and her headaches."

"She won't have to tiptoe around me."

No, she'd have to gallop to keep up. "If you think to turn her into a hoyden—"

"She looks a little peaked for that."

"Just so you remember. She's fragile, like her mother."

"Then you've made a poor choice in me, my lord. My gift lies with colts and fillies, spirited ones at that."

Could she be right? But he could not be wrong. Despite an excess of independence, Julia was the rational choice. She only needed his direction. Or a way out. "Cry off if you can't do it. Before it's too late. I'll take the blame."

She glared, giving tit for tat. "Very noble, my lord. But I would still look jilted."

Thinking any man would be a fool to jilt her, he raised a critical brow. "That's a poor reason to stand firm."

She crossed her arms beneath her breasts, obstinate and alluring all at once. "Oh, I have better reasons. I'd rather be your marchioness than my sister-in-law's footstool. Besides, I'd rather have my horses."

Horses? Surely she did not still think this was all about her precious horses.

"What about my daughter?"

"Girls, as you said, are flexible. I'm sure we'll rub along together well enough."

He didn't like her reasoning. She was stubborn and perverse—and needed taking down a peg or two. Or else he'd be kowtowing to his bride before the day was done. "Well then, you've made your bed. Luckily, you'll not have to lie in it."

"My lord," she acknowledged, and gave that little curtsy. Graceful, and endearing, but lacking in conviction.

She could not have the last word. He would not let her set the tone. Bowing formally, he brought her gloved hand to his mouth, brushing the middle knuckle with his lips. To remind her of her

31

new role, he told himself. The public and demanding one of being his bride, his marchioness.

Too late he saw the risk. Beneath the glove her hand was warm, obliging, and the scent of flowers floated all about her. *She had prepared herself for him.* Desire washed over him, weakened him, and the shards of his rational self cried silently, *mistake, mistake.*

Chapter Four

Independence I have long considered as the grand blessing of
life, the basis of every virtue.
    —Mary Wollstonecraft, *Vindication of the Rights of Woman*

Rayne released her hand, something like disgust suffusing his handsome face. Julia almost slumped in misery. She almost fled in mortification. She'd spent a solid quarter hour stuffing herself into her
matrimonial rigmarole—beaded slippers, yards of tulle, tiers of lace.
Hoping in vain to be pretty on her one and only wedding day.

Heaven help her, she'd even consented to wear this ridiculous
crown of flowers with a frothy cascading veil. Elaborate and expensive, the lace was her stepmother's fancy, "to do justice to her station."

It wasn't Julia's style. The annoying veil tickled her nose and itched
her face. Her bead-encrusted slippers pinched her feet. But she'd
gone along one last time as a sop to the impulsive woman who'd
made Julia's childhood wretched. When sober, the countess had set
standards of feminine behavior that a hopelessly horsy girl could
never meet. When glassy-eyed from opiates, the countess had set no
standards at all.

But also, Julia admitted, she'd agreed to wearing fancy dress in hopes of cracking Rayne's stiff control. The prospect had been irresistible.

The upshot hurt like the very devil.

Just beyond the robing room, an uneasy cough echoed in the tomblike hollow of the chapel. A boy yelped—one of her brother's rapscallion sons. A *shush!* hissed through the dank air—more of her sister-in-law's perpetual anger. Whatever lay in store with Rayne, Julia thought, she was right to go. Right to leave the devils that she knew, even if that meant leaving her dear, indulgent father.

Furtively she touched her kid gloves to an angry tear that threatened to betray her. Drat and blast! Rayne would think her a weak woman.

He merely gave her an inscrutable look. "Ready, my dear?"

His implacable courtesy shook her.

Then with long fingers, he tilted her chin and studied her expression. "You will go through with this," he commanded softly.

She jerked away, upset by his tone and unsettled by his touch. "Of course. I said I would," she said vehemently.

He merely blinked. But she had cracked his calm and felt restored. Then with a lordly sweep of a gloved hand, he parted the draperies into the ancient chapel. Storming in before the bride's processional, she'd missed the wedding decorations. Bright nosegays capped each pew, and several dozen candles in brass footed stands flared along the aisle, not quite lifting the gloom.

Her family sat in state, her father having been transferred from his chair to the peer's time-honored pew. The countess sat beside him, her eyes a little glazed. Lionel and his wife bracketed their six scrubbed sons. They wriggled with devilment. An arm shot up. Flanking pairs of shoulders shook. Lionel laid an arm along the top of the pew, no doubt to tweak an ear.

Julia rejoiced. She was escaping this . . . and yet, for what?

Rayne's family straggled in. A dejected Isabeau flung petals from a decorated basket. The sight tugged at Julia's heart. Skinny as she was, the child was lovely, like fine porcelain. And lonely, like an orphaned foal. Behind her, Henry's great aunt Augusta marched down the aisle with great dignity, her remarkable, old-fashioned skirts swaying from pew to pew, bumping up against the candle stands. Uncle Bertie scurried behind, his parrot bobbing on his shoulder as he swooped right and left, rescuing the flowers from his aunt's skirts and her skirts from the candles' flames.

Oh lord, Julia thought, amused and yet dismayed by their outlandish promenade. They were every bit as eccentric as Rayne had warned. When they reached the very front of the chapel, the trio bumped and shuffled into place on the groom's side. Aunt Augusta spread her voluminous skirts over half the pew, their hems spilling into the aisle. Uncle Bertie scooted nearest the wall. Isabeau sat small and lost between them, her little basket on her knees.

As if their quirks meant nothing to him, Rayne gently touched Julia's elbow. His touch had hinted of gentleness before, on the night they'd kissed. Fresh hope welled up in her, only to be flooded by new doubts. What kind of man was her mad marquis? What kind of husband would he be? Solicitous, as now? Or commanding and remote, as only moments ago? What if his fear that he was mad was true? And the swings in his temperament marked his madness?

How was she to tell? And what was she to do?

Uncertainty shivered down her spine as she turned, with him, to face Wraxham's rector and Henry's elegant Cousin Erskine and their marriage vows.

The beatific smile of Wraxham's elderly clergyman steadied her. He had baptized, cradled, and confirmed her. He, if no one else, seemed confident of the rightness of his task. He spoke kindly of her adventurous childhood, lectured her on willfulness, and commended her to her husband's guiding hand.

Guiding hand? No, more like his commanding rule and demanding presence next to her. She clenched her teeth and pasted on a smile, ignoring the rector's well-intentioned ramble through her past. If not Rayne's rule, she'd be subject to her brother's, she reminded herself sternly.

Lionel, his wife, and brood would smother her.

Would Rayne do less, or more?

Oblivious to her concerns, the rector joyfully meandered on about the fitness of joining two such ancient families. Fervently, he waxed eloquent on Rayne's duty to his estate and to the realm. When prayer was called, she closed her eyes, letting the significance—the loftiness—of her new order sink in. She prayed to be worthy of her new duties. She prayed to become an exemplary marchioness. She prayed not to be distracted by the smell of . . .

Smoke? Not the mere smoke of flickering candles, she thought, alarmed. Something was burning, neither wood nor wax. It was burning silently but near. She sniffed, opened her eyes, and turned to look at the pews, to look out for Isabeau. No hint of fire threatened her. No, she was sitting, bored, her gaze denying the procedure, avoiding Julia.

Then she saw it. In the aisle a trace of smoke smoldered up from Aunt Augusta's skirts. A tiny flame licked out from under their scalloped edges, retreated under crinolines, lanced up more boldly. Engaged, the moldering old brocade flared up with fury.

"Bertie! My skirts!" cried Augusta, fear in her voice.

"The candles!" Bertie answered, jumping up and sending Raj into a flutter about his head.

Instinctively, Julia dropped her bridal bouquet and dived, her gloved hands stretched to snuff the flames. She knotted fresh fabric all around the hungry blaze and pounded the knot, flat-handed, against the floor. Julia felt the heat searing through her gloves, felt a rush of air as Rayne raced to her aid. Clutching a vase of flowers from the altar, he flung out the blooms, upended the vessel, and drenched his aunt's skirts.

Besieged, the elderly Augusta Pelham scrambled across the pew, her little shrieks of alarm rousing the modest congregation. Lionel rushed from his seat to help, sons trailing like a fresh battalion of too-ready young recruits. The countess affected the vapors; the viscountess fanned her face. Julia's heart caught to see her father pull himself to his feet.

Terrified by all the commotion, Isabeau squealed, and Uncle Bertie's parrot hurled itself into the air, flapping its clipped wings furiously. Half a clumsy loop around the room, and it managed to land in the inviting rose bush crowning Julia's head.

On principle, she never screamed. Outbursts made horses bolt. But the bird's cut claws raked her scalp, and its stubby wings flailed her face. She batted at Raj to drive him off, only to feel stronger hands push her hands away.

And Rayne's voice hoarsely coaxed, "Be still, love. Steady. I've got him."

The thrashing stopped, and Rayne gently extricated the jabbering parrot's talons from her tangled hair. She sat stone still, cross-legged, on the cold, hard floor, admiring Rayne's efficiency and trying to make out the bird's barrage of words. To make out Rayne's words. Which she didn't dare pursue.

"What's he saying?" She asked instead, peering up from underneath her ravaged veil.

Rayne, livid, had stuffed the parrot under his arm and had a chokehold on its neck.

Rayne's cousin Erskine, barely repressing a grin, stepped in. "Believe me, my dear, you don't want to know."

Uncle Bertie hurried around the front, distressed, and wrenched the bird from Rayne's control. "He's cursing my nephew in Hindi, Lady Julia, as well he should. No call to be so rough, Henry. Poor Raj is frightened out of his wits."

"Wits!" Rayne snapped, giving Julia a perfunctory hand up, then resuming his scold. "You take that miserable excuse for a bird back to your pew, Uncle Albert. And hold onto it this time."

Huffing, Uncle Bertie pressed Raj safely to his chest. "He's not a bird, he's an African Grey parrot, and an exceptionally smart and talented one at that."

Comforted, Raj squawked freely. *"Mad marquis, mad is he, mad marquis."*

All elegance in his black and white and dove-gray morning suit, Rayne leaned toward the parrot, then threatened, "Another word out of you, birdbrain, and I'll roast you for supper."

Aunt Augusta rearranged her skirts. "Parrots aren't very tasty, dear, they say."

Isabeau whimpered. "But he's Uncle Bertie's only friend!"

Aunt Augusta whispered to Isabeau and patted the pew for her to sit.

The chaos eased, and Julia became aware that all the rest of the dearly beloved here assembled were resuming their appointed posts. The stately archdeacon and the shaken rector came back to the altar. Julia's father sat back down. The vaporous womenfolk fanned quietly. Lionel's sons, forcibly reined in and reseated, squirmed like fishing worms on hooks. She could almost hear them cheering: This was better than the circus, better than a schoolyard brawl.

And she would think so, too, she thought grimly, if she'd not been the one in center ring, the bedraggled bride, milling with a deranged parrot.

Beside her, Rayne was flushed and storm-faced, as if blaming himself for the spectacle his family made. He reached across the vast span of his aunt's damaged skirts, and plucked his weepy daughter from the pew. "And you, young lady, not another whimper. This is your father's wedding day."

Julia's wedding day, such as it was, was in ruins, and she didn't have a chance in Hades of impressing Henry with her aptitude for her new station. Or fulfilling a rare, feminine fantasy of showing up all dressed to the nines for her wedding and bowling her groom over with newfound stylish grace. Was that so much to ask?

Sighing, she tugged up her scorched gloves, vaguely thankful her hands were not burned. If only she hadn't lunged, tearing her really rather pretty clothes and destroying her fantasy of triumph. She'd been a boyish girl, and now she was a mannish woman. A hoyden then, a hoyden now. She wasn't pretty, or worthy, or fit.

But Henry was speaking through her shredded veil and tangled hair, not so gently as before. "You too, my lady. Take my daughter's hand. Let's get this over with."

Over with. At least he was honest. Julia pressed her lips together doggedly. Her present fiasco was not yet as humiliating as being dragged across the barnyard through the mud, her foot caught in the stirrup after a clumsy dismount, the grooms and stable boys all watching. And she wasn't a quitter. And she didn't go back on her word.

But oh, how ridiculous they must look. The bride, tousled and in disarray, and the groom, rigidly correct, standing to be married, with his unhappy daughter set between them.

Julia reached down to Isabeau, who sidled nearer to her father. He bent and spoke briefly. Isabeau straightened out, stepped over, and grudgingly offered her little hand. It was cold and limp. Julia held it, her heart shriveling. This could not bode well. Rayne had placed Isabeau between them like a wall, and the poor child found her repellent. They were a portrait of a family in misery.

They were in misery.

The rector must agree. He rattled off the Holy Scriptures as if the hounds of Hell were tearing at his heels. *Wives, submit . . . husbands, love . . . one flesh . . . one flesh . . . one flesh . . .*

Then it was the archdeacon's turn to lead them through their vows. His aristocratic tones restored a certain dignity to the day. Julia fixed her eyes on the gold and scarlet vestments that hung around his neck, and listened to her bridegroom vow to cherish her.

Heaven help her, she'd already fought with him twice today, before they'd even left the Wraxham web that held her in its snare. But Rayne's voice was firm and strong, almost as if he meant to keep his promises, almost as if he had not rejected her very womanhood.

Surely, this was madness, his blowing hot and cold when she could barely catch her breath.

". . . my lady," the archdeacon prodded, " 'to honor and obey.' "

"I do," she bit off, suddenly subsumed with anger at Rayne and at herself.

She'd held to her resolve. She'd saved her dream. She would have her horses—her childhood companions, her life's work—forever.

But in her zeal to secure a future with them, she hadn't looked deeply enough into her devil's bargain with a man she barely knew. A man who'd kissed her with something she imagined to be passion, rushed to her rescue, and then turned to stone.

A man she had just promised to honor and obey.

Chapter Five

A girl, whose spirits have not been damped by inactivity, or innocence tainted by false shame, will always be a romp . . .
—Mary Wollstonecraft, *Vindication of the Rights of Woman*

Henry stepped outside the chapel, his new bride on his arm. He looked about for his prized racing phaeton. Wat Nance was late, blast him, and Henry's fast getaway was foiled. Like everything he'd planned this wretched day.

The sky was lowering, and the wind cut through his waistcoat. A shower had passed through, and rainwater dripped from Wraxham's older yews.

He'd been mad to trust Uncle Bertie's knees to predict the weather.

Beneath the arched stoop of the chapel, Julia's grip on his forearm tightened. A funereal row of downcast household staff attempted to hold a proper line. Behind liveried footmen, a dozen grooms and youthful stable boys shot Henry evil looks.

A fine start to his marriage, Henry thought. Gloom and doom and tears. No one but he, it seemed, wanted Julia to go. Not even Julia.

But she smiled bravely for her minions. "You didn't have to all turn out for me today."

Mutters of dissent rippled from cook to scullery maid to tiger.

She hushed them with an upraised hand. "I thank you, everyone. Truly. I'll only be a few miles away."

"Three miles, five furlongs, ma'am." A wiry, graying redhead stepped out of the pack, flipping out a polished pocket watch of the sort used for timing races. He looked familiar. "Eleven minutes twenty on the likes of Meteor."

"You see, not far at all," Julia consoled them.

The stable crew dissented noisily, their cries muffling the servants' sniffles. The redhead, too, looked at a loss.

"Who is that man?" Henry found himself asking Julia privately, curiosity roused by the groom's obvious devotion.

Julia sighed dejectedly. "Jem Guthrie. My right hand."

She missed him already, Henry could see that. But she'd made her bargain for the horses and wouldn't ask for more. She dealt fair and square, he noted. It augured well for their arrangement.

To reward her, he said, "I'll get him for you." That was ill thought out, impulsive. Unlike him. But it was not ill received.

Approval lit her face. "Oh, Henry! I mean, my lord. That's positively brilliant. Jem babies all my horses. He'll make the move go so much smoother. And then the breeding, foaling, training—he taught me everything I know."

She was gushing, and Henry tamped down a sense of satisfaction he did not want to have. It pleased him too much to please his bride. Indulging her could set a dangerous precedent. Coddling horses, an even worse one.

He brushed back caution for her wedding day. "Consider it done. Your father can't say no."

Her free hand touched his arm. "But you said we ought not strip my brother lock, stock, and barrel."

Honest, too, he noted with admiration. "No doubt, he has his own man. And your man, Guthrie, if he knows everything, can take your place and ease your fears while you tend to duties in the castle."

She let go his arm.

He felt a protest coming and spoke fast to avert it. "It's a practical matter for all concerned."

Not fast enough. Her green eyes flashed with entirely too much spirit. "Do you do me a favor? Or confine me to the house?"

He put her hand back in its place and patted it. "I wouldn't confine

41

you, my dear. It would be to relieve you of extra work."

"It's no relief to sit at home worrying about my horses," she snapped.

Bugger all. He'd just dug himself in deep. She might be honest, fair and square, but she was far too willful. "You trust your man, do you not? And you will attend to your duties?"

She pressed her lips together, as if checking a violent outburst. Even so, a teardrop of vexation channeled down her cheek.

Or was it rain? He checked the sky, he checked the overhanging yew. Hard to say.

The family, impatient after their delay, surged around them. Uncle Bertie helped Isabeau fling petals in the air, petals by the handfuls, fistfuls.

They struck Henry's face, more impudent than rain. With an exasperated snort he blew them off, not a man to suffer public indignity for an instant. He turned, glowering at his uncle, only to see his aunt looking supremely satisfied. There was motion everywhere—aunts, uncles, falling flowers, servants, grooms, and nephews, their arms windmilling as they batted at the rain of petals falling down.

Henry stood transfixed. Julia bore up to a second hail of petals sticking damply to her face like jewels. Despite her russet hair, her creamy skin, his new bride was not a beautiful woman. He preferred delicacy. Deference. Dependence.

But she was dignified and proud, and that impressed him in spite of himself. He couldn't take his eyes off her, the random petals decorating her wet cheeks. Whether from rain or tears, who was to say? Her wedding day kept skidding off into lunacy, a Pelham-inspired lunacy that was now her lot in life. His stomach knotted with regret. Some lot in life he offered her.

"Here. Be strong for me today, my marchioness," he murmured, leaning close, plucking off the petals.

"A wedding requires a kiss, my dears," Great Aunt Augusta urged romantically.

The countess clapped her hands. "Oh yes, you mustn't disappoint us now."

Cousin Erskine and the rector watched benignly, hands folded in blessing.

The nephews, hellions all, took up a chant, soft at first, then rising, "Kiss her, kiss her, kiss her."

A public kiss. A simple kiss. It wasn't such a bad idea. In fact it seemed a sound one. A quick and dutiful kiss would reassure the servants and the families of his good intentions and of her consent. It would put an end to all this nonsense and hasten their escape.

With gloved fingers, he tipped up her chin, inclined his head, and claimed her cool, reluctant mouth, seasoned with salt tears.

Julia wished he wouldn't keep on kissing her when he didn't mean it. It was too confusing, too distracting. Too delicious. His richly whiskeyed breath caressed her face. She drew in air, drinking in his scent, his heat.

But she saw what he was up to. If he thought kisses could seduce her from her horses, he would soon see the error of his ways. She could resist the pull of his attractions. Why, she'd resisted the very thought of their steamy betrothal kiss for a solid month. Well, most days, and several nights, she amended.

So why did her knees go weak as the marvel of Henry Pelham all around her settled in? Because he was awfully good at kissing—almost good enough to make a woman give up anything.

But not her independence, she told herself.

Not her horses or her heart.

Julia heard her raucous nephews clamoring around them, cheering on the kiss. Oblivious to their ruckus, Henry stayed tender, knowing, firm. Just as in the library when she'd thrown herself at him. He'd gone about his business, controlling his anger and his interest. Except for that erection, she remembered.

Perhaps he hadn't minded so much after all.

Because this time he didn't stop, not even for the sound of hooves pounding in the distance. Unwillingly she stiffened under Henry's expert attention. He broke off the kiss and squinted, looking past her head.

"About damn time," he muttered.

Time for what? Self-conscious, she turned to face the stares, the teasing. But saw only relatives gathering around them, beaming approval. Approval! When the whole affair was such a fraud. She lowered her head and closed her eyes, her cheeks flaming.

They'd seen her kiss Henry, blatantly, brazenly. Let them, she thought, rallying. It was a legal, married kiss.

It was a pretend kiss.

A last kiss. For they had made promises, to themselves and to each other. No kisses, no lovemaking, no children. And they would keep them.

She had to face the families. She lifted her gaze, only to see their relatives drift away to say their goodbyes. Augusta Pelham nudged Isabeau toward Julia's ailing father. Tired and frail, he perked up for the child. Beyond the dripping yews, Bertie Pelham and his talking parrot charmed her stepmother into a rare smile. Just then, the thundering hooves wrested her attention from the little scene.

Rayne's sleek black phaeton sprayed gravel as it cleared the gate, rounding the massive pillars to her father's home.

Julia's confusion slid away. "It's Deal and Diamond!" Rayne's best team.

"A treat for you," he said.

Another wedding present. By far the best. She clapped her hands in sudden, girlish glee. "My lord, you shouldn't have."

"Greedy wench," he said, but good-naturedly. "They're for this trip only."

She was too happy at the prospect of a drive to cavil. "Of course, my lord. I'll settle for taking the reins."

He scowled. "They're strung tight as a bow."

"Just my sort of pair," she began. She itched to handle Rayne's best colts. She'd coveted the stunning pair of darkly dappled grays since last year when he raced them, newly trained, in a match. They'd won it running away. He'd scared off all the competition.

All but her. She wasn't scared of him or them. She just didn't have the team and rig she needed to defeat him yet.

But the wave of relatives was moving them along, toward their conveyances. Over by the Pelham carriage, Uncle Bertie assisted Aunt Augusta, then handed Isabeau inside. Rayne strode over to them, gave his daughter a word and a kiss, and returned. Among Julia's relations, quick goodbyes were said all around. After Julia hugged her father, he swiped away a tear, the first he'd ever let her see.

To her surprise, even her stepmother sniffled blearily, as if she really cared for Julia. "What will I do without you, my dear?"

But her concern was, as always, only about herself, Julia thought, relieved to be escaping her whims and demands. Relieved—but ever so slightly guilty to be leaving her father in that woman's hands.

"I'm sure you'll be strong for my father, madam," Julia said, hoping the idea would take root in the countess's opiate-dulled mind.

"You know I've never been strong . . ."

"If you need me," Julia reassured her, "I will not be all that far away." A quick gallop on horseback. Or atop Rayne's speedy phaeton. She eyed it longingly, then remembered to give the countess a dutiful peck on the cheek.

"It's time, my lady," Rayne said, as if cued to rescue her, and ushered her toward the carriage with its graceful curves.

There, at the archdeacon's elegant light trap, Henry urged his cousin to visit them at Pelham. But he offered warm congratulations and said a kind and courteous goodbye.

His matched team of bays was all the crack, and their dashing exit made Henry's horses champ their bits. Under the groom's uneasy control, Diamond pranced in place, neck arched, nostrils flared, and haunches taut with readiness to vault away. Gawking at the colt's sheer beauty, Julia stepped up to his side. She laid a hand just above his withers, noticing her scorched glove for the first time since snuffing out Aunt Augusta's fire. It was fairly ruined. But her hand was fine.

She was fine, she told herself. Married—but fine.

She focused on the colt, willing the stillness of her touch to quiet him. After a moment, his tense neck stretched down and he blew out a whuffle, the equine equivalent of a sigh.

She looked at her new husband. "I like his spirit . . . and his heart."

"We should go," Rayne said gruffly, his expression carefully blank. And with surprising strength, for she was so ungainly large, he handed her up into the box, her favorite perch above the world.

As if the entire rig belonged to her, she unwound the tapes and threaded them through her fingers. The leather lines vibrated in her hands, and she could feel each colt chewing at its bit. Rayne leapt up easily, took his seat beside her, and unlaced the reins from her grip.

"You're to sit back and enjoy your wedding day," he commanded in a vastly superior tone. It rankled her past caution.

"I'd enjoy it best driving."

He knotted his brows, disapproving of her cheek, no doubt. "This is our wedding. I won't let it turn into your funeral."

Julia was not a calculating woman. On the other hand, sitting back, a passenger, was deadly dull.

And she knew all too well from her older brothers' tales, Rayne never could resist a dare.

She slid him an innocent look beneath her ridiculous torn veil. "I bet you I can hold them to a walk from here to the gate."

Keeping this hot team in hand would show him her skill.

He crossed his arms over his chest. "Prove it."

She looked across her shoulder at him, pleased with her little victory. "If I make it to the gate at a walk, I drive us home."

Home! She'd rarely been to Pelham Castle, and already called it home. Part of Henry was gratified. Part, terrified, now that he was taking his young bride home. A gambler who calculated all his odds, he ignored the terror.

"Very well then," he said. "Show me."

Not a chance in hell that she'd succeed. Deal and Diamond were fresh. Some would say rank. Certainly more spirited than any mount he'd ever seen her ride. On any given day, they were challenge to him, a racing man, a sporting man. They could be an outright peril to a woman. No, Julia wouldn't have a chance of pulling off her plan alone. But she was in no danger.

Because he was sitting right beside her, completely in control.

Her form was correct, he granted that. She took up the whip in her right hand and the tapes in her left, making a perfectly straight line from her elbow to her hand to the colts' mouths. She sat erect and balanced, not leaning forward as inexperienced drivers invariably did. The gentle square of her shoulders showed no strain, no undue tension, no fear. Her waist was trim, her breasts were high and . . .

Sternly he reminded himself to ignore her attractions.

What mattered were her quiet hands. His usually headstrong colts flicked back their ears, giving her their attention. Her hand on the tapes eased forward slightly, nothing too sudden or startling. She gave a quiet cluck. With a skillful turn of her wrist, she cracked the end of the whip high above the colts' heads. They stepped into their collars and moved off quietly at a walk.

He let out a pent-up breath, betraying needless worry. Yes, there was a quivering eagerness about the colts he knew so well, he could sense it. One wrong move, and they'd explode. But she held them to a walk. She had them well in hand. The phaeton rolled past an avenue of chestnut trees, a few leaves here and there already turning, mingling the russet of her hair with the leaf green of her eyes.

Bloody hell, he kept noticing far too much about her. He swallowed hard. Normally he'd be absorbed in managing his team, and not give a thought to the charms of any woman who came near. But his hands were empty. He'd given over the reins. And she was practically sitting in his lap.

She drove them cleanly through the gate, quieting Diamond as he tossed his head, waiting to be sprung. She turned to Henry, almost tossing hers. "They're ready to trot now, my lord," she said, rather more pleased with herself than a man ought rightly to allow.

He leaned back against the waist-high seat, purposely at ease. "We didn't bargain for a trot."

She sat up, showing all the haughtiness she'd need in her new rank. "It would be a crime to try to hold this team to a walk all the way from Wraxham House to Pelham Castle."

"The crime, my lady, would be if you were injured."

"Horsefeathers. The crime would be if you had to admit I know what I'm doing."

He wasn't about to concede that. But he had a duty to avert disaster. "Tell me true, Julia. Have you ever handled a team this young, this keen?"

"A quieter team this young, and an older team this keen," she admitted.

"Hitched to a phaeton as fast as this?"

"Hitched to a . . ." Her voice dropped grudgingly. ". . . a pony cart, and a rumbling old landau."

"With permission?"

She gave an impatient shrug. "Jem knew. He said Father would fire him if he found out."

"Then," Henry said gently, grateful he'd banked on her honesty, "I'm sure you can see this is not the day, the team, or the carriage for you."

"It's the perfect day!" she protested, driving them smoothly around a jutting rock in the middle of the road. "It's the perfect present for my wedding day."

He grimaced. "I gave you the perfect present, Julia. Remember?" That necklace set was worth a fortune.

"Yes, thank you," she said, some schoolgirl manners kicking in. "The jewels are very nice, my lord."

Very nice? he grumbled to himself. This woman was not easily impressed. No, actually, she could be very easily impressed. All he had to do was let her romp around the countryside with his life and his best team's safety in her untried hands.

"No, Julia. I cannot allow it. The family couldn't endure another carriage accident," he said, playing his trump card.

Her face fell, and her genuine concern made him feel a perfect cad.

"Oh dear, my lord, of course not. How thoughtless of me not to consider that. But your father's accident was tragic—"

"My father's accident was suicidal. He meant to kill himself, proving once more our family's fatal madness." Henry couldn't keep the raw edge from his voice. He had put that ache behind him a dozen years ago. The end of his father's melancholia proved that madness was the family curse, quite possibly his own destiny.

Reining in the team, she laid the haft of the whip across her lap. Her freed hand touched his forearm in consolation. "I was going to say he was unlucky. And rather drunk."

"Who told you that?"

"Jem, and the boys. It was the talk of the stable."

"It was the talk of the county. And a highly questionable explanation of what was going on that night. He'd been low for weeks, hiding out in the stables in the harness room. Nothing I did had any—" He broke off. The memory was too dark for his wedding day. He'd found his father's broken body in the road, flung from his high perch. "Suffice it to say, I won't put Isabeau through that."

Undaunted, Julia gripped his arm. "Well, my lord, we're not melancholy, and we're not drunk. And you're right here to help me. What could go wrong?"

A very great deal. But her optimism beguiled him. Her determination made his head spin. And her confidence that he could handle anything touched a place in him long dead to praise.

"Put the whip away," he said gruffly, conceding to her plea. "I only use it when I race them."

She caught his meaning instantly. "Seriously, my lord?" she asked quietly, doubtless aware that too much jubilation could spook the team.

"You'll need both hands on the reins. Diamond pulls, and Deal needs the softest touch."

Silently she threaded the tapes between the scorched fingers of her gloves. He'd forgotten that she'd put out the fire in his aunt's skirts. "You're sure your hands are up to this?"

"The gloves might not be. But my hands are."

"Cluck twice to signal them to trot . . ."

"I know the usual commands, my lord."

He forced himself to sit back. "Walk first. Don't spring them, not even to trot. I don't want them—or you—getting the wrong idea."

She rolled her eyes in protest but went quietly about her work. Deal and Diamond stepped out smartly at a walk. "How are they through water?" she asked, a furlong farther on.

"Well-trained," he said, offended she'd expect anything less of a team he'd brought along himself.

"We'll just walk until we pass that stream up ahead."

They splashed through noisily, and she said calmly, "Hold on, my lord." Then clucked twice. The harness squeaked, and they trotted out briskly. Looking down, he saw their lean, sleek haunches ripple with contained power and checked speed. Rain-dark tree trunks flashed by, and at the verge, rock walls blurred like ribbons. A herd of grazing sheep bolted up the downs. Noticing that, the team half shied, but her calm hands steadied them.

No harm done, he admitted grudgingly.

"They're just superb, my lord," she said, another furlong on the way.

She was superb. It was impossible to resist her unbridled passion for the sport. Her face flushed with a joy he never showed and rarely felt. Five furlongs from Wraxham House, and she had them trotting at a spanking pace. Expertly, as he would do it.

"I could spring them," she said eagerly, rounding a curve and coming upon a gentle rise of straight, quiet lane.

She wouldn't dare, he thought. The colts' backs tensed, their haunches gathered. *Not here,* he started to say, in the second he assessed his team. She mistook hesitation for consent.

And sprang them.

Too bad he hadn't told her they were well nigh impossible to stop.

Two miles would take the edge off; four would bring them back in hand. By the time they got to Pelham Castle, they'd be flying. But he'd take over there, and his bride would get a stern and well-deserved comeuppance.

Henry sat back, one hand on the seat behind her, and casually stretched out a leg. He didn't want to alarm her any more than the horses, for he took her at her word. She was new to dangerous games. To rabbits leaping unexpectedly from hedgerows, to Purvis's rambling bull. To a husband wrestling with his growing lust.

They pounded up the lane, past farm fields and a country church, his grays flat out and his bride's veil and laces streaming behind them. Between the reckless lurching of the phaeton and his bride's jubilation, he was almost as exhilarated as if driving the team himself.

He barely felt the first rain splatter his face and barely heard the distant roll of thunder. It took a sudden deluge, and a lightning flash, and an unearthly shriek for him to notice. A great low limb on a giant oak splintered and crashed across the road not forty yards ahead. The colts lunged into a frenzied gallop.

Henry wrenched the reins from Julia's hands and started hauling on his horses' mouths—pull and release, pull and release—an uneven rhythm guaranteed to throw them off their pace before they charged into destruction. "Feather the brake," he shouted to his bride, for the brake was by the driver's seat and his hands were full.

Her wretched veil whipped around her face, and he knew in an instant she could barely see. "By your right knee!" He yelled into the pelting rain. "Grab it, pump it, now!"

She jerked off the veil, and with both hands, went to work, tugging the brake back again and again. He could feel the phaeton drag and see his team's distraction, but they bore down on the massive fallen limb, half trotting, half bucking, a little crazy with fear.

"Lock it," he called out. From the corner of his eye he could see her grab the handle with both hands and pull it into place. The phaeton shuddered, skidded, turned into dead weight. Diamond reared. Deal shied in terror, and both of their front legs tangled in the upper branches of the fallen limb.

Julia scrambled down the phaeton's side before Henry could even think to tie off the tapes and leap down himself. He met her standing next to Diamond. Gripping the reins, she patted his neck and whispered in his ear. The poor colt was trembling all over. Stepping into the branches, Henry took Deal's bridle and stroked the panting horse.

"Can we back them out now, do you think? I can't even see who's hurt," Julia said, a quiver in her voice.

"Gently," he said quietly. Working in tandem, they backed the horses free of their entanglement.

Laces and all, Julia dropped to her knees in the muddy road and ran her hands down Diamond's front legs. She looked up, stricken. "He's cut, Henry. Badly cut, on the fetlock."

Henry steadied Deal, and leaned over to look. Blood oozed from a gash. "It's no longer than a finger and not that deep. It will drain well and heal quickly," he reassured her.

Futilely. "I shouldn't have taken the reins," she berated herself. "I shouldn't be so bold with horses I don't know. It's all my fault."

"No more yours than mine. I know better than to subject a woman to such risk."

Any ground he might have gained by letting Julia drive his phaeton was suddenly treacherous as the shifting sands.

She stood up, wet, bedraggled, both hands set angrily on her hips. "You think we had this accident because I am a woman?"

Remorse washed over him. "We had an accident because lightning struck the tree. I should have been driving my team."

She took another look at Diamond's injury. "It's not so bad he can't walk home. You'd better drive your horses, my lord," she said frostily, and climbed back to her seat before he had a chance to help her.

He took his time checking the horses and their harness. No more cuts and nothing broken. By the time he finished his inspection, they were almost calm.

Which was a lot more than could be said for him.

Chapter Six

What acquirement exalts one being above another?
— Mary Wollstonecraft, *Vindication of the Rights of Woman*

A quarter hour later, Julia could smell the briny air and feel the ocean damp against her face. If she squinted, she could see Pelham Castle, its buff turrets ragged against the iron sky and roiling sea.

"Almost home," Rayne said. The horses knew. Despite his injury, Diamond pranced. "You must be cold."

Julia shivered. She was cold, and miserable, and cross. What else could go wrong on her first ever, only wedding day? "I need a bath."

"After we greet the staff. They've been waiting these three quarter hours to see their new mistress," Rayne said firmly.

Perhaps she should leave well enough alone. But she just couldn't.

"Diamond's walking out nicely at the moment," she ventured. Luckily, the injured colt showed no sign of favoring his left fore.

"So far," Rayne answered.

"When we get home," she hurried on, "they'll need bran mashes. And Diamond's cut needs whiskey and a wrap."

"Naturally, my lady," he said, still stern, but a corner of his mouth quirked.

He couldn't be amused. Could he?

Too aware of her bedraggled state, she was afraid he could.

"And blankets, after they've been rubbed down," she added automatically, then stopped. Whatever in the world did new brides talk about? Especially ones like her, who knew nothing but horses.

"Of course," he said. "And fresh bedding, don't you think?" There was a betraying quaver in his voice.

"*Bedding?*" she croaked. Her cheeks heated. But she couldn't let him get to her. "Quite right," she went on briskly. "Fresh oat straw, I'd think. The latest summer cutting. A team like this deserves the very best."

"Don't worry. My men will handle the team. And I'll take care of you."

She stared at him. The hard lines of his handsome face almost softened, and his large, warm hand reached out to cover hers.

Too large. Too warm. She didn't move a muscle.

"I should not have allowed you to drive," he said. "Deal and Diamond are a handful, even for me, even in the mildest weather. But Wat'll fix them up right, while we do our duty with the staff."

"I always treat my injured horses myself," she protested.

He withdrew his hand. "You have a household of servants to attend to now. We keep up appearances at Pelham."

"I'm all muck and tatters." Mud caked her beaded slippers, her ornate overskirts were slopped with dirt, and her veil was long since gone.

"I've seen you worse." His gaze raked her, and his lips compressed against a smile.

"That was in the hunt field after I was dunked in Potter's pond," she said crossly. He'd laughed that day with everybody else, and barely hid his amusement now. "This was supposed to be my wedding day."

"Our wedding day," he corrected smoothly as they crested the last rise. The golden castle loomed before them, massive and irregular. "And the staff expects to meet you. You can almost see them there, at the gatehouse."

She bolted to a safer topic, the sheep that dotted Pelham's fields. "Fine herds, my lord."

"Everyone wants to meet you, Julia," he said, calmly reining her back in.

She was not calmed. "Some new marchioness, perhaps, but not me."

"And they'll expect us to enter at a spanking trot." Bridging the reins in one hand, he lifted the driving whip.

"Diamond should be walked," she reminded him.

"Yes, he looks like he needs to walk," Rayne said dryly. Diamond's ears quirked back, eager to be sprung.

"Trotting will aggravate his cut."

"Trotting will drain it." He flicked his whip, and Deal and Diamond sprang into a trot. Lightly, the phaeton cleared a final copse of windswept yews, and there it was again, Pelham Castle, all battlements and towers, mullioned windows and lichened walls. Beneath an afternoon slant of sun, its mismatched pinnacles gleamed, some high, some low, some round, and one pair octagonal, as if erected at the whim of some mad—

Horsefeathers, Julia scolded herself. There was nothing mad about it, whatever Henry thought. His castle was a hodgepodge, put up over generations of Pelhams, Gothic, Tudor and baroque. A recent wing in the Palladian manner resembled Wraxham House. Each separate part of Henry's rambling pile was true to its time, formal and traditional.

Normal, she reassured herself.

Right down to the ranks of servants and upper household staff gathered in her honor. Henry wheeled the phaeton onto the broad paving stones before the east-facing gatehouse, and anxiety jigged through her. At the steps, he reined in the colts and vaulted down. She perched precariously alone on her high seat. Liveried grooms swarmed the team. The rig secured, Henry reached up from behind and clasped her waist to help her down. Blushing furiously, she backed into his arms, acutely aware of his view of her backside. The instant her filthy slippers touched the ground, she turned, hoping to recover her dignity.

He was examining her, his cool gray eyes unreadable.

Miserably she folded her hands and saw what he must see—scorched gloves, ruined slippers, muddied dress. Blast appearances. The servants would think he'd dragged the pond for his new marchioness.

Particularly as they were standing stiff and starched and ranged in orderly rows.

"Your staff, my lady."

"You could have warned me, my lord," she said privately. "Wraxham House has half as many." And they'd not been in her charge.

"Pelham Castle is twice as large," he said reasonably.

"I knew that," she snapped. She just hadn't faced it yet. Lifting her chin, she swept the assembly with a glance and gathered her muddy skirts. A legion of underlings were nothing, she told herself, compared to the six-foot oxer she had cleared on Meteor last week. "Very well then, my lord. Let's have at them."

Henry turned her toward his staff when the eeriest human cry she'd ever heard rang out over the grounds. She quailed. "Henry, some poor person . . ."

"Shhh," he said calmly. "It's only Uncle Bertie's peacocks."

His long fingers touched the small of her back, possessive and controlling, but surprisingly reassuring. Still, his people seemed a hundred strong, scowling as much disapproval as they dared, especially a great tall swarthy fellow whose turbaned head was wrapped in swirls of pristine white cloth. Before she could ask about his frankly frightening presence, her husband announced her in a commanding baritone.

"Lady Rayne, your new marchioness."

Marchioness! The very word had weight, and brought her attention back to her daunting new duties. A woman who had barreled over the downs in control of half a ton of horse had no hesitation, no fears.

Henry introduced a stout, oakish woman and bony elderly fellow. "Mrs. Lafferty, my lady. Your housekeeper. And Rutledge, our butler."

Rutledge bowed, his wrinkled face furrowing with respect. But Lafferty, her keys of office jangling, gave a perfunctory curtsy. Rayne pinned her with a cool stare, and she sank another inch.

"You're most welcome, my lady."

"Yes, so I see. Thank you, Mrs. Lafferty," Julia answered, determined to start well despite the woman's off-putting curtsy.

Mrs. Lafferty rattled off a barrage of names—the kitchen staff, the housemaids, the upper and the lower servants and a dairy maid or two, each turned out according to her state. Neat and rehearsed, they curtsied.

Julia's head spun. She could recite the names of fully eighty horses in her father's stables, stall by stall, but with people she was lost in seconds. She noticed only a girl with her hair plaited like a carriage horse, a rangy footman with coppery, chestnut hair. And the turbaned retainer. Had he come home with Uncle Bertie? Oh, she had so much to learn.

And which one had Mrs. Lafferty introduced as her new maid? She'd never had a maid. Never wanted one. All she wanted was to escape to the barn, and tend to Diamond's cut.

So did Henry. A high-pitched whinny pierced the air, and he fought his natural urge to rush to his colt's rescue. But it was his wedding day, and his poor bride needed him. She looked like a sheaf of last year's hay, left out in the rain, then trampled underfoot.

But she had pluck, a man couldn't deny it. Unlike Therese, Julia stood up to that old battleaxe Lafferty as one to the castle born. He had to admire the dignity it took to rise above her bedraggled state.

Dignity, or inattention. Like his, her gaze was drawn to the barnyard struggle they could not quite see. She stepped back to him and whispered urgently, "I'll just go look in on Diamond." Then she headed toward the racket.

He blocked her way. "Wat Nance knows his business," he said, much as he preferred to do everything himself. "And we're not finished here."

She straightened mutinously. "I take care of my hurt horses."

"Nance can manage."

A shriller whinny rang out, and shod hooves clattered on the cobblestones. *What the hell was Wat doing with the team?* His bride too looked about to bolt. He snagged her elbow as subtly as he could before the crowd. Her whole weight inclined toward the stables. "Not on your wedding day, my lady. Your staff is waiting for you," he prodded, his hand at her elbow, nudging her to duty.

She stiffened like a balky horse. Then he felt that sweet instant of give, of yielding to his mastery.

They turned as one. The staff looked on, fascinated . . . and approving.

Damnation. He and his bride must look like quarreling lovers. Henry could have roared. Instead, he led his lady down the line, praying for a distraction.

Which came, half a dozen fawning footmen later, as the family carriage lumbered up. Out spewed his relatives—daughter, uncle, and irate great aunt.

Augusta Pelham stalked over, her wide skirts flaring. Uncle Bertie, Isabeau in hand and Raj perched on his shoulder, hurried to catch up.

"Nephew! I am shocked, stunned, and astounded!" his aunt said, a scourge of indignation in her voice. "This is no way to treat your bride."

She shook Julia's tattered wedding veil in his face.

The servants' eyes popped. Mrs. Lafferty snorted, and Rutledge's lined face drew up like a prune.

Henry stood his ground. "Don't hold back, Aunt. Tell us what you really think."

"Yes, Aunt Augusta," Bertie Pelham chimed in. "Give him what for."

Augusta Pelham was on a rant. "It's what you well deserve for dragging your bride off on a miserable day in that flimsy, *fashionable*—" she spit out the word with a special aversion "—pretense of a carriage. A bride should have a proper covered carriage on her wedding day. No doubt, you thought it a lark, galloping home in a thunderstorm . . ."

She went on to condemn his preference for half-wild colts, his disregard for inclement weather—which brought on deadly ague, surely he had not forgotten that!—and his failure to provide even a flimsy spencer for his delicate bride to wear.

His dotty aunt hadn't strung that many thoughts together in months. Whatever made him think she couldn't manage his castle? Henry mused wryly. She was managing him just fine. And he ought to cut her off. But he never chastised family in front of staff.

The instant Augusta paused to draw a breath, Julia plunged in. "It wasn't his fault, Mrs. Pelham."

He did not need her defense, pleasing though he found it. He started to say so.

"Please," his aunt said first. "Call me Aunt Augusta, dear."

"Aunt Augusta," Julia repeated, more maddeningly deferential to her than him. "I bullied him to let me drive."

Henry raised an eyebrow. "Bullied?" Seduced, more like. He'd taken pleasure in her skill.

"Prevailed upon him, then," Julia amended, smiling on his aunt.

"I took advantage of his willingness to please me on our wedding day."

His aunt's mouth fell open. "His willingness to please? Oh dear, if you only . . ."

Julia hurried ahead. "Truly, Mrs. . . . Aunt Augusta. I cajoled him into giving me the reins. I sprang the horses when he asked me not to. The storm came up, the lightning struck, the tree came down. We barely stopped the team from crashing into the tree. As it was, Diamond was badly cut, and I think we should go and tend him," she concluded pointedly.

Her eyes gleamed at him in challenge. He should have known she'd use any route to get to her precious horses.

In any other circumstances, so would he.

"Ah, but Aunt Augusta is right. Your needs must take precedence over the horses, my dear. Let her show you to your room." Augusta could settle her into her new quarters far better than he.

Julia glared. "No, I—The horses . . ."

". . . need my attention," he finished for her. "I'll report back straightaway. You have time for a bath and a rest."

"Much better, Henry," Aunt Augusta interrupted.

"But I feel fine . . ." Julia started, her tone turning mutinous.

Without a second of premeditation, Henry quashed rebellion with a decisive kiss. He must be mad, he thought, tasting her cold, shocked lips, her delicious resistance, the hot cave of her mouth. Then her body swayed, into his. In front of everyone he savored the feel of her firm breasts, the warmth of her belly until he realized desire was pooling in his hardening member. He broke away, and she looked up, silenced, dazed.

Obedient.

He'd struck gold, Henry congratulated himself. In future, he would manage his fractious filly by surprise.

"All settled then," he said.

For, as he headed to the stable, he really thought it was.

Chapter Seven

Love, the common passion in which chance and sensation take
[the] place of choice and reason, is, in some degree, felt by the
mass of mankind.
—Mary Wollstonecraft, *Vindication of the Rights of Woman*

Harry's staff disbanded in disturbingly military rows, Julia noted as
her husband made his cowardly escape. She gave an indignant sigh,
steadfastly denying the fizz of pleasure Henry's hasty public kiss had
ignited in her body.

"Don't feel neglected, my dear," Aunt Augusta answered, patting
her hand in mistaken sympathy. "My nephew has all God's gifts, but
no way with women."

"Really?" Julia croaked.

He had a way with her. It might be blunt and unpredictable, but
if he made a practice of these hot public kisses, her pledge of celibacy
was doomed.

"Truly. But come. Let him run off to his horses. I'll make you feel
at home."

Home. Julia had almost forgotten Henry's rambling, stately pile.
Augusta Pelham passed a sulky Isabeau on to a nurse, then led Julia

through a dank, arched gateway and climbed a spiral of stone steps. An oak door swung open to admit them to the cavernous core of the house, its old Great Hall.

"This way, my dear."

At home Julia thought nothing of tracking in stable muck, but here? On Henry's gleaming marble?

Augusta Pelham ignored Julia's muddy prints and resolutely swept her past three suits of armor polished to a sheen. "Henry restored the first marquis's dining room and arsenal according to a sketch he found. Just as it once was," she explained approvingly.

Above a yawning hearth were rows of axes, broadswords, flint-locks, and small shields. Julia followed her hostess's massive skirts up half a flight of wooden stairs, listening to more praise of Henry. She recognized the finials, chevaux rampant, from the Pelham coat of arms.

Rearing horses. Fitting, but would she fit, too?

Three hallways and half a dozen stairs and landings later, she was thoroughly lost. Never mind Augusta Pelham's explanation: "Every room is on a separate level—you've heard that, have you not?"

"Yes, indeed," said Julia, bobbing up one step, down five, then spiraling up three.

Finally, puffing just a bit, Augusta Pelham turned a corner into a brightly lit passage. Rush mats covered old oak floors. "The gallery, my dear. Henry restored this, too."

Julia's jaw dropped. It was splendid. It was . . . hers? Treasure chests and china vases lined the hallway. The afternoon sun poured through high mullioned windows, illuminating canvas after canvas of dour aristocrats. Daunting ancestors, all with the imperious Pel-ham nose, all looked like Henry at his overbearing worst.

Augusta charged to the end, through a sturdy door, and two steps down. "Your chamber, dear."

Julia's throat lumped with sudden gratitude. How thoughtful Henry was. Here she'd been dreading laces and embroidery, but he'd fitted up her private suite exactly to her taste. A low fire in the fireplace chased away the September chill. She'd be right at home. Walls of warm, dark wood were covered by rich tapestries of antique hunting scenes and overhung with sporting prints of hunters, fox-hounds, a prized stallion. Opposite, a wall of carved wood displayed a chase. Lunging dogs and mounted hunters harried a noble, fleeing stag.

But mainly she saw horses everywhere. Even the windows opened up on fields. She rushed over. "Oooh, paddocks, I can see them from here. And the stables. How considerate of Henry to give me such a view."

Augusta Pelham looked a little puzzled, but went on. "You must want to change." She flung open a wardrobe and pointed to Julia's clothes, sent yesterday. "We've a few hours before dinner. I'll call your maid. The water won't be hot, but she can draw your bath."

Julia's guide left. And Julia stood by the window, excitement pumping through her. Everything—even her own new bedchamber—was twice as large as Wraxham House. Twice as many horses. Twice as many servants.

Twice as many duties. She sobered. She was quick and strong and smart, and this would be the greatest challenge of her life. But what if she had no gift for her new role?

That work did not begin today. She settled into the window seat, close enough to take a measure of Henry's breeding program. Oh dear, she thought, surveying an enormous paddock crowded with mares and foals. A recipe for disaster, quite the opposite of the plan she'd carried out at Wraxham Stud. She'd tell her new husband first thing in the morning. Not that he wanted her poking around in his pastures, but her improvements would win him over. She lost herself in planning. The sun was setting softly in the west when she heard a gentle rapping at the door.

"Your bath, my lady," chirped a youthful voice.

Julia rushed to help. It wasn't in her nature to sit idly by while others waited on her. At the door, a hearty farm girl led in a troop of scullery maids with buckets of water for her bath. Julia could only watch. They filled the thigh-high copper tub in her dressing closet with not-quite-steaming water. It was more than half full before she realized she was the object of great curiosity.

"That'll be quite enough . . ." she said sharply.

The girl had the decency to blush. "Yes, my lady, of course, my lady," she stammered, shooing out the scullery maids. "Can I bring ye aught else, mum?"

"Nothing," she said crisply. Too crisply. She was kind to servants, unlike her imperious, luxury-loving stepmother. "I mean, my towel, please. And is there a robe for me?" she added more gently, but couldn't remember the girl's name. "And you are . . . ?"

Embarrassment flickered across the girl's broad face. "Gillie, mum." She rummaged in a drawer and pulled out fine linens. "We're all sorry, my lady. Gawking, I mean. We just worried so, you know, him bringing home another wife after . . ." The girl looked down at her polished boots.

Julia tensed. "After . . . ?"

"Shouldn't say, my lady." She twisted a brown braid in obvious embarrassment. "Oh, I've ruined everything."

"Not my bath, I think, Gillie." Though brimful of questions, Julia had no intention of asking her new maid anything about Henry's first wife, not on her wedding day. She dipped a finger in the copper tub. Warm enough. "Very nice. This will do."

Gillie looked up cautiously. "If you're sure, my lady? Then I'll just leave you to it. The bell rope's there if you need me," she added hastily, bowing her way out. "Can I help you undress?"

"No, you may go," Julia said, running her fingers through the bell rope's silken tassel.

The girl stepped out and quietly closed the door behind her.

Julia hadn't been alone since this morning on her filly. Hugging herself, she spun around, taking in every luxurious foot of her magnificent new quarters. All this, and a warm bath waiting. Scuffing out of her ruined slippers, she peeled off her scorched gloves and flung them in the fire. Her dress she treated more respectfully, stretching her arms back to unbutton it, peeling it off her shoulders, skimming it down her body, and dropping it on the floor.

She looked down at her fine undergarments in dismay. Even they were soiled from her escapade with Henry's phaeton. But they were only clothes, she told herself, and she had more where they came from. Stripping down to skin, she piled them on top of her wedding dress and stepped into her bath, one cold toe first.

It was tepid. Perfect. At home, she never asked for heated water, but this private, lukewarm bath would soothe her after the upheaval of her day. Sinking to her chin, she drew in a deep breath and let it out.

She could get used to luxury and leisure. Despite Henry's irritating tendency to shoo her from the stables, he had brought her into a beautiful castle. Despite his annoying way of going all male and masterful on her, he'd provided her with a room that suited her tastes exactly.

Perhaps he was right about the bath.

Henry's colts were quite distraught, but not so much as he. What had he been thinking, kissing Julia again? Everyone would assume he was besotted when he was merely . . . intrigued. So what if his new bride had shown more mettle in a day than Therese in five years of marriage?

Julia was not his type.

Diamond's head bumped into Henry's chest. He firmed his hands on the colt's headstall. "Easy with that water, Wat."

"But we've got to clean the wound." Again Nance doused the fetlock, and again the horse danced.

"I'll do that, Wat."

Henry knelt at Diamond's hoof, soaked a piece of toweling, and pressed it to the cut, almost cursing the fretful colt. It needed time and patience for the wet rag to soften the caked mud and dried blood. Time which Julia had taken. Diamond had stood quietly for her ministrations.

He would have stood quietly, too, in the horse's place. For any ministrations she might offer him.

He squashed that thought like a summer fly. He could not afford to be intrigued with this singularly mannish woman. Julia, he mused, had given no thought to ruining her best lace—and no attention to his directions. She promised to be a handful.

No, never a handful. From here on out, it was strictly hands-off.

Hands behind his back.

Kisses forbidden.

Though he had enjoyed even that last quickest one. He liked her sweet, full lips and her high, firm breasts. She had a way of meeting his advances, yet yielding at the same time. For a virgin, she was fearless.

And virgin she would stay, he commanded himself.

"My lord?" Nance asked.

It occurred to Henry that Nance had been addressing him for some time.

"Yes, Wat."

Fiona Carr

"I was saying, my lord, you should mind the right wheel on your phaeton."

Half listening, Henry lifted the toweling around the colt's fetlock and inspected the wound. Rather nasty, after all. "Damaged when we hit the tree, no doubt. You take care of it."

"I wouldn't exactly call it damage, my lord. I'd prefer you saw it for yourself."

"No time, man. You handle it."

"If you insist, my lord," Nance answered, a note of disapproval in his voice.

"I insist. Good God, man, it's my wedding day." He scraped away the mud and clotted blood, than cleansed the wound with a gentle flood of water from a wine bottle. "A shot of whiskey. But brace yourself," he ordered to all the grooms who stood about to help. "This colt won't take insults lying down."

He poured, and Diamond reared. It took three men to bring him down. Afterwards, Henry walked the colt until it calmed. Then he closed it up in a box stall with fresh bedding. He ordered Nance to walk the colt at intervals throughout the night to stave off swelling, and headed for his castle.

He had a family dinner to attend with his new bride.

And he had to change. His man Grayson's deft brushwork would hardly rid him and his clothing of the day's dirt. Harry took the private stairs to his chambers three at a time, but he was exhausted. He'd met all challenges today—wedding, fire, thunderstorm, tempting bride, pouting daughter, indignant aunt. He flatly dreaded dinner, and looked forward to a few moments to collect himself before meeting with his wife. The well-oiled door opened onto a flood of candlelight . . .

A maidenly shriek . . .

A splash of water and a vision of . . .

Julia. She shot up from his deep copper tub, naked, water sluicing down her shoulders, between her breasts, along her long coltish thighs.

His manhood leapt to attention.

Her hands flew to her breasts. "Henry!" she shrieked. She criss-crossed her legs to hide her private parts, making the sight deliciously more tempting. "What are you doing in my chambers? It's not time for dinner. Aunt Augusta only just sent up my bath."

64

Henry froze, wishing she'd freeze, too, so he could admire her supple, healthy body at his leisure. She was sleek and wet and gleaming from her bath. All day, he'd managed not to think how she would look disrobed, telling himself the sight of her body wouldn't affect him. He'd never been attracted to tall, big-boned, small-breasted, and straight-waisted women.

Damnation, he was now. His bride was fully a woman, more woman than he'd encountered in his purposefully limited amours. The lush auburn delta at the joining of her legs glistened with water. When she moved, he glimpsed a pout of ruddy, secret flesh, inviting his caresses, even kisses, if they wouldn't spook his untried bride. Heaven help him, he liked the idea of an untried bride. Lust jolted through him.

Her hands shot down to cover her sweet fleece. Her breasts sprang free, jiggling a bit and swaying, rosy nipples puckering in his direction.

Harry stood transfixed, an ache of desire spreading through his groin to the root of his manhood. Interesting, he thought, through the daze of arousal. His masculine senses, it seemed, preferred her in motion. Preferred her.

"Henry, you're looking!"

Of course, he was looking. One more minute of this, and he'd strip to the skin and tackle her in the water. Heaven help him to remember she was just his wife.

Not his lover.

Not his taste.

"You could sit back down," he said, struggling manfully to suppress a wolfish grin. She sank underwater in a heap, splashing soap suds on his favorite old Turkish carpet. In moments, her head shot up, water streaming down her strong-boned face.

"Spying does not become you, my lord," she sputtered. "And spying on me in my bath does not bode well for our agreement."

A gentleman would be a cad to upbraid a bride at such disadvantage. He leaned against the doorframe and crossed his arms.

"Agreed," he said solemnly.

She eased back in the tub, still sitting up.

The better for him to see, he thought greedily. She seemed unaware of how the water floated the tops of her breasts up to his view. Not overly large, they would just fit his hands.

Not what he should be thinking. *Talking. He should be talking.* "So who put you up to bathing in my chambers?"

"No one put me up to anything!" Julia shot back, thoroughly out of sorts. She wriggled beneath the water but, under Henry's gaze, felt like a netted trout. "You suggested that I take a bath."

"In my chambers?"

She shrugged, which only made her breasts bob in the water. "Your aunt brought me here," she said as neutrally as she could.

"My aunt brought you here," Henry repeated.

"No need to sound so inhospitable, my lord. Unlike you, she made every effort to make me feel at home."

Her new husband's eye ticked with ill-concealed annoyance. "You are home. But your chambers are down the hall."

She listened with rising disillusionment. Any moment he would kick her out, to some brocaded and embroidered female bower. With no stables or paddocks in sight. But she would not betray her fears. Her disappointment. "And here I thought you'd fitted out the room for me," she made herself say lightly.

He stalked over and propped a lean hip on the edge of her tub, his gaze piercing the soapy water. She slid her hands to cover herself. Her breasts felt enormous, buoyant, separate from her body, but she vowed not to shrink before her husband like some timid virgin, virgin though she was.

"Who knows you're here?" he asked, watching her breasts bobbing in the water as if they were inadequate.

"Aunt Augusta, naturally," she offered, hiding her discomfort with a perfectly reasonable tone.

He arched a brow. "She filled the tub herself, I presume."

"She sent my maid for that."

"Gillie? And who else?" he prompted, leaning forward . . . to intimidate her or to inspect her, before he rejected her for all time?

"Three or four scullery maids," she recalled. "Looking me over."

"I'll bet they did," he said, his voice tight with disapproval. "You will have to move, that's all."

"You'll have to move my clothes first. They're already in the wardrobe."

He muttered a private oath, his face darkening. "A couple of footmen can move them in a moment."

Indignation fired in her chest. "Yes, that will do the trick. By all means, move your bride out, lock, stock, and barrel, on your wedding night."

He set his jaw. "You should never have been moved in. And there's not going to be a wedding night."

"That must be why you're leaning over the tub ogling me like I'm good enough to eat."

"I'm not ogling you."

"Leering then."

"Any man would look at a naked woman in his bath, Julia. But rest assured, I've no desire to consummate this marriage."

His blunt rejection capped all the petty humiliations of her day. Shaking with quick anger, she stood up, splashing his neat frockcoat with soapy, dirty water.

"If you're so immune to my non-existent charms, my lord, you won't mind fetching my towel."

"Of course not," he said in a gratifyingly choked voice. He swept the towel off its rack and, averting his gaze, unfurled it to cloak her. Something very wicked inside her clicked.

His turn, she thought, to squirm.

Ignoring the towel, she turned her dripping, naked body away from him and sweetened her voice. "Dry my back, my lord. Unless you'd prefer to ring for Gillie."

"The servants know too much already," he said grimly. He sounded hoarse. He looked disheveled. Desirable.

She shivered in response.

Idiot, she chastised herself.

He blotted her shoulders like a butcher plumping a loin of beef.

"Ouch! I must have wrenched a muscle driving the colts home," she said, continuing her charade. "Surely, you can be gentler."

Not even a little bit. Pat. Pat. Blot. Blot. But his hot breath streamed over her neck. "This is as gentle as it gets, you little vixen, unless you want me to throw you on the carpet and have my way with you."

She gulped. She wasn't ready for *that.* It was just that driving Henry to distraction thrilled her more than hurdling over the highest hedge. She'd never have hoped a great gangly, mannish woman like herself could have such power over any man. But to have it over Henry . . .

She snatched the towel from him and buried herself in its soft folds. "Don't be so literal, Henry. It was just a game."

He prowled around to face her and took her shoulders in his large hands. She'd never felt more vulnerable, naked beneath the towel and dripping bath water onto Henry's carpet.

"Make no mistake, my lady. This is not a game. This is an arrangement. You married me to escape your brother, and I married you to give you that escape. You have your horses, and my daughter has a new mother. You gave your word."

True. And her word was as good as any man's.

So why was her heart pinching with regret?

"Then you shouldn't keep on kissing me."

His face clouded. "I kissed you to satisfy our families, and then to shut you up."

But she didn't want to be shut up, not about his kisses, not about anything. "It's just that, Henry," she paused to give her point more weight, "it satisfied me."

He satisfied her. Fool that she was, she'd already broken every promise she'd made to herself. That she would do her duty. That nothing would come between her and her horses. That she would handle that old infatuation with Henry Pelham as she'd done long ago.

"Well, it didn't satisfy me by a long shot," he said harshly. "No more kisses, Julia. Neither of us can afford them. Now dry off and get your clothes. I'll change in there. Dinner is served shortly."

He stalked across the bedchamber and slammed his dressing room door. Julia even imagined she heard a boot strike the wall.

His arrogance annoyed her. Her attraction to him confused her. His control made her want to pitch a fit. She skinnied into her delicate French silk chemise and picked out a simple ruby velvet frock. It had a high neck and sleeves down to her knuckles. Best, after this close call, to cover up from throat to toe. She couldn't bear another merciless inspection, followed by rejection. So she sat on the hearth before the fire to towel the dampness from her hair, not caring if it curled as tightly as a judge's wig.

But Henry distracted her. A wall away, wardrobe doors jerked open. Drawers slammed shut.

She tried to dry her hair. But she couldn't help thinking she'd rather be toweling off and dressing up with her husband's help.

* * *

Henry stabbed a diamond pin into his spotless neckcloth and scouted out his bedchamber. Not a bride in sight. His heart lurched. Surely, she hadn't bolted. Julia was disingenuous, unformed, and rash, but courageous. His temper may have gotten the best of him for a moment, but she had not cowered. He stepped around the heavy hangings about his bed to the center of the room.

Ahh, there, by the hearth. He sucked in a breath of admiration. She bent to the fire to dry her hair, her straight spine gently curved. Lifting an arm to test her hair, she revealed a lovely breast, plump as a ripe fruit, and feminine. His heart raced. Her waist nipped in just there, her blood-red dress draping around her form. Her hips, which poked out provocatively, were just wide enough to please.

Mindlessly, his manhood sprang back to life.

She ran her fingers through her short-cut hair—her only nod to fashion—shaking water droplets on the fire.

It sizzled.

He sizzled.

For long moments of sheer lunacy, he allowed himself the luxury of watching lovely womanhood unawares at such a simple domestic ritual. Therese had had maids, had always needed privacy, had always . . .

Oh, banish memory to the flames.

Julia was here and now. He'd have to be a corpse not to appreciate her wholesome, unaffected country charms.

And a dolt to give in to them. Madness lay that way. If he could not control such thoughts, he was done for. His family was done for. His line was sunk. So much for keeping up appearances. Word would spread through his household like a barnfire. He could hear his staff speculating on how long, how loud, how often.

Ah, hell. He was speculating on all those things himself.

Aunt Augusta's meddling move had set him up. His long-denied desire could spell disaster to his plans.

Damn his aunt's good intentions. Damn his randy manhood, which would make the devil of a worrisome companion for his wedding dinner. He slid a hand inside his breeches and adjusted it down and sideways, reminding himself that Julia was not the type of woman he liked.

She arched her back and sighed.

His head and heart and manhood declared war. Biting back an

69

oath, he buttoned his waistcoat over his bulging breeches and cleared his throat.

From the distant dining room, Aunt Augusta's gong rang out, sounding time for dinner.

"Julia." He rasped, then tried again. "We'll be late."

She shot up, smoothing her unruly mop. With her hot red hair and hot red dress, she did look good enough to eat.

"I must look a fright," she mumbled wretchedly.

Only the cruelest husband would let her think that. "Ladies' maids in London put a morning's labor into achieving that effect."

"Horse apples," she said stoutly.

Damn, he liked her earthy retorts. He admired her earthy attractions. He would not play the cad. "Seriously, Julia, you look lovely."

Her cheeks, already flushed from the fire, reddened. And his mind careened to dangerous thoughts of reddening them with passion, here, on the deep down covers of his bed.

Not his mind, too. Yet another part of him that didn't care if she was not the type of woman he found attractive.

He offered her his neutral elbow.

"Come, my lady," he said gruffly, reining in runaway lust. "Our family must be waiting."

"Must we go?" Julia's emerald eyes pled for a reprieve.

The gong sounded a second time, ringing more urgently through the twisting halls.

"Aunt Augusta sets the evening meals at eight. I won't have my daughter thinking anything has changed."

Even though everything evidently had.

Chapter Eight

> . . . a girl, condemned to sit for hours together listening to the
> idle chat of weak nurses, or to attend at her mother's toilette
> . . . will imitate her mother or aunts, and amuse herself by
> adorning her lifeless doll . . .
> —Mary Wollstonecraft, *Vindication of the Rights of Woman*

He could have said it more nicely, Julia thought, though she approved that he put his daughter first. He could have done a lot of things differently on their first day. But before she could review what had gone awry, he was sweeping her down the halls of his amazing castle.

She tried really, really hard to commit to memory Rayne's twisting trek to the dining hall. She went so far as to count paces down corridors and steps up and down and around stairs. Eighty-seven paces later—to say nothing of a short flight up, two down, and another up again—she was completely turned around.

"We don't have time to take a ramble, my lord."

"This is as direct as we can go."

She gave an unladylike snort of disbelief.

"Think of it as a giant figure eight, wrapping around . . ." he started patiently.

" 'Two inner courtyards' . . . so Aunt Augusta said."

"I suppose she told you it was not quite square."

"And every room is on a different level. Why every room, do you suppose?" She stretched a bit to keep pace with his long-legged stride.

He shrugged. "Some say my great, great grandfather had a plan."

"A method to his madness?" Julia teased.

Henry was not amused. "Unlike our other mad ancestors, he set his insanity in stone. Watch your step." A footman came to life and swung open a door.

She blinked into a golden dining room. Up and down the polished table, candelabras sparkled. Great brass sconces glowed along the walls. Branches on the mantle flickered as Henry escorted her to her seat. They passed Uncle Bertie, but she didn't see Aunt Augusta. Suddenly Augusta Pelham's white-capped head popped up above the table.

"I must have left them in my room, Bertie," she complained.

Ever-present parrot on his shoulder, Bertie Pelham sighed. Aunt Augusta's antique brocade gown crackled as he helped her to her feet. "They're dangling from your necklace, Aunt."

Momentarily confused, she looked down at her bosom and spied her missing spectacles. "Oh, dear. Quite so, Bertie. Whatever would I do . . ." She broke off, spotting Henry and Julia. "I see you had your bath and found your way," she said.

"Henry helped."

Bertie and Augusta fairly twinkled.

Julia bit her lip in consternation. Everybody knew about the tub. And Aunt Augusta had arranged it. She might dodder about her spectacles, but she was up to something, Julia realized, suspicion galloping through her. Did Henry have any control over his aunt? After all, she'd put Julia in his chambers, evidently against his express wishes. She had ordered the scullery maids to bring the water.

Had she planned for him to find his virgin bride lolling in his bath?

A sudden flap of wings in the lofty space above her, and Julia ducked to escape a diving bird. Raj, in dapper gray, shed feathers as he ricocheted from mantelpiece to cornice.

72

The Mad Marquis

"For God's sake, Uncle," Henry exploded. "This is the dining room. Chain him to his perch."

"He hates the perch," Uncle Bertie grumbled, another relative not quite at Henry's command.

But Bertie Pelham chained the bird, then turned to Julia and bowed. His peacock-colored evening clothes glinted in the candlelight. "So very sorry, my dear. But welcome. A brilliant . . . no beautiful . . . yes, a brilliant *and* beautiful enhancement to our family," he said effusively.

Julia felt her face heat at the unaccustomed, and unlikely, compliments.

"Beautiful," Raj squawked, as if agreeing with his master. *"Beautiful, beautiful, beauti—"*

"Un-cle . . ." Henry grated. "Another word from that bird today . . ."

"I like it when Raj talks, Papa." Isabeau slipped out from behind her great-great aunt's skirts and took her father's hand. "We thought you'd never come down. Aunt Augusta says you have to get to know each other. Do you know each other now?"

Julia blushed hotter. Even Henry flushed, his high cheekbones dusky with discomfort.

"We understand each other perfectly," he said. He caught Julia's eye, admonished his aunt with a glare, then scooped his daughter into his arms. "But you must be starving, *ma petite,* and we should all sit down to eat."

"À côté de vous, Papa?"

"Beside me?" he echoed in English, obviously pleased. *"Mais certainmente, mignon."* With a flourish, he pulled out her chair. "Lady Isabeau, *asseyez-vous."*

Darting Julia a victorious look, Isabeau sat, skirts and lacy pantaloons foaming about her.

Julia endured a breathless moment of feeling out of place. But Rayne came over quickly, placed his hand at the small of her back in a reassuring touch, and directed her to the opposite end of the long—and growing longer by the minute—table. She felt banished, but told herself that he honored her in her new state. Publicly, if nowhere else, she was mistress of his house.

The moment everyone was seated Uncle Bertie called for toasts. Thirsty, Julia finished off a glass of something Uncle Bertie assured her was an exceptional vintage French wine. To go with her French silk undergarments, she thought wickedly. After they were served, the wedding day was reviewed with good humor and much laughter—mainly Augusta's and Bertie's. It was only when the staff set tiny stuffed quails and two plump partridges on the sideboard that matters took a downward turn.

Isabeau wriggled off her seat and whispered something in her father's ear.

He rolled his eyes and shook his head. "Not tonight," Julia thought she heard him say.

Isabeau was adamant. "She'll feel so left out."

"She's supposed to be left out," Henry clearly said.

Julia was shocked. Life in a vast, moldy castle must be lonely for an only child. If Isabeau had a little village friend or nursery companion, of course she'd want her at the celebration.

Augusta looked down her new-found spectacles. "Oh let her, Henry. Let's not contend with this tonight."

"Besides," Uncle Bertie pointed out with unflappable good cheer, "we all know your method isn't working."

Julia felt magnanimous . . . and touched by the child's dejection. "I wouldn't mind having her little friend for dinner."

"Really?" said Henry darkly, and snapped a finger at his staff. "Setting, Farley. Susannah, fill the plate. It seems this skeleton wants out tonight."

Oh lord, thought Julia, what ever had she wrought? Perhaps he had a secret child, a mad one. Or a ward. Or a by-blow. A shiver of foreboding trickled down her spine. Waiting uncertainly, Julia knocked back another glass of wine.

No one came. The ormolu clock on the mantel ticked loud minutes by, and no one came. And no one seemed to notice. Or to care. Uncle Bertie passed on eating partridge. Aunt Augusta signaled for more salt. Henry hacked his quail to bits.

But Julia agreed with Uncle Bertie. Dead partridge and live parrot made an uneasy mix. She pushed some bright green peas around her plate.

"You'll quite like the sauce," Isabeau finally said in a very grown-up voice.

The real grown-ups were silent. Expressionless.

Looking around, Julia was appalled, then realized she was the only one who'd taken any sauce. "It's delicious."

"I wasn't talking to you," Isabeau said curtly.

"Isabeau . . ." Henry's low warning rumbled up the table.

"Well, I wasn't," Isabeau said, a great deal more impertinent than Julia thought consistent with good manners and proper duty to one's father. It made her angry, for Henry's sake more than her own. Particularly as his aunt and uncle's attention was totally engaged with their third course.

"Who *were* you talking to, Isabeau?" Julia asked, sure no one had come in.

"Marie Claire," Isabeau mumbled, fixing her gaze on her mashed parsnips and potatoes.

But there wasn't another soul in sight. Isabeau had made this up! "Perhaps if you described her," she prompted her new charge.

Henry's glare shot up the table. "Don't encourage her."

She looked down the long table at Henry, aware of his and all other eyes upon her. "I can't see what it would hurt."

Isabeau gazed around, torn. "I know what she looks like, Papa."

Henry glowered.

Julia sympathized. "There were times with all my brothers, I wished I had an imaginary friend."

"She's not imaginary," Isabeau corrected, horrified. "She's really real, she's really here. She talks to me. We play dolls and cards and dress-up. She just won't let any grown-ups see her. *Especially* at supper."

"Oh," Julia said. So those were the rules. Isabeau's rules, not her father's.

Her father darted daggers of disapproval down the table.

How to handle this? Better yet . . . .

How would her brothers have handled it if she'd had a secret playmate?

Gathering imaginary weapons, Julia nibbled a tiny drumstick from her untouched quail and turned to Isabeau. "I'm afraid she must be rather thin, as she does not eat her food."

Startled to be taken seriously, Isabeau concocted a long face. "She's waiting for her pudding."

Very inventive! Julia almost choked on her tender quail.

But Aunt Augusta called her grand-niece's bluff. "Girls don't get pudding if they haven't cleaned their plates."

Isabeau's face lengthened but she rallied with near grown-up aplomb. "The plates were piled rather high for girls."

Henry rapped the hilt of his carving knife on the table and stood up.

Isabeau winced, obviously expecting a firm scold.

"That will be quite enough, all of you," he said, his voice more threatening for its reason and its calm. "It does not pay to play along, Aunt. As for you, Julia, now you know. Isabeau, clean your plate, or you will take your pudding in your room. Farley, remove that extra setting."

Isabeau's eyes welled up, perilously close to spilling over, and she pushed her plate away.

Julia chugged another glass of wine to cover her displeasure. Her new husband was acting like a tyrant, and tyranny always drove her to rebel.

Farley oozed around the table, picked up the disputed setting, then paused over Isabeau's plate as if to remove it as well.

"I'll take that, Farley," Julia said crisply. "No one should have pudding in her room on her father's wedding day."

Daggers, bayonets, and lances were metaphorically hurled her way from her tight-lipped spouse at the far end of the dining table.

Fearlessly, she polished off the contents of Isabeau's plate, washed it down with wine, then called out, "Pudding, everyone?"

Chapter Nine

For what purpose were the passions implanted? That man by struggling with them might attain a degree of knowledge denied to the brutes . . .
—Mary Wollstonecraft, *Vindication of the Rights of Woman*

The pudding was a family favorite, but all Henry wanted was a glass of port. There was no question of retiring with his uncle for that.

Aunt Augusta was nodding off, leaving his bride to her own devices. Besides, he had grave doubts about encouraging that friendship. Between his aunt's opinions and his new bride's independence, those two ladies had a cavalier disregard for his authority. He nearly shuddered. Disaster loomed.

Dinner mercifully ended.

Before Isabeau left with nurse, she bestowed a cool kiss on Henry's cheek but an approving smack on her new stepmother's. Julia had cleared her first hurdle in fine style. He couldn't approve of how she'd kowtowed to his conniving daughter, but he'd deal with the imaginary friend tomorrow.

The next hurdle was his. Pray heaven he was up for it. He looked at Julia across the room, her hot red dress, her warm pink

77

cheeks . . . oh, he was up for something. The wrong thing.

The forbidden thing.

Severely curbing his imagination, he grabbed a brace of candles and steered his bride into the cold, dark hallways of the family madhouse.

At the first stair step she stumbled.

He caught her just in time. "You're foxed," he said, taken aback. He'd lost track of how much of his uncle's prized wine she had imbibed. And he hadn't settled where she'd sleep.

If he could get her to their bedroom.

"Tipsy perhaps, but never foxed. I learned drinking at my brothers' knees," she boasted, and recovered from her near fall to glide beside him.

"Exactly how much did you drink?"

She shot him a reproving look. "You're awfully severe on a woman's wedding night."

"Not without provocation. How many glasses?"

"One or two." She gave a careless—tipsy—shrug. "Or three or four."

"That is unacceptable before my daughter." He'd vowed the day she was born that she'd never see grown-ups at such disadvantages as he'd been forced to see his father. "Although appearing drunk before her is not nearly as bad as indulging her fantasy."

"I think it was good for her," Julia said frankly. Soberly, in fact. "If she invented an imaginary friend, she must feel terribly alone. Someone in this household needs to take her loneliness to heart."

"You call delusion loneliness?"

"What do you call it?"

"Madness," he said grimly.

"Many children have imaginary friends, Henry," Julia said, touching his forearm in unasked-for commiseration.

Warning bells clanged through him. "And you know that how?"

She tilted her head as if puzzled by his intensity. "Common sense, of course."

He halted abruptly and spun her to face him. "You're sure you don't have imaginary friends of your own."

She reeled, then righted herself. "Why would I give the time of day to an imaginary friend? I have my horses."

Horse friends. He groaned. "I can see that's much more sane."

But Julia was off and galloping. "Oh, Henry. I am so relieved. We see eye to eye on that. In fact, horses would help Isabeau immensely. They would replace her imaginary friend—which you do not approve of—with horses, which you do."

He held up the branch of candles to navigate a narrow stair. Julia's enthusiasm was seductive, but horses would not work. How to explain that to a woman who had lived for the creatures?

Factually, he decided. "Isabeau is terrified of horses."

"Nonsense," Julia said heartily, then gave him a teasing nudge. "Are you sure she's your daughter?"

Quick wrath flooded him. His new bride had to take his daughter's mad obsession seriously. "I have not one particle of doubt. She may not have my love of horses, but she has the family lunacy in full measure."

Julia pokered up. "I found her an ordinary little girl with a lively imagination."

"There's nothing ordinary about putting food on a plate for someone who's not there."

"I'd prefer to form my own opinions, if you don't mind."

He minded very much, but they had reached his bedchamber, and he had more pressing problems: the awkward issue of where his bride would sleep, and the even trickier issue of pretending he didn't want to join her.

His dressing room was rather cramped for her to sleep there. It communicated with a second bedchamber where Therese had lived out the last sickly years of her life. Julia couldn't know that, but he didn't relish the association. In days to come, he didn't want his daughter to find her stepmother in her mother's deathbed. It could not be a permanent solution.

Still, it couldn't hurt tonight. No one would be the wiser if he and Julia took these separate rooms. Unhappy associations, to say nothing of two thick walls between them, would curb his baser instincts, should they arise to trouble him again.

Perhaps they wouldn't anyway. The disturbing spectacle of Isabeau championing her little friend renewed his vow to father no more children, ever. It hadn't, however, iced his earlier ardor for his bride. He couldn't be angry enough or Julia provoking enough to dampen his lust.

At the door, Henry dismissed Julia's new maid and his long-time valet, unwilling for anyone to be privy to any portion of his nuptial night. Julia glided in, her blood-red dress setting off her auburn hair and accenting the long straight lines of the body he once thought masculine. Strange, how feminine she looked tonight.

How desirable.

How available.

Desperate, he recited a litany of mad ancestors, the reason for the vow he'd made the night he found his despondent father, dead in his wrecked carriage. The reason for his vow seemed fuzzy.

Julia plopped on the upholstered benches at the foot of his four-poster bed as if it had been hers forever.

"Make yourself at home, my lady," he drawled.

She lifted her skirts and kicked off a pair of nankeen boots, suitable for the barn.

Catching his astonished look, she explained, "Ruined my wedding slippers, you remember, in the mud. Besides, these don't hurt my feet."

Harry scowled. "We have conventions for a reason."

"True, I suppose. But no one ever notices. Including you." Her fingers deftly worked off a pair of the finest French hosiery.

Barn boots with fine French hosiery? His mind reeled. His eyes goggled.

She had slender ankles, pretty feet.

Pretty feet? He must be stark, staring mad. Fisting his hands behind him, he backed up to the wall and staked out his position. Far distant from his appetizing bride. "Naturally, I expect you to keep our bargain."

"Our bargain?" She looked all innocence, then said gamely, "Oh that. You haven't bedded me, my lord."

Her candor shocked him. "I confess, I expected a show of shyness, even modesty."

She gave him an open look, her emerald eyes sparkling in the candlelight. "But why? You're not interested in me that way."

It wasn't that he wasn't interested. The problem was, he was. A couple hours ago, he'd almost bedded her, and his manhood was once again bang up to the mark.

It wasn't her, he told himself. It was his long years of self-imposed celibacy. Even a monk—and he'd very nearly lived like one—would be tempted by a beddable woman in his cell.

"That is our agreement," he said levelly, counting on her innocence to miss his erection.

"So it is, my lord." She gave a determined smile, and stood.

And wobbled.

"Oooh," she said cheerfully, clutching a handful of the bed's heavy draperies for balance. "I may be just the tiniest bit foxed after all." Giggling, she lurched around to the side of the bed and flopped across it, a picture of health and innocence and willingness, for all he could tell.

Drunk, she was disarming, too. But it annoyed the hell out of him to think she was too numb to notice him on their wedding night.

It was quite beside the point that he didn't want her to notice him.

The point was . . . not her hard-edged body, not the mixed messages in that velvet dress, not her naked vulnerable ankles bared to his sight for the first time . . . The point was . . .

Somewhere around the sweet, high arch of her foot, he'd lost track of the point. He had to keep talking or he'd be sunk.

"Christ, Julia," he said, deliberately harsh. "Is there nothing you don't do to excess?"

She stopped giggling, then said cavalierly, "Love, my lord. I have never loved, or been loved, to extremes." She flipped over on her back, scrunched a bolster under her head, and spoke conversationally as if in the presence of a friend. Or a brother. "I think that's quite sad, don't you? Once upon a time, it might have turned out differently. I had my day. They took me up to London for a Season. But not now. And not with you." She paused, then spoke as if thinking aloud. "Yes, sad. Very sad. But you and I—we struck a sound bargain. Very sound. Brilliant, in fact."

His thought exactly. But he could not come up with another thought, or a single, solitary thing to say. Nor could he risk standing here lusting after what could never be: a tumble with an uninhibited country girl. No doubt, she'd be at her luscious best if he offered her a roll in the hay.

Retreating to his dressing room, he almost stripped to small clothes, then thought better of it. His breeches with their complicated flaps and buttons seemed his last defense against himself. Wrapping the silk-lined luxury of his woolen dressing robe securely over his evening clothes, he formed his plan. He would permanently move her into Therese's quarters, after all. He could have them newly furnished, papered, painted in a style to suit. But he wouldn't kick her out, relegating her to the grand suite down the gallery as he'd intended.

Especially not tonight, despite the intolerable thrum of desire pulsing through him. Too many knew they'd begun their marriage in this room together. It was her duty to command the staff. He would not subject her to idle speculations that he'd rejected her only hours after they'd retired to bed.

In the bedchamber, he banked the fire and snuffed out candles all around, the only sounds the shuffle of his slippers and the peaceful rhythm of her breathing. He moved closer, thinking to rouse her gently and lead her to the adjoining room.

She was sleeping like the dead.

Damnation. He could carry her in. But he didn't want to test his flagging resolution by feeling her arm around his neck, her body against his belly, the side of her breast against his chest. He was too far gone. He marshaled his last bit of reason: He could take the cot himself, but he slept badly in strange beds. He could escape to the stables. He was no stranger there in foaling season or when a favorite horse was ill.

But that would jeopardize the way everyone saw his bride. He didn't care what anyone thought of him, but he wouldn't have grooms or stableboys laying bets on what was the matter with his wife.

For a few moments he stood over her, taking in her sensuous curves, her private womanliness, her perfect ease. He was exhausted and damned unwilling to be turned out of his own bed. Except for those pretty feet, she was still fully dressed. What could be the harm?

She was innocent; she wouldn't try to tempt him.

He pulled an extra blanket over her and tunneled in between the sheets, exhausted.

Wide awake. He checked his buttons.

He was buttoned up.

Nothing else protected her from him. Just quilting and down feathers and his troublesome vow.

Chapter Ten

Gentleness, docility, and a spaniel-like affection are . . . consistently recommended as the cardinal virtues of the [female] sex . . .

—Mary Wollstonecraft, *Vindication of the Rights of Woman*

Julia slept dreamlessly, and woke to a high horrible cry of human pain. Alarmed, she pushed up on her elbows and rubbed sleep from her eyes. What could it be? Ah, Uncle Bertie's peacocks, she remembered, and breathed in relief, only to feel stays pinching into her ribs. Puzzled, she ran her hands down her hips and encountered velvet. The dress she'd worn to dinner.

She'd not changed for bed last night. But whose bed? And who had covered her? And when?

She sat up, a blanket sliding off around her. The room was rich with garnet red and hunter green and dark mahogany—she had her bearings in an instant. Henry's bedchamber. Had he relinquished it to her?

He couldn't have. Yesterday afternoon he'd been awfully displeased to find her here. And last night after dinner he was obviously uncomfortable when he'd brought her up to bed. Not to *his* bed, she thought ruefully. But here she was, waking up in it.

And if she'd slept in his bed, where had he slept?

She hadn't even slept between the sheets.

But he had. Flabbergasted, she rolled over. *His* side of the bed showed a hasty attempt to make things nice. Had she and Henry Pelham slept together on their wedding night? She drew up her knees and hugged them close. Oh, he could not have bedded her. She more or less knew from breeding horses what married men and women did. People took their clothes off—hose, drawers, chemises.

She checked. Hose intact. Drawers in place. Chemise knotted around her knees. He hadn't even relieved her of her stays.

Besides, she didn't want to breed with Henry. Much as she liked his kisses, anything more would be a great mistake.

But if he'd let her share his bed, he must not find her repellent after all. She liked that. A lot.

She also liked it that he'd fled the scene quite early. She could get used to lazing about in Henry Pelham's private lair while he . . .

Blast it all! He'd beaten her to the stables, and she was worried about Minx and Meteor and Fidget and the rest of her horses due today.

Thankfully, she never dawdled over her toilette. In moments, she was buttoning up her best riding habit, the one not yet so frayed from constant use. She poked her head into the sweeping gallery. Up and down its walls, eccentric ancestors scowled. Now, if only she could contrive not to lose herself on the way to the stables . . .

A quarter hour later, she emerged, flush with victory, from Henry's labyrinthine stronghold into the stables' vaulted courtyard. Unlike his castle, Henry's stables were strictly built on an orderly European plan. The paving stones were immaculately swept. Brass finials were polished, leather lead ropes oiled. Several dozen horses stood in stalls. Half a dozen more lounged in spacious boxes. She breathed in sun-cured straw and hay, feeling more herself than at any time since her engagement.

In the courtyard, Wat Nance trotted Diamond out, glowering at her presence. A clump of men mulled over the colt's injury. Henry stood tall amongst them, his unruly ash-brown hair at odds with his immaculate attire and aristocratic bearing. Her stomach did a little somersault at the shock of him in public after private kisses, after . . .

What had happened in his bedchamber?

The Mad Marquis

Unfortunately, her memory blurred a bit there at the home stretch. Surely she hadn't let Uncle Bertie ply her with five glasses of wine. Surely she hadn't downed them like some strumpet in a public house. Surely she hadn't flung herself across Harry's bed and . . . and . . . what?

As if attuned to her befuddlement, Henry turned and spotted her. He had every reason to look daggers at her, she supposed. In their first short day of married life, she'd driven his best team into a fallen oak, made trouble with his daughter, and wound up foxed in his forbidden bed. But she refused to flinch beneath his glare and turned to mind the injured colt.

Despite her warning otherwise, someone had wrapped its wounded fetlock.

Bad idea. She stepped in closer.

Henry stalked up, inspecting her with a critical eye.

She folded her arms across her habit. Truth be told, over her breasts, for his disturbing gaze reminded her that he'd seen her naked as the day she was born when she'd rashly stood up in his tub. He apparently suffered no such memories, which was even more disturbing.

"Too early in the season for cubbing, my lady," he said firmly.

"I didn't come for that." She wasn't the least bit interested in training Henry's fledgling foxhounds.

"You needn't have come at all," he said. "There is nothing for you to do."

"The rest of my horses arrive today, do they not?"

"Of course, and we're ready for them."

"Good. I'd like to see that everyone arrives safe and sound."

"My men have everything under control," he said stiffly.

He was prickly as a hedge, and as unyielding. She didn't like it. "I know my horses better than anyone, and can help," she said. "And naturally I came to check on Diamond."

"Feeling responsible, are we?"

"You know I am."

Henry clasped his arms behind him. "He's doing fine."

Julia watched Nance walk the colt around the stable yard. "He's limping." She strode across the paving stones and told the groom to halt the horse. Henry, taken by surprise, caught up in a moment.

She turned on him. "I suppose you call that proper treatment."

85

"No doubt you have a better idea," he said darkly.

"The wrap alone goes against every tenet of good treatment I hold dear."

He bent over and slid a finger beneath it. "It's tight enough."

"I'd remove it straightaway so the wound can air."

His fine brow arched skeptically. "You would, would you?"

"I never used a wrap when Meteor sliced his hock."

"It's hard to wrap a hock."

"Not if you know what you're doing. Unwrap it if you please, and let me see what's festering under there."

"Festering, my lady? You're overstepping—"

But she knelt on the stones and unwound an admirably clean strip of linen. Admirable, that is, if it had been applied correctly. "Just as I thought," she muttered crossly. "Someone put salve on it. And they didn't properly trim the wound."

Henry hovered over his new bride, about to throttle her.

No, if truth be told, about to see if that kissing trick would shut her up. She looked positively edible in a forest-green habit that darkened her eyes, set off her hair, lifted her breasts, and snugged her curved bottom.

But there stood Nance, two grooms, and half a dozen stableboys privy to his ogling of his wife and to his looming marital crisis.

He'd be damned if he would kiss her in front of them. Or disparage her. Especially after Nance had taken the trouble to show him a suspiciously sheared-off spoke in the wrecked phaeton's right wheel. He'd gone so far as to suggest that Julia, or Julia's groom, had some nefarious scheme afoot. Worry-mongering, trouble-borrowing bloke. The phaeton had been crashed before he bought it, Henry remembered, and this had to be a failed repair.

"What would you suggest, my lady?" he asked evenly.

She didn't hesitate. "Hot water, soap, clean cloths, whiskey. And shears, your sharpest pair."

All agog, his men cast disbelieving glances at him.

"You heard your new marchioness," he barked.

Quickly, quietly, they piled up her inventory. Just as rapidly she went to work, her hands gentle and reassuring on the restive colt's fetlock. "No infection yet, thank God. But what were your men about? Fresh cuts need air, trimming, and daily washing. This ragged

86

edge will never heal, will just make a worse scar. And then there's the danger of it going to proud flesh."

Cheeky interfering female! As if he didn't know that irritated flesh would scar. But he stifled a rebuttal, too impressed by her knowledge and her fearlessness to be as angry as he ought.

She did good clean work and did it fast. He'd known she rode horses, and she'd said she bred them. But he'd had no idea her skill extended to treating their injuries. Who'd have thought she had the know-how or the grit to trim the ragged edges of a horse's flesh? The jury was out, however, on whether her treatment worked. If it failed, they would rewrap the colt after she left the barn.

She stood up, hands on her slim hips, satisfied. "There. That's that. I feel much better, Henry, and so will he. For now, he needs a quiet walk, Mr. Nance." With a quick glance for Henry's permission, Nance handed Diamond over to one of the boys.

Henry allowed himself a moment of self-congratulation. He'd defused an explosive incident, yet maintained control.

But Julia wasn't done. "I should like to see his stall."

He led her over. He was proud of his stables, the stalls well-drained and their bedding deep.

Lifting the hem of her habit halfway to her knees, she stomped around the stall in her nankeen boots. He watched, leaning against the doorway. Did she think she was a horse? he wondered, amused. But damnably attracted. He liked the confident way she focused on the task at hand. To his surprise, he was coming to admire her bold, forward stride. Worse yet, he seemed to see straight through her riding habit to the statuesque splendor he'd glimpsed last night when she stood, dripping wet, in his copper tub.

"The shavings are too deep," she concluded.

"Indeed," he said absently, remembering how her hands shot down to hide her auburn fleece.

But she was off and galloping again. "Damp the soil and put down just the thinnest layer of good clean straw—none of that late summer chaff to work into the wound."

Thoughts of her tempting charms evaporated as he grappled with her unexpected foray into his sacred turf. "That's what the bandages were for, my lady."

"A common mistake, Jem says. Diamond needs exercise, clean exercise, not bandages. If he stands in that stall all day, the fetlock will stock up. Oh, and Henry, your paddocks just won't do. Lumping all the mares and foals together in one large run is a certain recipe for more injuries."

"And you propose . . ."

She proposed a lot more fencing, smaller paddocks with only two mares and their foals in each. He'd heard of it on small estates and might have considered it, but not today, and not for his domain, and not at his pushy bride's behest.

"We've made quite enough changes in our routine for your first day," he said firmly.

"The fences aren't nearly as costly, Henry, as losing one good foal," she went on, her passion undiminished.

Passion. Henry ground his teeth in aggravation. He must not think of Julia and passion in the same breath. Last night had been hell. Her every breath, her every moan, and that last sweet unconscious snuggle had almost tempted him to break his vow. He wouldn't. Not in his bed, not in his barn.

He shouldn't kiss her, wouldn't upbraid her, but couldn't distract her from her present course. Wat, the grooms, and the stableboys were smothering smirks. He had to stop her gracefully.

"Come, my dear," he said in desperation. He moved his hand to the small of her back. To direct her, or simply touch her? Did it matter which if he removed her from the line of fire? "Hazard's in his box."

It worked. By the time he'd introduced her to his prized stallion, his stupid sensual fog had cleared and he had a plan. Two plans, in fact. He would give her tit for tat, starting tomorrow after she'd begun to settle in. Today, he'd turn her over to Aunt Augusta and Uncle Bertie, who were champing at their respective bits to show her her new home.

By the end of the afternoon, Julia's feet were steaming. So was she, as she schemed for a way to make Henry Pelham pay. She would not give him a chance to see her in the buff tonight. Her poor, tired, blistered feet—yes, he could see *them*. In fact, she intended to take them out of the bucket of hot water, stick them in his face and blame him for their wretched state. Then she'd waltz barefoot down to dinner, and he'd best not say a word.

She wriggled her toes in the cleansing water, letting the sting fuel her fire. Her husband's bedchamber was warm, but she was too angry with him to take the nap she needed.

The door creaked, and there he was, tall, unruffled, and still in control.

She marched up to him, her wet feet tracking soapy water on his prized Turkish carpet. "You palmed me off on them!"

He frowned. "I what?"

"Don't pretend you didn't know what would happen! You handed me over to your aunt and uncle to get me out from underfoot."

His mouth seemed to fight a smile. "You didn't enjoy your tours?"

"Not only did I not enjoy them, you made me miss the horses' arrival."

Ignoring the part about the horses, he said, "Surely Aunt Augusta and Uncle Bertie showed you every consideration."

And a very great deal more concern than she was willing to discuss in the few moments before dinner. Both of them exhibited a proprietary claim to the newest marchioness's person and were overly interested in her adjustment to her new wifely duties. Uncle Bertie even brought up the prospect of her soon bearing Pelham its long-awaited heir.

For now, their tours gave her plenty to complain about. "Between them, they must have shown me every nook and cranny of the house and grounds. The great rooms, the still room, the wine cellar, the orangery, the monkey house, and the rest of the menagerie. I have been walking all day."

She grabbed his arm, pulled her reluctant husband to the window seat, and clambered up on it. The sun beamed in. She hoisted a puckered, blistered foot into his unsuspecting hands. One blister had burst for best effect, and blood oozed from its edges.

"Hmmm." He scrutinized it with warm gray eyes, then gently set it down. "I'd say you walked too much," he said wryly.

"Obviously." Her heart sank. He wasn't the least bit moved. Probably because he didn't have the slightest interest in her body. She caught a tantalizing whiff of sweaty horse and well-oiled leather and something purely Henry, and marshaled all her anger. "And Aunt Augusta covered every floor of the entire castle. I thought you said she needed help with Isabeau."

"No doubt your arrival inspired her to new heights," he conceded, blandly courteous. "No one knows our twists and turns better than she."

"Twists and turns, my foot," she said, anger rising at his cool, superior control. "It's a maze, designed by a mad . . ." She clapped her hand over her mouth.

His eyes glinted with triumph. "I thought you'd see it my way."

"It's a figure of speech, my lord."

"Indeed," he said. "And how did you find Uncle Bertie's menagerie?"

Exotic. Fascinating, with monkeys, a pair of zebras, a small herd of gazelles, flocks of guinea hens and flamingos. Even the peacocks with their airy cries had been magnificent, fanning their shimmering tails. She chose her words carefully, determined not to slip again. "Amusing. Large."

"Is that all?"

"I particularly liked the cobra." Liked to think what it might do, turned loose on her provoking husband.

"A dangerous preference." For an instant, she was sure he caught her drift. But he turned on his heel and disappeared into the privacy of his dressing room to change for dinner.

Feeling reproached—reprieved—she took out the velvet gown and changed behind a screen, just in time to hear Aunt Augusta's gong summon them to dinner.

As they left the room, he paused to see if she was wearing boots and groaned. "Barefoot, my lady?"

"Unless you prefer that I subject myself to pain," she said, pleased she'd gotten some emotion out of him.

"Do you have no soft slippers?"

"Would you make me wear them?"

He gave an exasperated sigh. "I don't think I could make you do anything."

But he just had. He'd barred her from her own horses and subjected her to Aunt Augusta's and Uncle Bertie's endless interest in her marriage. On top of that, Julia had fretted all afternoon, knowing her horses were coming any minute. But so new to everything and everyone, she'd been unwilling to hurt her elders' feelings—or go back on her bargain—by rushing off to where she'd rather be. Besides, however daft, both aunt and uncle seemed well meaning, whereas Henry . . .

The Mad Marquis

He tucked her hand in the crook of his arm and escorted her through the maze of Pelham's twisted halls. The golden dining room was just as it had been last night, lavish and glowing.

Heavens, Julia thought, should she expect this every day? Aunt Augusta's dress, though worn, was gaudier, and she was rummaging through an ornate sideboard, muttering to herself. Uncle Bertie had replaced yesterday's boutonnière with a sea aster from their afternoon excursion. His beady-eyed parrot bobbing on his shoulder, he hurried over with a trusting grin and an overfull glass of ratafia.

After last night's overindulgence, she ought to turn him down. Henry was no help. He'd left her side to assist his resisting aunt to her seat.

"I'm looking for the silver salters, Henry," she protested.

He patted a knotted hand. "On the table, dearest," he said kindly, though his patience seemed stretched thin.

" 'On the table, dearest,' " Raj mimicked.

Harry pivoted. "You . . ." he growled at the bird ". . . can take your lettuce in the chicken coop."

Uncle Bertie puffed up. "Raj is not poultry, Henry."

Julia suppressed a grin. Henry was talking to parrots now? She glanced around to share a complicit smile with Isabeau, who talked to imaginary people. But Isabeau was nowhere to be seen.

Come to think of it, Julia hadn't seen the child all day. She'd been here for the wedding dinner, so Julia had assumed her presence in the evening was routine. What was going on? Julia saw Henry's hand in this, as it had been on her whole day. Having just upbraided him for managing her, she was reluctant to do so on this point before his aunt and uncle.

But exactly when, and how, did Henry expect her to take charge of his daughter if she never even saw her?

"I hope there's nothing wrong with Isabeau."

Henry and his aunt exchanged glances, then spoke in unison.

"Nothing at all," said Henry.

"Oh, everything," said his aunt.

Julia looked back and forth between the two. The aunt was worried. But Henry affected a studied calm.

Julia believed the aunt. "Perhaps if I went up . . . ?"

"Oh would you?" Augusta Pelham almost pled.

"There is absolutely no need," said Henry at the same time.

"You see, dear . . ." Augusta began again, inclining her head toward Julia in a confiding, hopeful way.

"Isabeau made her choice, Aunt," Henry warned.

". . . she refuses to come down without her . . . little friend."

"There is no little friend," Henry ground out, his patience splintering. "It's a figment of her imagination. The more we cater to it—to her—the deeper she will sink into fantasy, and the more lost to us she will be."

Julia preferred a firm hand too . . . with lazy stableboys, and with her brother's hellion sons. But with a lonely little girl, Henry's ploy felt harsh, hard-hearted. And it made an awkward place for a new stepmother to step in.

Or did it? True awkwardness would be leaving the child upstairs thinking Julia hadn't noticed her absence.

"If I am to help with Isabeau, I'd like to start now." Julia set down her untouched ratafia, put on her most obliging smile, and headed for the door, adding civilly to Henry, "Don't trouble yourself. I can find my way."

He caught up and stopped her in the hall. "Your way to where?"

"To Isabeau. To say goodnight. She is my duty now, is she not?"

"She will be in time, after you have made yourself at home."

"Why not now? Is she sick?"

"Not in the way you mean."

"So she's well? But not coming down to dinner?"

"It's her choice. I told her she could come to dinner with the grown-ups only if she didn't pretend her friend was there, too."

Julia's heart sank. "She'll think she's banned because of me."

"Rubbish. Her obsession with her friend has been getting out of hand for months."

"And your remedy is . . ."

"To make her face the truth. There is no Marie Claire."

Julia crossed her arms, affronted for the child's sake. Outraged, in fact. "That's bloody understanding of you."

Henry's face shuttered. "I do understand her. I understand what it means to need a father's guidance."

"If you're guiding her, where does her new stepmother fit in?"

"I'm sure we can arrive at a mutual understanding of your duty and her needs."

"Ha!" Julia had lived with too many male relatives too long to think his "mutual understanding" would give her opinion equal weight. "You mean that I am to agree with you, and everything will be shipshape."

"I have known her eight long years."

"But she is your first and only child."

He glared as if she'd accused him of philandering. "So far as I know."

That set her back, but not for long. "And you were an only child."

"I had a close friend in my cousin," he said, somewhat defensively, she thought. What had gone wrong for Henry as a little boy?

"I, on the other hand, was raised with four older brothers and a boatload of cousins. And I had a hand in raising the older of my dreadful nephews. So I bring something of practical experience to your daughter. As you intended."

He clasped his hands behind his back. "After last night, that remains to be seen."

"We can start over."

He cocked his head. "Not tonight. I sat with her through supper."

How admirable, except that he'd done it for the wrong reason. "Did you say her prayers and kiss her goodnight?"

He winced. "Nurse does that."

"And you . . . ?"

"We . . . read, then said goodnight," he said stiffly, as if an ordinary family ritual did not come easily for him. Julia yearned to break down his reticence, to introduce him to the rough-and-tumble family politics she'd enjoyed with her brothers. Her father may have spoiled her, but he doted on her. Henry loved his little girl enough to share her supper but didn't understand her needs enough to kiss her when he said goodnight. If only she could find out why.

"That's where I should start then," she offered.

His scowl did not invite her to explain.

She did so anyway. "I can take over nurse's bedtime duties."

"Surely not tonight, with your feet and your fatigue."

"Bother my feet and fatigue." An encounter with the child would distract her from her pain. She added, "You don't need to come. I'll be quick."

Henry wouldn't miss this encounter anymore than he would throw a race, in part because he couldn't believe she'd do it—and in part because he was afraid she would.

93

Upstairs, his daughter was decked out for bed in her linen shift, a blonde and white confection. But seeing her spacious room through Julia's eyes, he realized it looked almost empty, and its white floors and walls looked almost cold.

"You're back," Isabeau said, puzzled to see him. But she broke into a smile for Julia.

Henry shook his head, irked. Julia had won his daughter over too quickly, too cheaply, with a pudding and an invitation to her imaginary friend. But the damage, if damage it was, was done. Julia got right down to business. The prayers went smoothly, and the kiss was sweet. "Back tomorrow, *mignon*, for lunch and a little stroll," she said, then tucked Isabeau in and headed for the door.

From beneath the covers came a tiny voice. "Can you kiss Marie Claire before you go?"

The hair stood on the back of his neck. Julia had loosed a demon. His daughter probably did look lonely to an outsider. But was it true loneliness, or the family curse?

Next to him, he heard the whisper of Julia's dress and the slide of her bare feet across the floor. She was going back to Isabeau's bed. He stifled an oath. He could stop her but was not sure what she would do.

In a moment, the tall, bold redhead was murmuring, reassuring his blonde motherless child of . . . whatever mothers assured daughters of. Julia's voice was soft and full, his daughter's high and light. His heart tore. Was Julia succeeding where he so stubbornly had failed?

His bride leaned across the bed and kissed the empty air.

A pure, possessive and protective anger lanced Henry to the quick. This was bribery, pure and simple. Julia had ignored his injunctions. Had decided she knew better. Her independence, he could tolerate, even at times admire.

But he would not stand for her to throw over his instructions.

Catching her hand under his arm, he led her down the corridor until they were out of earshot. "That was imprudent, Julia. Hasty, ill-advised, and wrong," he exploded.

Undaunted, she snapped back. "Whereas you would leave her to her nightmares. I never had a hint that you were cruel, Henry. Never saw you beat a hound or whip a horse past its endurance. But your own daughter . . ."

The Mad Marquis

He lowered his voice. "I don't care if you're angry. I don't give a fig if you're disappointed in me. But damnation, Julia, this is the family Achilles' heel. Aunt Augusta's living in the past, Uncle Bertie's living in another country, and my poor daughter's living in a world that doesn't exist. If you'd been raised by my father, you would understand."

Oddly, Julia's hand clasped his forearm as if to say she was the one with wisdom and he was the one breaking all the rules. "Perhaps your aunt is growing a bit addled. Perhaps your uncle needs his menagerie. Whatever's wrong with them, Isabeau clearly needs a human friend."

"You're too new to us to make such guesses."

She gave an unladylike snort of pure disgust. "You're too deep in the forest to see the trees."

He didn't have a comeback, which set him off balance. It wasn't that people quailed before him. It wasn't that he thought they should. But no one stood up to him, either.

Julia didn't quail or shrink. Where the care of innocents was concerned—whether his horses or his little girl—she planted both feet on the floor and stood her ground.

He didn't think it feminine, or suitable for his wife.

But what to do about his new fixation on her pretty, blistered feet?

Chapter Eleven

If then women are not a swarm of ephemeron triflers, why should they be kept in ignorance under the specious name of innocence?
　　—Mary Wollstonecraft, *Vindication of the Rights of Woman*

"Perhaps you could explain something to me, my lord," Julia said in Henry's bedchamber after an awkward dinner with his aunt and uncle. Her short auburn curls bobbed cheerfully above the screen, but her voice was formal. Too formal. Henry heard the rustle of her undressing, savage as a scythe shearing hay. Too upset.

"Perhaps, my lady," he answered from deep in his favorite chair. He was thinking about the strain of sharing quarters, and the risk. But he'd taken steps toward a more suitable arrangement in the afternoon. Carpenters came tomorrow, and the plasterers next week, and he'd assigned his aunt to take charge of furniture and fabrics. He took a sip of brandy, wondering how to end their second evening on a cordial note.

Dinner had not gone well. From Isabeau to stable management to Uncle Bertie's plan to expand his menagerie, no more than two people at the table shared a view on anything.

The Mad Marquis

He and Julia had agreed on nothing.

"Your aunt was charming tonight," Julia observed.

"I found her to be her usual addled self."

Julia tossed her fine Persian shawl over the edge of the screen. "I don't suppose you instructed your addled aunt to pry into our love life."

No, he hadn't, he thought, taken aback.

"We don't have a love life," he said instead.

"She thinks we should. She spent our entire walk persuading me that we should fall in love."

"That presuming, interfering . . ." he sputtered.

"Loving, Henry." Julia must have stood on tiptoe. Suddenly her keen green eyes were peering at him over the screen. "Your aunt believes in love. Love between family members, and love between a husband and a wife."

"My aunt has her new-fangled notions."

"This was not a notion. She was promoting your attractions, Henry."

Not that he had no attractions, he supposed, but he'd rather Julia not notice them. Or would he rather that she did? "She always meddles," he said dryly. "Pay her no mind."

Julia flung her dress over the screen. It slithered into place. She was down to her petticoats. His renegade imagination dwelt on how stunning she must look, her high breasts peaked, silken fabric clinging to her coltish legs.

"And Uncle Bertie? I suppose I should pay him no mind, too."

"Especially when he's having one of his spells."

Julia's head popped up above the screen. "Your uncle has spells?"

"From time to time," Henry said, sounding a lot more at ease about it than he felt. "He hides out in his room, to indulge a fit of melancholia. Just like his brother, my father. It's another manifestation of the Pelham family madness."

"He doesn't seem mad to me," she said, dismissing Henry's observation out of hand. "He is, however," she went on, "relieved you married me. He's petrified he'll have to marry and produce The Heir."

Harry shuddered at the thought of Pelham ruled by the son of a madder man than he, but said, "I'm relieved our marriage sets his fears at rest."

Fiona Carr

"You're not listening to me." Julia angrily lobbed her chemise over the screen. "Your uncle thinks we plan on having children! And your aunt has her heart set on a love match for us."

The chemise missed the rim, then whispered to the floor. It was silk, he realized, mesmerized by her undressing so near to him and yet so far away. He'd bet her skin was silk, too. So it had appeared when he saw her standing there, gleaming, in his copper tub. That image had followed him all day, far more compelling than Nance's specious worries about the phaeton's spoke.

Far more disturbing. He took a sobering draught of brandy and said, "It's not really any of their business, is it?"

"No. But it's mine. They seem a great deal more interested in the state of our marriage than you are."

"Surely, you didn't expect me to tell the truth about our bargain."

"I didn't expect them to act as if they have a proprietary interest in my body."

"It's natural enough that they would. In their view, any son of ours would not be a just a son, but the new marquis, the future of the marquisate."

"Which is why you should have told them that we don't plan to have The Heir."

"Do you really want them to know our terms?"

"Well, no," came grudgingly from behind the screen.

"And it isn't as if I can control what they say to you," he added realistically.

Silk stockings, knotted into a ball, flew across the room and thumped against his chest. Julia swept out from behind the screen, unselfconsciously arrayed in her nuptial nightrail and gown. She strode up to him, barefoot, her breasts moving seductively beneath the sheerest tulle and lace. His breath hitched.

"I don't see why not," she said. "You control *me*—what I do and what I think."

"I don't even control myself," he muttered. He lowered his gaze from her breasts back to her innocent feet. No improvement. They peeked out beneath the lace that edged her gown.

"You kept me from my horses."

"Ah, but you treated Diamond," he pointed out, trying to focus on their argument and not her feet.

"You made me spend the day with your aunt and uncle."

"Yes, and you agreed to that," he countered. Her second toe was particularly attractive, slender and feminine.

"Anything less would have been an affront," she went on, not noticing his gaze. "But you could have excused me from that duty."

"They're keen on you. Which will smooth matters down the road," he added reasonably.

She drew herself up, indignant. "What road, my lord? Don't you mean, it will smooth things in the hallways, up and down the staircases, in and out of rooms? Isn't it your plan to confine me to the house?"

Stick to the argument, he told himself, or you are sunk. "You'll have plenty of days for riding, Julia."

"Hunt season only, I suppose, and only when the sun shines."

Her mounting anger animated her strong features and agitated her soft breasts.

"That could be arranged," he said through gritted teeth.

"Good God, Henry, no," she recanted. "You never heard me say that."

"All right. You can hunt in any weather," he conceded, all control eroded, both of himself and of her. Keep her talking. Keep from reaching out and touching her. "But I will have my way about Isabeau."

"As far as I can see, you've had nothing but your way with Isabeau."

"Except when you kissed Marie Claire." He tried to find his anger from that moment but the edge was gone. "Proof positive to my daughter that you believe her friend exists."

"I know she's not real." Indignantly Julia crossed her arms beneath her breasts.

Which plumped them up. "You may know that," he choked out. "But Isabeau thinks differently."

Whereas he was thinking dangerously. Not thinking. Thinking with his manhood. No doubt about it, Julia Westfall Pelham, marchioness of Rayne for one whole day, drove him to distraction. Oblivious to his man's needs, ignorant of her own—and yet almost completely uninhibited, she was any bridegroom's dream.

His nightmare. He rose. "We'll settle this in the morning."

In daylight, in public.

Fiona Carr

She let out a snort of disapproval and headed for his dressing closet.

He blocked her way, her breasts level with his ribs. "You can't sleep there." *He* would. *She* should have the bed.

"There you go again," she said triumphantly.

He must have looked puzzled. He was. He wanted her closer. He needed her very far away. "What?"

"You're trying to make me do things I don't want to do."

Irritation ripped him. Of course he was. It was his castle. He was its lord.

"No, my lady, *this* would be making you do things you don't want," he said, and pulled her body into his, lowered his head and claimed her mouth.

She made a small animal sound of surprise, but then amazingly surrendered, accepting his lips with a curious questing as her supple, big-boned mannish body melted into his. To hell with his conviction that she was not to his taste. He couldn't stop.

He didn't need to, he argued with himself. It was just a kiss. He probed with his tongue against her teeth until she accidentally opened her mouth. His tongue touched hers and tasted wine, heady wine. Then it struck him, like a kick to his chest.

His bride could be his next adventure. He set about exploring, astonished by her willingness to allow him in, by an odd sense of her own wonder. He took the kiss a little deeper, drinking in the even sweeter, headier feeling of being accepted. Of being wanted.

Monumental error. He ended the kiss with a muffled curse. He needed to set her aside, but she clung to him, her humid breath steaming through his crushed cravat and warming the skin of his chest.

"You're wrong, Henry," she murmured. "I want to do this. I want you to do this." She nuzzled a little closer. "We do this very well."

"Too well," he rasped, trying to control his agitated breathing. "That's the problem."

"It doesn't seem like a problem to me. It's all very . . . interesting. You're very interesting," she said, chatty as a nervous virgin. "Couldn't we just . . . ?"

"No. We couldn't," he said, desperate to convince himself.

But she was so yielding. So alive. So . . . not feminine, but womanly. His pulse roared in his ears and thundered through his veins.

His skin prickled, and his hard shaft burned. "No," he repeated. But just then she lifted her head, and her lips were close and sweet and swollen, and he had been alone so long.

He kissed her, a kiss more seeking and demanding than common sense or reason would recommend. Mad moments later, he came to his senses and broke off again. This time he stalked away to the marble mantelpiece and glared at the fire that crackled merrily in the hearth. As always, it was up to him and him alone. He had to protect them both. But how?

He could shut her in the other bedroom and bar the door. But some servant would find out. Talk would start. And Julia would never have a chance to establish herself as the respected mistress of the castle.

He could explain that she had night terrors and order a maid to keep her company. But Julia would look vulnerable.

He could tie her to the bed—no, bad idea, he warned himself, inflamed by the very thought.

He had to make her understand. Attraction between a man and a woman—any man and any woman—was simply too powerful to fool around with.

A light hand touched his shoulder and he jumped. She'd sneaked up behind him. "Henry, I'm sorry," she whispered, sounding mortified. "I know men can't help themselves when a woman is available, but you didn't marry me for this. I'm not the woman you want in your bed."

Damn, damn, damn. He couldn't help himself around her, and she *was* the woman he wanted in his bed. But if he corrected her assumptions, it would only make matters worse.

"Look, Julia," he started, his voice harsh from holding back. "I'm on the rack. I'm going to show you how a man feels with . . ." He laced his fingers in the tapes that tied her gown. ". . . temptation at his fingertips. I'm not that strong. And then you have to stop me."

She tilted her head. Her eyes glistened with unshed tears. "Anything," she whispered miserably.

He led her to his bed, sat her down, laid her back and looked, stunned by her health, her vigor, her womanly allure. She was a goddess, a Diana of the chase, armed and dangerous for any man. For him. He debated what to do. It wasn't seemly, it wasn't practical, for a woman in her position to be entirely ignorant. A marchioness, and married, she should have a woman's knowledge.

Using every ploy he knew, he started to arouse her body. He nibbled the nape of her neck, and was rewarded with a whimper. He nipped the peaks of her nipples, and she granted him a moan. He palmed the wide spread of her auburn thatch and had the pleasure of hearing her gasp. In moments she was writhing beneath his touch and tongue, her body arching up to him for more, her lips panting, her legs parting . . .

"Henry . . ." she breathed his name like manna. Like love. ". . . don't stop."

He wouldn't dream of it. He'd never left a woman high and dry, and he would not do that to his new bride. He eased his fingers inside her up to her virgin barrier and felt her shudder around them. Then he pressed his free hand to her mound and pressed and released and pressed again until her body moved to his hand's direction. He found her hot little nub and rubbed it slowly, deeply, and she arced off the covers, up into his touch. She was powerful, but in his power, and his manhood leaped and throbbed, angry in its isolation.

"Are you sure you want this?" he grated, bracing to restrain himself. "I can stop now." Just barely.

"There's more?" Her voice was husky with desire.

He nodded his head against her breasts, touched her nipple with his tongue.

She gasped at its touch. "Then please."

Her innocent courtesy rocked him, and he returned his fingers to her heat, slowing everything to drive her wild. She dug her fingers into his hair, pressing his head still closer to her breasts, until his instinct defeated sense. He sucked her pebbled nipples and stroked her lower nub gently, relentlessly, then harder. When she wriggled, wanting more, the blood pumped triumphantly through his veins.

She wanted it all. Breathless eons later she exploded around him, crying out his name. Trembling with unfulfilled desire, he wrapped his arms around her and waited for her to subside. Long moments later, he said hoarsely, "That's how a man feels. That's what a man wants."

"Oh God, Henry. We're fighting that?" she asked, awed.

His heart still hammered in his chest. "We're fighting that."

"Oh," she said again, but softer. "How could we give this up?"

The Mad Marquis

*   *   *

How indeed? The eerie cry of Uncle Bertie's peacocks rose above the patter of an early morning rain. Julia woke up feeling lethal. Blast Henry Pelham, he'd abandoned her again. She had a wine-soaked memory of his giving her the most blissful night of her life, the most scary, the most intimate, and then the most alone. Because after he sneaked up and seduced her—stripped her of innocence—he'd locked himself in his dressing room. For the first time since she'd been the victim of her brothers' slimy frog trick in her cot, she'd cried herself to sleep.

But if Henry could be up and about as if nothing had happened, she damn well could, too.

And yet, what to do? She didn't want to spend another day with dotty, wily Aunt Augusta talking about love. She didn't need another stroll into the depths of Uncle Bertie's jungle, admiring his peacocks' shimmering display while hearing about his hopes for The Heir and worrying if he would have a spell. And while she wanted to reach out to Isabeau, Henry had expressly ordered her not to do what she thought she ought.

Besides which, she'd not been on a horse in two whole days, had not exercised Minx or Meteor nor petted her beloved Fidget. No doubt her neglectful husband was already in the stables, riding to his heart's content while plotting more insidious ways to strip her life of all its real pleasures and confine her to his castle.

Time to assert her rights, before the marriage that was not a marriage got a minute older.

She slammed into her barn clothes and sped past the sideboard in the dining room, grabbing a handful of sausages and ham to wolf down as she went. No way would she face a hard day's work on a fashionably empty stomach. Racing through the labyrinthine castle halls, she did not miss a single turn. The stable block bustled with Henry's grays and bays, blacks and chestnuts being groomed and tacked, led up, walked out, cooled down. It must be business as usual.

Business without her. And Henry nowhere in sight.

Good, she thought vehemently. She'd rather kiss a horse.

But Minx and Fidget were not there, Meteor would be in the stallion's shed, and she didn't see Jem to ask.

She snugged her collar to her throat and headed for Henry's man

103

Wat Nance. His hands were full saddling an anxious colt. His fault, she thought, disapproving of his method. Any fool could see Wat hadn't run the stirrups up, and they were tickling the colt's flanks. Surely Henry didn't put up with such inept horsemanship from his head man.

"I'm looking for my husband," she demanded in her best brand-new-marchioness tone.

Henry's head groom flopped the saddle on the colt. It hunched its back.

"In the ménage, my lady," he said coldly. "Through there."

The schooling ring? That hurt. Last night's hot novelties had transported her into unimagined realms of sensual bliss, but nothing had kept her husband from his routine.

"Very well," she said, unable to resist adding, "The stirrups are banging that colt's sides. He'll stand better if you run them up."

The stableboy at the colt's head snickered, but she didn't admonish him. She was too intent on finding Henry and ripping into him.

The ménage was a large covered arena modeled on the French and Spanish schools, as best she could tell. Henry worked alone, drilling a strapping chestnut in slow, schooled figures, circles spiraling in then spiraling out.

As if last night meant nothing to him. Instead, he'd immersed himself in dreadfully boring Continental stuff, she thought, blanking out hot memories of his kiss and his touch. But ah, no matter how she wanted to deny it, man and horse were an eyeful. The man, no doubt about it, even more so than the horse. She shoved aside nagging thoughts of Henry's harsh profile softened by candlelight. Of Henry's tall physique striding across his bedchamber. Of Henry's muscled torso, bending over her on his bed.

Think of him as a horseman, she ordered herself. Not your husband.

Or she'd go mad, trying to reconcile last night's ecstasy with this morning's smell of horse and dust. This morning's indifference.

Henry was a consummate equestrian, whatever she thought of his rigid Continental training. Rigid but not cruel, she admitted that. Henry's seat in the saddle was flawless, too: light, balanced, proud. Almost arrogant, yet harmonious, man and beast as one. She particularly admired his leg, iron hard and quiet, gripping the horse's side. The horse's side, not hers.

The Mad Marquis

She shocked herself with her brazen thought. Last night, he'd had so much control—so little need of her—he hadn't even finished the mating process as she understood it. She hated it that he could up and walk away.

Ending the spiral, he trotted his horse over and halted square before her, his gray eyes unreadable but his broad shoulders relaxed, his ash-brown hair tousled, his frame on horseback towering over her, purely male, purely . . .

"Handsome," she muttered.

Henry caressed the horse's neck, almost proud. "Got him from Purvis for a steal."

Her face heated. She hadn't meant the horse.

"Good bones," she said, covering up. But her thoughts skidded out of control. From where she stood, Henry's bones were awesome, defining long, strong legs she'd felt pressed to hers only hours earlier.

Had he really slept beside her on their wedding night? Had he then deserted her last night? Her hand went to her throat, then to her mop of hair. Did she look rested? Fresh? Well kept? Was her riding habit neat and clean?

Was she out of her mind? she wondered crossly. She never fretted over frivolous feminine concerns. Her business, her work, her life, was in the barn.

"I did not expect you here," Henry said brusquely.

Idiot, she chastised herself. Here she'd been worrying about looking nice, and he didn't want to see her. "I took a morning gallop on our wedding day. So why not after my wedding night?"

The gray eyes shuttered, denying last night's pleasure. "You don't know your way around the grounds."

"You could show me after—" she said pointedly "—you show me all my horses."

He tensed. "They are taken care of, each and every one."

Her stomach clenched for battle. "I'd like to see them for myself."

"Your mares are in the west pasture," he said, his voice tight but courteous. "I'll finish here and take you."

A concession, she thought, pleased.

"Wat Nance can help you get your horse."

Her horse. That should help her put Henry's desertion behind her. But which horse? Henry would probably rule out Meteor. But Minx, the most promising filly she'd ever bred, would do nicely.

105

If she could find her. In the stable block, she stalked around the orderly square of stalls, growing grimmer by the minute. Meteor was in his stallion's box, no Minx anywhere.

She had just spotted Jem rugging up a Wraxham hunter when shod hooves rang out on the paving stones. They stopped square behind her.

"I'm sure we have a horse to please you," Henry said imperiously.

She spun around. "I can't find Minx."

"That filly you like? She's in the fillies' pasture near the mares," he said.

"I never pasture prized racing stock with the herd. You might just as well have put her in with Uncle Bertie's zebras!" Julia fired off. "She's in training. I shut her up for safety."

"She's with the fillies, not the tigers. I'm sure she's fine."

"Easy for you to say. She's the one I ride."

Henry dismounted with the ease of long practice and walked with her down the row of stalls. "We have other mounts for women."

"For women?"

"Yes, like Galleon, there." He patted an aged, flea-bitten gray, broad of beam and sluggish.

She snorted. "It probably swam in off the Armada." Julia respected elderly mounts. She honored them, in fact. But they were for fragile stepmothers or spineless sisters-in-law. She could even imagine this old fellow safely taking Great Aunt Augusta for a turn around the deer park. "I haven't ridden such an old crusader since I was a girl."

"Old Galley's the perfect gentleman," Harry said, somewhat huffily.

Wat Nance, his perpetual glower in place, backed the gelding out of its tie stall, and summoned a groom to tack it up.

"I did not strike a deal to ride only the old, the safe, the near-dead," she whispered vehemently to Henry. "My filly is in work. I plan to hunt her through the winter to leg her up and put her in a heat or two this spring."

His face closed. "We will not debate this publicly."

Indeed, she thought, inflamed. "I wouldn't dignify such a whole-sale usurpation of my rights with the term debate, my lord," she said for his ears only. "You might have managed me in your bedchamber, but you cannot dragoon me on my own turf." She stalked over to Jem, her unhelpful husband close behind. "Go get Minx."

To her great exasperation, her once-loyal Jem looked to Henry for permission.

A blink of Henry's eye said no. Then he sternly looked at her. "Take the gray, Julia. We'll ride up to see your filly."

She glared from Jem to Henry and back. Jem squirmed like a raw recruit in crossfire. "Don't worry, my lady," he stammered. "She fit in fine yesterday."

If she had an ounce of femininity, Julia thought, she would flounce off in fury. Her mare taken out of training! Herself demoted to a mount who was at death's door. Well, she'd make sure she saw her filly, then figure out a way to return her to her stall.

Feigning compliance, she walked over to Galleon and stood quietly at his head. Wat condescendingly brought out a ladies' saddle and cinched it on her mount. She didn't even protest the blasted thing. Sidesaddles felt crippled and constrained, even though she could ride one with both hands tied behind her back. It was just that with a man's saddle, she could take greater risks. Too late to complain. She'd kicked up enough muck before the stable hands for one day.

As for the elderly Galleon, he had a kind eye. He pushed a silken nose into her outstretched hand. She could compromise. After all, riding anything was better than another housebound day.

Her handsome husband mounted an equally handsome bay hack, and headed out into the morning mist. Just past the paddocks, Henry turned west and spurred his horse. Galleon pricked his ears and swung into a strong, long-legged trot. Perhaps she'd underestimated the old boy.

She'd definitely mistaken Henry.

Despite her anger, her heart lifted at the cool damp air on her face, the distant crashing of the surf, and the solid feel of a good horse between her legs. They covered half a furlong in silence, passing pastures of sturdy sheep, and fat cattle grazing here and there. Despite her sense of injustice, her temper cooled.

"Not quite dead, our Galley?" Henry called out, almost amiable.

"Too safe!" she shouted back, a stiff ocean breeze whipping the words from her mouth.

"He was a hell of a chaser in his day. Only Hazard's sire ever beat him."

"Before my time," she yelled back. But she was a little mollified Henry had put her on a horse that good.

Henry spurred his hack to a canter, as fit and fine a horseman as she could ever hope to follow. She'd always admired his quiet confidence on a horse, his back erect, his shoulders square, his hands steady, never hard. So why, since none of that had changed today, was everything about him different?

Because—she knew in a flash of conflicting emotions—everything had changed. Because in bed, his back had stiffened against her arms, because his shoulders had brushed her breasts, because his hands . . . his hands had touched her almost everywhere, his fingers . . .

Not that again. She mentally slapped herself back into the here and now, and spurred her horse. Henry's horse. There was no escaping it. Henry controlled her. Owned her. And her herd.

There was no future thinking thoughts in that direction.

Galleon could not have cared less about her thoughts. He had an easy, reaching gallop, so relaxed that she could hear him breathing rhythmically on each stride. In moments she pushed aside aggravation over the blasted sidesaddle and pique at her managing husband.

This was better, almost wonderful. The Pelham grounds were vast and beautiful, stretching north, east, west, and south to the sea. A bracing wind nipped her cheeks. A pewter sky vaulted overhead, and a well-bred horse surged beneath her. She could make the most of her new life. She could make it work. Never would she have imagined escaping the Wraxham family tangle. To riches, rank, to endless lands, and the sight and the sound of the sea only a short hack away.

Never would she have imagined herself galloping out on one of Pelham's honored chasers next to the only man she'd ever loved.

Julia's heart stuck in her chest. Horsefeathers! She couldn't be in love with Henry Pelham. She couldn't afford to be. The Pelham family madness must be contagious. True, she'd had a crush on him. Once. Ages ago. He'd been handsome, daring, bold. Now that he was her husband, she had to see him for what he really was—an illtempered, managing tyrant. An obstacle to her best ambition and her most cherished dreams.

In a pasture just ahead, a dozen horses grazed. Henry's bay cleared the gate, and Galleon popped up and over it with ease. Slowing,

Henry pointed to her herd, as placid as at home. Her gaze went instantly to Minx, munching the close-cropped grass as contentedly as any of the others.

"She'd have been happy with the zebras," Henry said dryly.

Julia snorted. Her sense of humor thinned where her horses were concerned. But Minx looked good. Safe and sleek. Julia vaulted off her horse, put her fingers to her lips, and whistled. The filly's head went up, her tail flagged out, and she galloped over, whuffling into Julia's hands in search of apple bits. Julia pulled a succulent date out of a deep pocket and offered it, palm up.

"So. You spoil not only my daughter," Henry observed.

"Some creatures are worth spoiling," she snapped, her back up under scrutiny. She managed her barn her way, and her pastures. Trying to ignore Henry's critical eye, she ran her fingers up and down the filly's legs, checking for injury or strain. In pasture games amongst her peers, Minx challenged all comers.

"Well?" Henry asked after Julia stood up.

"She's fine. She had a nice roll in the sand and needs a good currying."

"She looks content."

Julia walked up to him. It was now or never to take her stand. "I want her in a stall. I'm hunting her this winter and racing her next spring."

He scowled, granting nothing. "We have a lot more of Pelham to see."

Julia almost squealed in annoyance, like a mare nipped by a stallion. But she would fight this fight in human terms, and to her dying breath. With as much dignity as Henry, and every bit as much determination. "Very well, my lord. Show me."

They trotted to other pastures, to mares with foals, to colts kept in line by aging geldings. They cantered past fields of oats and corn and mangle-wurzels, fodder for them all. Side by side, she and her husband surveyed his—their!—vast estate. Hours later, they cleared the hill that gently rose before the castle and then dropped into the sea.

Without a backward glance, Henry plunged his bay down a cliff that defended ancient Pelham from the sea. A sheer incline. One moment she saw him, and then he was gone. Her heart stopped, and she saw his trick, a narrow but well-traveled path.

Fiona Carr

The cheat. From where she sat on Galleon, it looked daunting, steep, not easily negotiable. But Henry wasn't daunted. It was another test to see if she had what it took.

Beneath her, Galleon bunched in readiness. Julia grabbed a hank of mane and let the old crusader make his way, haunches tucked, head down, hooves nimble, as he plunged oh so fast straight down to the ocean's edge.

Where Henry waited, looking a little shocked to learn this lesson: His new bride did not scare easily.

And on horseback, she did not scare at all.

Chapter Twelve

I will use the preacher's own words. "Let it be observed, that in your sex manly exercises are never graceful; that in them a tone and figure, as well as an air of deportment, of the masculine kind, are always forbidding; and that men of sensibility desire in every woman soft features, and a flowing voice, a form, not robust, and demeanor delicate and gentle."
—Mary Wollstonecraft, *Vindication of the Rights of Woman*

He'd underestimated Julia by furlongs. As young bucks he and Galleon must have taken that cliff a hundred times. Bold as Julia was when she tore across the countryside, Henry never would have thought she had the knack for such a precipice. Or the nerve. Although after last night, he was starting to realize that she had the knack and nerve for anything.

She and her horse dropped down the bank in style, as clean fast as he had ever done. She reached the flat, her face aglow from her daring descent. Aglow, as she had been beneath him. He struggled to stifle that memory, but it was fresh and sweet. The tide was ebbing, he reminded himself, leaving the shore wide and flat, and his bay itching for a run.

111

Fiona Carr

"A gallop, my lady?" he offered.

She was patting Galleon's neck, her squabbles with Henry over her horses apparently forgotten. And last night? Did she remember anything?

He couldn't tell. But he remembered, ached, throbbed.

"How fast is this old campaigner?" she asked.

Fast, he thought. "Retired," he said firmly. "You just follow."

"We've been tagging along all morning, even down that little hill."

The wind garbled her protest. He nudged his bay into a canter, then let him out a notch just where the surf met sand. He recognized her cry of battle joined, too much like a cry of pleasure, and suddenly Julia and Galleon were bearing down on him.

It didn't seem quite sporting to race his bride, but Julia Westfall had beaten him once too often. He couldn't let her win on his own turf. He looked back over his shoulder. He would have guessed she hated sidesaddle, never having seen her use one. But her seat was elegant and secure, her waist accented by the twist of her legs off her mount's left flank.

And her slim, fit hips . . . he dare not dwell on them.

Galleon's ears pricked forward, and his solid forelegs pumped across the sand. The tide splattered under the gelding's hooves, and sea foam flecked his chest.

"Beat you to those rocks," Henry cried, his competitive urges overriding his last reservation.

"You'll be the first man!" she shouted back.

He would never be her first, Henry thought, if he could just hang on to his resolve. Grimly he urged the bay toward the pile of rocks before a seaside cave half a league away. The bay stretched out his neck and picked up his pace, sand and seawater splashing his belly and Henry's boots.

Halfway there, Julia pulled up even, Galleon's long strides threatening to overtake him and his handy hunter. But all he could think, all he could see, was the wind buffeting her habit's skirts up around her knees.

In public he couldn't approve. Here on his private beach, he couldn't look away.

"Retired, you say?" she yelled, evidently too drunk on speed to notice his distraction.

He saw her loosen her reins, saw her ask her horse for more. The gray lowered his head, dug into the surf, and passed him.

"Consider yourself beaten!" she shouted breathlessly.

Over his dead body. He laid his crop on his mount's flank and touched him with a spur. Younger, fitter than Julia's old campaigner, the bay found a burst of speed and pulled away, a length, two lengths, three. Henry raced along the flat, the thrill pumping through his veins, his horse all out, himself reaching for that moment of perfect exhilaration, the win. He reined in at the rocks.

Julia came in three strides behind, a priceless grin of sheer exuberance lighting her face beyond any satisfaction he'd brought her to last night. Her vagrant skirts settled around her boot tops. Her brilliant auburn curls kinked into tighter curls from the drizzle and the damp . . . just like in his bath. Just as last night when he'd touched her, there.

But she was taunting him, as if no touch of his would ever tame her. "A coup for you, my lord," she ragged him cheerfully, "putting your wife on your oldest chaser, and beating her on your own beach!"

Every fiber in his body responded to her taunt. He wanted to throw off the rank and mantle of responsibility, and shout back boyishly, *You started it!*

He froze. He *had* thrown off rank and mantle, leading his new bride down Pelham's sheerest cliff, then racing her neck or nothing on the flat, heedless of her safety or propriety. All to show his mastery.

He edged his winded horse near hers, and apologized. "I had no right, my lady, to let you take such risks."

It was almost worth riling her to see her eyes flash and cheeks color, while her breasts trembled with indignation. Then he remembered the taste of her nipples.

"I do this every day," she protested. "Have done for years. With my father's blessing."

"Thankfully," he said, "you no longer need to take such risks."

Pointing her crop in Henry's face, she exploded.

"Horse apples! I live for such risks, and you do, too. You ought to understand. But you married me for my father's horses, and nothing else."

Both horses danced. And he wanted to rebut her. But he didn't

113

because she looked abandoned in her anger, as she had last night when he'd taken her halfway to ecstasy.

As if nothing of the sort had happened between them, she plowed into him. "If you think you can confine me to the house, you'd better think again. I love my horses, I know my horses, and I know racing, too. Minx won't run for you, my lord, or Meteor either, not the way you think they will. I know their secrets."

Passionate, and willful, too. He'd never known a woman quite like her. "I did not say you could not ride." He'd meant she could, with certain stipulations. All right, a lot of stipulations. A lot more than she was willing to accept.

"With all due respect to Galleon, you might as well have said I couldn't," she said. "Even if he does still have a flash of speed, he's gentle enough for Isabeau."

"No, not for her," Henry insisted.

She shrugged, dismissing his opinion. "You took my mare out of training. You haven't a clue who to breed Meteor to. And I haven't seen poor little Fidget since I left home."

"Fidget's with the weanlings, just as he was at Wraxham." Henry mustered indifference.

"That doesn't settle the issue of my training Minx and working Meteor."

He didn't want her training her filly or working with her stallion. He didn't want her racing hell bent for leather against every buck and wag in this parish and the county.

Because he didn't want other men lusting after her the way he did.

"Jem can breed and exercise the stallion. And he can train Minx."

"He doesn't handle my stallion, and he never rides my mare," she said majestically. "I do both. Me, and only me."

Henry had never felt so backed into a corner as he did on this wide beach under this bleak gray sky. Had never felt so inadequate to deal with a woman who wanted, he realized too late, to love like a woman but live like a man.

He wouldn't stoop to bargaining. A husband didn't need to. "Then I'm sure she'll make a fine broodmare," he said. He hadn't expected Julia to look so stricken—or to cover it so fast.

"We should prove her first, for the reputation of her offspring," she urged.

To hell with reputation, prudence, contracts, common sense. To hell with her being practical and right. He just wanted them to dismount so he could shut her up with a kiss.

She could have cared less.

Because she didn't understand. He cleared his throat. "I'm afraid for you, Julia. I'll not have my wife, my marchioness, take these risks. It's far too dangerous."

Her brows snapped together. "Do you mean, too dangerous for a woman? Shouldn't you have thought of that before we married? Before we struck our bargain?"

Perhaps he should have. Perhaps he should have guessed that he would turn madly protective of Julia Westfall's safety the moment he had made her his. But he wasn't ready to examine that, and he was sure she would reject his instinct to protect her out of hand. "I did not marry you so you could go on taking risks your father never should have allowed. I married you because you are young and strong and healthy. Everyone at Pelham needs you to stay that way."

"You know, my lord, I would even concede your point, if I was breeding. But I'm not. So it can't possibly matter if I take a risk or two. Besides, I've been racing for years."

Stubborn lass, blind to danger, immune to fear. It went beyond his family's reputation and his daughter's need. It went to his old griefs and fears. "Julia," he said quietly, demanding her full attention. "I couldn't bear another loss."

"Another loss?" she asked.

"Like my father."

She rolled her eyes. "Henry, he was drunk. The hour was late. The night was black. Everybody knows that."

"People see what they want to see. I see my bride too willing to take risks."

"I am not your father," she said carefully, as to a backwards child. "I don't drink and ride."

True enough, he thought, and she also did not seem to have his father's debilitating melancholia. But still . . . "You've been lucky for years," he pointed out.

"You think it's luck?" She stuck her crop under her arm, engaged his gaze and said, supremely confident, "I'd wager it isn't." Then she wove the reins around her fingers, one finger at a time. "I'd venture a bet that it's my skill and talent."

His pulse picked up, as always with the stakes out on the table. "Don't even think to tempt me with a wager," he warned.

Her green eyes glittered anyway. "I'll bet you a race, 'cross Pelham's fields—my choice of my best horse and your choice of yours—that I'm the better trainer and the better rider."

He swore a ripe barnyard oath. "You left out 'the better breeder.'"

"That goes without saying. My best horse is one I bred. You, however, can choose any horse you want. It wouldn't have to be from your stud."

He wished she hadn't used that last word so comfortably, wished she were more ladylike, less mannish. But his interest was damnably piqued. He never passed up a bet.

He'd always chalked it up to his fighting spirit. Today it seemed like Pelham's curse. He must be mad to strike another bargain with his bride. Mad to risk giving her a scintilla of control.

"Your stakes?" he asked.

"If I win, I continue with my horses as I did for my father. I breed them, train them, race them." Then, as if she couldn't stop herself, she added in a rush, "You won't regret it, Henry. This is all I know how to do, and I do it very well."

He was sure she would do quite a few other, more intimate, activities extremely well, but forbore to say so. He didn't like her proposal. He felt responsible for her safety, and for the dignity of his marchioness, both threatened, both compromised whether she won or lost.

But he'd always been a betting fool. "What if you lose?" he asked evenly. "You might consider that."

She fidgeted with her crop and looked desolately out to sea. "I will abide by your wishes."

"On your honor?"

She made a face. "I honor my bets, Henry."

Of course, she would. He knew that she'd accept it when she lost. So it shouldn't tug at him that he would win and she'd surrender, except that he'd be asking her to deny her heart. He didn't want to tame her, he couldn't crush the feisty woman who seemed a mirror to his soul. He would just contain her, as her negligent father should have done. He would protect her from herself, and probably, in doing so, save her life.

"Very well then, we race on Monday."

"Oh no. I need six weeks to condition my horse."

"Two," he countered.

"Too soon. A month. At least, a month. And until then, free run."

He scowled. "Free run of my stables?"

She nodded. "You won't regret it, Henry. I know each and every one of my horses' needs and habits and peculiarities. It can only help your men to get to know them and get them settled in."

His new marchioness was a hell of a haggler, he'd give her that. "One month, and that's generous."

"A small concession," she said gamely, "to a woman who has as much to lose as I have."

"I suppose you'd say I have everything to gain," he said grimly. It was a damned good thing he wasn't in love with the wench. She'd toast him for breakfast.

"Horse apples! You're a man. If you lose, you won't be giving up the only thing you've ever been good at, and the only thing you've ever loved."

Well, he could fix that, he thought, the notion socking him in the stomach. He'd already felt her passion. But he could show her more. His country wench of a marchioness would be an awesome bedmate, and sublime when she fell in love. He clenched his jaw against the thought, and said instead, "Perhaps it's time to set your sights in a safer direction."

She screwed up her face, rejecting that idea outright. "Not until I've been soundly beaten. Which you can't do."

Henry picked up his reins and turned his horse toward home, Julia at his side. He wouldn't have to trounce her; he wouldn't want to break that spirit.

Just harness it to his own ends.

Chapter Thirteen

How then are the tender minds of children to be cultivated?
—Mary Wollstonecraft, *Thoughts on the Education of Daughters*

"Marie Claire has the sniffles," Isabeau confided to Julia three days later. A proper little lady, she fussed over serving a simple luncheon of fruit, cucumber sandwiches, and the world's blandest porridge.

"Sniffles, too?" Julia asked, still feeling her way with Harry's perplexing daughter. Why would Isabeau make her imaginary friend too sick join them for the only meal where she was allowed? Fearing some new strategy afoot, Julia called her bluff. "I know the cure for sniffles."

"Garlic," Isabeau said fatally. "And mustard wraps."

"Goodness. She must be very ill," Julia answered gravely, then pointed out ruthlessly, "Too ill, then, to join our afternoon excursion." After luncheon, they usually hiked an hour exploring the castle hallways. Yesterday they'd added a few turns around an enormous inner courtyard. The real girl and her invisible friend had shown unexpected reservoirs of energy, giving Julia hope for longer rambles. She was itching to get her new stepdaughter out of the house and on a pony, convinced it was the surest way to free her from her fears and help her become strong.

Isabeau bent to confer with Marie Claire, then reported brightly, "She thinks she'll be fine if it's not too far."

"The stables are very near," Julia said, fiercely stamping out images of the man she might encounter there. Of the man who was avoiding her.

Isabeau and her friend whispered violently. "Marie Claire adores Uncle Bertie's peacocks," Isabeau counteroffered.

Caged and harmless peacocks, Julia realized. Nothing like Henry's fearsome steeds. "The stables are much nearer than the peacocks' pens," Julia pointed out. "That long walk might harm her lungs."

The girls conferred again. "No, she wants to see the monkeys, too. She thinks they're funny."

Julia casually stirred her porridge. "Ponies are funny."

Isabeau's pale blonde brows furrowed. "Marie Claire did not think it the least bit funny when Papa's big old hunter sneezed all over her fresh frock."

Julia bit back a smile. She could just see her proper little hostess fretting over a ruined frock. "Oh dear. We'd better teach that horse to use a handkerchief."

Isabeau failed to suppress a giggle. "Horses don't have hands, silly."

"No they don't," Julia agreed. "I suppose he couldn't help it then."

"I suppose," Isabeau said uncertainly. "But I—but Marie Claire still had to change clothes."

Julia ignored the slip. "Of course, someone should tell a girl not to wear her best frock to the stables."

Isabeau looked miffed, but she lowered her voice to share a confidence. "Marie Claire finds all of Papa's horses really rather large and dangerous."

So that was the way of it. Isabeau attributed to Marie Claire her own wishes and her fears. How to combat that? Julia thoughtfully peeled an orange from a silver fruit bowl. "Did you know I brought my pony Fidget from my father's farm?"

Isabeau looked skeptical. "Grown-ups don't ride ponies. Even I know that."

"True. But I learned to ride on Fidget. He was my best friend. Uphill and down, and even over fences." She had been so proud.

With an intensity that surprised her, she wanted Isabeau to find that pride.

Isabeau shuddered. "I'll bet you took a lot of tumbles."

If she had a prayer of getting Harry's daughter on a pony, she'd better not sugarcoat this issue. "Not at first. Jem—did you meet Jem, my groom?" Julia separated her orange into its dozen segments and arranged them around the plate. "He's moved here, too—Jem taught me, you know. Fidget was very careful. The only times he ever let me fall were when I got careless."

"How many times?" Isabeau ask breathlessly.

"Oh," Julia said casually, offering a slice of orange, "I lost count."

Isabeau took the orange, so engrossed in horror and adventure she forgot to relay Julia's story to her friend. "Didn't it hurt?"

Julia gave her a wry, honest smile. "Not as much as when my brothers laughed."

"You have brothers?"

"Four."

"Marie Claire and I think brothers would be most inconvenient," Isabeau said in a very grown-up voice. "They would laugh at us."

"But you have your Papa. He wouldn't laugh at you."

Isabeau's mouth pursed in disapproval. "Papa doesn't laugh. He scolds. He is very disappointed that we don't like his horses. He wishes I were a boy."

Julia sighed. At least she could give an honest answer. "Your papa doesn't want a son. He loves you just as you are, Isabeau. He's proud of his beautiful daughter."

"He'd be more proud if I liked his dirty horses," she said sadly.

Horses weren't dirty, Julia almost said. She popped an orange bit into her mouth instead. She had to think. If she'd learned anything in the last few days, she'd learned that Henry's daughter was terribly lonely. Loneliness she understood from her own childhood, and she knew the cure. "You wouldn't have to like them. But I know one pony who needs you."

"Needs me?" Isabeau's blonde brows arched. "I don't see how."

"When I saw Fidget this morning, he was very lonely. Two new friends, bearing carrots, could really lift his spirits."

Isabeau curled her fingers into her fists. "How do I know he'd eat the carrots . . . and not us?"

The Mad Marquis

Julia smiled, but privately she worried. How in the world would she get this child on a horse? "Come on, I'll show you how."

Henry was growing more short-tempered by the day. Aunt Augusta cheerfully assured him that Julia's new bedchamber was rapidly taking shape. But he knew for a fact that the carpenters were still banging around, so the plasterers couldn't start, and he hadn't seen any sign that the fabric and furniture ordered from London had arrived. He would spend every night of this week as he'd spent the last one. In his dressing room. On the bench. On the rack.

It didn't make it easier that he was doing it to protect his wife. If, indeed, he was having any effect. From butler to scullery maid, from magistrate to rector, sly, approving looks came his way. Clearly, everyone inside the castle and beyond assumed that he and his wife had vigorously set about making babies.

They had not. Which, he told himself daily, was what he wanted. What she wanted. Besides, he was up to his neck supervising estate affairs while his new marchioness supervised his stables. Or rather, turned his once sacrosanct male haunt upside down.

"She wants this horse there and that horse here, and saddles oiled too lightly, and rugs put up inside out," Wat Nance had grumbled after her first day, and the second, and the third.

Henry had thrown up his hands. "You follow her orders when she's here."

"And when she's not, my lord?"

"Do as you see fit."

He'd stalked off. He had books to balance, harvest to oversee, tenants' cottages to improve, and a dozen favors and intercessions to render to his people. Then he had a horse to train. Not that he didn't believe Hazard could take her on today. Not that his stallion wouldn't peak with another month of training.

It was just that in another month, they'd be carting Henry off to an asylum, bound, gagged and blindfolded, a victim of his own overreaching plans. He'd done some insane things in his time, foolhardy races, reckless leaps over impossible ditches, daring descents down harrowing cliffs. But marrying Julia to get Wraxham's horses and a mother for his daughter was top of the dust heap.

Marrying her, and taking on that bet.

At least he could count on having his stables to himself in the early afternoon, he thought, pacing from his steward's office across the grounds. His dotty great Aunt Augusta had gleefully taken Julia under her wing. And out from under his, except for nights. His nights alone with Julia in adjoining quarters flayed his nerves, shredding his vaunted control. He'd snapped at the grooms all day. A nice cross-country gallop on his stud would take the edge off Henry's temper.

If not dull his lust. He hadn't had a decent night's sleep since introducing Julia to the marvels of her body. He'd been out of his mind. An unsettling thought which did nothing to slake his thirst. Night after night, he'd lain there, hearing her toss and turn, one thin wall away. Even her silences aroused him, the deep and blissful sleep of an innocent.

One night when the moon shone full, flooding her bed with a silvery light, he'd stood in the doorway watching. She'd flung out an arm, alabaster against his wine-red counterpane. She'd kicked it off, struck out with a leg, shapely as any statuary in his pleasure grounds, but vital and alive.

For a woman who saw herself as homely, her bedtime beauty was his forbidden pleasure. For a man on the rack, her easy abandonment in sleep invited him in.

In his obsession, he pretended their children would not be stained. Then and only then, he remembered the wine-sweet taste of her humid mouth, the clink of teeth on teeth, and the arousing duel of tongues. He imagined freeing her from her filmy nightrail. He would stroke her silk-sleek skin.

His obsession deepened, and he dreamed of sinking his manhood into her hot, slick depths, and thrusting home, until she screamed for him, until she surrendered.

Which proved that he was well and truly mad. Any lunatic could see surrender wasn't in her nature. Could see how quickly she'd already stamped out any yen for the pleasure he'd introduced her to.

He returned to his narrow bed, aching and disgusted, his bulging erection a testament to the madness of his passion. A nagging, simmering craving for his bride tormented him from bed to breakfast to barn. He had to control it. Work, he ordered himself. Bury your cravings in work. Mind your tenants and fields and sheep and cattle. Attend to your horses, each and everyone. Race the wind.

So he stalked down to the stables, counting on a hard, unstinting gallop for relief.

He did not count on seeing Julia, bent over cleaning out a pony's hooves. Her buttocks stuck up in the air, on display for any of his grooms and stable help who happened to pass by.

"First we pick out his hooves and remove any stones. They would make him lame, and that would be our fault," she was saying, obviously demonstrating the first principle of good hoof care to some hapless stable boy. "She can try her hand next."

She?

From behind the pony's rounded rump, Isabeau's blonde curls bobbed an enthusiastic *yes*.

Good God. What was his daughter doing here? The last time he'd dragged her down to see his horses, she'd fled in tears, terrified of them and him and, for all he knew, her shadow.

Her small, trusting hand patted the milk-white and chestnut-spotted pony's flank. Isabeau was safe, he could see that. But what had turned her brave? Surely not Julia, not overnight.

"She really didn't think Fidget would like her," Isabeau said cheerfully.

She who? Harry's suspicions peaked. What was Julia up to?

No scenes, he reminded himself. Aunt Augusta stirred up scenes. Uncle Bertie stirred up spectacles. His father, bless his memory, stirred up mayhem when he wasn't sunk in melancholia. Only Henry kept his madness under wraps.

"They say horses have a sixth sense," Julia went on. "I think he knows Marie Claire likes him."

A hot anger boiled in Henry's chest. How dare Julia continue to act as if Marie Claire was real! But he would not create a scene, he told himself. He would not chastise Isabeau or Julia before his staff, and he would protect his daughter from her own disturbed imagination and return her to the safety of her schoolroom. After that, his wife was in serious trouble.

He stepped through the carriage gate and managed to stroll up. Managed to speak calmly, managed to sound sane.

"Well, well, *mignon,* what do you think of Julia's pony?"

Isabeau's eyes widened at the sight of him. "He's very . . . gentle, Papa," she said, anxiously.

His heart twisted. A moment before, with Julia, his daughter had been cheerful, confident. "And you are being very brave," he said.

She ducked her head.

He patted the pony. The sturdy little Dartmoor wight flattened his ears.

Oh, bugger all. Henry hated ponies with their opinions and their wit. That's why he'd tried to start Isabeau on a horse, as his father had started him.

It's all in your head, he'd tried to reassure her. *Horses don't know how small you are.*

I know how small I am, she'd said miserably.

Julia glared at him, siding with her pony. "Isabeau helped groom him, and now we're learning to pick out his hooves."

And what did Marie Claire do? Henry wondered acidly, but complimented Isabeau. "Excellent, *ma petite*. I think your lessons are done for the day."

Isabeau's lower lip threatened, but she added, very brave indeed, "Can I give him just one more carrot? We don't want him to feel lonely."

"By all means," Henry said, grudgingly acknowledging the improvement Julia had brought about.

Isabeau reached into her apron pocket, pulled out a broken bit of carrot, and extended it on her outstretched hand.

Such courage. There might be hope for his fragile daughter yet. Fidget lipped the carrot off her palm.

Isabeau looked at Julia. "Just one more?"

Julia shook her head worriedly, but Isabeau plunged ahead. "This one's from Marie Claire, Fidget."

Henry's anger spiked so, he saw fireworks in the air. By the time the pony had gobbled a second treat from the friend who didn't exist, Henry had summoned Wat Nance to lead his daughter home.

Nance scowled distrustfully at Julia, all but telling Henry to remember about the severed spoke. Not now, Henry thought irritably. He could handle only one defection at a time—well two, counting his daughter's.

"You can see Fidget again tomorrow, *mignon*."

She looked like a kite when the wind failed. "I patted a pony, Papa. I wasn't even scared."

He felt like an ogre. He felt almost proud. But mostly he worried that Julia had gone too far. "We'll tell everyone at dinner. Aunt Augusta, Uncle Bertie—they will be so pleased."

He simply did not know a better way to get his daughter out of danger. But when she walked off crestfallen, he fervently wished she could have a little friend.

He passed the pony to a stable boy, then grabbed his bride by her elbow as subtly as he could with his men looking on. "Upstairs, madam, to the hay loft, and not one word, one sign of anything untoward."

Chapter Fourteen

> . . . it is the rarest thing in the world, to meet with a man with
> sufficient delicacy of feeling to govern desire.
> —Mary Wollstonecraft, *Letter to Imlay*, Todd

Henry just didn't get it, Julia thought, fuming. It wasn't right or fair
or practical to assign her the difficult task of helping his daughter,
then cut her off midstream. She had a plan for weaning Isabeau from
her dependence on Marie Claire. He was ruining it with his interfering, controlling ways. A possessive hand at the small of her back
directed her up a ladder. The hayloft, brimful of summer's harvest,
smelled sweet, like sun-baked summer fields.

Henry grimly latched the hatch behind them. "How dare you feed
my daughter's fantasies. We have only the slimmest chance of re-
claiming her. Instead you indulge her."

Julia curbed an angry sense of his injustice. "Isabeau needs a
friend, willing to lend an ear."

"Marie Claire is a figment of my daughter's imagination. If you
cared one jot for her welfare, you would not pretend otherwise."

His cold control was worse than any outburst. "Please. I can see that you're upset," she said gently, as if approaching a distraught horse.

"Upset!" he exploded.

So, Henry was not a horse. "All right," she conceded. "Furious." She had other ways to calm an agitated animal. She put her hand on Henry's shoulder, and went on earnestly. "You could not know this. But Isabeau forgets about Marie Claire the minute anything else interests or distracts her."

"Only to remember her tomorrow," he said, stiffening beneath her touch.

She softened her palm on his hard muscles, but pushed her argument. "Only because the distraction was not strong enough. Horses are a strong distraction."

"For God's sake, Julia, she hates horses. Where did you come up with that?"

Julia turned up her palms. "I wanted her to care for something real. Something mute and cute and furry. A real companion who would trot her around the paddocks and gallop her across the fields."

He paced about the loft's plank floor. "You should have asked me before undertaking this dangerous path—a path I obviously do not approve—all on your own."

Angrily, she thought of pointing out that he had left her all on her own, that he'd avoided her the last three days as effectively as if he'd run off to London. But he was remote with righteous anger—more than she thought the situation warranted. But she was new to mothering, and not quite sure. "Perhaps it was wrong of me."

He was still pacing, his hands behind his back. "You're bloody right it was wrong. And one more thing," he added. "My marchioness does not clean her horses' hooves. She does not bend over, her very fine bottom in the air, for all my men to ogle."

Julia felt a hot blush rise. After these last days of totally avoiding her, he couldn't possibly be saying he liked her rear end. If it weren't so crude and unromantic, she'd be flattered.

"No one noticed when I was at home."

"Believe me, they noticed."

"You noticed. And I'd really rather you not ogle my behind in public."

His hot gaze raked her up and down. She knew how far short her

127

body fell of feminine perfection. But then, she'd never seen a stallion turn down an ugly mare.

"I did not ogle your behind," he said.

She dropped her hands to her side and drew in a breath for courage. "You're ogling my breasts right now."

Two quick strides, and his arm went round her back, a hand cupped the back of her head, and he pulled her to him. "A man can ogle his wife any time he wants." He took her in a hard and deep and thorough kiss, his last syllables humming against her lips. It was a masterful kiss, like nothing that had gone before between them. Her heart pelted in her chest. He wasn't exploring the texture of her lips. He was claiming her mouth, teeth, tongue, palate. Her stomach dipped with the thrill of his authority. He wasn't trying to please her. He was insisting on surrender.

The private, secret space between her legs clenched and burned.

But he broke off, and she felt abandoned.

Not only did he reject her attempts at mothering his daughter, but her kisses fell short, too.

"What was that for?" she asked, hurt.

"To shut you up," he said hoarsely.

Julia was so thrown off course, she began to chatter. "I have a right to talk, I have a right to my own ideas, and I have a right to the month you granted me to prove them. I should have made Isabeau a condition of our bar—"

He cut her off with another kiss, a longer deeper kiss, her breasts crushed to his chest, her belly to his belly, the place where her legs met to . . . his . . . private . . . she'd guessed about men's parts . . .

But she hadn't guessed a man's erection would be so large, would throb against her belly, would cast its heat deep inside her.

Then his hands began to move over her habit, cupping breasts, defining ribs, sculpting the spread of her hips. She was aware of everything at once, his hot hands, his thick shaft, her gangly frame, her quickening pulse.

Through thick wool, his warm fingers found and tweaked one nipple. Hard.

"Henry!" she cried out, astonished at the insult. Astonished, when he stopped, that her nipple ached with need.

"Ummm?" His mouth did not leave hers.

"What was that for?" she asked, indignant against his lips.

"It wasn't working," he muttered roughly.

Not working? She was offended. She was mesmerized, besotted. What did he want? What did he mean? He buried his face at her neck, and thrills of pleasure started at her throat and raced down her body. Her insides were on fire. Waiting these three days, thinking, dreaming in the dark, only made it worse.

Better. "I think it's working very well," she gasped.

Almost independently, his insistent fingers unbuttoned her bodice and pushed it aside to expose her chemise. His fingers brushed the silk and stopped. "Silk for riding, too?"

It was her only vanity. She wore it every day. She might be gangly, she might be homely, but she refused to be rebuked for this single, secret luxury. "I have a right to wear anything I want, especially where no one can see."

"No one?" he rasped.

No one but you.

"Do you want me in muslin? In sackcloth? I'm sure it can be arranged—" she was chattering. She was scared.

"I just want you . . . to stop talking . . ." He was untying the tapes that laced her chemise, and her breasts sprang free, and his gaze grew heavy. ". . . want . . . to feel . . . this . . ." His hands cupped her breasts, making her aware of the shape of them. The weight of them. Of a tremor in his fingers playing with them. His mouth moved across her chest to the swell of one breast and captured the nipple he had pinched before.

She felt his tongue.

She felt his teeth.

"Henry!" she protested nervously. She knew everything there was to know about animals mating, she told herself. But nips and nibbles? Teeth? She had married Henry Pelham thinking she could handle anything. She never imagined she had so much to learn. The other evening her foray into married bliss had held surprises, yes, but not this whirlpool of anger and desire. But he suckled her nipple insistently where before he'd only teased it. She held her breath, waiting, watching as if he were doing it to someone else.

Could he be mad after all?

But he seemed to know what he was doing, trading patience for haste, tenderness for passion. Her nipple grew hot and taut. He sucked harder, and an unexpected tingle spiraled inward, from his mouth through her breast, then shockingly down to the parting of her thighs . . . So soon.

"Good God, Henry!" she exclaimed, unable not to.

"Better still," he murmured, and stormed the other nipple.

She didn't want to stop him. But her body baffled her and he confused her. She was a masculine woman, a homely woman, and he did not marry her for this. Worrying, she closed her eyes. Again, the tingle spiraled inward, downward. Her breath tickled in her throat. Her stomach twinged and fluttered. Then *there* between her legs, it turned into a glowing ache. How could this feel deeper, hotter than she'd felt the other night?

No wonder housemaids giggled. And her brothers closed their doors. But she and Henry had a different bargain.

"I have to tell you, Henry—Henry!—this is not a good idea."

Her chin brushed his ash-brown hair as he moved to her other breast, nibbling, suckling still. Her tingling, twinging, burning deepened.

"Henry?"

Abruptly he let loose. The cool air fired her damp nipples. "I've not had my way with you, wench."

Good, she thought to her astonishment. She wanted more of Henry Pelham, fierce and angry, exploring her body and making it sing. Those confident, roaming, prowling hands tore at the tapes that held her skirts. Released them. Shoved them down her hips, shucked them over her thighs, and then bared her stockinged legs for him to see.

People ripped their clothes off, she marveled, wondering if she should strip her stockings, too.

Oh, but she had gone too far. Too far in feeling. Too far in fact. Should she stop him? Could she?

"I know I made you angry," she offered desperately.

"I just want you to shut up," he said, in a growl wrenched from his chest. He pulled her roughly back to him as if he had no choice.

"Oh," she answered, loving the sudden knowledge that Henry was at the edge. *Not so indifferent, after all, my lord, and not so controlled.* But it was crystal clear that in this gripping, clutching moment his growing frenzy was the madness that he feared.

He made an animal sound she knew from the breeding shed. Her stallions sounded almost human, covering their mares. Her husband, covering her, sounded raw and feral. Possessive. Magnificent.

Warmth rioted inside her belly, heat slid into her depths.

Her husband was taking her to wife.

She put aside her doubts. His fingers trailed down her stomach into her private thatch of hair, and she knew nothing—nothing—from barnyard lore or rumor to explain the paths of fire they conjured once again. His insistent fingers, hot and individual, explored her womanhood, and she was all confusion. Again they outlined a tender nub. She squirmed. Again he parted her secret lips. She waited, curious. Would it work this time? He probed into her core. Alarmed but eager, she wanted to press into him.

He flattened the heel of his hand exactly where she needed pressure, and her body rocked with need.

"Henry!" she cried out, baffled, hungry.

He lifted his head from somewhere near the pulse in her throat, the throbbing in her breasts.

"I don't understand," she said. Asked.

"You don't have to. Feel me."

She felt him everywhere but didn't understand it anymore sober in the light of day than that night on his bed when she'd been foxed. Why did his fingers feel so good? Why did she need to move? Why didn't he stop? Then his fingers returned and touched that nub and stroked it, back and forth. Her buttocks clenched, her stomach coiled, her breath grew short, and she wanted more. More.

Her fanny wanted to wiggle into him.

Wiggle? She felt so conspicuous. So large and ungainly, graceless.

Had she really done this that night? If he didn't want her to speak, could he want her to move? No matter. She simply could not help herself. She moved, not knowing why but knowing Henry's hands, Henry's mouth, Henry's body hot against her required her to.

She was pushing toward his fingers, trying to get them closer to that spot, to that nub he seemed to need to touch.

She needed his touch, too.

"Henry," she whispered. "Please."

"At last," he said, his voice husky, his actions swift and sure.

"At last . . . what?"

A beam of sunlight slanted across the planes of his tortured face. "If it's not a moan," he said, "don't say a word."

He spread her skirts on a pile of hay like the finest sheets, and rearranged her on their new bed, his chest heaving under his crisp linen shirt. When had his coat come off? She'd not seen him in less than his coat or dressing gown. How could he seem larger wearing less? Even more virile than before, even more strong. How had she not noticed that purple pulse in the dent of his throat? That lovely bronze of hair in the vee of his chest? That golden skin?

"Part your legs," he said, his voice strained, urgent.

It was more personal, stone-cold sober. Intimate in daylight. She parted her knees a few inches, embarrassed her thighs were long and muscled. Embarrassed to expose her most private self to the naked air. To him. He pushed them apart wider. Suddenly his lips trailed kisses between her breasts, to the hollow below her ribs, down her stomach, to the mound beneath her bush of hair.

"Henry?" she asked, her voice trembling.

Her whole self trembling.

"Let me teach you," he said, too rough for any comfort. She felt his hot mouth at the nub his fingers had discovered.

She was too stunned to move. Not even the most lascivious mating animals did anything remotely similar.

He kissed her there, earnestly, tenderly, insistently.

The sweet pain almost killed her.

In the strangest confusion she had ever known, he was suckling that nub, too, as rhythmically, as systematically as anything that had gone before. He raised his hands to grasp her breasts again, and tweaked them both, everywhere all at once, and suddenly she was all sensation.

She might have moaned. She might have screamed. She arched her heat up to his mouth. Her body of its own will lurched and jerked and shook and shuddered. She sank her fingers into his ash-brown hair and pressed his head more tightly to her bush, her yearning. Perhaps she called his name, perhaps she cried, but then the dam broke, flooding her, releasing her, and she sagged, limply, for him.

They were silent, gasping for their breaths.

"Henry?" she said at last, nothing left but whispers. She wanted to draw him near. She wanted a simple kiss. She wanted to reassure him that she knew he wasn't done.

Her eyes closed, she felt for his face, and found moisture, sweat or tears, she couldn't even tell. But he said nothing. Nothing. The hay crackled beneath her as she breathed. He breathed beside her, agitated. Fabric tore, and she opened her eyes. He'd raised up on his knees before her, and his strong square hands jerked at the buttons on his breeches' fall.

She froze on a breath of anticipation. He would take her after all. Which she fervently wanted him to do, despite her promise and their plan.

The fall fell, and he pulled his shirt free, and his shaft thrust up, pearled with juicy fluids, all for her.

"So I get to ogle you," she said shakily, awed to see him, intimate and individual, his manhood swollen with desire. In the village, the sight of nursing women's breasts was commonplace, she remembered lucidly.

No one saw men's members but their wives.

"Touch me," he said, a raw, urgent ache in his voice. It gave the lie to all she'd ever seen of Henry's iron control. It made him human, and it made him hers.

Clumsy, eager, and reluctant all at once, she lifted her hand carefully as if to an overwrought stallion.

Henry's shaft was satin, hot, and hard beneath her fingers, and her heart squeezed with tenderness. Who knew him so but she? Who dared touch her mad marquis?

He shuddered at her touch, and she felt beautiful and powerful, her awkwardness, her ungainliness banished by his desire.

He rolled off her on to unprotected hay, saying hoarsely, "Another lesson, my sweet. Now you see what drives men crazy."

"But you didn't—"

A shaken laugh. "I'm not that crazy."

"But we're not finished. You're not finished," she protested, certain there was more. And positive she liked him better rattled than reasonable.

He propped up on an elbow, and seemed large again. Furious again. "I'd damned well better be finished, or we'll have that baby we both don't want."

"Can't you just pull out?"

"How do you know about that?" he asked, dark suspicion in his voice.

From eavesdropping on her brothers and their randy friends. Which would not sit well with him. But she knew from other ways.

"Breeding my horses. If a stallion doesn't finish . . . If a mare is difficult . . ."

He gave a hollow laugh. "You are difficult, my sweet. That wouldn't protect us."

My sweet, he'd said, in an unguarded moment. She must not put stock in that.

"Pulling out would protect us, too," she insisted.

He reached across the little distance between them and tilted up her chin. "Why do you want this? I showed you a woman's pleasure. Safe pleasure."

She pressed her lips together, hoping for the right words. "You did not show me yours."

With a rough groan, he bent over her. "My pleasure will be our curse. You don't need to know it."

"They think I do already. They look at me with knowing looks, approval—"

"You can't want their approval."

"I want yours. I want you. Inside me once, just once. I want you."

His steely gaze softened, and he looked almost vulnerable. "You're making this complicated."

Dust motes floated through the shadows of the loft. "I'm trying."

He pulled her to him, her cheek against his chest, against the pounding of his heart. "It's a risk."

"Is it such a very great one?"

"No . . . I don't know. We could. We shouldn't."

She heard the waver in his tone, the not-quite change of heart, the not-quite giving in.

"I dare you," she breathed. Her blood was already pumping, in rhythm with his pulse. Mad or not, her husband was taking her to wife. She was mad enough to want him to.

He swore a ripe barnyard oath. "I will hurt you," he said through gritted teeth.

"I've heard mares squeal." And it was always awesome.

So when she spread her legs and he drove into her and the sharp pain lanced her, she just accepted him. Where he belonged, hot and shuddering. "Goodness, Henry," she breathed as her pain eased.

"Goodness has nothing to do with it," he bit off, driving in and out, his hard, large shaft probing deeper than his fingers. "Married people can do anything they want."

The Mad Marquis

Married. Paired. One. His flesh was her flesh. His pulse was hers. Then bracing himself on one arm only, he moved a hand over her breasts, tweaking her nipples in a rhythm to his steady thrusts. She hissed an oath of complete surrender. His hand moved lower, found her tender nub, and gave it deep, firm pinches, too.

"Hen-ree!" She squealed. He covered her cry with his mouth. Suddenly, she was beyond herself with a shuddering pleasure, waves and waves of pleasure. This time she heard it when she screamed.

And her husband pounded at her gates, pounded, and then pulled away, withdrew. He pressed his shaft against her belly and with an agonized shout of release, spurted his hot fluids on her.

She felt she should thank him.

She felt she could cry. But then he held her close.

"Bloody reckless thing to do," he panted vehemently, his weight propped on his elbows, his body heating hers.

"But safe?" she asked, even though she wasn't thinking about safety. She was thinking how strong he'd been, how careful of her pleasure. She was thinking that she loved him like this. She was thinking how it hurt that he hadn't even said her name.

"I got out." He reached down with the hem of his shirt and wiped his seed off her belly. Bloody. It was tinged with blood. "And we've got that out of our systems, once and for all. Satisfied?"

"Satisfied," she answered, but she wasn't. She couldn't imagine being with her husband like this only once. Whatever his intentions, she couldn't imagine stopping now.

Chapter Fifteen

Passions are spurs to action, and open the mind.
—Mary Wollstonecraft, *Vindication of the Rights of Woman*

From below, Henry heard a whinny. Oh for God's sake, he'd gone and tupped his bride in the hayloft of his barn.

He had lost his mind. But the thought didn't send the usual rivers of self-loathing through him. If loving Julia was mad, he probably ought to give lunacy a chance. Because her hot sweet passion pleased him more than anything had . . . since . . . when?

He couldn't remember when he'd felt so alive. He lifted his weight off her body and rolled over on the hay, inordinately pleased when she reached out for his hand and laced her fingers through his. He closed his eyes and allowed himself lazy moments of pure, undiluted pleasure. To hell with Nance's glowering looks and suspicions about his bride. Something flowed between him and Julia, something rare and fine. Something innocent.

She had been innocent and had given him the proof, despite his expectations. Riding astride broke women's maidenheads, young men speculated over ale in pubs at night. It left a man in doubt if he took a horsy bride. Given Julia's equestrian activities, he'd have bet on it.

Well, he chuckled to himself, he'd never make that bet again.

Worse, he thought, extracting his fingers from Julia's clasp, he'd never take his wife again.

And he'd been a damn fool to risk taking her this time. He knew why he'd denied his passion all these years. What if he hadn't gotten out of her in time? Which variation of the family curse would his son display? His obsessions? His daughter's and his aunt's imagined worlds? Or his father's and his uncle's melancholia?

He stood and shook out his hacking jacket, snapping it in the loft's still, fragrant air, then inspecting it for bits of chaff. Better to straighten his clothes, than indulge the sight of his bride sprawled luxuriantly on a makeshift bed of her riding habit. He'd brought her up here to upbraid her, yes, but privately, as befitted a lord and his willful lady. How had he managed to throw sense and caution to the wind?

"Henry?" she murmured lazily, probably triumphing that she'd broken him down. Still, there was a note of such contentment in her voice.

He should have known he'd be vulnerable, even to her, after his monkish life. And she, like any woman, couldn't keep a promise. Not that he could fault her, when he hadn't kept his either. Savagely, he drove his arms into his shirtsleeves, one leg after the other into his breeches, then jammed his feet into his boots.

So much for the future of the marquisate.

After all his caution, the next mad Pelham heir might well be on his way.

"Time to dress," he said bluntly, pulling his bride to her feet and facing her away from him. Which was no solution whatsoever. Her back, which he'd not yet seen naked, was perfect. Her shoulders were gently rounded, not drooping in the current style, and her shoulder blades were flat, not poked out as when women fashionably slumped. Then there was her straight spine, that gentle taper to her waist, leading to . . .

He swept down, grabbed her silken underclothes, and shook them free of straw. "Here."

He handed them off, capturing her habit next. "And here."

But bits of hay and straw clung to the fabric she scrambled into, and he stood in the loft's soft light, picking off every bit. Whatever transpired between them in private, he would preserve her modesty and her dignity before his staff.

From below, someone shouted, and horses' hooves clattered on the cobbles.

Julia wheeled to face him, her rosy face stricken. "Good lord, Henry, I wasn't even thinking. Everyone will know . . ."

"Of course they'll know," he said, suppressing a smile at her self-consciousness. "We're man and wife. They have *known* all week."

"But we hadn't . . . you mean, they thought . . . when I knew . . . nothing . . ." she protested. Then came a tone of wonder. "I had no idea."

She had some ideas now. Quick male pride jigged through him. He had pleasured his wife. And it felt wonderful.

But not for long. She scowled at the low loft, piled high with summer's bounty. "There isn't a back way, I suppose."

"None," he said, and then with a sudden, cozy sense that she now belonged to him, he patted her behind and pointed her toward the hatch that opened down onto the stableyard. "Do me a favor. Look like you enjoyed it." Because she had. He had. This first time.

This last time. The sober truth stalked him like one of Uncle Bertie's tigers, and so he forced himself to add, "Because we're not taking any more chances, Julia. No matter how much you infuriate me."

Every luxurious bone in her body stiffened, and the real Julia snapped back. "I infuriate *you* . . . ? What about you, blowing hot and cold, *allowing* this, *forbidding* that, and then taking my . . . my . . . innocence in your hayloft!"

"You appeared to enjoy yourself," he pointed out, feeling a little smug.

"Which is neither here nor there! Abstinence was your idea, not mine."

"You assented readily enough."

She drew herself up wrathfully. "In ignorance! Whereas you . . . you knew what I'd be giving up."

But he hadn't. He could not have imagined she'd turn into the wholehearted, uninhibited country wench of every gentleman's secret fantasy. Or his, he realized, with stunning clarity. Where he had thought her not to his taste. Was there no end to his capacity for self-deception?

The Mad Marquis

"And furthermore," she continued, inhaling an irate breath, "let's not forget that you brought me here on the pretext of attending to your daughter. Now you're paying us no mind—except to tell me that I'm doing it all wrong. Well, I'm not. Isabeau is improving, and she's improving fast. You may be hands-on with all your tenants, but you've virtually abandoned the person who needs you most. You gave your word—"

He stopped her with a quick, hard kiss.

She looked up, this time without shock.

Spirited, loquacious country wench, he amended, stunned by how much he liked her just like this. When he must not like her.

"What was that for? Really, Henry, just because I like your kisses, don't think they'll bring me to my knees."

She liked his kisses.

He pressed his lips together to keep from grinning like a dolt.

"Far from it!" she went on. "If I were your horse, I'd balk at every hedgerow—"

"You are decidedly not a horse," he said as soberly as he could manage. But the image of riding her again shot flames to the root of his manhood.

She bridled. "That is not the point. The point is . . ."

He forced himself back to the subject at hand. "I know. My daughter." Julia deserved to know. He heaved a sigh. "I didn't have a childhood. My father's moods and excesses ruled us all, but especially me. He either expected too much, or he wanted nothing. I couldn't be the sportsman he demanded or the nurse his moods required. I made a mistake when I tried to force Isabeau to learn to ride." Julia was shaking her head. "I want her to have a chance to be a regular little girl, with a love of dolls and dresses, and no demands from me, or you, that she cannot meet."

"She will build up to that. It's the only thing I know how to do."

He had to put his foot down. "You will have to think of something else."

Her brow darkened, whether in frustration or outright anger, he could not tell. "You brought me to Pelham to help her, but you're tying my hands."

"I want you to take one step at a time. Continue your luncheons, and your walks. Her aunt couldn't even do that. And Julia—" he checked to see that he had her attention "—no more bending over

139

and picking out the horses' hooves for all my men to see."

She snorted. "Horse apples. I did it every day at home. No one said a word."

"I can't think why they were silent. Can you?"

She blushed scarlet. He was sure her own men had leered at her, and she must not have noticed. "No doubt I overstate the case," he said more gently, compassion overcoming the possessive jealousy that raked him.

"No doubt," she said uncomfortably.

He touched her stubborn chin. "Promise you won't let that happen here."

"I'll have Jem do the hooves, then."

"And Isabeau and the pony?"

"I'll have to think of something else," she said testily.

He opened the hatch and went down the ladder first, taking care to keep her skirts from flaring out and betraying all her charms.

It was days before he realized she hadn't promised anything.

Henry's concern for putting her clothing and her hair aright was heavy-handed but thoughtful. As Julia backed down the ladder into the solemn hush below, all hands stopped to watch. But her feet were barely going where her mind directed them. Her body, on public view, was still luxuriating in Henry's ravishment. How long would these feelings last?

And how far would they extend?

As her feet reached from rung to rung, she was terribly aware of a damp rawness between her legs, of a still spreading warmth, of lassitude. Her clothes felt heavy and confining, and her breasts chafed against the bodice of her habit, her nipples tender from his rough caress. Hastily she reassured herself no one could see. But what if they could tell? Hot embarrassment washed through her.

How would she ever face those men to give another order?

Harry stood squarely behind her in support. She could imagine his stern look. It produced respectful silence, then an awkward bustle with horses' rugs or currycombs or buckets as men returned to work.

Chin high, she strolled through the barnyard and headed for the castle, pretending not to notice the occasional curious eyes sliding from her glance. Outside she picked up her pace, already late for her daily lesson in managing Henry's crazy castle.

Henry's aunt was waiting in the yellow drawing room, tea unpoured and hot toast cooling, a knowing twinkle in her eyes.

"That took you two long enough."

Not her, too! Julia sank into a brightly tapestried chair and hid behind a cup of tea. "We two?" she asked innocently.

Aunt Augusta's kindly gaze dropped to Julia's bosom.

Julia looked down. Her habit was misbuttoned, the fabric all bunched up, and her lapels all askew. As they had been as she marched past Henry's men. Caught, dead to rights. Although, after Henry's scrupulous effort to protect her, it was almost funny.

Rallying, she bluffed, "I left in a terrible hurry."

"You needn't pretend to me, my dear. I'd say it was past time."

"You knew?" Julia croaked, noting approval in the older woman's sympathetic face.

"I consider it my duty to mind everyone else's business, especially my nephew's marriage," she said cheerfully.

"So what gave us away?"

"Your sheets, at first. No blood, you see. And now, even without the enchanting evidence of your badly buttoned habit, there's no hiding the flush of a woman who has been well loved." She leaned over the tiny tea table and touched parchment-dry fingers to Julia's face. "Just look at your pretty mouth."

Julia's fingers flew to her lips, which felt sensitive and full. Well and truly kissed. And not just her mouth but everywhere. After the astonishing things Henry had done to her in the hay, she'd have thought she was done blushing for a lifetime. Her face burned.

Then his parting words crashed down on her.

"It isn't as if he plans to make a practice of it," she blurted.

Aunt Augusta's Pelham-gray eyes narrowed. "Pardon me?"

A dry toast point turned to dust in Julia's mouth. "Nothing. Never mind."

Aunt Augusta sat up, soldier-straight. "Oh, no, my dear. No stopping now. What has my great-nephew done this time?"

Julia tried evasion. "Nothing, really. He is, as you said, a good provider and an attentive husband."

Not good enough. "But a one-time lover? Oooh!" Augusta's simple expletive seemed like a scurrilous oath. "That is just like Henry.

Listen, my dear, everyone knows he's not sleeping in your bed, which would be well and good ten or fifteen years down the— poppycock! What am I saying? It's never good. Husbands and wives sleep together through thick and thin. It's too private, too precious—" she broke off, a hint of tears welling up in her eyes. She poured Julia more tea, pushed more toast points toward her, and resumed her seat and her self-command.

"I won't stand by and watch him ruin another marriage. Not after all my planning," she said wrathfully.

Julia's jaw dropped. *Ruin?* she wondered.

"Your planning?" she asked.

Aunt Augusta huffed. "I tried so hard to make him eligible, no small task with his obsessions. Who do you think planted the idea to link our houses? Not Henry, no matter how he coveted your father's horses. And your father! It took me a year of correspondence to persuade him that if he isn't dying now, he will soon enough, and his precious herd is wasted on that cit of a son of his."

Julia felt like she just tumbled into a fox's den. Where everything was very dark. "You? And my father? But why?"

"I didn't count you stupid, gel," Aunt Augusta said, but fondly. "Why do you think?"

Julia couldn't think. She could barely breathe. "If you could just give me a clue . . . A moment to catch up . . . Henry seems perfectly capable of managing his own life. Too capable, in fact."

"Precisely. He is too capable. And manages too much. And imagines things that couldn't be. Why, he's decided we're all mad!"

For one truly dizzying moment, Julia thought him in the right. But she had to start trusting her impressions sometime. Had she seen madness here? No. Eccentricity abounded, but mad they certainly were not.

And yet this intelligent, scheming side of Augusta Pelham was the last straw. She had to get to the bottom of the woman's machinations. Up to now Henry's aunt had seemed quite harmless. Benign. Amusingly addled. Not stirring up some witches' brew of familial politics, with the marquis and the marchioness its ingredients.

Extreme caution seemed in order.

"I don't understand," Julia said carefully, "why you took the trouble. How could our sham marriage benefit you?"

Aunt Augusta looked quite keen to tell her story. Quite a bit keener one-on-one than when she did her addled old lady bit at dinner. "First of all, my dear," she confided, "Henry is driving Bertie and me quite batty, scrutinizing our every word and deed for evidence of the so-called Pelham curse."

So far, so true. They were more than odd, and Henry was right to notice. "Is there a Pelham curse?"

Aunt Augusta gestured to the room, replete with rich, brocaded draperies, costly wooden carvings, mahogany and rosewood furniture, and deep-piled carpet over marble floors. "Would an accursed family amass all this magnificence?"

A point, but was it to the point? "Such success as the Pelhams have had would seem to require stability and skill," Julia said, reaching for rare diplomacy.

"Precisely! If we were mad, we would have dribbled away our wealth to folly generations ago. And second, Henry is stifling the life—to say nothing of the heart and soul—out of a perfectly normal little girl." She paused as if awaiting Julia's next question.

Despite doubts, Julia stood up for her husband. "To his credit, I believe, he asked me to help her—and to relieve you of her care, if I may be frank."

Aunt Augusta waved an impatient hand. "Oh, do be frank, my dear. I'm much too old to beat about the shrubbery. At my advanced age, I confess I've neither the energy nor the inclination to play mother to an eight-year-old child. Even if I hadn't gone so shatter-brained."

Julia gulped. The old lady was forthright. "You do seem to misplace things."

"Everything! As I grow older, I can barely keep track of my spectacles. I can't be expected to take care of a little girl. Especially with Henry's expectations."

"I think Henry's concern for his daughter commendable."

"Commendable? Now don't get me wrong. But he seats the child with us for dinner." Aunt Augusta removed her spectacles and jabbed them in the air. "In my time, it was not done."

"I find it rather touching."

Henry's aunt harrumphed. "Overly fond, indulgent, and controlling."

"Then you did right to facilitate his suit. I will do my best to help Isabeau."

143

Aunt Augusta waved her glasses. "That child will do fine, with or without you or me. Pretty gels always do."

Julia stifled a rebuttal. Far be it from her to criticize her elders. But his aunt's indifference toward Isabeau put Henry's concerns in a whole new light. However misguided he might be about his daughter, Julia could see why he'd recruited her to help.

"Your time is better spent," Aunt Augusta went on in her single-minded way, "if you help my nephew."

"Help Henry?"

"He's wound tighter than a Swiss clock. He fears he's mad, don't you see? And he thinks he can outrun it by tearing across the countryside, denying he has feelings, denying he's a man capable of love."

Julia was speechless. Aunt Augusta was right. Blunt, but right. And devious. "You want me to fix him."

Aunt Augusta's dark bombazine positively rustled with her self-satisfaction. "*Exactement*, as our dear Isabeau would say. A little love would go a long way."

"Henry doesn't love me, Aunt."

"Nonsense, gel, he can't take his eyes off you."

"I think he's doing that rather well." Except for that aberration in the hayloft.

Augusta Pelham nodded knowingly. "Proof positive. He's fighting it."

"And winning," Julia persisted.

Aunt Augusta wagged her finger. "Ah, gel, you have a lot to learn."

"About Henry?"

"About love." Henry's aunt said earnestly, planting her cane with a flourish as she stood. "Well, well, enough of that. We have much to do for Pelham Castle's fall hunt ball."

Not the ball! Julia almost blurted. Yesterday, knee-deep in crates and boxes, they had taken stock of the stillroom with a view of what was needed. Who knew what came next?

But protest would be sacrilege. The Pelham Hunt's fall ball at Pelham Castle was the crown jewel of the county's social calendar, but its nadir for her. She'd fought and pled for years to be excused from the awful crush of people—people who talked like city wits and danced like courtiers. Where she was tongue-tied, and moved on two left feet.

But the sicker her father got, the more emphatically he insisted that she represent the family. So she'd come, dreading to set foot inside.

Year after year Henry turned out every inch the lord, and she turned up the wallflower, nipping out to the stables on the slightest pretext to escape the crush. She couldn't possibly be thrust into the role of Pelham's marchioness, hostess to a castle full of strangers. If she'd had her wits about her when Henry offered marriage, she'd have refused him on that account, alone.

"Menus, lighting, tables, dance floor, rooms for guests—off to the cellars and the storage rooms!" announced Aunt Augusta in full cry, forgetting her spectacles and aches and pains. She marched across the room and charged down the hall, her cane cocked up and body tilting forward.

Objections tumbled through Julia's mind. But she was too flummoxed to lodge a single one of them. Should she try to help Henry, who didn't want it, but not Isabeau who needed it so badly? She followed her mentor along twisting corridors, down spiral stairs to Aunt Augusta's office, more lost in Henry's crazy castle than the day he brought her home.

She had to help them both.

Chapter Sixteen

In order to fulfil the duties of life, and to be able to pursue with vigour the various employments which form the moral character, a master and mistress of a family ought not to continue to love each other with passion.
——Mary Wollstonecraft, *Vindication of the Rights of Woman*

By dinner, Julia observed, Henry had resumed his tight control. He didn't blink when Augusta Pelham announced she'd lost her pearls.

"Look to your neck, dear aunt," he said complacently, too used to her dotty behavior to question it. It wasn't her behavior Julia questioned now: It was her designs.

Uncle Bertie sauntered in with his newest Capuchin monkey. Julia scrutinized him for any sign of the spells Henry had darkly hinted at. Nothing tonight. At some invisible signal, the monkey started beating a tiny drum.

Henry merely smiled. "How long to train him to do that, Uncle?"

That launched Uncle Bertie into a heartfelt but tedious quarter-hour discourse on not only how long it takes one to train a monkey, but how one finds a drum for a monkey, fits that drum to said monkey, and keeps the blasted monkey interested in it.

The Mad Marquis

Henry took in every word without a sign of boredom.

Fascinated by the doll-sized creature, Isabeau forgot to complain about her least favorite sorrel soup.

As for Julia, her head still spun from Aunt Augusta's command of details for the ball. A thousand candles, two-hundred-eighteen servants, ninety square yards of flooring, forty-three cases of wine, twenty-seven baskets of bread, a dozen bushels of lemons, countless cakes, and one beleaguered bride. In Julia's mind, it kept her from making progress on the bedchamber renovations, the last of Julia's concerns.

Henry was treating her as if she were Aunt Augusta's guest. Or Isabeau's companion. Or Uncle Bertie's long-lost niece. He did make small talk about her horses—which one shied to the right, required special horseshoes, took a light whip or needed none. He'd claimed her horses for his own. Just not her. She was hurt. Something spectacular had happened between them in the afternoon.

They'd been lovers. They'd been one.

But Henry's message—spoken then, implied tonight—was that she had best get over it. Get over him. But how?

Despite his courteous distance now, she saw him as he'd been for her in the hayloft. Tonight, his tailored coat of superfine cruelly hid the landscape of his chest. But not from her sharp memory. His pressed cravat covered his corded neck, which had strained for her in the throes of love. And under the table, skintight breeches clung to thighs as hard as iron. In the loft she'd welcomed them between hers like some wanton woman . . . And his manhood . . . was it rampant now?

Vexed by her fascination with her husband's body, she stole glances up and down the table. Could the grown-ups tell what she was thinking? Doubtful. Aunt Augusta asked for more parsnips when they were piled high on her plate. Uncle Bertie passed peas and honeyed carrots down to a grateful monkey.

Henry's mind, judging from his conversation, went on to his tenants' woes.

Leaving her behind.

You couldn't disgrace yourself sleeping with your husband. Could you? Brotherly vulgarities swarmed through her head, the upshot of many misspent hours spying on them in their cups. Henry had tumbled her in the hay. Swived her in the afternoon. Gone bollocking,

147

gone bird-nesting, oooh, she had heard them say it all. Laughing drunkenly, crudely, coarsely.

Men didn't care about love, not like women.

Henry didn't care about her, not like she did him.

Succulent boiled chicken fell off the bone at a touch, but she half choked chewing it. She refused dessert.

Supper done, her husband rose, helped her from her seat, drew her hand to his mouth, and lightly kissed her knuckle.

"Until tomorrow, my sweet."

"About tomorrow . . ." she started to protest. She'd barely seen him yesterday or the day before.

A fragment of a frown crossed his face.

But Isabeau, bouncing with enthusiasm, inserted herself between them. *"Moi aussi, Papa."*

Under his daughter's flattering attention, his hard gaze softened. Flattery? Julia wondered. She could try that, if she got desperate enough. Henry hoisted Isabeau to eye level, landed a smacking kiss on her pale cheek, and without a word exited the room.

Tamping back murderous feelings, Julia dutifully took Isabeau up to the nursery, read her a story, and put her to bed. Then she stalked back to her own.

In the garnet and green and mahogany hues of Henry's stronghold, Julia paced furiously. What did tonight's little performance mean? For now that she'd seen a tender and attentive side to Henry, performance it clearly was.

Did he love her? Like her? Hate her? Did he want her?

Did he not?

And what did he mean, *tomorrow?* Besides the obvious: He had no intention of coming to their bed tonight.

Well, she accepted that. She'd made a bargain. Whereas her afternoon delight with Henry in the hay was merely an ill-considered interlude.

Possibly even a reckless one. She pressed a hand to her flat stomach. He had pulled out, she tried to reassure herself. That ought to work. She'd seen stallions interrupted. Sure that the mare had failed to catch, Jem had taught her to put the stallion to his work again. And again and again.

There would be no *again* with Henry Pelham, the mad marquis of Rayne.

But no child, either. She tried to remember why she had never wanted children. Why she hadn't wanted marriage. Why she hadn't wanted love.

The fire sputtered and went out, and she flung herself across the wide reaches of her husband's bed. Not her best move, for images rose up in quick succession of Henry with her in his bed, of Henry in the hay, of Henry with his shirt off, of Henry nibbling at her breast, bringing a nipple to a tender peak.

Of Henry spilling his seed on her barren belly.

She bolted up, jerked off her evening gown, and angrily tossed it over the carved-ivory folding screen. Her silks were next, her stockings last. Naked, she was too overwrought to feel a chill. Still, after she put on the lacy nightgown her stepmother had insisted on, she slid between the sheets with a bleak sob of frustration.

Would no man ever want her? How could Henry be passionate and then turn remote? What was so wrong with her body? What was so lacking in her charms? He'd taken her, and left her. Claimed her, spurned her. In private, he'd kissed the center of her with passion. In public, the knuckles of her hand.

She would not cry.

She would not. But it had been so awesome when he'd aroused her, *there.* She touched herself, remembering the press of his palm to her soft mound of flesh, crisp curls, secret lips. Here in her evening solitude, the afternoon's sweet sensation left her with an ache, a lack. Henry's manhood had pierced her, stretched her, filled her. He was the only husband she would ever have. The only man. She doubled over as she held herself, the throb of yearning there finally driving her to tears.

She wanted to belong to Henry. She wanted him to want her.

What was she doing? she berated herself. Whimpering and bemoaning her fate. A first for Julia Westfall, who stood up in her stirrups and took her fences hard. What was she to do?

She'd do what she'd always done.

Never allow rejection, and never accept defeat. Henry might turn away from her, but in the end she'd win. Tomorrow, she'd find a way around his prohibition about the pony. Tomorrow, she would plan his blasted ball.

And somehow, every day for the next month, she would train her filly. And she would win their race.

*   *   *

None of which proved to be as easy as she'd thought, when black night turned to foggy morning gray.

First, she tackled the problem of Isabeau's riding lessons. She was disturbed by Henry's revelations about his childhood, and sympathetic, too. It touched her that he confused it with Isabeau's in any way. But she vehemently disagreed that his daughter needed to be protected. Learning to trot and even gallop would make Isabeau strong, and braver, too. But where? Julia couldn't very well conduct the lessons where Henry's staff could see and report back to him. Not until Isabeau had overcome her first fears. Thank God, Jem Guthrie still worked for her.

She found him forking fresh straw into Minx's stall.

"All due respect, mum," he murmured. "M'heart's with ye, helping that poor child. You got the right idea, and Fidget's the properest pony. But don't ask me to go behind his lordship's back. He'd kick me on out me bum—beg pardon, mum—and where would ye be without me?"

Alone. With no one to rely on for her horses. "You're a good man, Jem," she forced herself to say, then lightly chided him to hide her disappointment. "You'll not tell, now."

"Not one word, mum, never."

Clutching the pony's tiny bridle in her hand, Julia explored the pebbled path around the landscaped lake, Pelham's pleasure grounds. She came across a fanciful huntsman's cottage, nestled in a stand of yews. No use whatsoever. There was a grotto, deep, damp, and dark, and a temple crowned a little man-made hill. She could imagine trysts—with Henry, blast her futile yearning—in any of these secret places. But she couldn't hide her pony in them. Discouraged, she scuffed along the path as it circled back to the castle.

She needed a private shooting range, a secret grove, something close. Not only was her young charge timid; she was not yet strong enough to go traipsing off to distant rendezvous. An hour later, Julia's feet were aching. She should have brought a horse. An arched bridge crossed a charming stream that burbled into the lake, and Julia turned onto an open vista she had never seen.

Plop in the middle of it, twenty feet high if they were a foot, boxwood hedges formed an antique maze.

Perfect. Once inside, they would be safe from prying eyes. And patriarchal eyes. The tall green walls might make the child feel more secure.

"I'm not supposed to go there. Ever," Isabeau said by rote at lunch after Julia proposed her scheme.

"Ever? Or just by yourself?"

Isabeau's lower lip trembled. "I wouldn't want to go there by myself. It's very tall and very . . . scary."

"Hmm," Julia temporized. "I don't think I'd be scared. I'd be curious."

"I'd get lost."

"We can take string. A very, very long string."

Isabeau's brows drew together skeptically. "Strings break."

Julia shrugged. "A very, very, very strong string, then."

"Do you think it would work?"

"Absolutely."

Isabeau blinked. "Papa would enjoy that."

Julia's heart sank. She hated deception, and she had the gravest doubts about helping a child deceive her father. But Isabeau would never conquer her fears with Henry in the wings. His smothering ways left Julia no choice.

But what to say, short of outright lies? "Why, I'm sure he will, in time. But let's keep it our secret until we know our way around the maze. Then we can surprise him."

Isabeau brightened. "If he's not coming, I can bring my friend."

"Hmm," Julia repeated, casting about for a way to say no. Getting rid of Marie Claire was even more important than getting Isabeau on the pony. She needed a substitute for her imaginary friend first, but she had not yet lost her heart to Fidget. "Won't Marie Claire be afraid?"

Isabeau was crisp and confident. "I'll explain everything to her."

It was a tricky plan, born of desperation, Julia thought, heading to the stillroom in search of a ball of sturdy string. Tomorrow she would have to steal Fidget from the barn, sneak across the lawn unseen, and coax both him and Isabeau into the monster jaws of the maze. She couldn't guess whether he would balk or try to eat it. But she was sure Isabeau would take convincing.

So would Jem, as she marshaled arguments to change his mind.

* * *

Fiona Carr

That afternoon, in Augusta Pelham's office, Julia was offered sherry.

She eyed the sparkling spirits askance. "Tippling in the afternoon, Aunt?"

The older woman twinkled. "Fortification, my dear." She bunched up her voluminous skirts, crowded onto the settee with Julia, and piled a stack of invitations atop her tiny rosewood desk.

Julia tippled, smiling wanly. "Aren't we a little late?"

Can't we put this off forever?

"Late? Only with these. The usual ones went out weeks ago. Two hundred and eighty-nine, to be exact. This year's ball will be our largest to date," she went on cheerily.

"Oh," Julia let out the word in a whoosh of defeat. There was no escape.

"These are all *your* relatives and neighbors." Aunt Augusta handed Julia a list of addresses in an elegant hand.

Julia glumly dipped her pen in ink. Her writing was a thready scrawl, hardly an elegant welcome.

"Everyone will want to see Henry's new marchioness in all her splendor."

"Splendor?" Julia half laughed. "I don't even have a decent dress."

"I've sent for Mademoiselle Le Brun, my modiste from London. Frightfully clever with a needle."

Julia gawked. She couldn't see herself in anything remotely resembling Aunt Augusta's old-fashioned dress. Clever didn't begin to describe the cumbersome garment. Its massive side rolls pressed Julia to the edge of their shared settee.

Aunt Augusta acknowledged Julia's look of disbelief. "Never fear, my dear. Polly Brown renamed herself Le Brun for business. 'Twas her grandmother made these old rags. Polly can hardly bear to mend them. She would sell her soul to bring me up to date."

Julia scrutinized Augusta Pelham's antique dress. "What would be so wrong with that? I think you'd look splendid in the modern style."

"I wear these for my own . . . reasons," the older woman stammered, obviously holding back. Julia let the subject drop, for now. "But Polly sewed for Isabeau's mother. She'll know exactly how to show you off to greet our guests and lead the dancing."

Dancing. The point of Julia's quill pen broke and ruined her envelope. "Oh bother!" She found a knife to trim the quill. "I cannot possibly lead the dancing."

Join the Historical Romance Book Club
and GET 4 FREE* BOOKS NOW!

A $23.96 Value!

The Mad Marquis

"But my dear, it's your duty," Aunt Augusta said in a decided tone. "Here, you sand and stamp and seal." And passed her the box of sand.

Julia took another, welcome swallow of the sherry. Perhaps Aunt Augusta was hard of hearing. "I have two left feet."

Augusta Pelham handed her the sealing wax and the marquisate's formal seal. "Oh, Bertie can fix that, my dear."

"Bertie can fix what, my dears?" boomed Uncle Bertie, striding in in peacock colors, sober gray Raj perched upon his shoulder.

"Fix what, my dears," said Raj.

"You don't understand," Julia said, without acknowledging the interruption. She was too dismayed at the thought of dancing at the center of attention. "Four brothers coached me. Nothing took."

Aunt Augusta passed her a finished envelope to sand and seal. "Bertie's very good."

"Indeed I am, my dear. Danced my way from London to Calcutta."

Julia studied him for any sign of spells, but saw only the charming optimism that had marked him from the first.

"Introduced the waltz to India, in fact," he continued energetically. "Smashing hit with those company men."

"He means East India Company men, gel." With a flourish Aunt Augusta addressed another envelope and passed it on. "Now, Henry is very particular about his seals. Center the wax on the page, and the seal in the middle of the wax, right and tight and perfect."

Julia indulged a moment of despair as she sanded, stamped, and sealed. She didn't belong in Henry's perfect world. She looked like a post in formal dress and danced like a drunken goose. To say nothing of her graces on a receiving line.

Her slight hope of fixing her husband's affections vanished in a puff of dust.

At dusk on his shooting range, Henry steadied his pistol and took aim. "Bull's-eye on the far target, man, two out of three. Lay down your bet."

Grayson cleared his throat, as close as a refusal as he had ever come. "I'd prefer not to, my lord."

"Won't break you. You're paid in pounds sterling."

"It's against my principles, my lord."

"Religious?" He hadn't thought his dour, dapper man to be religious.

"Professional, my lord."

"And you have served me how long?"

"Since your last year at university, my lord. Eighteen years, nine months and three—"

"Long enough for me to have ample evidence of your professional conduct."

"—weeks, my lord," Grayson finished, somehow without a hint of insubordination. "So long as I maintain my conduct, I should think, yes, my lord. But"—his shoulder hitched—"if I may ask, why now?"

Because he hoped a manly, sporting competition would take his mind off his bedeviling bride.

Which Grayson no doubt suspected. "I shoot more keenly under pressure, Grayson, if you would be so kind as to set aside your standards and oblige me."

"A sovereign, then, my lord, if you insist," he conceded tonelessly, but a corner of his mouth turned down.

"A sovereign, against what?"

Grayson sighed. "A sovereign that you cannot possibly hit the bull's-eye of that target twice in three tries."

"Double you, I can hit it twice in two," Henry countered, and aimed and fired. The pistol kicked his hand. He fired, it kicked again.

Satisfying, that. They paced across the greensward to the target. Both shots had ripped its one-inch eye. The pistol was his favorite, designed and forged for him by a friend from university who lived up north. A perquisite of status. One had friends who did interesting work, and sometimes did one an unexpected kindness. He turned the pistol in his hand, and the butt snugged into his palm. A perfect fit.

Like Julia's breasts.

"Damnation," he swore softly. Nothing overrode his obsession with his bride.

"My lord?" asked Grayson.

"Reset the target," he said grimly. "And up the stakes."

"You are late to dress for dinner, my lord," Grayson prompted gently.

Gently as a razor at his neck. As if he knew Henry had been avoiding the sight of his wife in anything approaching a state of undress.

"I know I'm late for dinner." Purposefully so, as he had been every evening since he'd made love to Julia. Correct that: every evening since he'd lost his mind and made love to his wife.

"My lord," Grayson began, neither hesitating nor asking.

"Yes, Grayson."

"If I may be so bold, my lord . . ."

"You may be bold."

"Given your aunt's expectations, being on time is practical, my lord."

Being on time was the very devil, with Julia in the room.

"I have been late before."

There was a hint of a gleam of a smile, instantly suppressed. "In the year ought-two, my lord."

Grayson was a master of obliging indirection, but Henry saw where this was leading. "Are you saying the servants are talking?"

"I wouldn't say that, my lord."

"Are you saying I am neglecting my bride?"

A twinge about the corner of his mouth betrayed him. "My lord. I would never presume."

"Yet we are having this conversation. Are you saying I am a callous brute not to share her bed?"

"I had no idea," he said, so hastily he left off the obligatory *my lord.*

"Flummery, Grayson. I'd wager you know how many times I turn over in the night."

"I don't—"

"Wager. Right. So I'm not a callous brute."

Grayson stiffened stuffily. Man and master's conversation had never gone this far. "I have no opinion, my lord. Decidedly no opinion, public or private."

"Good man. But you know that I'm a fool."

"It is not for me to judge."

"Excellent, my man. You don't judge me a fool for avoiding my wife, and I won't judge you a fool for putting up with me. We'll go in then."

But he could judge himself. He was a fool for marrying, a fool for making love to his wife, a fool for avoiding her and exposing her to servants' chatter, a fool for letting temptation run him out of his own chambers.

But he could not—would not—allow himself to avoid her forever. He was a stronger man than that.

Chapter Seventeen

. . . for if men eat of the tree of knowledge, women will come in for a taste . . .
— Mary Wollstonecraft, *Vindication of the Rights of Woman*

Under the setting moon, a heavy dawn fog rolled in, obscuring white caps on all but the nearest waves. One broke at Minx's hooves, and the filly gave a playful buck. Julia sat easily and felt herself again. She was pleased with her mare's spirit.

Pleased with her own. She'd endured a week of Isabeau and pokey pony rides, Aunt Augusta's incessant organizing, and Uncle Bertie's animal enthusiasms. Nothing had kept her off her horse.

Even so, this morning she'd fled her castle obligations at first light. Never mind she hadn't had a wink of sleep, worrying about the ball that was only four days away. Worrying about Henry. He hadn't spent the night in their shared chambers since they'd made love.

She would not care. She would not let his absence get her down. If this truly was a marriage of convenience, all the more critical for her to win her race and claim her freedom. She was too miffed, and too determined to go about her business, to pay much mind to Wat Nance's warning not to disturb his master. How could she disturb him when she didn't even know where he was at this ungodly hour of the day?

Half an hour into Minx's workout on the shore, Julia's spirits were restored. Spotting a tempting outcropping, she let out the reins a fraction and nudged her filly toward it. Still fresh, the youngster gave a dazzling burst of speed, showing some of the reserve Julia knew she had. Julia exulted in the lash of the wind and the power of the filly she'd bred. She wouldn't just win her bet. They would astonish Henry.

Two fast furlongs down the shore, she reined Minx to a trot, only to hear a pounding gallop at her back. She glanced over her shoulder.

It was Henry on his stallion. He pulled up, his handsome features flushed with exercise and anger. He looked dark and mysterious in a caped coat that flapped in a stiff ocean breeze, perhaps even a little mad. Minx sidestepped, squealing like a mare in heat. Hazard arched his neck and pranced.

Ah, true love, thought Julia a trifle ruefully, and the way of the world it was—just not her world.

"Where do you think you're going?" Henry asked.

"Good morning to you, too, my lord," Julia said, forcing cheer at his cold greeting. Forcing calm over her racing heart. "To the outcropping, as if you couldn't tell."

He glowered disapproval. "There are jagged rocks under the sand flats, and a cave on the dune's side hidden at high tide."

"Where you played as a child, no doubt," she baited him.

His look said he had not played at all. But he evidently checked his anger and his need to order her around, and took another tack. "You're out early."

"And you are late. Rumor says you train at midnight." Or so Jem had explained. On her sleepless nights, she'd practically had to rope herself in bed, so keen was her urge to spy on her mad marquis racing his stallion on the moonlit shore. "It's dawn."

He lifted a shoulder. "We nearly lost a mare last night."

She tensed. "One of mine?" Her filly tensed beneath her.

"Ours, Julia," Henry corrected. "One of ours. But yes, one of the Wraxham broodmares. Juno colicked."

Minx's mother. "And she's . . . ?" Julia prodded, worrying.

"Eating hay again. She's fine. We drenched her, walked her, watched her through the night."

All night long. Without her. His oversight flew all over Julia.

"I should have been there. You should have sent for me. Jem would have."

At her sharp words, Minx jigged, and Henry's stallion gave a throaty, urgent whicker, courting her maiden filly. Julia stifled envy. Animal attraction was so much simpler than human entanglements. Henry slapped his stallion on its neck to regain its attention.

"Jem's off to Gloucestershire to see a colt."

"All the more reason to send for me."

Henry sidled Hazard nearer. Hazard was a full hand taller than the filly. On top of him, Henry towered over Julia. Glowered down at her. "I am not your employee, my lady. Nor am I your indulgent father. At Pelham, we have men to nurse sick horses in the night."

She wasn't reassured. "So did I. But I worked and watched right alongside of them. As I should have done last night. If you had any respect for our bargain, you would consult me when my best brood-mare almost dies."

"She had a bellyache," he said with patronizing patience.

"Did it occur to you to ask if this was her first colic?"

He set his jaw. "I'm asking now."

"Last fall. On acorns, as best we can determine, so you should have her in a paddock with no oaks."

"Our paddocks don't have oaks."

Julia glared. "Then we have a mystery, do we not?"

"Horses colic, Julia. It's a fact of life."

She hated condescension. She hated sitting on her filly with Henry towering over her. "Not if I can help it," she said sharply. She whirled Minx around and kicked her into a gallop. Henry's, *"Don't"* was muffled by the fog.

Julia did not press for her filly's top speed. Indeed, she thought, as the wind whipped tears from her eyes, she didn't *know* her filly's top speed. Up ahead loomed the precipitous path she'd first negotiated on Galleon. She knew Minx could take it. Her filly's ears flicked forward.

No need to take it slow, Julia thought, not with Henry thundering behind her. She leaned forward, grabbed a fistful of mane, and pointed her mare up the hill. Minx's hindquarters bunched, and she hurdled Julia upwards with great leaping lunges.

Loosened chunks from the chalky cliffs rained down behind them.

Henry's ripe curses echoed upwards. Julia laughed, not even looking down. Henry couldn't catch her here. His stallion was too big and bulky, her filly compact and clever with her hooves.

Moments later, Minx leapt onto the flat, out of sight of Henry and of Hazard. The stallion's protest trumpeted through the morning mists, echoing up and down the cliffs to all the birds and all the fishes of the sea. Compelled by the primeval mating call, Minx balked and whinnied back. Her frantic love-struck call vibrated her body so hard it shook Julia to her bones.

Then Hazard and Henry cleared the edge, and the filly curved her neck around to . . .

Flirt? Drat and blast, Julia thought, kicking hard, but uselessly.

Her filly was head over ears in love . . . and beyond control. Standing in his stirrups, Henry reached for Minx's bridle. Perversely, Minx reared, her front legs churning empty air. Arms around the filly's neck, Julia felt her rise too close to vertical, felt the filly's desperate lunge to right herself, and flung herself off and rolled onto the ground.

Heart sinking, she glimpsed her prized filly flip over, almost onto Julia, her delicate, tapered legs flailing in the air.

Henry leapt off his heaving stallion and bent over Julia. From her position on the sandy turf, she barely noticed him. Julia saw Minx scramble up, shake herself and gallop off, obviously unhurt. She looped giant circles across the downs, stirrups flapping, tail flagging in the breeze.

Such spirit, and such speed.

Julia's punctilious husband, it seemed, disapproved of both of them.

"She's never done that!" Julia said, unable to take her eyes off her hot-blooded filly. Couldn't Henry see her promise?

"From the looks of it, you can't control your filly," he said brutally.

And that was all he saw! "Something about Pelham makes everyone go mad." She turned to give him the set down of his life.

A nasty cut jagged across his high cheekbone. "Good God, Henry! What happened?" She reached to stanch the blood.

"Don't move," he ordered.

"What about your cheek!"

His brow knotted. His fingers found his wound, tested it, and found blood, but he shrugged. "That's from those boulders you

159

kicked up. Good thing you weren't trying to kill me."

"Of course I wasn't."

Ignoring his own injury, he knelt down, all business as his fingers probed for tenderness, for broken bones. He straightened the leg she'd landed on, then gingerly ran his fingers up and down it. "Where are you hurt?"

In my pride, she thought.

"Everywhere," she said.

"Bloody hell," he said fiercely, and scooped her in his arms.

"Bloody hell, yourself, Henry." She wriggled in indignation, though almost mollified to see he cared. "For God's sake, put me down. I was bamming you. Don't be so grim. I've been tossed off in hedgerows. I've taken spills from a dead gallop. This was nothing. I'd tell you if I'd broken anything."

Somewhat unceremoniously, he deposited her on her feet.

"You mean if your filly had broken anything. I never should have agreed to let you ride that half-tamed creature."

"She's not half-tamed, and it's not her fault," Julia said. She never blamed her horse. Horses didn't do stupid things unless their riders put them in stupid positions. "And we're neither of us hurt." She took a few test steps and held out her hands, wiggling her fingers as proof. "See. All in working order. I am not quite, however, up to walking all the way back."

Shading her eyes, she looked across the gently sloping downs and admired her filly. Minx was still looping great circles around them, cutting up the turf, despite Hazard's bellowing to her to come to him.

"Thought your filly came if you just whistled," Henry said provokingly.

"In the pasture, yes. Under commands from some overbearing stallion, she's having second thoughts."

"You can't even handle your own horse."

"Oh for heaven's sake, Henry. She's in season, and she's trying to seduce Hazard. Just put me on him, and let's get back to the stables."

He arched an imperious brow. "Hazard is not a woman's mount."

She wouldn't take offense and lose this chance. "We can share," she propositioned.

"He's never carried two."

She cut her husband a daring look. "You don't think he can."

"He's seventeen hands tall, eighty, perhaps ninety stones, and in peak condition. Of course he can."

She'd trapped him in his own words, and his look said he knew it.

"Then there you are," she said, trying not to gloat as he gave in and gave her a leg up. The thought of riding home with her arms around her husband sparked an itch of anticipation in her.

Proximity was damned awkward, Henry thought. Damned awful.

Damned arousing. So arousing he barely noticed the burn that throbbed across his cheek. No, the throbbing burn he noticed was lower, and a great deal more vexing. He'd handled the sight of Julia's fine bum as she galloped her horse ahead of him. He'd handled the curves of her fallen body molding to his arms.

But he could not handle this.

Behind her on the horse, he could bury his face in her flame-red hair, darkened by the heavy fog and kinked by the ocean spray. He could smell her scent of salt and surf and leather, an outrageously unfeminine but heady aphrodisiac. He wrapped his arms around her rib cage just below her breasts. With his horse's every stride, he could feel her muscles moving. His bride was a healthy handful of woman, willing but not vulgar, eager but not quite lewd.

Then he remembered her silk underwear.

Did she wear it in the mornings? Did she have it on right now? Under her riding habit?

Desire coursed through his body, racing down his spine into his loins. His manhood swelled, nothing between it and her but the pommel of his saddle, the low, flat, almost nonexistent pommel of the lightweight saddle he'd had specially made for racing. He floundered for a way to stifle his desire. An argument should do the trick.

"Spying on the competition isn't very sporting, Julia," he chided, using the patently superior tone he knew provoked his bride.

"You weren't supposed to be there," she shot back.

He scowled at her wanton curls. She always had an answer.

"You know where I train. I call that spying."

"I was told you trained at midnight."

"Right. Away from all distractions."

"Such as our bed," she said, provoking him.

161

No, such as you.

"It is not our bed," he reminded her.

"Everyone knows that, my lord," she said lightly. Too lightly.

"What do you mean, everyone knows?"

"That we don't share that bed. That you don't really want to. But what they say is none of your concern."

"They can say what they want of me, but I won't have them asking about my wife."

His wife. She had never felt more so, rocking gently in his arms to the movement of his horse, her body relaxed if her tone was not quite.

"They aren't asking," she said. "They're talking."

"Talking?" He had plainly instructed his staff never to gossip about anyone under his protection.

"Your man, my maid, your aunt, and for all I know your uncle and your daughter. It's nothing I can't manage," she said stoutly, but a tremor in her voice betrayed her.

And finally sank in. His injunctions had not worked. Gossip was hurting his bride. His rejection had compromised his household's respect for her. "I never meant for our arrangement to hurt you, Julia."

"I'm not hurt. I'm busy. Busy training for our race."

He was not deceived. Being busy hid hurt. But she had pluck, and he respected that.

"And you can spy on us, my lord, any time of the day or night. I plan to win."

"Ha!" he said, relieved at her recovery. "You'll never get that mare fit the way you stop and start."

"Wait and see, Henry."

"I saw enough this morning. She's good, though, for a mare. I'd breed her first thing in the spring, hands down."

"Oooh, men!" she all but swore. "Can you only think of us for breeding?"

No. At this moment, he only thought of her for love.

Clop *clop* clop *clop*. Clop *clop* clop *clop*. An awkward silence reigned. Not even Hazard's regular footfalls overrode his discomfort.

"I didn't marry you for breeding, Julia."

I married you for this. For passion, and adventure.

Had he? He must have. He mulled over the wild, random thought.

162

The Mad Marquis

He was having a lot of wild, random thoughts this morning, nothing like the controlled reason he prided himself on and struggled to maintain.

"What did you marry me for, Henry?" she asked indignantly, shifting in the saddle to confront him.

Her short, thick hair tickled his face, caught on his morning stubble.

To hell with reason.

"This," he said. *"This."*

Arms crossed below her breasts, he let his fingers find her nipples. Already they were peaked and hard. Rosy, he remembered, and responsive to a pinch.

She sighed through her teeth at his touch.

"I married you for this," he said roughly.

For he knew, the instant the words crossed his lips, he'd spoken a terrible truth.

All his other rationales were lies.

Already hard, his manhood swelled. Nudged at the parting of her bottom.

She hissed a sigh of shock. "Henry," she whispered back at him, "I thought you couldn't do it from behind."

He dropped his head, his lips brushing the lee of her neck. "We're not doing it. But we could try." He tightened his grip, snugged his erection closer.

"But we're . . . on . . . a horse." Breathlessly.

"We could try that, too."

The thought inflamed him. Bloody hell, any thought of Julia inflamed him, but this dalliance on his fiery stallion was reckless, mad. He thought of that hayloft interlude, of his lady's country wench temptations . . . And madness seemed like reason; reason, madness; and he wasn't sure he cared to split the difference anymore.

The morning fog was lifting. Before the sweep of landscaped grounds that led to his ancient family's ancient castle, the last copse of windswept yews sparkled. They were the last privacy he and his wife would have all day.

At some instruction Henry neither saw nor felt, Hazard halted. Had Julia signaled the stallion to stop?

"How did you do that?" he asked.

163

She laughed at him. "Magic. What do you think I am, Henry? An untutored stableboy?" She kicked free of her stirrups.

"You don't know my cues and aids."

"Did you invent them?"

She swung her leg over the stallion's neck and slid to the ground, her habit's skirts too well weighted to fly up. Unfortunately, he thought, once again unable to control his fascination with his bride. His fixation on her.

Looking up, she said earnestly, "I know almost everything there is to know about my horses, Henry. My problem is that I know nothing about love."

Her eyes held an unmistakable invitation, and he slid to the ground beside her, his heart hammering in his chest. "You don't know what you're asking."

"I just want to know what I'm missing."

He tied his horse's reins to the rough-barked limb of an ancient yew. She braced against its trunk, flung her arms around Henry's neck, and pulled him to her.

Kiss me, Henry, teach me. Love me.

She might not have said the words aloud, but he heard them in his heart. He felt the fissure there, like an old iron chest cracked open. With a black oath of surrender, he claimed her mouth with his teeth and his tongue, wanting the feel of all that stubborn vitality streaming into him. Damn the risk.

She responded as she had before. As he remembered she was capable of. Under the shelter of the copse, he explored the sweet moist cave of her mouth with his tongue and let his hands explore her body.

Uncoached, she opened to him, pressing her body to his like some Lady Knight-Errant hell-bound upon some quest. She tensed with a virgin's arousal, uncertain but eager. He knelt and ran quick kisses down her shielded breastbone. His mouth found the soft flat of her belly, and he went lower still.

He lifted the skirts of her habit to get to the center of her pleasure and found horrible, snug, laced and buttoned breeches—so odd on a woman, so daring. So impenetrable. He groaned with irritation.

"I can slip out of these," she said, her breath hot, filled with need.

Her heat, her need thoroughly undid him. "My responsibility," he muttered, fumbling at her buttons and tearing at the lacings. Whichever would give way first. One button popped off, another yielded, and he jerked the laces free.

Eagerly, she rucked up her skirt, wriggled her breeches down, and balanced her hands in his hair. Too eagerly. If he was to show her what she was missing, he had to slow her down. He began with his tongue, outlining lazy circles on the pearly white skin of her stomach.

"Tickles," she murmured, her voice gone husky with desire.

He slowed, bringing one hand to her buttocks and the other to her tempting bush. Treasures lay there, pleasures. He raked through its crisp abundance, his fingers feeling for the silky skin of her lower lips, feeling them, and slipping in between them. He wanted her moisture and her heat.

She shuddered when he touched her, a deep, full woman's answer to his careful exploration.

All his desire pooled in his balls and the root of his manhood, demanding that he'd go at her, hard and fast and furious. But he held off with steely determination. He could make it better for her, longer, deeper. Patiently he moved his mouth down her generous mound toward her taut crest. Her nails tightened in his scalp.

In anticipation.

"I will kiss you there again," he managed to mutter before closing his mouth on her craving. He tasted the salty damp of her desire, felt the tender skin that hooded it, breathed in the lusty scent of woman and musk and leather. He kept his kisses light. He wanted her to ask this time. Her buttocks tensed and she shifted her legs, trying to bring him closer.

But no, he was in control.

"What are you waiting for, Henry?" she asked with agonized impatience.

He was waiting for her to moan.

She moaned with her body and asked with her hands, pulling his head tighter to her mons. He gave in to her will, jabbing and stroking with his tongue. She vibrated for him. He steadied her with one hand on her behind and the other pressing above her bush, then tenderly he took her crest between his teeth, and sucked it in an ancient rhythm. Clutching his hair, she trembled beneath his mouth.

Her orgasm started in waves beneath his hands, and she gave him her release. Standing, he pulled her, limp and bendable, to him. He was close to bursting, too. Her surrendered body conformed to his, and she felt almost liquid. It was too sweet for words, too sweet for him, a man unused to tenderness.

Unused to love.

Long, silent moments passed. Finally he noticed he could hear the distant, rhythmic sea. He had never heard it sound so raw or so elemental in his life.

And then before he could act to stop her, she slipped to the ground, knelt and opened his breeches, and took his aching manhood with burning hands.

What was a man to do? Closing his eyes to feel the pleasure deeper, he placed his hands on top of hers, guiding her to slow moves that made him groan from delicious torture. To faster, firmer movements, wet by his own juices, that made him growl with painful pleasure.

She stopped and studied his rampant shaft. Then she looked up at him, her face a wonder of curiosity and tenderness. "I could do more."

Sweet heaven, please.

But through the fog of arousal, it occurred to him that her offer was very odd. He found his voice. "Whatever gave you that idea?"

Still flushed from loving, she blushed scarlet. "I have brothers . . ."

Ah! That explained it. "Did you spy on them, you wench?"

She gave a guilty laugh. "Only by accident."

He raised a brow. "You make a habit of being in the wrong place at the right time. So what did they say?"

She could barely look him in the eye. "They said nothing. Something was bound to happen. With four of them and two dozen maids always about—"

"Bounders, cads!" Harry ground out the words. He was no prude, but he would never have been so heedless with a young female relative around, or any female whatsoever in his household.

"It wasn't like that," Julia huffed. "When I stumbled across them, it appeared to me that all concerned where having fun."

"All concerned?" Orgiastic visions thundered in his head. With Julia forced to watch. Madness, and more madness, pressed in on him. "Just exactly how many are we talking about?" he grated.

"You cannot ask me to say who I saw. Really, Henry, I would never betray my brothers, not even in their indiscretions."

The Mad Marquis

"A brother," he said, lethal with suspicion. "Or all your brothers?"

Her brow knitted in bewilderment. His anger must seem mad to her. She puffed up, offended. "One brother—whom I shall not under any circumstances name—was . . . dallying with one of the under-servants. Of course, I didn't know what I was seeing at the time," she went on rapidly, uncomfortably. "I only saw them at it twice, or well, perhaps three times. But she looked willing and my brother looked intense, a dairy maid in the milking shed kneeling at his feet and his pants were—"

"*Yes,*" Harry stopped her, his fears of incest and orgies set to rest. *She* was unharmed, still innocent, just wiser.

His pressing urges thudded back to life. She had offered. A man would be mad to refuse such generosity in a wife.

Said wife looked up, blinking in confusion.

"Yes," he repeated, trying not to sound like a slavering schoolboy or a lecherous old coot. "In answer to your question. Earlier. You can do a very great deal more for me. If you don't mind."

She smiled gamely. "I don't mind. Not at all."

His manhood jerked, spilling hot drops in anticipation.

Her brow knotted at the sight. "Ah. Well, then. I can do this. Here we go."

They were hardly the words of a practiced courtesan, but he did not feel particular. From where he stood, looking down, the tip of her tongue parting her lips was pink and shy. Gently he took her head in his hands, closed his eyes, and prayed his country wench of a wife would go far, far beyond her bounden duty.

Her tongue's first touch along his shaft was tentative but hot and seeking. He swallowed a bone-deep groan, afraid of scaring her off with the intensity that walloped him. She lightly licked the length of him, stopping at its head to explore its crown, its ridges, and its opening, pearled with unspent seed.

With the keenest pleasure he had ever known, he groaned.

She closed her mouth and looked up, worried. "Did that hurt?"

"Not the way it sounds," he rasped.

"You liked it?"

"Yes, until you stopped."

"Oh. I see. I can go on," she said factually. Modestly. And so she did. She toyed with his desire with a devilish innocence. Like a cat with a mouse about to die. With manly forbearance, he endured her

167

version of all the different tongue touches he had given her, lingering licks and little jabs and at last, at the head of his manhood, an insanity of sweet sucking.

He felt like he was dying, or never more alive.

"Just please take me in your mouth," he grated out at last, driven by her fearlessness so far to hope that she might do so.

Driven by his own mad need.

"I don't quite understand."

Desperate, he dropped to his knees, clasped her hand and took three fingers into his mouth, moving them in and out to show her how he wanted pleasure.

Her eyes widened in understanding. "But my . . . teeth," she protested.

He blew out a harsh breath. "Don't worry about your teeth."

"What if you . . . finish?"

He tried to shrug off the thought, but he suddenly wanted to come in her mouth so badly he would have given her every last horse in the stables if she would just let him in. "I could pull out, as I did when I was in you, or . . ." He began almost fierce in his hot need, but broke off. He didn't want to frighten her away.

"Or . . . ?" she studied his face as if he might answer her.

But he couldn't. He wasn't a prude, he told himself. Or an innocent. But if he explained and she said no, he would expire on the spot.

"Oh," she said. As if, perhaps, she understood. "You wouldn't have to pull out. After all, it wouldn't make me pregnant."

"It couldn't make you pregnant," he assured her, if a scraping voice of desperation could assure anyone.

She tilted her head, puzzling over her new choices. "Very well, then. Which way would you prefer?"

Like a double malt Scotch whiskey straight up, her earnest candor vibrated in his bones. Still he could barely speak. He'd never known a woman so open or so unafraid of something so entirely new. He'd never imagined himself having such a conversation with his wife.

"I would like for you to take me in your mouth and make me come there," he said steadily. But his heart thumped in his chest. She couldn't be that bold, or that obliging. In his experience, limited though it was, women hated such an imposition.

Not his Julia. Her boldness over fences was nothing to her boldness in his bed. Or rather, here, on his estate, under the copse of yews, in the open air.

"I would like to do that, too," she said, only the slightest hesitation in her throaty voice. Then, resolutely, "I've missed out on everything too long."

Shaft throbbing and balls aching, he pushed himself up and sat back in a crotch of the low-slung yew. Parting his legs to let her near, he gently drew her toward him, amazed and awed when she rocked back on her heels, and knelt, and willingly closed her mouth around him. Inside and out, he shuddered from the shock of teeth and tongue and humid sucking heat. It was the most unexpected gift, the most moving intimacy.

The most grinding pleasure. She took only an inch or two at first, as if tasting, testing her way along his engorged shaft. The very awkwardness of her mouth moving up and down, a little farther down each time, utterly undid him. The scrape of her teeth brought him to the edge of exploding into her. He was barely holding back, and he didn't even know for what.

Then suddenly, she found more room for him, and took him in, almost all of him, to the back of her throat, swallowing around him, and he heard himself asking her to hold him, hold him with her hands. No longer tentative, she cupped his balls, feeling their weight and size, firming them up to the base of his manhood, and he was lost, crying out, not his usual roar of climax, but something more desperate, more final.

Gently, tenderly, she let him go and sensibly blotted her mouth with the hem of her habit. He was inert, a spent cartridge, a sated stone, but she seemed to be in tears. With an effort he pulled himself back into the world where waves crashed on the shore and gulls cried overhead. The world where his bride lay, pliant and humiliated, in his arms. His triumph turned to self-disgust. Drawing her to his chest, he held her there and rubbed small circles on her back for comfort.

He was the cad, the bounder.

"I am so sorry, my sweet," he whispered. "I never should have asked."

She looked up, tears shining in her soft green eyes. "You had every right."

169

"You don't know what you're saying. That was the most selfish thing I have ever done in my entire life."

"It was the most beautiful to me."

He looked at her in disbelief. What was beautiful about a man in rut taking his pleasure and leaving his near virgin bride high and dry? Or not so dry. He should have taken weeks, no, months, to prepare her for this, and then maybe even never. "Pelham makes us mad."

"Then I love you mad."

His heart lurched. Had she said she loved him? No. No, it was a figure of speech, a compliment in the heat of love. She kissed the corner of his mouth, her lips still moist with him, then tilted her head in that way she had, and grinned. "It must be all those years I spent breeding horses."

Right. *In the heat of love.* His imagination rioted indecently. "What in bloody hell . . . ?"

"Even Aunt Augusta seemed to think I'd be afraid."

"My *aunt* talked with you about doing *this?*"

"Not specifically about this, you nodcock. What kind of teller of tales do you think I am? But she said I should trust you to take care of me in this respect."

"I did nothing for you."

Her expression softened. "Henry. You delivered me from innocence. You gave me pleasure. You freely showed me yours. If husband and wife can do this, I am going to love being married to you."

Bloody hell. She thought this would work. He'd thought so, too, some play, a dalliance, nothing more. "Julia, we can't keep doing this."

She stiffened in the hollow of his arms. "I don't see why not. You said it wouldn't make me pregnant."

"No. But, damn it all, if we kept going at this pace, I'd want everything. All the time."

"Would everything be bad?" Her green eyes, bright with love—the heat of love—only a moment ago, darkened with hurt.

"Everything would be wonderful. For a while."

She looked affronted. "And then you'd tire of me. Is that what you're saying?"

He would tire of her when he tired of breathing.

He knew it in his bones. But temptation would lead to consummation, consummation to obsession, and obsession to offspring. And the pain of their children's madness—however it would manifest—would burden this fragile burgeoning . . . love? No, he knew it was not that. Love was play, and life was serious. And making love to Julia would destroy her. As it had destroyed Therese.

He steeled himself to instruct his bride in what she couldn't know. "Lovemaking is transient, ephemeral. It is not what lasts."

Her stubborn chin said she did not believe him. "What lasts then? Family? Because you are trying to destroy that, too."

"We Pelhams destroy ourselves. The house of Rayne has had generations of practice."

"You're stuck on that."

"I'm stuck on that," he said grimly.

Chapter Eighteen

. . . an unhappy marriage is often very advantageous to a family,
and the neglected wife is, in general, the best mother.
—Mary Wollstonecraft, *Vindication of the Rights of Woman*

Julia was stunned. How could Harry deny the wonder and the rightness of what they had just done? She refused his offer to let her ride
Hazard home. "I am perfectly capable of walking this last bit by
myself," she said.

And see if I ever let you touch me again.

"Not by yourself, and not without me," he grated, taking his stallion's reins in one hand and her elbow in the other. His stubborn
courtesy moved her and provoked her. She wanted to be alone. Their
passionate tryst had drastically transformed the way it felt to be in
her body. Her hands shook. Her feet were leaden and her knees
wobbled like a newborn foal's.

Yet she felt as if she was walking above the carefully scythed sward.
On air. In sinking sand. She ran her tongue around inside her mouth,
tasting a rich brine, all that was left for her of his heart-stopping
surrender. She wanted to feel that again, Henry yielding to her. Not
her to him.

Could he tell how his powerful desire affected her? Newly sensitized, the private space between her legs pulsed as she walked along beside her husband, reminding her with every step of pleasure and rejection. Henry had awakened her to astonishing sensations and then left her in a welter of elation and confusion. Where to take those feelings as he led her and his horse back home? Minx flirted around his stallion, reins flapping and stirrups banging at her sides.

"I could catch her now," Julia urged.

"Too dangerous," he said and tightened his hold on her elbow. Without another word, they passed fruit trees, clipped hedges, and a tortured topiary garden of gnomes and medieval beasts, and then entered the stable yard. A stableboy secured her filly, and she retreated to the castle, nothing left to do.

She was late for being fitted for a gown designed to impress the husband who rejected her. Polly Le Brun and Aunt Augusta met her in Henry's chambers, armed with tapes and pins and feathers. And the most meaningful looks.

Could they know? Did it show? Anxiously, she fingered the buttons on her bodice. This time they were in order. She breathed out in relief.

Never mind how odd it felt, standing behind the screen and taking off the silks and riding habit she had shed for Henry only a short while ago. Oh, but she minded very much. Her skin had lost its sensitivity, and her body the warm glow he had aroused in her. And yet here, in Henry's inner sanctum, all she had to do was think of his private kisses, and her stomach dipped in a hum of hot sensation.

She wanted him again.

She slipped into the silken folds of her elegant new dress, feeling unloved and hopelessly horsy. She wanted to be alone, not adorning her body with a useless gown for these two determined women to drape and tuck and tug and hem. She stepped out on Henry's posh expensive carpet in her bare flat feet and presented herself to scrutiny.

Mademoiselle Le Brun yelped approval, and her white, chubby hand flew to adjust the fabric gathered beneath Julia's still-sensitive breasts. Everything about her new gown seemed to flow from that one focal point—its undulating skirt, its low draping bodice, its narrow shoulders.

"You should ask Polly to make you a gown after the modern

173

fashion, Aunt," Julia said to deflect attention from herself.

"Poppycock, my dear! I'm just fine the way I am," exclaimed Aunt Augusta, fussing with the gown's amazing slitted sleeves.

"You'd probably attract a suitor," Julia persisted. Unlike the protective armor of her riding habit, her new gown displayed all the parts of her body that Henry had made her so acutely aware of—a neck he'd nipped, hands he'd kissed, nipples he'd tweaked, length of leg he had admired.

"Look how that green sets off your gorgeous eyes, your flaming hair," said Augusta, fretting with a rosette.

Julia gave in. "Like a bonfire in a hayfield."

Augusta focused on her face. "And roses in your cheeks—you look positively delicious."

"To tigers," Julia grumbled. But her face heated. So Henry had seemed to find her delicious, but then he walked away. "Uncle Bertie's lot would not be particular."

"Pshaw, child. Not even your stuffy husband could resist this," Henry's aunt said gently. Too gently.

Julia burst into tears. She could not keep up this pretense. It barely registered with her how efficiently Augusta Pelham shooed the chubby modiste out the door, and led Julia to sit at the edge of Henry's massive bed. Julia plucked at the pale yellow folds that defined the swell of her too small breasts and the lines of her too long legs.

Spurned breasts, scorned legs.

"If he can walk away from my naked body, he can surely resist me in a dress."

"Oh, dear, not again."

"Worse," she sobbed. "Never again. I gave him . . . all I could, but it's not enough. He wants no more of me, because then he would want everything, all the time. And that would lead to children, which would be disaster. No, no, dear aunt, you shouldn't have encouraged me."

Tears stained the dark fabric on Julia's lap.

"I had to encourage you," Augusta said fervently, folding her hand over Julia's sapphire wedding band. "I couldn't bear to stand by and watch. You and my nephew are throwing away a chance at the only thing that matters."

The Mad Marquis

Julia shook her head. "His daughter matters, his family matters, Pelham matters."

"Oh, no, my dear. Love matters. True love. An all-encompassing, sharing, lasting joining."

"Harry says love is transient."

"Then he's a fool. True love never dies. And I should know."

"You? You never married."

"Regrettably, my dear. Irrevocably. But I could have."

Augusta Pelham had that faraway look, too sad for tears, that Julia had seen before.

"If I had been braver, more . . . original . . . I would have followed him to the ends of the earth. Which he begged me to do."

"He . . . ?" She waited, thinking Henry might be right about his aunt.

She did seem a trifle batty.

"He was the son of my father's trusted estate agent. As children we had played together innocently. As we grew, our childhood attachment turned to love. Had they known, our families would have had none of it. Too soon, time came for my Season. There were balls and dresses, dresses, balls. He—we—never had a chance."

The old woman's voice was toneless, and yet sad.

"Papa chose for me. A distant cousin of impeccable lineage and some scattered properties he wanted back in the family. I didn't love Edward. I couldn't. So I refused. Papa locked me up in my room. . . ."

"Your room, here at Pelham Castle?"

She drifted into memory again. "We met there, loved each other there, eloped from there. Papa and Edward caught us and brought me back and locked me up again. Ruined, they said. True, but it was they who ruined me."

Julia murmured commiserations. Augusta Pelham had been sad so long.

"After the duel, Liam had to flee the country."

"A duel? Not your father?"

"No, just as bad. He killed Edward. It was horrible. I never would have married Edward, but I didn't want him dead."

"Of course not," Julia said, touched by the depth of the older woman's regret.

"Liam released me from my vow and fled to the colonies. I will

175

wish to my dying day that I had followed him, but by the time I escaped, word came that he had died."

It was a tragic story, Julia thought, the stuff of those awful romances her stepmother whiled away her life on. Surely Augusta Pelham was made of sterner stuff. Filling with sympathy, she patted her hand. "Surely, Aunt, you've grieved for him long enough."

Henry's aunt looked stricken. "Oh, my tears have long since dried. This is a memorial to what we had . . ."

"Which is why," Julia suddenly realized, "you live in your old room, wear your old dresses, and—"

"Which is why, my dear, I know how to advise you."

Julia thought Augusta Pelham could use some advice herself. "With all due respect, Aunt, I think you're overdue for a change. Polly would love to do you a new dress along modern lines."

The old lady would have none of it. "You must not miss this opportunity," she persisted. "Go after my nephew. Don't turn away from love."

Julia sighed. "It's not love. Henry and I are at war."

"Nonsense. Henry is at war with his demons. Only you can help him."

"I can't even help myself. He's determined that we must not produce The Heir."

"But I thought . . . we all thought . . . you were enjoying your marital pleasures."

Julia's face heated. She simply could not get used to everyone in the family assuming they had a stake in her body. But she could be as frank as they. "Not so we could produce The Heir. Henry won't risk it."

"Who's mad now? If he's afraid of breeding," Henry's aunt huffed, "that's easily surmounted."

"Not according to Henry."

Augusta Pelham scoffed. "The boy knows better than that. French gloves should do the trick."

Julia flushed, mortified. When she touched him, should she have been wearing . . .

". . . French gloves?" she croaked.

But Henry's aunt was deep in strategies. "Although where to get them . . ."

"Why would I need gloves from France?"

The Mad Marquis

". . . we will require an agent, and it could take time. Worse yet, I don't quite know whom to trust. I might inquire of Grayson," Aunt Augusta went on, ignoring Julia's question.

"Why ever would we bring Grayson in on this?"

"Grayson knows everything. And we can trust him absolutely. Of course he might not be able to get them—"

"The gloves, Aunt Augusta! Why do I need French gloves? Or any gloves at all?"

"Because they work, my dear."

Nothing else had. Not even catering to her husband's desires. But still, Julia took affront. "I thought I did extremely well without gloves. At least Henry seemed to enjoy my hands—"

Blast! Julia clamped her mouth shut, tricked by the older woman's candor into divulging a far too private matter.

Aunt Augusta locked her shoulders straight, obviously suppressing laughter.

Surely Julia's discomfort was no laughing matter! For an instant, she entertained the notion that Pelham's affliction was contagious and she herself was going stark, staring mad.

After long moments, Augusta said gravely, "I'm sure you did Henry a very great service with your hands, my dear. The gloves we want are not for hands. They're for him . . . to put on his—" A peachy stain started in the older woman's face "—ah, member . . . before he, ah, enters you. They're made of finest sheepskin and they form a barrier between, ah—I didn't think this would be so difficult, but Henry is my *nephew*—" she blurted, blushing deeper. Then she sucked in a determined breath and soldiered on. "A barrier between his seed and your womb."

Julia made an incoherent murmur.

"So you won't conceive, my dear, you see."

Julia remembered a talk with Henry, weeks ago. "He says prophylactic measures don't work."

His aunt tilted her head, mulling over that new bit of information. "He must have used our English ones. Like him to rush in heedlessly. Everyone knows ours are second best, always were," she added, blushing full blown red and standing hastily.

"We have four days to get them. You have four days to set your mind to do your duty and seduce your husband."

And a ball to prepare, and a daughter to rescue. Oh, deliver me from stratagems of domesticity, Julia thought, longing to outrun her obligations with a good gallop.

Aunt Augusta jangled a silver bell and called out for Polly. And Julia submitted to yet another trial for her absent husband.

"*One,* two, three." Uncle Bertie counted out the rhythm like a metronome. A perpetual motion metronome, tireless and unstoppable, whereas Julia was tired and wished that he would stop. After luncheon with a grumpy Isabeau and her whiny imaginary friend, Julia wanted nothing more than a little lie down. Riding horses all day long was easier than riding herd on Isabeau and her shadow. Marie Claire fretted about galloping while Isabeau worried that the maze's lanes were way too narrow even for a walk.

But any riding had to wait until later in the day. In preparation for the ball, Uncle Bertie had engaged her for dancing lessons in the South Gallery every afternoon at two for the rest of the week.

He had not once been a minute late nor a shade less than enthusiastic.

"Might do better with a spot of music. Henry's man plays the pianoforte."

Pianoforte, mimicked Raj, tied to his ornate iron perch.

She lost her stride. Since her morning's dalliance with Henry, her concentration was shot to kingdom come. "Music confuses me, and so does talking. Face it, Uncle Bertie, Pelham's new marchioness cannot hold a candle to its first one."

"Zebra's spots," he protested. "That one couldn't ride a horse at a walk on a sunny day in Henry's covered ménage!"

Julia grinned weakly. "You're trying to make me feel better."

He grinned down at her, his Pelham-gray eyes twinkling. "I am, indeed. You look sadly peaked. But the ball is four days away, and I'm under the strictest instructions to ensure your success. You will be its shining diamond."

Weariness and distraction aside, she almost floated on his compliment. With athletic grace and skill, he whirled her round the room, a slighter, slightly taller man, remarkably like her handsome but neglectful husband. What would it be like to dance with the Henry who'd made love to her this morning?

Bliss. She closed her eyes and wished he was her partner.

The Mad Marquis

"That's it, my girl! You're getting it! *One,* two, three. *One,* two, three. *Ouch!*"

Horse apples, and then some! "Oh, oh, oh, oh, I am so dreadfully sorry. I am so terrible at this," Julia exclaimed. Her wretched dance with Henry on their betrothal night flooded back to her. Anxious to look good for Henry at his ball, she had only gotten worse.

But Uncle Bertie held her in a firm avuncular grasp. "*One,* two, three. *One,* two, three," he said, his words in rhythm with the waltz's beat.

"This didn't work with Henry either, Uncle."

"You're fighting the rhythm of the dance."

"I'm fighting fatigue."

"Tail feathers." He spun her effortlessly about the room, faster than they had gone. She struggled mightily to keep pace. He might be Henry's uncle, but he was strong and young at heart.

"We haven't stopped in half an hour."

"You gallop horses all day long," he said. "Dancing don't tire a gel like you. You should love it."

She wished she could. She wished she was nimble and beautiful and she wished desperately that she was . . . whatever a woman needed to be to keep Henry as interested in her as he had been for a short time this morning.

Uncle Bertie lowered his voice and said softly, "The dance is about love, my dear. Think about Henry. Think about love."

She skidded to a stop flat in the center of the marble floor. "I cannot think about love and Henry in the same breath."

Uncle Bertie stopped, too. "Good God, it's true."

"Yes, if you've heard—"

"—that you're not sleeping together. Heard that, I did, in fact. This old castle bears more tales than mice," he said heartily.

Julia scowled, and his face fell. "Everybody in the family has a proprietary interest in my love life."

"Very sorry about that, my dear. But we do. It's a fact. And I hoped he'd come around. Because if you two don't start on a family right away, I shall, as next in line, be forced to hunt down some poor unsuspecting girl to make my wife. Don't suppose you have a sister?" he teased, his good humor restored.

"Uncle Bertie!"

"Too bad you're taken."

Fiona Carr

"A man shouldn't flirt with his nephew's bride," she scolded.

He mimed dismay. "Quite right. It's just the thought of going to all that trouble to produce The Heir myself."

"I thought the woman had all the trouble," Julia joked in turn. But she was taken aback that Albert Pelham had his own considered plan. "You can rest easy there, Uncle. Henry fully means for Pelham to go to Cousin Erskine."

Uncle Bertie snorted. Raj aped his snort dead-on.

"*Archdeacon* cousin Erskine?" Julia prodded.

"That ramshackle imposter? Pettifogger. Mountebank. Cares no more for Pelham Castle, its tenants and traditions than I care for his chasuble."

"Henry trusts him. They are friends from childhood."

Uncle Bertie smoothed his cravat. "Henry sees what he sees. I know what I know."

"Which is what, Uncle Bertie?"

"Do you think Cousin Erskine will let our aunt stay on at Pelham Castle for one minute? *Au contraire.* Off to the dower house, he will say, or worse. Some tatty London flat, where she'll live out her days—shortened, by his cruelty—lonely, away from family, away from all she holds dear."

Julia's head spun with this new picture of Henry's relative. Not that he'd offered any evidence to support his doubts. "Cousin Erskine did not impress me as unfeeling."

"Equally as bad," Uncle Bertie went on, "where would I and my poor animals be? Zebra steak, that's what. Peacock under glass. Lion rugs. Monkey muffs and mittens."

"Surely not," Julia exclaimed, her love for animals swaying her from the courteous cousin back to the eccentric uncle's side.

"Surely so. I overheard him at the wedding, mocking me to your brother."

"But he seemed so . . ."

". . . considerate, well-spoken, urbane, and erudite."

"Precisely."

Uncle Bertie patted his cravat. "Hm. Forgot reverent. Best imitation of reverent I ever saw in a man of the cloth."

"And you say this because . . ."

"Knew his father. The apple don't fall far from the tree. Or is that acorn? That branch of Pelhams has been lurking about for half a dozen generations waiting for us to destroy ourselves."

Once again she felt herself on the shifting shoals of Pelham's domestic landscape. "Uncle Bertie, that is a scandalous accusation."

He looked put out. "Don't have to believe me."

"I want to believe *you,* just not *this.*"

"She suspects my motives," he said with sudden, sane clarity. Except when he turned to Raj, offering a bit of lettuce from a pocket. "Tell her I've had done with that marriage bit."

Done with marriage, done with marriage, Raj parroted obligingly.

"Unless Pelham needs you to rescue it."

"Altruistic, my dear, I assure you. Erskine won't do. But you and my nevvy are by far the better instrument for continuing the line." He bowed and assumed his position for the waltz. "Shall we resume our lesson? Time's awasting, and my nevvy won't be an easy nut to crack."

He whirled her, dipped her, but her mind spun worse. Somehow, she didn't think Uncle Bertie would agree with Aunt Augusta's plan to keep her from getting in a family way.

A short time later, she met a very put-out Jem waiting in the maze with Fidget and Isabeau and her nurse. Determined to make progress, Julia had threatened him with dismissal if he either reported her to Henry or refused to help.

"Good afternoon, everyone," she said brightly, determined to put behind her the private world she'd shared with Henry in the shrouded dawn. It had taken all her resolution to resume her domestic duties, to be a social being, no longer her husband's lover, no longer speaking with her flesh.

Jem's eyes shuttered as if he knew about their tryst. Could anyone have seen them? Could Jem have heard by now?

Isabeau wore an adorable sky-blue riding habit that brought out the gentle blue of her eyes. But her protruding lower lip spoiled any illusion she was either gentle or adorable. Days of difficult negotiations lay behind them. And very little progress. Isabeau could mount and dismount, take up the reins, hold her little crop, walk the pony forward, turn him left and right, back him, and halt him. Over and over, and not a faster gait, and Julia or Jem could not let go.

"I've been waiting half an hour," little Lady Isabeau complained.

"It's rude to tell me that I'm late. Little girls wait patiently for their elders. Time to mount."

Bending deeply, she laced her fingers to give Isabeau a leg up.

Isabeau set her jaw. "Marie Claire wants to go first."

"Marie Claire doesn't have a pony," Julia said, deliberately repressive.

Isabeau cast Jem a conspiratorial smile. "Yes, she does. We brought Sir Galahad."

Julia could have throttled Jem. "As if we need a knight in shining armor."

"He is silver, mum, dapple gray," Jem said soberly, but the corners of his eyes crinkled. "Our young lady preferred her friend to have a pony that did not match her own."

"And a spirited one, no doubt."

"Not overmuch for his young rider."

Deciding to trust Jem's instincts with children, Julia gave Marie Claire a pretend leg up and began her lesson. How to stop, how to start, how to ask for the next gait.

"She's a natural," she said to Isabeau, then pressed her lips together in consternation. Bad enough she was going against Henry's express instructions and teaching his daughter to ride. Now she was catering to the imaginary friend, instead of getting rid of her.

Isabeau watched the pretend performance with grave attention. "Oops," she said, "She's slipping off."

Julia sighed and pretended, too. "Marie Claire! Grab a handful of that mane. Quick! Now right yourself, steady . . . heels down, sit deep, and . . . oh no, oh wait, don't bounce *against* your pony. Go with him." She turned to Isabeau. The fragile blonde peeked through wary fingers at her friend's difficulties. "That's right, Marie Claire," Julia went on, throwing in everything she could imagine could go wrong. "Better . . . Steady . . . Don't look down, look straight ahead. Galahad will go where you are looking."

"He bucked!" Isabeau shrieked.

"That was just a little hop. Listen, Marie Claire is laughing."

Isabeau covered her eyes completely.

There was nothing to do but stop the lesson. Julia clapped twice to summon her rider back. "Excellent, Marie Claire. Jem, lead Sir Galahad," she said firmly. "Isabeau and I will take a turn on Fidget."

Isabeau gave a mutinous glare, so like her father's grim determination that Julia's memory was jolted back to his parting from her at the yews. She banished the thought in a surge of anger. Henry had been her problem there. His daughter presented an entirely different set of problems.

But after a week and a half of fits and starts and high jinx, Julia didn't have the slightest worry that the child was actually scared of trotting. In fact, she was gratified to see the improvements riding lessons had wrought in Henry's fragile daughter. She grew stronger and bolder by the day. No one, but no one, told little Lady Isabeau what to do.

"Today we trot, just like Marie Claire." And Julia began her litany of proper conduct for girls on pony rides.

"I don't have to listen to you," Isabeau broke in. "My father doesn't like you. He doesn't even visit your bed."

A kick in the chest hurt less. Julia thought she'd made more progress with the child than that. The servants must have been talking, perhaps even the nurse.

"Your father expects you to mind Aunt Augusta, nurse, and me," she said briskly, and picked up her contrary stepdaughter and put her on the placid pony. Then she bent to her eye level and gave her an ultimatum. "We trot, or no more Marie Claire at luncheon, and no new dress for Papa's hunt ball."

Isabeau's bright blue eyes glinted with mutiny. "You'll be sorry when I fall off and die."

Julia stuffed Isabeau's feet in their miniature riding boots into child-sized stirrups. "You'll be sorry when you see how much fun you've been missing. Jem, you tie Galahad to that statue, and come lead us out."

His mouth crimped against laughter or censure—Julia could not tell which—Jem elaborately mimed leading the imaginary mount to a granite cherub shooting an arrow. Once there, he carefully tied off the non-existent reins.

Julia put Fidget's real reins in Isabeau's small hands and adjusted her wrists and fists into the correct position. "Don't forget, I'll be running right along beside to catch you if you fall."

Isabeau blinked, and swallowed hard, and pressed her lips together.

Julia didn't have to run that hard. Fidget had a clear sense of a revered elderly pony's obligations. Trotting fast was not among them.

Isabeau did in fact list precariously sideways once, but she grabbed a handful of mane just as Julia had instructed Marie Claire to do. Remembering the pony's bone-jarring trot, Julia felt a dash of sympathy.

Until Isabeau asked for more. "Faster," she demanded, obviously feeling secure.

"Check your hands, head up, heels down," Julia called out.

Isabeau carefully obeyed.

"Cluck and squeeze."

More obedience. And at last, Henry's daughter was truly trotting, straight down a lane of the boxwood maze, a smile splitting her face. Except for almost beating Henry on the sands at dawn, this was Julia's most gratifying moment since arriving at Pelham Castle. It thrilled her to give her not-so-fragile stepdaughter a chance for her spirit to run free. It thrilled her to think of Henry's pleasure when he saw the rescue. He'd have to admit she knew what she was doing. He'd want to thank her. . . .

Isabeau's father blocked their way, his face stony with disapproval.

Chapter Nineteen

I do not mean to allude to the romantic passion, which is the
concomitant of genius. Who can clip its wing?
—Mary Wollstonecraft, *Vindication of the Rights of Woman*

After an amazing morning interlude, Henry's day had gone steadily
downhill. Back at the barn he couldn't believe what he was hearing.
He'd known his men resented Jem Guthrie and suspected they resented Julia even more. Then Wat Nance had confided his latest
worry: Perhaps the stone that hit Henry's cheek this morning on the
cliffs had been cast purposely.

"Not even remotely possible," he'd said, uncinching Hazard's girth
himself. "There wasn't another soul in sight."

"But there are outcroppings and crevasses to hide in up and down
the cliff, and boulders at the top."

"No one would harm Julia," Henry had answered placidly, easing
the saddle off his stallion's back and onto his arm.

"Not her, my lord. You."

He'd snorted. "Preposterous. My enemies have had thirty-eight
years to come after me. Why start now? And who?"

Nance hadn't answered that, and he'd stored his saddle in the harness room. But later that afternoon, Nance had urged him to check out what Julia was doing in the maze with her groom. Henry had blasted out a jealous oath worthy of a besotted husband. Worse than besotted. He'd already spent the day trying to outride his mad obsession with his tempting bride.

Not the easiest task with his mind and his member in a state of rut. Five horses, five workouts hadn't quelled his lust. Nance's disgusting hint had come close.

"Not what yer thinkin', my lord," Nance had backtracked hastily. "For God's sake, no. But did you not forbid riding lessons for Lady Isabeau?"

Yes, he'd forbidden them, damn it. But he'd forced a bland response. "How long has this been going on?"

Nance had studied his muck-covered boots. "Couldn't say, my lord, several days, p'rhaps. You didn't ask me to keep tabs on that."

Because I trusted her.

"You do right to tell me now, Nance," he'd said stiffly, unable to hide his aggravation. He owed the man for stepping beyond duty, for risking wrath, for protecting Isabeau.

And he hated owing anybody anything.

Nance had given a deferential bow. "Your servant, my lord."

And Henry had charged off, gathering an arsenal of accusations. Headstrong, willful bride. No, she was a wench. A hoyden. But he'd always known that about her. He had to admit it was a damnably clever ploy, hiding her deception behind the overgrown green depths of the abandoned maze. If not for his faithful Nance, she could have pushed his fragile daughter beyond what she could endure. Could have done so already. The thought made his blood run cold. Stopping at the entrance, he had looked down the first long lane, keenly attuned to protests, weeping, threats. To cries of fear. Instead he heard . . .

Giggles. Hysterical giggles.

Ruination! he cried out inwardly. He should have seen it coming. Julia—bold, daring, *heedless*—had pushed poor little Isabeau over the edge. This was the very madness he had feared, had predicted for his daughter.

With a great effort, he mastered his urge to rush in. He couldn't afford to startle the child and spook the pony.

The little triumvirate rounded the final turn unawares at an out-

and-out trot. Isabeau's blonde curls bounced out of control, and her porcelain face sported a forced grin. It turned to fear.

Julia glared at him ferociously. As if he were in the wrong. One arm at his daughter's back, she took the pony's reins and gently tugged him to a walk, talking to Isabeau or the pony—he could not tell which—too softly to be heard. But he could see her lips move, luscious as they had been on him that morning. A need to ravish her ripped through him.

He squelched it savagely.

"Take the pony, Guthrie," he ordered, as they came even, and he gently plucked his daughter from danger. Julia must have terrified her, but she was putting on a brave face.

"Very pretty, *ma petite*," he said quietly. "We're going back inside."

She gave him the oddest calculating look. "But Sir Galahad . . ."

Julia shushed her. "Not now, Isabeau."

"But Marie Claire will want . . ." Isabeau began, then trailed off.

Julia's eyes slid away from his.

And Henry understood everything. The forbidden pony, and the forbidden friend. Like a farrier at his forge, Julia fanned the flames of disrespect and insurrection.

He stifled a blistering impulse to haul her onto his lap and spank her speechless. "Wait for me in the library, my lady," he commanded. "I will return my daughter to her nurse's care."

She paled at his insult and skulked off.

He did not feel one grain of pity.

Her nurse's care! Hopelessly misguided man. That nurse had smothered Isabeau, at his express orders.

Julia fumed all the way back to Henry's moldy castle. Once there, she paced the dark commodious book room, waiting for Henry, and pretending Isabeau's nasty little charge had not hurt. The library's claret-colored velvet draperies muffled sound and cut off the late afternoon's low light. Along two inner walls, new and musty leather volumes ranged in rank from floor to ceiling. She'd have thought a man of Henry's learning and intelligence would see past his daughter's ploys for his attention and stop coddling her.

Julia had had to peel off layers of her stepdaughter's insecurities just to make a dent in the poor child's learned fragility. Engendering her interest in freedom and adventure had been an uphill battle.

Today, they'd been within a hair's breadth of success. If only Isabeau hadn't mentioned Marie Claire, Julia's plan might have worked. It still stood a chance. She'd gotten out of worse scrapes.

Just never against such a formidable antagonist as Henry.

Who strode in, ash-brown hair tousled temptingly. The lips that had kissed her passionately at dawn were drawn in a thin line. Wordlessly, he rested a lean hip on the edge of a heavy mahogany desk, tapping his glossy boots with his black riding crop. Tap. Her breath caught at his air of command. Tap. Tap. She wondered if he knew how attractive he looked, furious and unattainable. She wondered if he knew how he affected her.

Not if she could help it. She wasn't about to break the silence. Let him explain why he'd lowered himself to spying.

Explanation, she discovered, wasn't in his aristocratic nature.

"I trusted you," he said at last, more as fact than accusation.

She drew herself up. "As well you should have done."

Another glaring silence. Did he expect apologies?

"My daughter is not strong enough to ride."

"True, she lacks the strength to ride all day," Julia made herself say smoothly. "Even as a boy, you had to build up strength."

"No one ever ran alongside to hold me on a horse. Nor you, I imagine."

"I ran alongside to encourage her."

He snorted. "No doubt, she needed that."

"And for safety."

"Isabeau is afraid of horses. Horses sense fear, and riding them cannot be safe."

Aha, Julia thought. She had him there. "Perhaps you could explain, my lord, how you saw fear in gleeful giggles."

"Gleeful, or hysterical, madam?"

He really didn't understand. "She was starting to enjoy herself," Julia protested. She had worked so hard to overcome Henry's joyless discipline.

"You presume to know her very well, indeed, on such short acquaintance."

Blast her best intentions. Julia threw civility to the wind. "Our short acquaintance is not my fault, my lord. You failed to prepare her before we married—no introductions, no visits, no warning. I had a right job of it to break through the barriers you set up. I had to assure her I would not replace her mother, that her mother still loves her, that her father loves her best.

"Which," she added pointedly, "I am sure he does, in his own distant way. Yes, indeed, I do presume to know her rather better than that distant father, whose idea of a good riding lesson was to mount her on a fearsome hunter stout enough to carry a man. After which he fussed and criticized her every move."

His smile did not reach his eyes. "Temper, my love."

Not now. Not after all these days of walking on eggshells around him, of trying to help and aiming to please. "Holding my temper won't do Isabeau the least bit of good. With only your fears of the supposed family madness, you cosseted and spoiled your daughter. Let me put you on notice, my lord. Your daughter is neither fragile nor mad. With me, she has toured the house, the grounds, the barn. She has picnicked on the shore. She never tired. She has strength and energy to spare, and a healthy curiosity, too, if only you would let her. Her fragility and her fears are the only way she can get your attention."

He scowled briefly, then put down his crop and brought his hands together. Clap. Clap. Clap. "Very good, my love. Therese would be proud to see her daughter turn into a hoyden, romping over the countryside."

"I am the hoyden who romps over the countryside, my lord. I'm merely taking your daughter out for a healthy turn in the open air."

"Which no doubt accounts for her continued need for her imaginary friend. Or is that my fault, as well?"

"Indeed it is. She only trots out Marie Claire when she is scared or wants to have her way. Marie Claire is the very best weapon a lonely little girl could contrive to get her father's attention."

"Rubbish," Henry said, not even appearing to be upset.

"Do you ever just let them talk?"

"Certainly not. There is no *them*."

"Of course there is. When I play along, Marie Claire is soon forgotten. All your daughter wants is your full attention."

"Which I give her."

"You give it to Marie Claire by working so hard to deny her. So Marie Claire assumes an importance that she doesn't have, and Isabeau desperately clings to her to ensure your attention."

He paused, as if she'd struck home, but said, "Sophistry, Julia.

You're too new at this to know. Pelham madness take many shapes and forms."

Somehow, he had wrested control of their confrontation. But the truth would wrest it back. "Everybody knows about us," she persisted.

He arched a brow. "Everybody?"

"Aunt Augusta, Uncle Bertie, and the entire household staff." And Isabeau. But she couldn't admit to that.

"What precisely about us do they know?"

"That we do not sleep together."

He scowled at her. "And your complaint about that is . . ."

"I'm not complaining. I'm merely observing. They will sooner accept your new marchioness if you appear to." And so would Isabeau. But she was determined to earn Isabeau's acceptance on her own.

He shrugged. "My people will accept what I tell them to accept."

"And laugh at me behind my back."

"Not if I forbid it."

She snorted. "Not even you can forbid household gossip, Henry. But—" she said brightly, determined to be as offhanded as he was being obtuse "—I don't mind if you don't. I've been laughed at all my life."

A frown flashed across his face. "I won't have my wife laughed at."

It wasn't a victory. But his willingness to defend her pleased her. "They won't laugh if we appear together."

"Not a good idea, Julia. How much together?"

A lot more than they had been lately, but she flattened any yearning from her tone. "We should come to dinner arm in arm, as we did on our wedding night. As if we'd dressed together. That would quiet a few tongues."

Desperation crossed his face before detachment settled in.

Heartened, she struck again. "And at night. You aren't in our bed."

He groaned. "You well know why I'm not."

She had a vision of him yielding to her in the foggy dawn. It hadn't lasted. "You rode off easily enough this morning. Surely you can resist me in our rooms."

He stood and joined her on the settle. She wanted another kiss. But he leaned close, his gray eyes like flint. "I can master anything. Even you."

The Mad Marquis

She wasn't sure she believed him anymore. She spurred him a little harder. "And your fears for Isabeau? Can you master them? She's thriving, Henry. Don't ask me to stop her lessons."

He stood, tapping his crop against his boots, considering. She'd never seen him hesitate. Could this be progress? A chink in the armor of his control?

"I will talk to her."

An hour before supper Henry climbed the stairs to his daughter's nursery, in a state. His valued, vaunted control of home and hearth, of castle and kith and kin, was being wrested from him. His daughter had ridden a horse and was not in tears. His lusty bride dared him to prove he could abstain. His household staff and stableboys gossiped about his unconsummated marriage.

If only they knew how gloriously he had consummated it. And not consummated it.

Julia was right about one thing. He was learning to deny his carnal appetites. He'd just done so in the library, despite the fact that she tempted him most when she stood up to him, however wrong she was. It had taken all his command to keep his hands to himself. To say nothing of less governable parts. Which protested now with an insistent ache.

But he had mastered himself, as he had had to do.

He was less sure where his chat with Isabeau would lead. He could not simply accept Julia's assurance that his daughter loved riding now. He'd seen real fear on her face this afternoon. Upstairs, he found her curled up alone, her pale blonde brows knitted over a wooden puzzle. What if Julia was right, and he was the ogre in her life, not the horses?

Not possible, he told himself. He adored her to the alabaster nails on her little toes.

"Papa!" she said with a start, then a flash of a fear that tore his heart. "Are you very angry with us?"

"Angry with whom, *ma petite?*" he asked gently, but cautiously. Given Julia's accusation, he would not give Marie Claire a toehold.

Isabeau tilted her head, as if confused. "Me and Julia."

"Should I be?"

"In the maze. When you saw me on the pony. You looked mad."

Her bed sank beneath his weight. "Why would I be angry, *mignon?*"

She studied a piece of her puzzle and fixed it in place. "I'm not a very good rider, am I?"

Anger jabbed him. "Who told you that? Julia?"

"No. She says I'm doing very, very well, and promises I'll do better." She blushed pink with pride.

Now there, he thought, Julia had embarked on a dangerous stratagem. Instilling overconfidence set a child up for a hard fall. Or had Julia set his daughter up to succeed? He forced himself to compare what he'd seen in the maze with what he saw here. What Julia had said. Did Isabeau fear the pony more, or him? Had she giggled from terror or delight? Was she ashamed of her performance? Or proud?

True, he'd corrected her flaws, but patiently, and one by one. That was merely rational, the way he improved himself. It hadn't occurred him to treat his daughter any other way.

"I'm sure you will do better, every day, *mignon.*"

She gave him a fleeting, not quite trusting, smile, which turned into a frown. "Papa?" she asked gravely.

"Yes, Isabeau," he answered gravely, too.

"Is it all right if I like Julia, even if you don't?"

His gut twisted. "Of course. I want you to like Julia. But what makes you think I don't?"

She fiddled with a puzzle piece. "Cook said so to nurse yesterday at tea."

For Isabeau's sake, he tried to laugh it off. "Rubbish. They don't even know I don't like peas. Which I don't."

"They said you don't like her bed."

Her in *bed,* he amended silently. He was indifferent to her bed. He craved her body. Bloody hell, he hated gossip and its consequences. Julia had been right about people talking about them, and right to feel hurt.

"Don't you listen to them. I like her bed just fine, and I like her, too. So you can like her just as much as you wish."

She tried the puzzle piece in several slots, then wiggled it into place with new confidence. "Papa?" she asked, so much more gravely that his heart twisted.

"Yes, Isabeau."

"If you don't mind . . ."

"Mind what?"

She sucked in a breath of courage. "If you don't mind, I should very much like it if you would not watch me ride just yet."

His eyes burned with mortification. Julia had been right there, too. His daughter was frightened of him.

Isabeau laid a small white hand on his sun-darkened one. "I had so much rather show you when I can do it right." He felt like a boy again, desperate to please a demanding father. He'd never meant to do that to his little girl.

"I'm certain you'll turn out to be a splendid rider." He bent and kissed her forehead, and the sweet, fresh smell of little girl eddied around him. He had lost her. Could regain her. "Then we'll gallop together across the downs. You and me and Julia."

"I'd like that, Papa," she whispered, in a tone that said his consent was almost too good to be true.

"I'll see you at dinner then," he said, taking his leave and heading off to dress.

It wasn't until he reached his chambers that he noticed: His daughter had not once mentioned Marie Claire. Which surprised him and relieved him. But it jagged his conscience more. What if Julia's schemes were working to liberate his daughter from her little friend? He should be overjoyed. But he wasn't sure he was ready to admit that Julia had bested him.

The minute Henry joined Julia to dress for dinner, she saw the folly of her challenge. She'd meant for the domestic ritual to stir him up, not her.

Dispassionate, objective, he showed no interest in her toilette. Whereas she, trollopy wench that she'd become for him, noticed his every move.

"I talked to Isabeau," he said evenly. He was peeling off his skin-tight buckskin breeches. The seat and legs were slick, worn from constant riding. And dark, from saddle oil. Half naked, he stood unselfconsciously—indifferently—wearing nothing but a shirt, a long shirt, long enough to conceal . . .

Almost gawking with unbridled interest, she turned away. Which did no good. In her mind's eye, she could still see his muscled calves and his perfectly sculpted knees and ankles, a vision of manliness she'd studied in marble statues in the Long Gallery at Wraxham.

Never had she hoped to see such splendid manliness for herself.

"You found her well?" she asked blandly.

But the thought of his powerful thighs made her knees go weak. This morning she had touched him there. Inside, where sinewy muscles would hug the saddle, his skin was tender as a child's. The dark dusting of hair, crisp and surprising, had brushed her cheeks this morning when she had lowered her mouth to . . .

Her face heated when she realized where her thoughts were headed.

"Very well," Henry was saying dispassionately. "And eager to continue her riding lessons with you. Without me, I might add. She prefers that I not see her until she is really, really good."

"She will be good," Julia croaked.

We were good together.

She wanted him. Remote and maddening as he was, her body really wanted him. Everything they had done together, she wanted to do again. Her heart thudded, and her nipples spiked, and the burn returned to her private mound, spreading to her lower lips, and inside, deeper, to her womb. All the feelings he had aroused in her this morning would be at his fingertips.

All he had to do was ask. He didn't.

How humiliating. She consoled herself that he'd conceded to Isabeau's request. That was progress of a sort, just not for her.

He walked into the dressing room, his open shirt showing his corded neck, the beginnings of the tawny thatch of hair she now knew covered his muscled chest. How many women knew that, she could only guess. But oddly, the thought of other women didn't worry her. She had seen him in the hunt field, raced him over the most challenging courses. Horses were his passion. Women a distant second-best. Especially her. When she looked up, he emerged fully dressed, expertly tying a fresh cravat.

He caught her eye with a detached gaze. "If you will, then, continue her lessons. You need not hide out in the maze."

It was a monumental concession, but not the one she wanted. "For now, we feel safer in the maze, if you don't mind," she answered as detached as she could be. Which was not detached at all.

He nodded his consent and shrugged into his jacket.

Accepted, and rejected. She pulled herself together. She'd won half and lost all, her way with his daughter but nothing for herself. Between her own desires and Augusta and Bertie Pelham's meddling encouragement, she had a half-baked scheme of seducing her husband. That was why she'd dared him to come back to their room.

He had come. He had undressed, washed, and dressed again.

Would he be interested? She sneaked a peak as she pulled on her velvet evening gown.

There was his usual erection, his hard shaft saluting her dishabille. Or, as she had hoped, her charms. How could he not act on it? From all she knew of stallions and the little she knew of men, being aroused was going slightly mad. Their actions were not quite within their control. From the very first at her father's harvest ball, her presence had aroused her husband. Up to now, he had hardened for her on the dance floor, in the bedroom, in the barn, on a horse, and out in the open air.

Always before, it had led to something, even if only a kiss.

Leave it to her controlling husband to quash his natural desire. This was his ultimate madness.

A fine anger raced through her. This was war. French gloves, or no French gloves, starting tomorrow evening, she would drive him to the breaking point, deliberately, with all the seductive powers she could muster.

She wouldn't let him touch her till he begged.

Dinner was a subdued affair. Isabeau cried off, and Uncle Bertie, too. Henry escorted Julia to her usual chair, a very long way away. Then he escorted his aunt to her place of honor. Farley bustled around the table, serving far more food than the three diners could eat.

Julia's exile at the far end of the table perfectly fitted her wretched day. She felt overworked, overdressed, and underappreciated. Doggedly she piled her plate with crisp mutton chops and greasy sausages and juicy slices of roast beef and tore into them, hearty bite by bite. Her cutlery clinked in the grand, empty room.

"I suppose Bertie's having one of his spells, nephew?" Augusta Pelham said between removes.

"Very likely, Aunt," Henry answered.

Julia disliked their indifference and doubted anything was wrong. "He was fine this afternoon."

Aunt Augusta speared a hapless parsnip from a silver salver Farley passed around. "Oh, it always hits him suddenly."

195

Julia's indignation rose. "Henry, what's the matter with your uncle?"

Henry scowled. "You know. I told you."

Uncle Bertie was having one of his spells? "But he was his cheerful self in the afternoon, even a hopeless tease."

"We don't think the case is hopeless, my dear." Aunt Augusta calmly cut her parsnip into rounds. "He always pops up a few days later."

"*If*," Henry said ominously, "the past is any predictor of the future."

Julia gaped at Uncle Bertie's two nearest and dearest. Neither one showed the slightest actual concern for his absence or his well-being. She crumpled her napkin, flung it on the table, and stood. "I shall just go see him now."

"No!" Henry said.

"No!" Aunt Augusta chimed at the exact same moment.

Julia swung her gaze between them, glowering with disbelief. "Why ever not?"

"He locks his door against us," Aunt Augusta said, not a little petulant.

"A man has a right to privacy when he wants it," Henry added with conviction.

All the aggravations and humiliations of her day spurred Julia to rebut him. "A family has an obligation to look out for one another," Julia said, glaring down on both of them. Sometimes it was good to be a tall, strong woman. "Henry, animals take to the woods to hide when they are sick or wounded, and you well know it's the very worst thing that they can do. We cannot help them if they're lost. We go and find them and bring them back."

Henry was watching her with the most inscrutable expression. Well, bugger him. Between his ardor in the morning and aloofness in the afternoon, she had done with trying to figure him out.

"I am going after Uncle Bertie," she said, and stalked out of the room.

Finding Albert Pelham was easier said than done. The fact that his quarters were in the remote north wing of the rambling castle had not seemed odd to her till now. Had he chosen secret lodgings for a retreat when he succumbed to spells? And what kind of spells, exactly, did he have? Why didn't Henry or Aunt Augusta seem to know or want to know? And what was she getting herself into now?

She picked up her pace as she walked down the ancient dank stone hall at the dark periphery of Henry Pelham's castle. Built centuries ago, it was the only part of the structure where everything was on the level. Her boots thumped down the empty hallway, and she worried that someone would hear her—or would not. Door after heavy oak door barred the way to every chamber that she passed. Then she heard a cry, the high keening sound of an animal in pain.

Her heart thudded in her chest. "Uncle Bertie?" she called out.

A bizarre chattering next echoed down the hallway. The monkey, it had to be that obnoxious little monkey.

"Uncle Bertie!" She cried louder, hurrying toward the sounds.

To her left the door cracked open, creaking, and an enormous white-turbaned, swarthy-skinned head poked through. Buvenish Goswami.

She lifted her chin. "I've come to see Albert Pelham."

"Albert Pelham does not wish to see madam," the man said in a cheerful singsong accent at odds with his fierce foreign face. Pungent, exotic scents, more intriguing than spices or perfumes, wafted past him from inside.

"You would admit my husband," she said. If he asked. Perhaps he had, it struck her. Confronting this stern giant, she was no longer certain that Henry's indifference had kept him away.

"No, madam, no one is allowed."

"I only want to see if my husband's uncle is well."

"I am taking care of husband's uncle. Family of no help." And he closed the door in her face with all the authority of an obviously powerful and trusted retainer.

She slumped against the door jam, plotting. Whatever condition Uncle Bertie was in, was it his will that no one saw him? Or was it his servant's? And did that matter?

No, it didn't, she decided, not nearly as much as not finding out what was wrong.

She straightened herself, made a fist, and rapped hard three times on the door. Raj squawked, and the monkey chattered briefly, and then silence reigned.

She rapped longer, louder. "Uncle Bertie, it's Julia. Can I come in? I just want to help."

The door swept open, and Buvenish met her with a ferocious scowl. "He is resting, madam."

Gathering up courage, she pushed past Bertie Pelham's pillar of defense. "Surely, he won't mind a little cheering up." *And you could use some, too,* she thought but forbore to say.

Henry's uncle lay sprawled on his bed beneath thin sheets, pillows mounded around him. She came closer and was dismayed to see the sweaty pallor of his face. "Oh, how dreadful," just slipped out.

"Dreadful, indeed," Uncle Bertie said faintly, and patted the edge of the bed for her to sit.

"Dear me. That's not at all what I meant to say."

He weakly propped himself up. "But true, nonetheless. That's why family is not permitted. Although I congratulate you on being the first to try to pound down my door when I am in the throes . . ."

She cupped his hand in hers. It was burning hot. "The throes of what, Uncle? Spells? Madness? That's what your nephew thinks."

"Ah, madness would be preferable to this. It wouldn't feel so wretched."

"This what? I would help, if only I knew what to do."

"There's nothing to do, beyond what Buvenish does for me, the wraps, and the incense, and the bark."

"Bark?" Julia repeated. Suddenly everything was clear. "Uncle Bertie, you're not mad. You're taking quinine for malaria."

"Zebra's spots!" A sheepish look spread across Bertie Pelham's sallow face. "You clever girl. You found me out. But don't tell Henry."

"Why in the world not? It would take a great load off his mind. Your spells are further proof to him of the family madness."

"True enough, my dear. But if he realizes I'm not mad, he might expect me to produce The Heir he's so afraid of. Besides, my little spells give me a break from Aunt Augusta."

Julia didn't laugh at his feeble humor. "Uncle Bertie, you know this isn't right."

"I know no such thing, my dear. We all do the best we can to protect our family. And I expect you to keep my secret. You're a straight up girl, you are, and you wouldn't rat on your favorite dancing master."

"For my husband, I might," she threatened.

He made a face of mock horror, but she couldn't help noticing beads of sweat gathering on his white forehead. "Trust me, my dear.

Your husband is better off facing his delusions and attending to his business. He owes it to all of us—to history—to produce The Heir with you."

Julia started to say whole truths were better than half ones.

But two large hands grasped her shoulders respectfully but firmly. "Madam, you go now. He's slipping back."

"Yes dear, do go. It isn't a pleasant sight."

"But—" The hands lifted her to stand. "How long until you're better?"

Buvenish was gently pushing her toward the door.

"I will make it to the ball, dear girl," Bertie Pelham called out bravely. But his teeth were chattering, and he turned his face toward the wall.

She had a long walk back to Henry's bedchamber, arguing with herself whether or not Henry ought to know.

Chapter Twenty

*. . . is she, I say, to condescend to use art . . . in order to secure
her husband's affection?*
    —Mary Wollstonescraft, *Vindication of the Rights of Woman*

Setting his rifle to his shoulder, Henry aimed skyward, squeezed the
trigger, and—ka-blam!—blew another pheasant out of the sky. It
sagged and plummeted, broken feathers listing idly down.

The third shot, the third bird today. Very satisfying.

Dick, his best dog, held point flawlessly. Henry flicked a hand
signal, and Dick dashed to retrieve their dinner. Mouthing it in his
gentle jaws, he ran back and dropped the bird at Henry's feet. Henry
strung it with the others, its body limp but warm beneath his fingers.

"You won't believe the rest," he said, resuming conversation.

"Try me," said Cousin Erskine, down from London for the ball.

"Name the most preposterous thing you can imagine."

"She's having an affair with her groom," Erskine suggested,
worldly-wise and without judgment. Two of his best traits. Those,
and his slant wit.

Harry cut him a look of incredulity. "You haven't seen Jem Guthrie."

"Guthrie's that bad, eh?" Erskine asked.

"Not bad. Just older than her father." Henry swung the leash of pheasants over his shoulder and headed home. Reluctantly. His stables and his castle were in chaos with the annual frenzy of preparations. The annual shooting party was his best escape . . . and the best way to handle early houseguests and nosy neighbors keen to see how married life was treating him. Squire Purvis and a couple of yeoman farmers trailed behind, dangling their own kills.

"It was Wat Nance," Henry went on. "He tried to convince me that an enemy threw the rock." He wasn't about to mention the mysteriously severed spoke, even though Nance still brought it up from time to time, uncannily when things with Julia were at their worst.

"The old fusspot! Worrying trouble to death." Erskine laughed, then soberly checked the safety on his gun. "But seriously, man, think. What if the rock had been thrown? Could you have such deadly enemies?"

Henry shrugged, amused by his cousin's appetite for intrigue. Too many years of ecclesiastical politics, no doubt. "Only a few dozen men who've lost their horses or their shirts to me at racing."

"No need to be so bloody cool about it."

"Besides, the sooner I'm done in, the sooner all this is yours." Henry made a sweeping gesture that almost set his leash of birds to fluttering again.

Erskine groaned and gave his usual response. "The present marquis should get the heir. Besides, what would a city cleric do with all this space?"

"Manage it. You have heirs and assigns enough to do the job," Henry said easily. But Erskine's oblique concern pleased him. Nance and his insinuations did not. "Damnable thing was, Nance blamed Julia."

Erskine's brows lifted in what was, for him, a horrified expression. "You should have fired the bloke. Ages ago."

"Too keen an eye for horseflesh."

"But had he any evidence? Better yet—supposing, just supposing his hint has any merit—does your bride have any motivation?"

"None. On either point." But Henry mulled over his cousin's questions as they crossed the field in a companionable silence, matching stride for stride. What else would Julia do? Truth be told, Wat

Fiona Carr

Nance's latest outrageous insinuation had nagged at him for days. Nagged because it was preposterous. Nagged because it was just possible to a worry-mongerer like Nance. Had he seen something Henry hadn't? A lot more of Julia, Henry admitted, in and about the stables. And a very great deal more of her devoted groom. Could Guthrie be Nance's perpetrator? Julia couldn't be plotting against his person, not when she was scheming to seduce him.

"Because," Henry began, more to himself than to his cousin, "the evidence is against it being her or anyone. I was there by chance, not my usual time. She was there by chance, as well. She couldn't have met me or even tracked me down. No one could have done. She was scrambling up the cliff herself. Rocks were falling all around us. They had to be accidental, could not have been aimed. The chalk is brittle, easily dislodged from up above when only a single horse gallops up the hill. They could have as easily fallen on her."

"You're confident then that she has no motive?" Erskine's brows drew down with concern.

"Perhaps her feelings have been hurt. Who knows how a woman thinks?"

"True enough," Erskine commiserated. "But seriously . . . would your death benefit her in any way?"

Henry gave that some thought. Up till now, he'd focused on why Nance was making such inapt insinuations. Jealousy, he'd determined, because Julia had a month's free rein to meddle in his realm.

"No benefit I can think of."

"No provisions in the marriage articles that would . . . forgive me, Henry—" Erskine slipped into a familiarity born of rough and tumble boyhood games, of pacts and secrets shared. The familiarity of a trusted family cleric and advisor. "—no provisions that would leave her better off without you?"

"She would be better off without me," Henry answered. "I don't deceive myself in that. A privileged, wealthy widow, freed of a husband and children she never wanted. Free to bestow her affections on the horses."

A pregnant pause. Then Erskine said warily, "In the event of your death, your wife gets the horses?"

"Wraxham insisted."

"Ah, a father looking out for his daughter's best interests."

"Any man would," Henry said. He'd looked out for his. Julia's

202

seductions had tortured him for days. He'd endured them to stop castle gossip. By now, Isabeau must have heard that her new mother's place was secure.

"If that doesn't bother you, I'll not give it another thought."

Henry didn't have time to let it bother him. Hunt balls and revelers bothered him most now, and stables full of nosy neighbors' horses for the night, and a castle at sixes and sevens. Whether his bride was dead-set on seducing him or killing him, he couldn't guess. Would a shower of rocks or a storm of seduction do him in first?

In his present mood, he didn't much care which.

Three long days and three long nights later, and Julia hadn't breathed a word of Uncle Bertie's condition to Henry. Instead, as planned, she'd embarked on a carefully calculated seduction. Henry hadn't cracked.

Julia was seething inside, dying a little every day.

He had watched her take off her boots, breeches, stockings, drawers, habits, and the flimsiest chemises she had in her trousseau. He hadn't bothered hiding his erection, but he'd not acted on it.

As for dressing, she had slithered into her silks, shimmied into velvets, and slid on her sheerest stockings. Like a bidder at an auction, he'd watched her every move.

He'd been interested—she could see his interest, blast him—but not enough to bid on the merchandise.

She had walked across the bedchamber in corsets and camisoles, and—at Polly Le Brun's insistence and Aunt Augusta's advice—in lacy nightgowns Julia imagined best suited for a brothel.

Her husband seemed immune to courtesans and lightskirts. Or perhaps he was just immune to his gangly wife, no matter how she tricked herself out.

She had, on his aunt's counsel, presented herself naked in the copper tub, with soapsuds and without.

"Charming, my sweet," he'd said once, granting her a smile of appreciation. Then he had picked up a branch of candles and settled down to read a book.

Growing desperate, she'd reclined before the hearth, draped herself across his favorite upholstered chair, struck half-dressed poses on his bed she concocted from forbidden drawings secreted away in her brothers' wardrobes.

Fiona Carr

Henry had been impervious, invulnerable, untouchable.

But she'd not survived untouched. Out of the blue one evening, he'd given her a sapphire necklace and helped her put it on for dinner. His hands were so close she could feel their heat on her neck, and his breath stirred her hair.

He must have felt nothing. Or as his daughter would say, *pas de tout*. Nothing at all.

Standing for the final fitting of her gown, she was at the edge of tears. "He doesn't even have the courtesy to look relieved when I put my clothes on," she complained to Polly and her aunt.

"The ball, my dear, is your best chance to fix his attention," Aunt Augusta, ever ready with advice, advised.

"I can't imagine how."

Polly and Aunt Augusta shared a conspiratorial glance. Augusta grinned. Polly hid a decorous giggle behind her chubby hand.

"Oh no. What do you two have in mind?" Julia demanded, bracing for some new humiliation.

"Should you tell her? Or shall I?" Augusta asked.

"That pleasure is all yours, madam," Polly choked out, her giggles spiraling out of control.

Augusta took a quick breath, then whispered something in Julia's ear.

Julia gasped. It was too scandalous, too bold. For years, she'd defied convention, vaulting over fences and making herself the match of any man. But this was a woman's way of battle, and she wasn't sure she had the nerve to follow through. To say nothing of having the body or the beauty.

"I don't have the looks to carry off a trick like that!"

Augusta drew herself up, as if offended. "And you say that because . . ."

"All my life, they called me Horse-face, and now my husband finds me utterly . . . resistible." Julia bit her lower lip, too mortified to say that he had tried her and not come back for more.

Augusta muttered imprecations against her nephew. "Never mind how stupidly Henry behaves. If we say you have the looks, you have the looks."

"But I'm too tall—"

"Stately, my dear," Henry's aunt corrected.

"And gangly—"

"Willowy." Polly Le Brun amended.

"Clumsy," Julia persisted.

Augusta tilted her head. "Not according to Bertie, now that he's up and about again. He says you're a natural. You've made great strides."

"On his poor toes."

"He *was* soaking them last night," Augusta teased. "Oh, for heaven's sake, Julia. You'll be the belle of your own ball."

"I'm not even pretty."

Augusta adjusted the folds of silk that formed the risqué décolletage of the ball gown. Creamery-butter yellow, it really was quite stunning, with crisp mossy green and coral rosettes outlining its sheer overskirt and crisscrossing her breasts. Long, slitted, see-through sleeves were tied at intervals with half a dozen of the same rosettes running up and down Julia's arms. And the train, while not so very long, was gathered up in triple rows.

At any other entertainment, its beauty and its elegance would have made her feel pretty—except that she felt almost naked, too.

But Augusta seemed to see only Julia's face. "No, I wouldn't call you pretty. Would you, Polly?"

"Madam!" Polly said in horror. Clearly the modistes' code of etiquette forbade the slightest hint of the painful truth for their homely patrons.

Julia's heart shriveled. "I never pretended to be attractive."

"Not attractive in the current style," Augusta amended, fluffing Julia's hair, and twirling its short curls into what must be fashionable disarray. "Better." Then she re-examined her work. "Our Julia is classically formed, with good strong cheekbones, intelligent eyes, and a patrician nose. And she carries herself with pride."

Julia did not recognize herself in Aunt Augusta's portrait. But with guests arriving this afternoon and the orchestra setting up, it was too late to correct her misconceptions.

"Quite right, madam, yes, precisely." Polly sighed, with obvious relief. "Classically formed, the very pattern of a marchioness."

"Transcending fashion," Aunt Augusta added.

Polly clasped her hands together. "Setting style."

Aunt Augusta harrumphed. "Doing it a bit too brown, Polly. But at the very least she will bring city ways to country revelries. Impress her guests. And seduce her husband."

Fiona Carr

A rockslide would be easier to stop than Aunt Augusta and her minion on a mission. Still, Julia tried. "It would be a great deal more appropriate, Aunt, for you to wear down the new fashion. I cannot think I should defy convention on my debut as Henry's bride."

"*Au contraire, cherie.* You'll never have him more at your mercy. Just don't forget to tuck an extra glove or two into your reticule." The old lady winked. Augusta Pelham didn't mean the kid gloves Polly Le Brun would furnish for her hands.

"Aunt!" Julia choked. "There will be guests to meet and greet, even dance with, if I must. I will be a slave to duty all night long."

"One way or the other," Aunt Augusta said, aglow with hope and satisfaction. "What do you think is going on when married couples absent themselves from balls? Surely, you never believed my lady's nattering about the migraine."

Julia had never thought about it. Balls gave her headaches and her partners aching feet. Besides, the most risqué conduct she'd ever noticed at a ball happened in plain sight. A couple would be waltzing close enough to kiss. A man would unmistakably pinch his partner's derrière. She'd seen kisses stolen in a hallway. . . . Did couples really repair to bedrooms to make love in a castle filled with revelers and revelry?

Would Henry? Would she have the nerve to carry out their scheme? Would she, could she, break him down tonight?

Daunted by the thought, Julia sank into a chair.

Both women hurried over. "Don't sit!"

"You'll ruin our gown!"

"Stand, and we'll undress you. Courage, child," Aunt Augusta added, pulling her to her feet with surprisingly strong hands. Then her Pelham-gray eyes caught Julia's gaze, and she said earnestly, "Yes, the stakes are high. But the reward. Ah, the reward."

But oh, the price if she should fail, Julia thought. The consequences for her pride, her marriage, and her heart. She squeezed her eyes shut and welcomed blessed darkness as they eased the gossamer gown over her head. It wasn't like her to quake before her fences.

Henry wasn't a fence. Henry was her husband.

What if he didn't break, but snapped in anger? She could lose even the appearance of friendly commerce between them. Or lose him altogether. Or what if he simply snapped?

206

Chapter Twenty-one

Women of quality seldom do any of the manual part of their dress, consequently only their taste is exercised, and they acquire, by thinking less of the finery, when the business of their toilet is over, that ease, which seldom appears in the deportment of women who dress merely for the sake of dressing.

—Mary Wollstonescraft, *Vindication of the Rights of Woman*

"Enough, man!" Henry said. Grayson had been fiddling with his formal finery for half an hour. His dressing room door was closed while the women carried on with Julia's ball gown in his bedchamber.

"But your cravat, my lord. That fleck just there."

With deft disobedience, Grayson unknotted his own creation and consigned it to a mounting pile of discards. Then he began again, humming tunelessly.

It drove Henry mad. "It doesn't have to be original, and it doesn't need a name," he said irritably, angling his chin away from Grayson's knuckles. But Grayson's tongue wagged on.

"Regrettably, my lord, The Waterfall is taken. But we would do well to refer to some similar natural feature. To evoke your sporting life. Not steps, even though my design has these stepwise creases. Steps betoken buildings. Not streams nor waves, which I might consider . . ."

Losing himself in his work, Grayson hummed and fiddled.

"The Castle was a fine name last year. So much better than The Turret," Henry said acidly. Grayson had campaigned for "The Turret" until Henry pointed out its similarity to cruder words.

"Shh, my lord, bear with me if you will. We cannot call it The Castle. This year's creation is altogether different," Grayson said, so intent upon his task that he nudged Henry's chin out of his way. "It makes me think of those outcroppings by the shore. Rocks tumbling down the cliff."

Tumbling down a cliff would suit Henry fine. "Better than standing here and being trussed up like a capon."

"Pardon me, my lord?"

"The cliff. A few more minutes of this, and you can toss me off it."

"The cliff. That's it! Very apt, my lord." Finishing with a flourish, he held up a mirror for Henry's scrutiny. "Yes, we shall call this The Cliff."

Grayson always expected Henry to admire his artistry, but too much attention to his dress smacked of preening. Henry glanced uncomfortably at his reflection and saw a sun-browned man with a thin, beaked face. And a cravat tied exactly like last year's.

"Well done," he said peremptorily, and turned on his heel to make his escape.

The dressing room door cracked open. "Papa? Julia said I could present myself to you."

Better than escape, Henry thought. "Did she, indeed? Come in, *mignon.*"

Excitement glittered in Isabeau's blue eyes. Just as her mother's would have done.

Isabeau curtsied ably, showing crisp crinolines and ruffled leggings. "Do you like it?"

His heart twisted as he picked her up. She sounded so unsure of herself. Her starched skirts crackled against his topcoat. He gave her a smacking kiss on the baby-soft skin of her porcelain cheek.

"*Je t'adore, ma fille.* Let's go get Julia."

"I'm supposed to tell you she's not ready."

"Not ready?" He tried not to scowl. He'd reminded her they had to be on time.

"It's her dress," Isabeau confided in a stage whisper.

He set her down, pleased that his daughter and his bride were talking. Making a show of sharing his bedchamber must be paying off—for someone. For him, the price had been too high. Aching, agonizing arousals had plagued him day and night.

Still, Isabeau's cheerful intervention seemed quite natural. He swallowed hard. He was touched, and troubled. There was a family feeling about this that made him uncomfortable. He hadn't had it with his father or with his first wife, and he wasn't sure he knew enough to make it work this time around.

"Very well then, let's go see that dress," he offered, cutting off that thought.

Isabeau's blonde curls shook in refusal. "That would spoil the secret."

"Secret or no, she's just on the other side." He pushed through the door.

And there she was, barricaded behind the screen with a rustle of fabric and a tittering maid.

"Secrets, my lady?" he asked, prowling toward her, feeling slightly dangerous. He saw a tumble of dressed auburn curls and undressed alabaster shoulders. Nothing else. If his unpredictable, addled aunt had contrived to deck out his bride in an immodest gown, he'd toast her for breakfast. The evening would be long enough without his bride snaring all men's eyes.

Without her snaring his.

"Oh no, Henry," Julia said, her gaiety a trifle forced. "I will be only a few moments. If you would just go down with Isabeau, we will be right along."

"*We*—" he said, his tone corrective "—the marquis and the marchioness—enter together."

"But you must be on time. Gillie is repairing the rosettes on my train."

His imagination went riot. Ladies did not rip rosettes or any other frills and fripperies off their gowns. With Julia, however . . .

"Never say you trotted down to the stables in your presentation gown," he said dryly.

"If you must know," she said, "my reticule went missing. I had to borrow one from your aunt. On my way, a rosette snagged on the short steps in the narrow passageway."

She sounded nervous. Bloody insensitive of him. He hadn't given a thought to what a new bride might feel at her presentation ball. Telling himself to make allowances, he filled with sympathy. But duty was duty. As host, he could not delay.

"Don't be long. More than a few moments will raise eyebrows."

"Could you not take Isabeau down before the crush? She has such a short time to enjoy the festivities before she must go to bed."

That seemed supremely sensible, even thoughtful, and so he led a delighted daughter down with him to meet the gathering assembly. He had already introduced her to half a dozen guests when it struck him.

What did Julia need with a reticule at her own ball?

She would raise more than eyebrows, Julia realized, as she finished dressing for the ball after Henry had left. All alone, she removed her underclothes and corsetry and dipped them in a basin of lukewarm water. Hands shaking, she gave them a quick twist and slipped them on. Aunt Augusta called Julia out from behind the safety of her screen and reached over her own vast old-fashioned hoops to hand Julia the flimsy gown. "Here you go, my dear."

The underdress was the merest slip of gossamer, its overdress essentially the same. With a gulp of courage, Julia slid it over her head, shifted her shoulders, and wriggled it down her naked body. It clung to her cold, conforming petticoats. She looked down and gasped.

Such a revealing gown. The wet of her petticoats had soaked through. She could make out her puckered nipples, the outline of her breasts, her waist, her legs.

It was scandalous. She was scandalous. She would raise ridicule and ribald remarks and rude interest. And she would never live this down. Cowardice swamped her. "Aunt Augusta, are you *sure*?"

Sure I can carry this off? Sure I won't be a laughingstock? Sure I can seduce my husband in . . . worse than nothing?

Augusta Pelham stepped back and admired her. "Oh, *child*," she murmured. "You look . . . you *are* Diana huntress, chaste and fair."

Then she giggled, almost girlishly. "Although, as to the chaste part . . . I'd say, not for long. Do you have the gloves?"

Julia tapped her reticule and swept a hand beneath her bosom. "Two here, and the other two here."

"Very resourceful, my dear gel," Aunt Augusta said.

In an anxiety of practicality, Julia had supplied herself with four— two tucked inside her bodice beneath her breasts—and two jammed into her borrowed reticule. If dancing dislodged the first two, she'd still have her reticule. But if she misplaced the purse, she could only hope the gloves beneath her breasts survived the dancing she would have to do.

Julia never knew how she made it to the ballroom. From the balcony she could hear the orchestra tuning up, people talking, laughing, shuffling about. She was cold and hot at once, and gripped with fear.

Henry looked around the ancient dining hall, its armor and weaponry polished to a gleam. His hall had been transformed, decorated in sheaves of wheat, dried stalks of corn, apples, gourds, and turning leaves. And it pulsed with the milling bodies of the members of his hunt, neighbors, and friends. Lateness might be fashionable in London, but not for a county ball.

A hush rippled across the crush, and he followed its gaze to the top of the stairs.

Julia hesitated, one hand tentative on the marble newel post. His bride was a picture of pride, boldness, and an enticing hint of vulnerability. The last chains that bound Henry's heart clanked free. She was all a man could dare to love. He didn't even flinch before the thought.

His aunt hadn't done badly, either, fitting her out in the height of fashion, in colors becoming, and a style . . . he could barely describe it. Her gown was simple and complex all at once. Evoking Julia's very spirit, his country wench, his marchioness. A man had to fall for a woman who came bang up to the mark in her new roles practically overnight.

Even from afar, he was so attuned to Julia that he could see her fine high breasts rise on a breath of courage. She surveyed the watching crowd with a regal regard. And then, descend she did, all on her own, with confidence. The marble steps were wide and low. Unescorted, she took each one with a firm, deliberate grace.

His heart thumped with pride. No hanging on to rails or demand-

Fiona Carr

ing a gentleman's elbow for this lady. What had he been thinking when he'd fallen for his first wife, a woman in the current romantic style who was faint of heart and weak of limb?

He'd take his Julia any time over them. No false delicacy, no fake dependencies. Evidently his guests thought so, too, as heads bent to whisper. A smattering of applause broke out.

The squire's wife tittered.

A fresh-scrubbed youth pointed. A plump matron looked away.

The orchestra went still.

The back of Henry's neck prickled with a sense of doom descending.

Isabeau made a girlish sound of confusion. "Papa?" she asked in a reedy, puzzled voice. "Why is Julia's dress all wet? It isn't raining out."

Out of the mouths of babes, he thought, anger branding him like hot, forged iron. He could see every luscious contour of his bride's stunning body, the round of her breasts, the indent of her waist, the inviting length of her long legs.

Beneath his satin breeches, he hardened instantly.

So much for his plan to introduce Julia to the county in a manner befitting her new dignity as his wife.

"*Exactement, ma petite,*" he said to his daughter through clenched teeth. Speaking French somehow put Julia's ill-advised audacity at a distance. "*Il ne pleut pas ce soir. Sa robe est très élégant à Londres.*"

"*Vraiment?*" Isabeau asked doubtfully.

No, not really. Only among sex-starved widows and courtesans on the prowl for their next protector. How had Julia lowered herself to that?

His aunt and uncle conspired by the stairs, approval lighting their faces.

Surely not. He would throw them to the tigers.

Isabeau in hand, he marched over, mayhem on his mind.

Julia paused at the landing, halfway down, a smile plastered on her face. He thought he saw her smile twitch, he thought she faltered.

She had better, at the sight of him.

A thousand candles lit the ballroom, and in their brightness, through her clinging gown, he could see . . . almost everything. The divide between her legs. The exact swell of her breasts. The darker oval of her nipples.

212

The Mad Marquis

Nipples. A mad possessiveness skidded through his brain, his torso, his groin. He tried to ignore it. He tried to think.

From the corner of his eye, he could see Cousin Erskine striding to the rescue. Perhaps, Harry thought grimly, Erskine was prepared to offer up a prayer over their aunt and uncle's murdered bodies. Did he intercede for them as well?

At the foot of the stairs, Henry bumped into his aunt's enormous belled skirts. They bobbed merrily against him.

"You two put her up to this." He ground out the accusation, angrier than he had been in his entire adult life. A man could hardly find more proof that his whole family was stark, staring mad.

Uncle Bertie ran a bejeweled finger down Raj's feathered wing.

"Not I," said he, all innocence. "*I* taught her how to dance." Nevertheless, Henry had the sneaking suspicion that he heartily endorsed Julia's audacity.

"Aunt . . ." Henry growled, imagining wildly inappropriate punishments for an elderly, addled lady. Bread and water. Stocks and shackles.

His aunt had her share of the Pelham bearing . . . and the mad Pelham propensity for neck-breaking risk. "It is the very pinnacle of fashion," she said, majestic in the face of Henry's rage. "Most becoming, too, don't you think, Nephew?"

"Not even in the boudoir, madam," he bit off.

"Oh Henry, I didn't think you chicken-hearted. The gel has spirit and . . ."

With a glare Henry dared her to say anything unseemly before his daughter.

". . . sizzle," she concluded. But a suggestive wink told him exactly how unseemly her thoughts were. The old bat.

Halfway down the lower run of stairs, Julia kept descending, her confidence apparently on the rise. Perhaps she thought her collaborators could protect her.

They couldn't.

"The match is made, Aunt. We don't need your interference—or your advice."

Augusta smiled regally. "I wouldn't presume to advise you, Henry. You are clearly a man who knows exactly what he wants."

At this minute, yes, he did. He wanted Julia upstairs; he would strip her, spank her impudent bottom to a rosy red, and turn her over on her back, spread her legs, sink himself into her hot, brazen center, and rut with her like a madman. By the time he let her up for air, this unwelcome band of revelers would be vanished into air, and he would have her all to himself forever—

Bloody hell, he was *thinking* like a madman.

Sobering thought. He'd vowed no more madness.

Handing his daughter off to his aunt, he salvaged sense and said, "Would you be so kind, Aunt, to see that Isabeau gets punch and cake?"

Then he pushed through the phalanx of protection his uncle and his cousin had set up for Julia and confronted her on the stairs. A carved-ivory fan dangled from a silk cord on one not-so-dainty wrist, giving an illusion of femininity to any fool who did not know better. A tiny gem-encrusted reticule swung down from the other.

To his surprise, they trembled, betraying her wrought state, but she met his gaze.

"Overfaced your fences this time, I see, my dear," he said conversationally, fighting to present himself as calm and in control. For, whatever she had done, whatever consequences he would devise for her afterwards, he would not make a scene and chastise her before their guests. "With a little help, no doubt, from my uncle and my aunt."

She gave a wobbly smile. "This was my idea, Henry."

He'd believe that when horses talked. "And where did a country wench like you learn to damp her dress? From your brothers? Or my uncle? Or my aunt?"

He took her hand, and found it clammy cold. But she faced this hurdle as boldly as any he had ever seen. "I take full responsibility."

He bent his head, deliberately intimate for all to see, but said, "Then take responsibility for this. We will lead out the first dance. Then we will do what the marquis and marchioness of Rayne have always done, dance with our honored guests."

Undaunted, she gave back an obliging look—a ploy for him or for their audience? Could it be that she was reckless, brazen, and an actress, too? "I am well prepared to dance."

"I heard as much," he said, allowing himself to look down and take in the full effect of his wife dressed up for the ball. She was noticeably shorter in evening slippers than in her usual thick-soled boots. Noticeably slimmer in the shockingly sensuous folds of her

The Mad Marquis

wet dress. Noticeably seductive, her gown too scandalous for words. His mouth went dry.

"Uncle Bertie says I show great promise," she said, a little of the tension in her easing. She must think he'd let her off the hook. Not likely.

"The question is, my dear, whether I let you show anything ever again," he said mildly, with a smile. "Anywhere."

That jarred her. She bit her lower lip in consternation. And he found himself wanting to bite it, too. Just a nibble, followed by the tip of his tongue, exploring . . .

Lunacy. He reproached himself. One of them must remain sane. And both of them must lead out the first dance. Wordlessly—for words deserted him—he tipped a finger to the orchestra, and they struck their bows, tuning for the opening minuet.

He summoned revelers with an upraised hand. Men and women lined up in rows opposite, by rank and age and, among the unattached, attraction and intent. Every year, it pleased him to organize the hunt ball, to gather neighbors to his home and let them frolic. Frolic with them. The odd thing was, Henry liked country frolics. He was good at dancing. To him, it was a pleasurable way to burn off the mad energy that drove him over fields and fences. Julia, unfortunately, had been hopeless at her father's ball. He'd taken it as a certain sign they were physically mismatched and so, he'd assumed, would be unsuited in bed.

It would be interesting to see how Uncle Bertie, a lightfoot famed for expertise and grace, had fared with her.

Brilliantly, he realized, the moment they took the floor. And Henry suffered the second—or was it the third or fourth—shock to his once orderly existence. Julia had learned to dance. They led the minuet, a devilishly demanding dance, with twirls and pirouettes, crisscrosses and exchanges.

She twirled, and the gossamer material wrapped around her waist. He wanted to encircle it with his hands.

She lifted a leg, and it outlined her shapely knee. He wanted to start the kissing there.

She lifted an arm, and the slitted sleeve exposed the creamy skin of an arm he'd seen bare only by candlelight. He wanted her, all of her, naked in his bed.

She didn't miss a beat, a step, a twist. When their hands touched,

215

Fiona Carr

she was light and balanced, warm, gay. When they parted, he felt a little mad with loss. At the end of the dance, she was gasping and aglow.

He shattered with desire.

Uncle Bertie, beaming, met them the minute the set broke up. "My turn, nevvy. If I may have your bride for the next waltz."

Henry nodded, but a wave of possession nearly bent him double. How could he let her go? The scandal of her dress took a back seat to the scandal brewing in his heart and in his loins.

He had to let her go. He had a tradition to uphold, a yearly festival of celebration with a role to play. There were men to notice, wives to please, a picture of sanity to restore after generations to the contrary.

But how the devil was he going to keep the vow he'd made—on his father's grave and in the family's name—to stop the ill-fated Pelham line with him?

Chapter Twenty-two

But women only dress to gratify men of gallantry; for the lover
is always best pleased with the simple garb that fits close to the
shape. There is an impertinence in ornaments that rebuffs affection, because love always clings round the idea of home.
  —Mary Wollstonescraft, *Vindication of the Rights of Woman*

She'd won. Julia knew it as surely as she recognized Henry's expression. He'd looked like that when he'd tupped her in the barn. And
again, when she'd taken him in her mouth under the copse of yews.
Conquering, and conquered.

But she couldn't stop shaking. The cold, damp dress clung to her
body, and her nerve was flagging. She would never live this down.
Nearby clumps of gentlewomen tittered. Julia sucked in a strength-
ening breath to resist their curious stares. Laughter rose and fell,
words, phrases, jibes, she could not make out. She was being talked
about, and watched. They couldn't know what was on her mind,
what she had hidden in her reticule and the bodice of her dress.

Perhaps she'd overdone it just a tad, trying to hide all four French
gloves, but in the heat of preparation, she could only think of safety.

Safety, and her determination to make a real marriage with Henry

Pelham. Henry sent Uncle Bertie over—to bring her back in line?
Still a little pale from his recent ailment, Albert Pelham bowed over
her hand, then kissed her, Continental style, on each cheek.

"Heartiest congratulations, m'dear, on your success this splendid
evening."

"Are you quite well enough to come out tonight?" she asked. He'd
first sat down with them for dinner again only last night.

He adjusted a wildflower boutonnière. "I have been conserving
my energy, Lady Julia, purely in hopes that we might have the pleasure of this dance."

"*We?*" There sat his parrot, head bobbing as he surveyed the crowd
from his usual perch on his master's shoulder. "You and me and
Raj?"

Uncle Bertie gave a disarming grin. "Raj gets knocked about during
the minuets, m'dear, but he quite loves to waltz."

He quite loved to squawk, Julia thought. The blasted bird started
a stream of nonsense syllables, garbling the words of the tittering
ladies.

"Dancing with a bird!" Julia said as gaily as she could. "A little
more scandal shouldn't hurt."

She tightened her fingers around Aunt Augusta's tiny reticule for
reassurance. She felt, rather than heard, the crackle of the two papered packets. They were still safe. After Grayson had secured the
French gloves, she and Aunt Augusta had laughed themselves to
tears.

However could the contents of these smallish packets protect a
man endowed like Henry?

Only afterwards, lying beside her husband in their dark, unhappy
bed, had it occurred to her: His aunt still knew more of men and
lovemaking than she'd let on.

Driven by curiosity and worry, Julia had unwrapped a costly
sheath by candlelight in the secrecy of the dressing room. Buttery-
soft and flat, it did indeed appear inadequate to contain Henry's
brash invading shaft. She had seen it, had touched it, had even tasted
it. No, she thought, this meager, shrunken casing could not stretch
to accommodate that member. Especially judging from the bulge her
newly experienced eye detected under his satin evening breeches.
But it had to work. Henry would never take her now without a
guarantee. And that was not her only worry.

The Mad Marquis

What if she mislaid her reticule?

She crossed her arms under her filmy bodice, hugging her breasts. She was chilled from her cold, damp petticoats, and needed to dance again. Were the other two skins still hidden under her breasts, unseen, where she had stashed them?

They'd slipped dangerously out of place. Nothing she could do. Unbearably aware of all eyes on her every move, she squared her shoulders and said a prayer that her desperate measure didn't show.

On her dancing master's arm, Julia promenaded to the center of the floor, jumbled snips of conversation coming at her from every side.

One wayward scrap of gossip reached her, and she cringed.

Bubbies. See her bubbies, see her bubbies. Raj repeated, squawking, and flapping his clipped wings

Even Uncle Bertie blanched.

"Stifle yourself, bird," he hissed, his hand steadying Julia.

Her face scalding, she assumed the position for the waltz, the reticule at Uncle Bertie's shoulder, in plain sight where anyone could guess what it carried. Violins picked up the music, and Uncle Bertie nervously hummed along. Numbly, Julia fell in with his easy lead.

Halfway round the ballroom they found their rhythm. Around again, and he circumspectly glanced down her scandalous wet dress.

"Daring, that," he said, straight-faced.

"You disapprove." She met his gaze. His eyes were twinkling. Twinkling!

"Far from it. I applaud your courage. If this don't win him, nothing will. All future Pelham generations will thank you for, ahem . . . charming my nevvy into doing his duty."

Put like that, she sounded rather noble. She didn't have the heart to tell him that getting pregnant wasn't in her plan at all. "So, do you think I have a chance with him?"

"If Henry were a nag," Uncle Bertie reflected, "I'd call him done for—knackered."

"A grisly turn of phrase, Uncle."

He spun her around, almost dislodging the impertinent bird. Raj flapped for balance, squawked a foul complaint, then fluffed his feathers back in place.

"Smitten then. Besotted. Struck down." They whirled. "Pierced by the arrow of love. Head over ears in love." They spun. "You see, m'dear, all metaphors for love are of injury and death. Which is wha holds my nevvy to his course. Fear of letting anyone hurt or contro him the way his father did."

Julia's jaw dropped. She hadn't expected illumination in the mid dle of a dance.

Uncle Bertie went on earnestly, "Make sure he knows he's getting something well worthwhile for everything he thinks he's lost."

"Thank you." Where her wrist and reticule rested on Uncle Bertie' shoulder, she gave him a grateful squeeze. "Thank you."

But what worthwhile thing could she offer Henry Pelham? A scan dalous appearance at his hunt ball designed to entertain the locals Her inadequate, unfeminine self?

Uncle Bertie gazed down earnestly. "Words are free, m'dear. The execution is up to you."

"*Execution,* Uncle? There you go again."

"Humph. Might feel like that to him." Uncle Bertie went ab stracted. "Felt like that to me once upon a time."

Julia regretted she couldn't pursue that hint tonight. She regretted her ill-chosen dress. She regretted the dance was ending, forcing her back amongst the revelers. And the family.

Aunt Augusta dragged Isabeau over, struggling to hold on to her across the span of her enormous belled skirts. Pink with excitement and too much cake, Isabeau had no intention of going quietly to bed.

"One more dance, Auntie," Isabeau begged.

"Ask Julia," Augusta Pelham said, at the end of her tether.

Julia groaned, and hitched herself up. She'd been so intent on seducing the father that she hadn't given a thought to mothering his difficult child. "Time for good girls to go to bed, my dear."

Isabeau stamped her slippered foot. "Marie Claire and I are alway very good. Which means we get to stay up late."

Henry was fast bearing down on them after a vigorous country dance partnered with Squire Purvis's wife.

Could it be he hadn't heard the ladies? Had he missed Raj's out burst? And his daughter's?

Disheveled, his color high, and a light sheen of effort beading his high forehead, he darkened at the sight of Julia. No, he hadn't missed a thing.

The Mad Marquis

"Papa won't make me," Isabeau said, pulling in her pout to charm her father.

He bent down for his daughter. "Papa won't make you what?"

"Go to bed. One more dance first, Papa, please."

"One more, pet, and this one with me. But no complaining after," he said agreeably, and cast Julia a reined-in smile.

The orchestra struck up a lively gavotte, and Henry hoisted Isabeau into his arms. Suddenly, amidst the throng of dancers, the mad marquis was galloping his little girl around the room.

Julia's heart stirred. Had he been like this before she'd married him? There was a touch of madness in her husband, and more than a touch of play. Lovely in a father, she mused. What a father he would make to any children she might bear him. A sudden longing for what could never be streamed through her.

But he didn't want them, she told herself, and she didn't either.

Her wretched dress showed no signs of drying out tonight, Julia realized several dances later. Not in the humid crush of people on a cool October evening. The orchestra was striking up its second set. And she was doomed to brazen it out with partner after partner. Every man in the entire county seemed willing to take her on.

Except her husband.

She'd taken a miserable spin with Squire Purvis, who cared for her feet no more than his wretched dogs, and a quick turn with the local magistrate, who danced about as well as she once had, and a stately pavane with Henry's aging rector. Boring, proper partners, each in his different way, so careful not to notice her damp dress that it was all she could think about.

She slunk miserably to a chair, her dress now cold and feet the worse for wear, her emotions shredded. How incredibly stupid of her to risk Henry's good opinion by wearing a scandalous dress. How incredibly shortsighted to overlook his position in the county. She should have stood by him on her best behavior, like the lady she'd been born and raised to be.

"Lemonade, my lady? Or champagne?" said a rumbling voice, very like her husband's.

"Cousin Erskine!" she said, hiding her surprise by picking at a coral and moss-green rosette. Unlike her, they had not begun to wilt. "Both! May I have both? Lemonade to quench my thirst, and then champagne . . ."

To wash away my misery . . .

". . . to celebrate, perhaps, your introduction to the cream of the county and their wives?" He came round with lemonade, and glanced at the fine, caned chair beside her, like a hundred others lining the walls for dancers' rest. With his striking Pelham looks, it was second-best to having Henry there, a fairer, softer, gentler Henry. A less irate, less rejecting Henry.

"May I join you?" he asked, with reverent consideration. "Or do you need a moment to yourself? You are the center of attention."

"I rather thought my husband was, and rightly so."

He glanced across the floor where Henry escorted an elderly woman to a glass of negus. "The old fellow has a knack for mingling with his guests. Or should I say subjects? Always did. But you have pleased every man you danced with."

"You mean the dress amused them," she said glumly, still stinging from Raj's public announcement. "It does not please my husband."

Archdeacon Erskine looked so puzzled that she almost laughed. She must have misread his sophisticated ways.

"Only the dullest country parson, sir, could fail to notice my scandalous attire."

He looked her up and down, dispassionately, inscrutably, and said, "Ah, that." He turned up a hand as if dampened ball gowns were the slightest matter imaginable. " 'Tis common enough in town."

"Common being the operative word."

"You are a married woman."

"I never should have let myself be talked into it."

He lifted an ironic brow. "Do I sniff the hand of Aunt Augusta, plotter of romantic stratagems?"

"You guessed?"

"I was born into the bosom of this family a full year before my cousin. She has long been a tireless matchmaker in her nephew's behalf. Although," he said, a little puzzled, "I thought the match already made. Well made, if I might add. You and Henry seem suited to one another."

I will do well by you and you . . . suit me.

It had not quite worked out. To her horror, she felt her eyes fill with betraying tears.

The Mad Marquis

Cousin Erskine's warm hand covered the back of hers, just where the silver cord of Aunt Augusta's reticule wrapped around her wrist. He couldn't see, he couldn't guess, that it contained Julia's hopes and his cousin's protection. She'd never felt such an odd irony in her life. Irony, except that Cousin Erskine was the archdeacon before whom she and Henry had said their vows.

"My dear girl," he said with sympathy. "Anything I can do to help? Anything at all?"

"Our plan is mapped out. It's just that . . . Horse feathers! I'm sure you can't be bothered." He was an important man in his own right, likely successor to the bishop of London. A man of the town who condescended to rusticate with Henry to keep up family ties.

"No bother at all. Remember, Henry and I go back to our infant days in dresses." Was he a man to confide in, or was he the fraud Uncle Bertie warned of? As Uncle Bertie had been away for years, and Henry had known the archdeacon all his life, she was inclined to side with her husband.

She looked into his startlingly blue eyes and decided she needed a man's perspective. A married man's, not a clergyman's and not a bachelor uncle's. She cleared her throat and forged ahead. "We agreed to a marriage of convenience, Henry and I. We neither one of us want children."

"I realize that," he said gently.

"Henry told you!" Never mind her own indiscretions, she started getting angry.

The soothing voice again. "I repeat, I have known Henry from our cradles. I am well versed in his fears."

"But you're a married man."

"With far too many children," he said, although she detected a note of pride.

"It isn't that I want children . . ."

"My cousin will be relieved."

"But the rest . . ." *This* was awkward. A lifetime spent with the bawdiest brothers hadn't prepared her to speak openly with a clergyman about matters of the . . . was it the body? Or was it the heart? Horse feathers, had she ever stepped in deep. ". . . I mean, what comes before the childbearing . . ."

"Conjugal relations," he supplied.

"Yes," she said with relief. "Conjugal relations."

Henry's cousin nodded thoughtfully. "Henry considers it a risk."

"But it seems like such a loss. That is, not to do it . . . when one is married . . . that is, with a man like Henry."

"Quite a man, our Henry," Cousin Erskine said gently. His expression mellowed, and for an instant he looked like Henry when comforting his daughter. "You're in love with him," Erskine concluded.

Her hand flew to her breasts, to cover her thumping heart. "I feared it was merely that baser emotion, lust."

He leaned back in the caned chair and said, a knowing glitter in his eye, "Very difficult to split the difference between love and lust, my lady, when a couple is young and vigorous and handsome."

"Fustian, Archdeacon!" she cried. "Henry is not exactly young, and I am hardly handsome."

"Vigor, alone, has its virtues in a case like yours," he said, dryly dismissing her objections just as Henry might have done. Truly, Julia thought, their likeness was unnerving. Then Erskine sobered. "If you want my cousin in your bed, I am certain you'll succeed."

She scanned the ballroom floor. Henry was graciously leading out another county gentlewoman, as he must have done at annual hunt balls for years.

But he had not come back for her. She had strong doubts that she might succeed tonight, or any other night. Her silence must have shown them to his cousin.

"Oh ye of little faith!" Erskine said in sonorous pulpit tones, yet with a note of humor. "Never fear. My handsome cousin will not break your heart." He went dead serious. "Henry has a greater worry than whether or not to sleep with you. Which is indeed what I wished to speak to you about."

Another, greater worry? Julia felt poleaxed. What news could Erskine Pelham, Henry's trusted confidant, impart to her? Her imagination galloped like a stabled filly turned out into a paddock. Another wife? A mistress? Children lost or dead or not acknowledged? An estate so in arrears that they would have to sell the horses? "I beg your pardon?" she asked, as neutrally as she could muster.

"He hasn't mentioned anything?"

"We talk about his daughter, his aunt and uncle, and the horses."

Gravity settled in about the corners of the archdeacon's mouth. "I take it he did not tell you about the sheared-off spoke. Just like Henry, taking all the worry on himself."

"What sheared-off spoke?"

"On the phaeton, on your wedding day. There was an accident, was there not? A tree struck by lightning fell before you, am I correct?"

"Yes," she said carefully.

"But you made it home, injured horses, and damaged carriage?"

"The carriage was not much damaged."

"One wheel was." He sighed heavily. "How like Henry not to tell you. A spoke was sheared off. Cleanly broken, as if cut by a knife. Had you not run into the tree, making you walk the horses home, the wheel would surely have given way. One of you, or both, would have been injured. Or killed."

"Rubbish," Julia said, but her still-damp petticoats clung coldly to her body.

"I am certain there was a reason my cousin did not tell you, my lady."

Yes, like he wanted her dead in an accident. He wanted to rid himself of his troublesome bride before he'd even crossed the threshold. The thoughts tumbled across her mind in quick succession. And she dismissed them.

"Henry always has his reasons," she said, searching Erskine's face for a hint of what he really thought. There was none.

She trusted Henry not to kill her. She just couldn't trust him to love her the way she now hoped he would. She was dying by inches in this damned uncomfortable gown. Perishing, for want of his attention. But Henry? Conspire in such an underhanded and unpredictable way to murder her? Never.

"Of course, he has his reasons," said Erskine. "No one more rational than my cousin. No one I ever trusted more with my life."

"Me either," she said, very quietly.

She had trusted Henry with everything.

Chapter Twenty-three

Men are certainly more under the influence of their appetites than women.
—Mary Wollstonecraft, *Vindication of the Rights of Woman*

Henry galloped his daughter to the end of the gavotte, lifted her over his head, and set her down.

So what if he defied convention and looked a little mad? Better him than Julia, whom he'd protected every way he could think of. He'd not scolded her in front of all their guests. He'd not banished her to their rooms. He'd matched her with men he could entrust not to paw her dress to shreds—thickheaded Purvis, who had eyes only for his horses and his dogs, the magistrate, the rector, and his uncle.

And he'd made sure no county bucks, deeper in their cups as the night progressed, got more than a distant sight of her.

So far, his strategy was working. Appalled as he was by her attire, he'd gone on as if she had done no wrong. Attracted as he was to her in it, he'd not molested her.

His control was wearing thin. Marshaling restraint, he escorted his daughter back to a cozy family gathering—Julia, Cousin Erskine, Uncle Bertie and his perpetual parrot Raj.

The Mad Marquis

But where was Aunt Augusta? Cooking up trouble, no doubt.

A quick glance showed her leaving the hunting set and bearing down on Julia with Squire Purvis's son and heir in hand. Handsome Eldon Purvis, hellion to his bones, had a keener eye for a willing lass than his father for a setter. And so was the worst possible partner for his bride in her current state of dress.

Feeling a plot afoot, he snared Julia's guilty gaze.

"Time, my dear, to take Isabeau to bed."

Julia's green eyes glittered mutinously but she rose from her chair, a vision of bedraggled dampness. "I'd rather attend our guests, my lord. But if you insist, I will retire with Isabeau . . ."

"No, no, Julia," Aunt Augusta intervened, arriving just in time to hear. Purvis dangled at her elbow. "Mr. Purvis so wished the pleasure of a dance. Lady Julia, Mr. Purvis."

Julia hesitated, evidently torn between Henry's curt order and his aunt's bright meddling, then said graciously, "Mr. Purvis. I quite admired your new gray 'chaser at the summer fair."

Purvis, overfaced for once, stammered something feeble about Julia's filly. Julia responded in kind, and the two were off and running on the subject of racing.

Aunt Augusta tugged on the jewel-encrusted reticule that dangled from Julia's wrist, then gave her a knowing wink. "You stay down here and dance, my dear. I'll take care of Isabeau."

Henry's theory hardened. There was a plot, and his nearest and dearest were its chief conspirators. Worse, he knew young Purvis from the hunt field and the tavern. He was guaranteed to grope Julia during a dance and talk about it afterwards. Damn his aunt! She'd championed the very kind of partner he'd fended off all night.

Damn himself for standing here and letting her.

Eldon Purvis was bowing low over Julia's hand, having recovered his rough country charm. "My lady, I would be honored—"

"—more honor than you need tonight, my man," Henry cut him off, a lunatic jealousy melding with the fierce possessiveness that had obsessed him since he'd looked up and seen Julia at the top of the stairs. "My bride promised her last waltz to me."

Julia endured a wordless couple of circuits about the room in the strong, resisting arms of her husband, gratified and worried. Gratified that Henry's iron control had slipped. Worried that he'd shown a flare of jealousy she'd not thought possible.

Why jealous, if he was plotting murder?

She almost missed a step on that wild, ironic thought. Curse Cousin Erskine for planting the seed of such a hateful and absurd idea. It had blighted her evening, which had been trial enough. There had to be a reason the spoke was severed. There had to be a reason Henry hadn't told her. There had to be a reason there had been no further threats.

No further threats, she repeated, taking reassurance where she could.

The reason was, it was coincidence. It couldn't have been Henry. It didn't square with either his tenderness or this last display of jealousy. If she were a foolish woman, she would think it looked like love. Like love? Or lust? She wished she had enough experience to know.

She closed her eyes to feel his strength. His solid grace. His manliness. For on a whirl, he caught her up to him just close enough that she could feel the ridge of his heat. Another reason. He couldn't want her and want to get rid of her, could he?

Her reticule with its secret packages banged against his shoulder, reminding her what she'd set out to do. Under her breasts, she could feel the sheaths, stuck to her skin from perspiration. She had not finished with him yet.

But could she finish? Had she mangled her chance by damping her dress? Had her behavior so repulsed him that he would only dance with her to repel a man like Purvis? In these last days, she'd aroused her husband, time and again, and he'd resisted her. Did she have the female arts to entice him be her lover?

Henry fought an urge to smash young Purvis's face, and thought about his contradictory wife.

In his arms she was as light as air. Tall, proud, agile, womanly. Defiant hoyden though she was, her body responded to his slightest touch like the best-trained horse he'd ever ridden. But what aroused him most, what he could not deny, was her daring. Tonight, whatever or whoever was behind that scandalous dress, she'd put it on and faced the consequences. Fearlessly. A grinding desire settled in his groin.

And a grinding necessity to protect her from other men.

To say nothing of himself.

"You dance beautifully, my lord," she said brightly, just as their silence had stretched past comfort.

"I have my uncle to thank for your improvement, I suppose," he said stiffly.

She gave him a jaunty smile. "And me, my lord. I aim to please."

Provoked, he glanced down grimly. "You fell short by a long shot."

"Oh, this?" She glanced down at her audacious dampened dress, too confident. Too pleased. "A whim. Everyone approves but you."

Her breezy disregard of good manners and good sense goaded him to rebuke her. "That's not approval, Julia. That's lust. I have protected you from your folly, but I can't keep it up all night."

She leveled him a triumphant emerald gaze. "Lately you've been expert at keeping it up all night. Less adept, however, at knowing where to put it."

Brazen hussy. Henry's face burned with anger and arousal. "I know where to put it, Julia. And we both know why I won't. It's a damned nuisance walking around every waking hour distracted by your . . . charms." He gave the word a sarcastic twist.

"So terribly sorry I've inconvenienced you, my lord," she said crisply, then looked directly into his eyes. "I'm not so comfortable, myself."

Her hands were cold, chill bumps dotted her bare arms, and he could see her nipples were hard peaks. From hours in her dampened dress? He wondered if her bodice irritated them. Images of irritating them himself—of squeezing, nibbling, sucking them—ran away with him. He reined in his runaway imagination. "The remedy for your discomfort is within your grasp."

Her brow knotted. "Too late to start the evening over, Henry."

"Go upstairs and change."

She shook her auburn curls, her headdress tousled. "If I change now, everyone will know you're disciplining me like a sulky schoolgirl."

He gave a hollow laugh. "No one can suspect me of disciplining you. Successfully, at any rate. I've had no success whatsoever getting you to do things my way." Then he admitted ruefully, "I'd merely hoped to introduce my bride tonight and show that all was harmony and bliss with the Raynes."

"It will be clear that we have neither if you send me upstairs like a child."

"It will be clear, my dear, when you return in a warmer gown, that you were merely cold."

"Ah, but my lord, what if you escort me up and we return in charity with one another? Your guests will see us in a different light. And I will be warm. And my reputation intact."

Probably. His guests wanted a happy marriage. Gossips nodded sanction as he and Julia waltzed, and county luminaries cast approving looks their way.

He didn't approve. Not of her and especially not of himself. He hadn't meant to touch her, let alone enjoy her in his arms. He hadn't meant to find her argument sensible, inevitable. But he put great store in appearances, and held public family fights in great disgust.

It only needed a quarter hour more of resisting her, he promised himself. Five minutes to and from their bedchamber, and five for her to change. And then back downstairs to duty. To safety.

"Which gown do you prefer? The green velvet, or the ruby sarcenet?" Julia asked neutrally, once they had navigated the twisting halls and erratic stairs back to their bedchamber.

But her heart and mind raced, worrying what to do, and when, and how best to bring him to his knees. According to her plan. According to her vow.

"I have only dinner dresses, which can serve in a pinch," she added, draping them over the bed's rich, heavy coverlet and returning to her wardrobe in the dressing room for more. "The scarlet's out. It's cut too low for warmth," she said airily over her shoulder.

"Um-hmm," came a distant and indifferent murmur. At the hearth, logs crashed and crackled. Her heart clutched, and she dug into her trousseau. She could only hope he was fighting wanting her, not plotting her demise. Henry had resisted her with iron control when she'd paraded nude about the room. What if Cousin Erskine's suspicion explained that? What if it did not?

Of course, she thought, seducing him should answer those questions. If he made love to her as he had before, that would prove him innocent of any nefarious schemes.

Bolstered by that thought, she scavenged through her wardrobe, and pulled out the black silk. Its elegant overdress was thinly layered over a quilted bodice and heavy velvet skirt. She padded over the Turkish carpet to the hearth and held out the dress for Henry to consider. "This is my warmest gown."

He poked the guiltless fire.

"Really, Henry, since you disapprove my first choice, you must choose."

He glanced over his shoulder and decided in a snap.

"The green. Red is too . . . suggestive, and black—no, black is mourning."

"Very well, then. Green it is." She stalked back to get the green, feeling a little hopeless. Inscrutable, infuriating man! She'd meant to have him on the ropes by now, but she'd barely turned his head.

What if he couldn't chance a look? she wondered, clinging to faint hope. What if his iron control was his last stand? What if this was her moment to disrobe, to walk up to him naked, and then begin . . . to what?

Heaven help her, exactly what came next?

Hadn't she tried everything already?

The dress, Julia scolded herself. Remember the way he looked at the dampened dress. Take it off slowly, but take it off now. Throw your heart over, like leaping the scariest hedge, and the rest will follow.

Henry will follow.

She folded her arms behind her and twisted up to untie her tapes, aware of her breasts jutting out, her fingers numb. Too numb. She pulled on the tapes and yanked and jerked. They snarled into a knot. Clumsy, stupid. No, she had the power to turn a reversal into good.

"Blast!" she cried, convincingly as she could. "I made a tangle, Henry."

Another log crashed down, sparks sizzled.

"Henry?"

She turned and saw him, standing by the hearth, an arm draped on the mantel, and heavy-lidded hot desire burning in his gaze.

Her stomach dipped and throbbed.

"Come here," he said, his voice a rasp of barely mastered passion. "I want to see you by the fire."

Suddenly she was walking toward him, shaking.

"Turn around," he instructed as she joined him at the hearth. She turned and felt his warm hands work the knot, his hot knuckles braced against her skin. Her breath went shallow, and her knees went weak.

"So," he said harshly, "you and my aunt hatched a plan for you to seduce me."

Yes. But she would say so only to his face. She tried to turn.

"Stand still," he ordered. His voice was rough. His hands on the back of her bodice tugged her into place. Moments more of his kneading, nudging knuckles, and the knot gave way. She sucked in a breath as her breasts came free. Then she felt the soft sheepskin of the hidden sheaths.

"Here's what I don't understand," he ground out, easing the bodice off her shoulders, so it gaped away from her breasts. "You are honest to a fault in trading horses. I believe that you'll be faithful to our wedding vows. But we agreed not to perpetuate my family's madness. Isabeau's imaginary friend is alive and well in her imagination. My uncle and my aunt demonstrate their follies daily. You must see my concern."

How to say she didn't share it? He was so convinced, so wrong.

And how to get out of her dress without spilling her secret weapons on the floor? The sheepskin sheaths half stuck to the lining of her dress, half clung to her skin. Thank God he was behind her, she thought, scheming furiously how to get them out and where to hide them. She had no pockets, and her reticule was full.

"But Henry, your concern is—"

"Shhh," he said, his breath hot against her ear. It tickled into her throat, shivered down her neck. Backing her up to him, he pressed his arousal against her buttocks, hard and hot and intimidating. "You've tormented me all week. It's my turn to torment you."

"You're doing a damnably good job of it," she muttered. His hands came round and claimed her breasts. She gasped with pleasure.

Then dismay.

"What the devil is this?"

His hands plunged inside the gaping neckline of her bodice and his fingers ran around the tender underside of her breasts and pulled out . . .

"Our protection," she said firmly.

Softened by the damp dress and her body's heat, the sheaths hung limply from his fingers. "You little vixen. Where did you get these?"

"Our hounds chase vixens," she said, mustering a cool dignity. "I'm your wife."

"And I am still lord of Pelham Castle," he bit off, and flung them at the fire.

"Henry! I went to a lot of trouble to get those!" she burst out, racing for the hearth, arms outstretched to salvage her investment, her hope. Midway there, he clamped his arms around her body and brought her down onto the rug. Blast and damnation. He had been too quick. Wriggling in protest, she could only hear the sizzle of the sheaths and smell the acrid burn of leather.

He pinned her body to the floor with his hard, athletic one. "Who's in on this with you?"

She grunted under his not-unwelcome weight. "My lips are sealed."

"Not to me, they're not," he said, grinding out the words against her tight-lipped mouth.

His heat and strength and force were irresistible. What she'd fought for, Julia thought moments later. Henry, uncontrolled. Parting her lips, she gave in to his insistent tongue. It swept the insides of her mouth, prodded against her clamped teeth.

He pulled back briefly. "Open, damn it. You wanted this."

"Not here. Not in anger."

"Not anger, my lady," he muttered at her mouth. "Unbridled, raging lust."

"Oh—" she began, but the fierceness of his kiss swallowed her words, and swamped her senses. His tongue invaded her open mouth, probing past her teeth to explore its roof, to duel with her tongue, and then probing deeper, a hot adamant reminder of how she'd taken his shaft that dawn beneath the yews. Eyes closed, remembering, she drank his angry lust, imbibed his turbulence.

Oh . . . he could have his way with her.

When he'd finally kissed her to an agony of expectation, he came up for air, his breath wracked, his gaze tormented.

"Am I performing according to your plan, my lady?" he gritted out.

She forced a crooked smile. "The carpet helps, but the floor is rather hard."

Despite the fire's low light, his sun-darkened skin flushed darker. "Bloody hell, I'm acting like a beast."

My beast, she thought, oddly touched. Mine, and almost wild.

He dragged her to her feet, wrapping his arms around her, pulling her back into his front, reaching around to fondle her nipples. "It's just that you've been driving me mad for days," he breathed against her neck.

She reached for a sultry tone, almost overwhelmed by his admission, his passion. "I had planned our consummation for the bed."

"Did you, now?" he said, his voice rumbling with . . . promise, or with threat?

She shivered with uncertainty. She was sure she wanted him to lose control, less sure what that meant. He walked her awkwardly across the room, stride for stride, like a hostage he couldn't trust, a captive on delivery. With each step his breath burned her neck, his strength grasped her arms, his erection throbbed at her behind. Branded, she felt branded, and for the first time, possessed.

"There," he said at the bed's edge, turning her around and sweeping away discarded dresses. Then he tumbled her across the coverlet, a dark knight claiming her as plunder. He swept aside the filmy overskirt of her gown, bunching its orderly rosettes into a riot of pink and moss-green flowers that fell beside her hips. Then he rucked up the underskirts to the joining of her legs, and let out a low hiss of approval. "Nothing underneath, not even a scrap. Are there no limits with you, wife?"

She swallowed hard and found the nerve to say, "None, my lord. Not if it will get me what I want."

With a low rumble in his throat, he knelt before her, parted her legs, and his expert blunt-tipped fingers worked their hot magic at her secret folds. Her husband's skillful touch sent sparkles of sensation throbbing through her, and she arched for more.

"Never doubt I can give you what you want," he rasped.

But she wanted something else. "I want what we did in the hayloft, Henry."

His shock of ash-brown hair brushed the insides of her legs. She tried to hide a shiver.

"Absurd to take that risk," he grumbled.

"Absurd to forgo it," she countered.

"You promised otherwise." But his breath blew puffs of hot moist air where his fingers played with her, and she fought not to wiggle into their exquisite pressure.

She fought to speak. "I promised in ignorance."

He growled an oath against her tenderest skin, asserting his will, not stopping. She pitched forward, her strength and the surprise knocking him on his heels. Sitting up, her bodice gaping open, she added, "Henry, I'm not asking anything so very difficult. You want this, too."

His handsome profile flushed with provocation. "All right. I want you so badly I'm thinking about risking my family's future."

"This isn't a risk."

"I burnt the sheaths," he said, unmoved and in control again.

She reached across the wide wide bed, retrieving Aunt Augusta's reticule with a heady sense of her own power. "Not all of them."

Chapter Twenty-four

The two sexes mutually corrupt and improve each other.
—Mary Wollstonescraft, *Vindication of the Rights of Woman*

Henry instantly saw her plan, and his erection went rock hard. She'd danced all night with their protection on her wrist. With the one thing that might let him satisfy his hunger.

"Clever wench," he said, half scolding, purely shocked. And aroused and flattered. It touched some deep male pride that she wanted him enough to come up with such an ingenious and deliberate plan. It touched his heart. But his mad, endearing daughter was proof it was a risk.

Julia unlatched the reticule with a self-conscious tremor. Which only made him harder. Damn. It shook him that she was both bold and shy.

He put a knuckle to her cheek, tipped up her face and gentled his voice. "You have doubts?"

She flashed a jaunty smile. "Not even for a minute." Then she upended the purse. Fresh-wrapped sheepskin sheaths bounced onto his bed. Not one sheath, but two. The wench had aspirations. Damn, and damn.

The Mad Marquis

Aspirations he could meet. He'd been stalwart for weeks, resisting almost every lure she'd thrown his way. But he was not invincible. Not when he could take her twice tonight. Once and then again. The thought pounded through the most primitive center of his brain.

She picked at a paper wrapper, but he covered her nervous hands with his. She jerked her hoard away to safety.

"No tricks, Henry. The fire bit wasn't fair."

"Nothing's fair, my dear," he muttered. "It wasn't fair to make you swear off marital relations, and it's not fair for me to want you now. But I do. So bad it hurts. I want to skip all that kissing stuff and bury myself inside you."

Her green gaze searched his, testing him for truth. "Then do it, Henry. Love me." Taking a bold initiative, she melted against him, hot and pliant, pressing her belly tight to his burning shaft. "Let the sheath protect us," she whispered.

He wasn't sure it would. But her demand rocked him, and her daring pushed him over the edge. He pulled away from their hot embrace. If he was going against his principles, it would be his way.

"Undress for me first," he ordered. But his voice cracked with the quick intensity of his desire.

Her eyes went wide with shock. "I can't do that!"

"I thought you could do anything," he pressed, pleased to throw her off her stride.

"I'm not . . . you know . . . you're supposed to . . ."

"Everything changes when the orders come from me, doesn't it? Or are you afraid I'll accept your offer?"

Her brow furrowed. "I am not afraid."

"Good. I wouldn't want that," he said, deliberately smooth. "I just want you to undress. A little more of what you've been doing to torment me for days."

"I . . ." she started, and broke off in confusion.

Desire walloped him. Julia flummoxed was a sight to behold. But he said coolly, "Do it for my pleasure. And," he added, "for your edification."

Her blush spread down her throat and to her bosom. But she lifted her chin and planted her feet and took her stand between him and the glowing hearth. Firelight outlined her legs, and they were saddle-fit. Man-fit. The flimsy fabric of her drying dress fluttered from anxiety.

237

Fiona Carr

Biting her lower lip, she fumbled with the fastenings of the over-dress, shucked it off, and dropped it on the carpet. He absorbed her slightest move with a keen new pleasure. All week she'd been brash with her hopeless little schemes. Now that he was waiting, really ready, it pleased him to see her tremble beneath his greedy gaze. Until she froze.

"Go on. Start with your bodice," he coached.

She hastily slipped a shoulder free.

He leaned forward and pulled the gown back up, gently correcting her. "I want you to slow down, like untacking a high-strung horse. And look at me while you take off your dress."

This time she went slower, her fingers skimming creamy skin, first one shoulder then the other. Her hands tight fists of anxiety, she hesitated, and he exulted, not because he wanted to break her spirit but because he wanted her to be fully conscious of his attention.

"Now the sleeves, but take your time . . ." he instructed, his pulse pounding in his throat.

Half a dozen rosettes marched along her arm, each one catching up a swag of gossamer fabric. Julia struggled to release something—hidden buttons? hooks? pins?—whatever sartorial devices women designed to drive men mad. She bared her arm a few ivory inches at a time. He was in heaven.

He was in hell, his erection straining against the fitted satin of his evening clothes. For relief he stretched his legs out on the bed and unbuttoned the fall of his breeches. His burning manhood sprang free.

She goggled.

He chuckled. "You have seen me, Julia."

She gave her head a nervous shake. "I merely touched you . . . Tasted . . ." she trailed off, not yet so bold that she could put in words what she'd really done.

It wasn't false modesty or cowardice, and his heart shifted in his chest. He loved her flustered and confused. For him. And at his mercy. She bowed her head to her task, to more mysterious under-pinnings, even in a dress so slight. He wanted to rip off all his clothes and go and rip off hers. But he thought of the pleasure if his naked bride disrobed him, and refrained from doing what she could do ably. If he could only get her to undress.

She watched him as if he might pounce.

Pouncing, and devouring her, was distinctly possible. "Don't worry, Julia. I'm not one of Uncle Bertie's tigers. I won't eat you. I just want to see your breasts."

Pressing her lips together, she edged the gown a little farther down, clearing the coral peaks of her nipples and the soft rounds of ivory flesh. The slim dress snagged on her hips, a wanton drapery. She looked like an antique statue of a goddess, hidden in a private maze from any prying eyes but his.

He blew out a whistle of appreciation, and then with a mad, unthinking urgency, he pushed to see how far she would really go. "Touch yourself, caress your breasts."

Her face clouded with mortification, and she covered them instead.

"Don't," he burst out, harsh with his need to see.

Her hands dropped to her sides, leaving breasts and nipples bare and proud.

It took all his will not to stand and show her what to do. Instead he said, "You didn't hesitate to do this to torment me."

She was taken aback. "It was easier when you didn't ask."

"Because you were trying to defeat me. As if we were in a race."

"Yes. No. I don't know."

"You do know. Do you want me, or do you not?"

She swallowed hard. "I do," she said softly.

"Do you want to please me?"

"Yes," she said, softer still, as if mortified to put it into words.

His chest tightened. He had to push her back as she'd pushed him, to even up the score, to regain control. Besides, he loved the answers she was giving him. "It will please me if you fondle your breasts. Show me what it is you'd like for me to do."

She sucked in an anxious breath, and her ivory breasts quivered. Hot lust bolted to his groin. Then she recovered herself, his brave country wench, his fearless hunter goddess. Closing her eyes, she cupped her hands beneath her breasts and lifted them toward him. Trancelike, she splayed her fingers over them and pressed them to her chest. A coral nipple peeked through slender fingers. She tested it, then squeezed it awkwardly. Its coral hue darkened. Growing bold, she rolled it between the pads of a finger and a thumb.

As he had done. As he craved to do, there and lower down.

But he reined himself in, watching her carry out his commands,

239

watching her explore her body. It was almost more than he could bear. And yet he bore it, his gaze roving her body, breasts, face, drinking it all in. When her expression changed to pleasure, he almost spurted his desire into empty air.

"Julia," he rasped, his pulse pounding in his throat. "Look at me."

She looked up, heavy-lidded, sloe-eyed, dazed. Seduced. Converted.

"You asked for this," he reminded her, his voice thick with desire. "Tell me what you're feeling."

Her throat worked, but she met his gaze, a glitter of yearning in her green eyes. "You. I want your hands on me. Your hands and mouth all over me."

His manhood quaked, and he shook off his last qualms. "Come here. Now." And added, after drawn-out seconds when it seemed she could not move, "Please. Julia, undress, and come and love me."

She freed her gown from her hips. With a sigh, it rippled down around her slippers, and she curled her toes and pushed them off and stepped out of the dress. Her trim bare feet carried her the few short strides into his waiting arms. She wasn't self-conscious about undressing him, he noted, for she tore at his shirt and started on his breeches.

"Wait," he said, inspired to put her to another test. "My boots."

"I'm not your valet, my lord," she protested. But she turned and took a leg between her knees, bending forward to give him an unrestricted view of her curvy, tempting bottom.

"I'd much rather look at your behind than his." He curled up, and braced her hips with outspread hands. She wrenched one boot off. It yielded with a sucking sound, and thudded on the carpet. She mounted his other leg, her crisp curls and silky private folds resting on his thigh.

Tantalized, he let out a groan of anticipation.

But she flipped an arch smile over her bare shoulder. "I could say the same for yours. I always liked to see you on a horse."

His arousal throbbed. He had no idea she'd ever even noticed him that way. Had it been that last time he'd bested her on Hazard? He dragged her up his naked body, relishing the slide of her soft skin against the rough textures of his legs and chest. She let go of inhibitions, rubbing her body against his, spreading her naked heat against his chest, his groin, his steely erection. She must like him that way best, for she rubbed her mound against him with her first moan of satisfaction.

Taking her moan into his mouth, he kissed her again, a kiss steeped in haste and want and hunger, a devouring, drinking, melding kiss, abandoned to propriety and sense. He rolled them onto their sides, enjoying her almost equal length and health and strength, her womanly—

With a jerk, he remembered precautions. Fingers scrabbling across the bed, he found a sheepskin sheath, stretched it to fit his swollen member, and worked it on with suddenly shaky fingers. He'd come so, so close to danger. He was so close now.

Too late to turn back. Every ounce of flesh in his body demanded he go on. He rolled another quarter turn to cover her. He pressed his sheathed shaft against her hidden folds, and his member spasmed with hot hunger. But he felt . . . next to nothing—no crisp curls, no tender lips, no moisture. The wretched leather sheath was thin and softly oiled, but it masked all sensation. He wanted to strip it off and burrow home. Wanted to. Wouldn't risk it.

So when she gripped his arms and looked into his eyes and said, "Ride me, Henry, ride me," he plunged his stone-hard member into her tight center, burying himself where he belonged. He couldn't feel her sensuous slick skin, only her tightness and her warmth.

In his wrought state that was enough. She enfolded him, accepted his driving, thrusting, and withdrawing, his driving again and thrusting home.

Ah, he had missed tupping. Her hands and heat and forthright moans of pleasure drove him to push higher, deeper, and she met his every move, his brazen country wench.

And, oh, he'd wanted Julia, his fearless equestrienne. He rode her hard, rode out days of pain and abstinence, rode out weeks of worrying, pumping her to meet his final charge.

His hoyden came through true to form, lunging beneath him, bucking against him to a shattering release. With a roar, he emptied into her all his hopes and all his fears. Madness, he told himself, even as he spurted out more and again and more.

If loving Julia was madness, madness didn't seem so bad.

For long moments after, he lay across her body, braced on his elbows, their pulses racing in harmony. Little spasms of aftershocks pulsed from him to her and back. Rapture. Bliss.

Perhaps she was right. Perhaps they could always have this, and his fears for his offspring—

"Bloody hell," he muttered, and his hand shot down to retrieve the wasted sheath. He'd gone wild. Mindlessly, splendidly wild. But he could have lost their protection in her, torn it, rubbed it off. Where her curls still tangled with his rough hair, he found its edge, clamped his thumb and forefinger around it, and very, very carefully withdrew.

"Don't go," she said dreamily, as he slid out of her hot depths. She looked up, her eyes sated, her lips swollen from kissing.

He had bossed her, worked her, plundered her, and she had taken him in without a whimper, and she wanted him to stay. His heart filled with tenderness, rare and terrifying. He brushed his mouth across her nose, her cheeks, her chin, claiming her bit by bit. Thanking her, for freeing him from years of loneliness and onerous self-control.

Not that he could say so yet.

"I'm not going anywhere, my love, but this . . ." He pushed the sheath off his still-hard shaft, exposing himself to the shock of cool castle air. "This must be taken care of."

He held the brown sack up to the firelight. It was limp and sad. Her brow wrinkled. "Oh blast!" she moaned. "It didn't work."

He turned it around. "I don't see any tears."

"That's good?"

"Very." Then he pinched it at the top and squeezed downward to its tip, as though stripping a cow's teat. "This will show if anything leaked through."

She inspected the sheath with that practical, unfeminine objectivity of hers that kept him so off balance. She looked like a woman, she made love like a woman, but she acted like a companion, an equal, a friend. Not that he tupped friends, or wanted to kiss them again so soon after . . .

"I don't see any," she pronounced, as detached as if she'd just checked her filly's shoe and found no stones.

"Me either," he said, repressing an inappropriate smile.

"Do you know what that means?"

"No more children," he said soberly. But he wanted to laugh with relief.

"That's obvious! But no, Henry. It means it works. It means . . ."

She actually gave him a lustful look. ". . . we can do it again."

And with a restorative power he thought he'd left far behind him in his youth, he grew hard again.

His bride watched his member swell, fascinated. "I never thought about that," she said, in that objective voice again.

"What?" he asked lazily, not even put out that she sounded unimpressed. He was painfully halfway between the delicious lethargy of aftermath and the sweet ache of mounting hunger.

"A stallion can service several mares a day. I hadn't thought that men could, too—that is, service several women," she seamlessly corrected.

"I could," he said. Which had once been true, at any rate, but he only tossed it out to goad her.

Instantly indignant, she crossed her arms below her naked breasts. Which only plumped them up to tempt his greedy eyes. "Men! Thinking they can have every woman they see."

"Not necessarily," he murmured, loving her provoked. He tweaked a tender nipple, not quite offered, not withdrawn, and saw her bite her lower lip. "I'd settle for one woman, my love. For you, again, right here, right now."

"You would?" She examined his arousal with questing fingers and dancing eyes. Then she sat up, her face grave. "We're forgetting our guests."

"Plague on our guests." The first drops pearled at the tip of his shaft to corroborate his oath. "They have food for three days, and cider for a week."

"Oh, right. Aunt Augusta told me people expected married couples to—"

"Plague on her, too." He could just imagine what Augusta Pelham told her. "I walked through fire to do right by my family and deny our marriage bed. I'm not backing out on you now."

She gave him an alluring grin. "I didn't mean for us to go downstairs, Henry. I meant . . ."

And to his astonishment, she tenderly sucked the tip of his shaft, testing how far she could take him in. Again. A potent seed boiled up from his depths. He didn't dare move and stop her experiment, but he didn't want to spend again so soon. There was so much more to savor and to teach his curious bride. He took her head in his hands to stop her.

"Julia, please, no more, I beg you. I want you with me when I come again."

She released him and rocked back on her heels, her jaunty breasts tempting in his line of vision, but a triumphant grin on her face. *"You begged.* You actually begged."

He scowled at her swift turnabout. "I never beg."

"Julia, please, I beg you." She mimicked his low voice.

" 'I beg you' is a figure of speech," he huffed, feeling foolish to dispute the point.

"Sheer sophistry, Henry. When you ignored my efforts to attract your attention—"

"You mean, your efforts to seduce me underhand, outside the bounds of our agreement—"

"—when you ignored my efforts, I vowed I'd make you beg."

"Knowing you, you probably wanted me on my knees."

"That would have been quite satisfactory," she said saucily.

He laughed because he loved her spirit, then drawled, "But I'd much rather take you on yours."

Julia's stomach dropped. "What?"

"I'd like to put you on your knees and bend you over and take you from behind," Henry said, his voice suddenly sounding hoarse with desire.

"Absolutely not. Not here, not anywhere!" Julia blurted, not even taking an instant to consider his request.

A corner of his mouth crooked. "Where's my brave country—"

"Running! She's running." Julia scrambled for the other side of the bed. But his hand clamped implacably on her ankle, hobbling her.

"What happened to my fearless seductress?" he asked, amusement in his voice.

She was appalled, and a little frightened. Another hand clamped down higher on her leg, and she squirmed and struggled to get away.

"Your fearless seductress overheard her brothers making fun of a tavern strumpet who liked it like . . . because she couldn't get pregnant . . . Oooh, Henry, how could you even think I would . . ." she panted from exertion and embarrassment, even as he arranged his lean, hard body behind her with a firm but gentle strength.

"You mistake my best intentions, Julia," he said with due deliberation. "I just want to come inside you, like before. But from behind. We'd still need that sheath."

Oh. "Well, that changes everything, my lord," she said on an ironic note. It sounded bestial, like horses mating. Forbidden. And exciting. But she wasn't about to admit to that. "We were doing just fine the regular way."

"We don't have a regular way, Julia," he said quietly, and snugged up to her and lay silent for a while. She could feel her heart pounding inside her ribcage, could hear his breathing, could try to imagine how it would feel to do something that risky. That wild.

"Try it," he whispered in her ear, a hot puff of breath spiraling down through her. "You might like it."

"Might not," she countered emphatically. But to her dismay—and amazement, she was liking it a little bit already. Henry was so solid and sure behind her, his moist breath at her neck, the rough texture of his chest at her bare back, his powerful erection burning at her bottom. He seemed endlessly patient, as if waiting for a sign from her. Her breathing calmed, but her insides churned with a hot mix of fear and anticipation.

"You could trust me, Julia," he said quietly.

She could. She even thought she did. Cousin Erskine's dire warning seemed ever more mistaken. Henry had controlled his gentle violence, his fierce urgency in the name of pleasure. Her pleasure.

He put on the remaining sheath, rose to his knees, and pulled her up in front of him. She couldn't help stiffening a little as he placed her where he wanted her. On her knees, her legs a little parted. Awkward, and exposed. But to him and him, alone. Then he nibbled her ear and trailed trial kisses down her neck, perfectly situated to do so. A sigh swooshed out of her, a pale shadow of the sparkles that swirled throughout her body.

Maybe he was right. "Ummm," she murmured her consent.

"I'm not done with you, wench," his voice rumbled at her ear. His arms closed over her front, and he played her nipples with one hand, and with the other, caressed the cleft between her legs.

"Ooooh," she said, wriggling for him and pressing back against his erection. "This feels scandalous."

"And this?" he asked. Reaching lower, he dipped long warm fingers into her core, wrenching a groan of acceptance from her throat. Relentlessly he drove them deeper inside her and worked them in and out. For the first time she felt her own wet readiness. Weakened with pleasure, she moaned.

"Now, my lady," he whispered hotly, "bend over on your hands."

Her back went rigid. "Oh Henry, I just can't," she muttered, shocked by the indignity of the position after all.

"You're the bravest woman I've ever known. Don't back down now," he said, a stark urgency rimming the edge of his voice. "I know I can please you. Trust me, my love."

She trusted him, she realized.

She just didn't trust herself, not with something so outside her experience, something so shockingly new. She dropped down on her hands, her arms as stiff as fence posts, her body shuddering from the exposure. But he entered her respectfully, gently parting her sensitive lower lips with his fingers, then with the head of his protected shaft. She could feel him edging up inside her in tiny increments of tenderness.

Marvel of marvels, she thought, Henry was inside her, establishing his claim, possessing her. When he tunneled in and touched her womb, she nearly collapsed with an urgent need to put her arms around him. But he stopped and waited for her, apparently as astounded by their intimacy as she. He worked her taut nipples and the swollen crest below, and she could feel his iron hot erection throbbing in her, pulse by pulse by pulse. Exquisite moments passed, and she softened with desire. He bent forward over her and whispered hot, racy promises in her ear.

It was more than she could bear. She murmured something, "hurry," maybe, and he began driving, stroking her rigid crest as he thrust in and out. He pounded against her, strong and male and driven, and she gloried in his power. His thrusts grew wilder, and she absorbed them, amazed by his animal frenzy, and so astonished to discover that she craved him that she called out for more.

For his hand—clever and relentless and in rhythm with his thrusts—was compelling her to a more profound release than any she had felt. He rent her, opened her, widened her, and then she closed around him, pulsing, gasping, shattering when he did, and they collapsed together on their sides. Stunned. She was stunned. He seemed as stunned as she. His arms encircled her, and his leg hooked over her hip, and he nestled her back and bottom into the curve he made for her between his chest and his knees.

She loved him, she murmured, slick and hot and wild. Tender, mad, and sure. They drifted together like summer clouds above a grassy paddock, over the ocean's waves at the foot of the chalk cliffs, elemental and at one.

She rolled her head against the damask pillowslip, relieved to know something so very intimate about her husband. He could lose control. Even better, he was just as neck or nothing in his bed as he was on a horse.

Relieved, too, as she luxuriated in his warm embrace, about one more pressing matter. She wound her fingers about his hand that rested on her breast, and whispered with all the tenderness in her being, "I do trust you, Henry." She sighed, contented, and stretched a leg alongside his long one, feeling for the bump of his knee and the point of his ankle. "You couldn't possibly have been the one to shear that spoke."

Chapter Twenty-five

Do passive, indolent women make the best wives?
  —Mary Wollstonecraft, *Vindication of the Rights of Woman*

Henry rested, emptied and replete, awash in remorse and self-condemnation. His country wench had just transported him beyond his most private, fevered fantasies into untold bliss.

And for that, he'd risked the one certainty of his life and exposed them to the dreadful prospect of having a mad child. Stupid, selfish lout.

His heart's hammering slowed. Through a daze of sensual exhaustion, Henry heard *I do trust you,* and his gut twisted. She shouldn't trust him. He could barely trust himself. He'd faced madness all his life, and fended it off as best he could. No heirs, no byblows. All precautions.

Until Julia. For her, he'd caved like a house of straw. What would a mad heir do to his family? What would a mad child do to Julia, so forthright and full of life and aching to live like a man? he tormented himself.

So he'd been unprepared when she'd gone on with languid confidence, "You couldn't possibly have been the one to shear that spoke."

He hadn't flinched, a tribute to his decades of self-control. "Of course, I wasn't." He forced a tone of wry amusement to match her lazy cool.

She half rolled over to face him, her gaze narrowing with accusation. "But you knew, didn't you, and you didn't tell me."

Of course, he hadn't told her. Between the broken spoke and the falling rocks, he was watching, waiting, looking out for evidence and finding none. "Didn't want to worry you."

"I'm worried now."

He didn't want to pursue the subject but couldn't help asking, "How long have you known?"

She shrugged off his question. "Not long."

"What exactly do you know?"

"On your phaeton, on our wedding day, you found a spoke that had been cut. A spoke not damaged by almost crashing into that tree."

"You know that for a fact." He'd seen the severed spoke and still didn't know what happened.

"I heard it as a rumor. I'm sure my source was all mixed up."

"Rumors don't drift in on the ocean breeze. They have bearers," he pointed out. He didn't want to suspect her. He couldn't. Not after their night of love.

"I won't bear the story outside our bedchamber. If I hear another word of it, I'll stamp it out."

She turned in the circle of his arms and nuzzled into his chest as if seeking comfort. As if she wanted him to love her again. Another proof of innocence? he wondered. If he weren't such a cad, he wouldn't even speculate. If he hadn't been such a selfish bounder, he wouldn't tell her what he had to next.

"No more, Julia. We cannot risk this again."

Hurt rimmed her steady gaze. "Not even kissing?"

His heart pinched. "Given where that leads us, no," he said, trying to sound firm instead of regretful. Convinced, rather than assailed with doubt. "It's too great a risk."

"What's it going to take with you, Henry?" she cried, her body no longer pliant in his arms. "I give you my trust, my body, everything, and you turn away."

"We have to wait a month, six weeks, until we know you're not with child. Until then, we return to what we were doing."

"Training for our match race," she said bleakly.

"Yes, training for our race." Limb by limb, finger by finger, he reluctantly disengaged from her charms. But not from her demands.

"I need another week."

He raised a brow. "I thought you stood by your deals."

"If we go on as scheduled, Minx will be in season again, as it was that morning we raced on the shore."

"You're afraid you can't handle her."

"Can you control Hazard? I just want to beat you fair and square."

He wanted to argue, but saw her point. "One extra week, three weeks in all."

"And Isabeau's lessons? I want her riding outside the ménage," she said.

"She's not ready for that."

"You're not ready for that. She is. She's making remarkable progress, even if she's not yet ready for you to see."

"You must take someone along for safety. And I don't mean my daughter's little friend. It's past time for that to stop."

Her eyes flashed, insulted by his insinuation. "Jem Guthrie, then."

"No, Wat Nance. He knows the estate."

She lifted her chin, apparently accepting his terms without approving of them. Then she scooted to the far side of the bed and pulled on a concealing cotton nightshift, the beauty of her body unlit by the dwindling fire. He didn't need a fire. He still could see her body moving beneath the tent-like shelter of her shift. Jaunty breasts, shapely legs, tempting bottom. She thought he was indifferent. Hardly. He would want her morning, noon, and night.

But he went on otherwise. "And Julia?"

She looked at him, unable to hide her hurt.

"You're a desirable woman. You proved you can seduce me. Don't try seducing me again."

She threw a heavy robe over her thick cotton, jammed herself under the covers, and lay silent as a brick.

He lay silent, too, questioning his judgment. He wanted to believe that Julia had only lately heard of that damnable spoke. He wanted to trust her. But independent spirit that she was, she'd gone behind his back in many ways. Up to now, they'd seemed harmless—rebellious, yes—but never mean, or criminal. She'd given Isabeau secret riding lessons, and pleased her. She'd allowed Marie Claire who was less and less a problem every day. She'd plotted his seduction—and how could a man fault that? Then she'd involved his aunt—and who knew who else?—in a scheme to supply them with sheaths, to ensure they could make love.

His judgment warned him these things taken altogether made her suspect. But suspect of what? Wanting him? Or wanting to overthrow him? His heart told him it was not the latter. He flattered himself that she had not feigned loving him, and he cursed himself that he had caused her pain.

He'd have to make it up to her . . . if he could let go. For the fear that nudged him in the darkness of his chamber crystallized. Reason and control were the hallmarks of his life. For Julia, he'd thrown them out the window, giving her whatever she asked whenever she asked for it. He hadn't been able to deny her. But what would she want next? And how would he say no?

"It couldn't have been Julia, Cousin," Harry said offhandedly as he could. Erskine, elegant in his caped town coat, stood by his light town trap ready to return to London the next afternoon.

Erskine's refined features knotted in concern. "You suspected your bride of something?"

"The wheel, on our wedding day."

"Right, that. You found the person behind it," he said, in a hearty congratulatory tone.

"No. But whatever happened there, I trust she had nothing to do with it."

"I am so glad, Henry. So glad you trust your judgment."

But Henry didn't. His judgment had never been so called into question. He took another tack. "Now to see if I can trust my horse to beat hers. You are coming back for our match race. She's won over everyone else. I could use a man on my side."

"I wouldn't miss that contest for a bishopric." Erskine cuffed his shoulder, a mark of their old ties, and swung into his seat, his gleaming team of blacks snorting to get underway.

"Good morning, Jem. Good morning, Wat," Julia said, not even breaking stride as she entered the stable yard. The last guests left yesterday, and she had three weeks, less one day, to get Minx fit enough to race.

"You're early, ma'am," Jem said. With a look of pure disgust at Wat, he headed for the filly's stall. She didn't stop to straighten out their latest spat.

"Never mind, Jem. What with my duties for the ball, it's been days since I could get away. I want to check her out myself."

Jem huffed and stalked off. Julia watched Wat watching him, a bellicose expression on his thin face. She gave an exasperated sigh. The stable was at sixes and sevens. Her man and Harry's were at odds. Most of the visiting animals had carried their owners home, but many of the usual residents still grazed in paddocks and pastures. Squabbling stable boys spread fresh straw for bedding. Grumpy grooms led horses back to their boxes and their stalls.

The men's moods were nothing, Julia thought, to her state of mind. She was alternately weepy and rejected, and plotting murder. Well, not *murder* per se. She and Henry would never murder each other. They would just murder love. But still . . . why hadn't Henry trusted her with the news about his phaeton? Why had she found out about it from his cousin? His lack of confidence made her stomach queasy. She had fretted over his fussy daughter and accommodated both his addled aunt and daft uncle. And then—*and then*—she thought, indignation rising, she had contorted her body into the most unseemly, even undignified, positions just to please him.

After all that, he thought her capable of harm.

She entered her filly's quiet, dark stall with a feeling of relief. Minx, so spirited under saddle, stood quietly in a corner, placidly eating mouthfuls of sun-dried hay. Horses could be trusted, not like men. With a horse you knew exactly where you stood—or sat, if it decided to unload you on the ground. There was a bee, a barking dog, and a sheet flapping in the breeze. The horse evaded it. You didn't. You ended up in dirt. The horse had no ulterior motives. No overwrought rationales. No promises. Its needs and wants were simple: Eat, sleep, exercise. Exercise, eat, sleep. Evade the enemy.

She wasn't sleeping worth a hoot. The very thought of food—such as her usual morning breakfast of sausages and toast—made her stomach heave. And as for the enemy . . . she hadn't exerted herself in days, except that night in Henry's bed. She craved a nice brisk gallop over the downs. It always perked her up. Not so with Henry and their bedside exertions.

Instead of feeling better, she felt sore and used.

She laid a hand softly on Minx's neck, and her filly gave an anxious whuffle. "That's my girl. I know I was gone too long," she murmured, and a host of other compliments and confidences. Minx was beautiful, and Henry growing old. Her filly was steadfast, and Henry as unpredictable as the weather. She was light as wind, swift as fire, *cooperative*, and Henry stubborn as a goat.

Julia rested her forehead on Minx's sloping shoulder. "I will never, ever breed you to a handsome, well-built, false-hearted, two-timing stallion with an eye on all the other fillies on the stud and a mind to break your heart."

Not that Henry looked at any other women, either. Tears, real tears, held back for an entire day and night, slid down Julia's cheeks and plopped onto the sympathetic straw. "No matter how much you think you love him."

She'd been fool enough to tell him that she did. Had she really expected him to answer her in kind?

To hell with Henry Pelham, she fumed, running her hands along the filly's flanks, over hipbones, and down powerful hindquarters.

Over faint, thin ridges. Long, crisscrossed welts. Her heart plummeted. She removed her gloves and felt again, gingerly. The filly's sensitive skin shuddered beneath her hand, and Julia ran to the box stall's door and cried out over the top.

"Jem! Come!" Which was their long-standing call for help.

He rushed up, grooms and stable boys and Wat Nance at his heels. She let Jem in, and closed the upper and the lower door to shut the others out.

Jem stood in the darkened box, puzzled. "Don't ye need help, mum? Ever'body's ready."

She placed his hand on the worst spot she'd found, and watched his face flame with rage, a shadow of her own.

"What the devil?"

"She's been whipped. The question is by whom."

"We've all been busier than a swarm of bees. I had Thomas take her to her paddock, and walk her out for exercise."

"Thomas, from home?"

"Our Thomas, yes, mum."

253

Her mind spun. "Thomas would never—"

"—never hurt a fly, mum. There's deeper cruelty afoot than he's capable of."

She scrubbed a hand across her face. Thinking. "With so many guests, how will we ever know?"

"We saw few o' them, mum, what with the dancin' and the drink."

"But you stayed here?"

He ducked his head guiltily. " 'Twas good ale, mum. Every man jack of us slipped out for a toot."

Julia was furious. It was not the answer she wanted. "Tell no one. I will ride as planned. When we get back, cleanse the welts and cover them with cool, wet cloths. And you and Thomas guard her round the clock."

Jem glanced at the door. "What to tell them? You did call urgent-like."

She waved her arm. "Tell them I . . . found weeds in the hay . . . a stone in the straw. Tell them I was overwrought after so much company." She patted his arm. "I'm sure you'll think of something."

Jem slipped out, and Julia pored over the filly's injuries. Damn and blast. Who would do this to an innocent horse? And why?

She found her answer to that second question when she trotted Minx out across the downs. Her spirited filly shied at shadows, spooked at rocks. Julia got one decent gallop out of her at the end, and Minx quieted down a bit—only to panic on passing the ménage.

What had happened there? And how long would it take to calm her filly down? Julia enlisted Thomas to cool Minx down, and checked every square inch of tack before hanging it in the harness room. She couldn't be sure who had beaten her horse.

But she knew why. A distracted animal was a poor candidate to win a race. She believed with all her heart that Henry could not have done it, but she couldn't confide in him. He trusted his men implicitly and would deny they had any role whatsoever. He would probably guess Squire Purvis, and in any other set of circumstances, she might, too. But not after Henry's reaction to the severed spoke. The upshot of it was, Julia faced three weeks of vigilance to protect her filly.

Julia looked over the precipice and felt Galleon tense beneath her, eager to plummet down.

The Mad Marquis

Isabeau hung back. Never mind that the child's seat had improved every day in the two weeks since the ball, and that she was popping over knee-high logs and arms-wide streams with her father's flair for risk and execution.

"Perhaps big horses can scramble down and get back up," she said with grown-up certainty. "But Fidget's just a little pony."

"There's a safer path, my lady, just on th'other side of those rocks," Wat Nance said, seated on a sturdy cob. He nudged his cob over to the jagged crest of the chalk cliffs, and Julia and Isabeau followed. "You see. It zigzags down, so it's not so steep."

"Very inviting, Wat. Look, Isabeau."

Isabeau's blue eyes filled with patently fake fear. "Any steep is too steep for Fidget."

"Fidget's perfectly capable. Especially of a zigzag."

Isabeau drew herself up, her perfect posture commendable if it weren't so contrary. "He'd feel a lot safer with Marie Claire and Galahad along."

Julia had been waiting for that. "You mean you'd feel safer. But you wouldn't be."

Isabeau's lower lip thrust out. "I should like to see another pony do it first."

"As you well know, there is no Galahad," Julia said cheerfully. "Marie Claire comes only for luncheon in the nursery."

After Henry's censure, Julia had banned Marie Claire from riding lessons, satisfied that Isabeau took lessons perfectly well without her imaginary companion, and had only used her to gain attention and control. Every day, she insisted on her presence, only to drop the subject the instant an unexplored path or challenging jump captured her interest.

Today's lesson: cliffs and caves. As recommended by Wat Nance. Julia was so caught up in training Minx that she'd yet to see the cave herself. From the stables, a seaside trek had seemed a good idea.

"Go on," she told Wat grimly. "We're right behind you."

Acting as obliging guide and safety net, Wat pointed his cob downward. If anything, he looked amused. Isabeau's protests and Julia's stratagems of mothering had entertained him all week.

Isabeau held Fidget back and said in remarkably adult tones, "I am simply too young to take a risk like that. Aunt Augusta would most certainly agree."

Julia ground her teeth. No spoiled eight-year-old would outtalk or outthink her. "I don't, and neither does your father. He's pleased as punch about your progress."

"But it's steep, and I'll be all alone."

"You're far from alone, and I would never put you to a path too steep. You have to trust me on that. Fidget is a very clever pony on chalk cliffs, and Galleon and I will be right in front of you."

"You'll be very sorry if I fall."

"You'll be very sorry if you miss the cave. I hear it's ancient and mysterious. I'm going down. If you decide to join us, grab a hunk of mane."

Julia did not look back, sure Isabeau would follow. Galleon pricked his ears and picked his way along the gently sloping path. In moments chalky pebbles pelted down. Isabeau had changed her mind. Julia indulged a smile. Her strategy had worked, but it wasn't the way she planned to treat *her* children.

Her children? Where did that thought come from? She had no plan for children. No desire for them. She'd be an awful mother. Although she had to admit that Isabeau was getting under her skin. Worming her way into her heart. It was, in fact, deeply gratifying to guide the child away from the delicacy that had been instilled in her.

The waves slapped the flat shore lazily with the ebbing tide. A pair of gulls careened overhead, fighting for possession of a fish. A crab scrabbled across the wide gray sand.

Eyes dancing, Isabeau reined in her miniature mount. "That was . . . exhilarating."

Julia smiled down on her wind-blown curls. No I-told-you-so's. "Where did you learn words like that, *mignon?*"

"Aunt Augusta, I think." Very matter of fact. "Can we see the cave now?" It was a short trot down the shore.

Ooohs and aaahs echoed in its entrance, Julia's as well as Isabeau's.

"Pelham's best-kept secret, my lady," Nance said with a touch of intrigue.

The entrance was twice the height of a person mounted on a horse. Trickles of ebbing seawater etched a delta of streams in its floor.

"It looks like a dining room for giants," Isabeau said breathlessly. The tide had carved out uneven walls, making shelves and cubbyholes and steps. A great ungainly slab of rock jutted out, a giants' banquet table.

"Not very big giants," Julia observed.

Isabeau gave a pretend shudder. "Big enough for me."

They rode their horse and pony in as far as they could go, their hooves sucking in the wet sand.

"How high does the water go?" Isabeau asked, her words hollow under the vaulted ceiling.

Julia squinted, her vision sharpening in the shadows. "Way higher than that rock. As high as the barnacles go."

"Oh . . ." said Isabeau, awed.

And the child stayed awed, shrieking with delight when Julia urged her to trot the last few feet up the cliff, and laughing as they cantered home. Back at the stables, tucking her pony's saddle under her arm to hang in the tack room, Isabeau said formally, "Thank you, Julia."

This was a first. "For what?"

"For marrying my papa, so I could learn to ride. Can we go back to the cave soon?"

Her marriage to Isabeau's papa didn't feel like much of a marriage, Julia thought. She was dressing for dinner that night behind the screen out of Henry's sight in case he came in early. Which he had not done since before the ball. She'd chosen again one of her most straitlaced gowns, a high-necked ruby brocade that flattened her breasts and fitted like a suit of armor. Not that she needed one to repel her husband.

Running late, he slammed through the doors and dove into the dressing room without a word. Shortly he emerged wearing black dinner dress, neat and precise and devastatingly handsome, hands clamped repressively behind his back.

"For you," he said without preliminaries, and handed her a box.

His third gift to her in the two weeks since the ball. A handsome leather box, gilt-stamped, and with a little latch.

Puzzled again, she opened it and gasped. More of the family jewels. A diamond and ruby choker, and perfect for this dress.

"How did you know . . . ?" she blurted, before she could regain her poise.

He waved it off as a matter of no significance. "This morning you asked Gillie to freshen up that dress."

She arched a brow. "Spying on me, my lord?"

"If you say so," he muttered, then added awkwardly, "It was my mother's. May you wear it in good health."

"Why, thank you, my lord. It's beautiful," she said as gracefully as she could. But two weeks of repressing feelings in the name of duty put the devil in her. "If I didn't know better, I would say you're trying to seduce me. I should warn you, my lord. Unlike yourself, I can be seduced."

A half a dozen unreadable expressions played across his face. Formal courtesy won out. "I was remiss, my dear, in not giving you a few family baubles sooner."

"Baubles! These three pieces, alone, are worth a fortune."

He bowed with great ceremony. "As are you, my lady."

She laughed. "Fustian, Henry. You're either besotted, or gone quite mad. Mad, I think, much as I might prefer the former. After all, madness is the family curse," she teased, because she'd given up tiptoeing around her husband's prejudices and fears.

His lips pursed to form a word of protest, but he cleared his throat instead. "These jewels signify our family's station. My marchioness must have adornments worthy of her contribution to the household."

She simply couldn't help herself. Two weeks was her upper limit for restraint. "Does this mean our race is off? And I can go about my business?"

He scowled, an expression that emphasized the strong bones of his face, and made her want to touch the line of his square jaw. "It is my plan to beat you soundly next week, my lady, ending all debate about who does what and when and where."

"Beat me soundly," she scoffed, bracing to give him the setdown he deserved. "You've rarely beaten me by a nose."

But Aunt Augusta's gong sounded, and he coolly offered her his arm. "Time for our evening show of harmony, if not quite bliss."

Downstairs in the dining room, Isabeau was chattering. ". . . big enough for giants, Uncle Bertie. Big giants."

"An excellent adventure. You know, I explored that cave when I was a boy."

"Then it is truly ancient, just like Julia said," Isabeau commented.

Uncle Bertie peered at her as if unsure whether she was serious or teasing. Raj sat on his shoulder, bobbing his head as if waiting for a juicy phrase to mimic. A neat black and white monkey danced at the end of its leash. "Perhaps tomorrow you would like to try the zebras hitched to the donkey cart."

"Zebras are wild animals, Uncle, not suitable for driving with girls," Henry intervened.

Bertie Pelham seemed to notice his nephew for the first time . . . and Julia at his side. "Ah, the happy couple," he said beaming, and gave Julia an avuncular buss of approval on her cheek.

Happy couple, happy couple, Raj repeated, cheerful and content to have found such a tasty phrase.

"Careful, Uncle," Henry said. His light man-to-man tone staked his claim.

Some claim, Julia thought, and shrank a little inside. Here was Uncle Bertie, naively trusting that she and Henry were working on The Heir, and Henry wasn't even kissing her goodnight.

"Must we entertain that monkey, Bertie?" Aunt Augusta asked. Tonight her spectacles dangled on their proper chain, and keys hung from her belt, her world in temporary order.

Bertie pulled his monkey to him. "You've maligned this innocent creature every evening for a week, Aunt. He's not committed one single, solitary sin."

"It breaks out in shrieks! A positive detriment to the appetite. Julia, my dear, come here." She segued to another topic without missing a beat.

Julia reluctantly extracted her hand from Henry's warm, solid arm. She would not touch him again until tomorrow evening. That was their routine. Present a solid front at dinner, but afterward go their carefully planned ways. Henry and Uncle Bertie removed to the library for a smoke and port, and Julia wound her way upstairs to put Isabeau to bed. Afterward, Henry rode his stallion to the shore to train, and Julia went to bed. She made sure she was up and out at the crack of dawn before Henry came in to sleep.

"Yes, Aunt." Julia walked over to her, offering herself up to she knew not what.

Augusta Pelham touched the ruby choker, and her eyes shimmered with unshed tears. "Your mother's favorite. Excellent choice, Rayne," she said to Henry. "About time you showed your bride you love her."

Henry's sun-darkened face flushed. "It's no less than she deserves, Aunt," he said smoothly.

Fiona Carr

Blurry-eyed, Julia found her seat. Why hadn't Henry told her it was his mother's necklace? Why was he giving her specially meaningful presents? Why would he give her anything at all? This wasn't more of Henry running hot and cold. This was worse. He might be honoring his marchioness, but he was rejecting his wife. She hadn't seen a sign that he would ever crack again.

Neither would she. She would take what comfort she could in her progress with Isabeau. She would train her mare. She would race next week to preserve her old rights and privileges.

There was no hope for it but to win.

Chapter Twenty-six

In the name of truth and common sense, why should not one woman acknowledge that she can take more exercise than another?

—Mary Wollstonecraft, *Vindication of the Rights of Woman*

"Here's a present for you, ma'am," Gillie whispered, pulling back the bed's canopy to interrupt Julia's afternoon nap.

"Go away," Julia muttered, deep in a dream of a horrifying auction. Her father's London banker was selling off her herd. She had to stop that outrage before she attended to anything else. "Way away."

Paper crinkled. Gillie prodded. "It's just in from London, ma'am. We'll want to see if it fits."

Julia rolled over and blinked. "If what fits?" She was too tired for frocks, and she had to rest for tomorrow's race. Minx was still edgy from her beating, and had been throwing shoes all week—so many shoes that Julia suspected foul play. The filly had hooves like flint; her shoes stayed on for ages. Frequent shoeing weakened the hoof's walls, and created the risk of Minx throwing another shoe, which created the risk of bruising her sole on the rocks, which created the risk of laming her and losing the race.

Julia was now taking turns with Jem and Thomas guarding the filly round the clock. And she was constantly exhausted. "This, ma'am." Gillie plunked a large lumpy package wrapped in heavy paper on the bed. Too thick for a frock.

Julia turned away. "I don't need another spencer."

"It's not a coat, ma'am, least ways I think not. Come, come. Let's give it a look, even if you are a little out of sorts . . ." she urged solicitously.

Julia propped up on an elbow, drained and dizzy. She was just too worn out for anything.

In contrast, Gillie bounced with anticipation.

"Very well, take the paper off, and let's have a look."

Ever eager to please, Gillie untied the hemp string and began winding it round her fist with slow, infinite precision.

"Oh, for heaven's sake!" Julia exclaimed, coming fully awake and tearing into the bundle. She was a bundle of nerves herself, of moods and fears and worries. Never had she been so missish before a race.

Never had so much hung in the balance.

The rasp of paper tearing cheered her. She crushed the tissue paper lining in her fist and tossed it aside, revealing . . . a brilliant forest-green riding habit, with military trim and braid on the lapels. It alone would strike fear in her adversary tomorrow.

"Oooh, she shouldn't have," Julia cooed, taking out the dashing cap to match and setting it on her uncombed curls.

"She, ma'am?"

"Aunt Augusta, my fashion advisor."

"I wouldn't be jumping to conclusions, my lady. There's the card right there in the breast pocket, see?"

It had her name on it. *Julia*, in Henry's bold, aristocratic hand. Julia's heart thumped. What was this? A gift before the race? A bribe? A jest? She opened the heavy linen deckle envelope and slipped out Henry's thick, masculine notepaper.

Wear this in good health, and all safety.

Yours, R.

Blindsided, Julia lay back on the bed. How thoughtful. How kind. How *sneaky*, playing on her emotions the day before the race. Was this just more of what he had been doing for weeks, bestowing price-less family heirlooms on her for no reason whatsoever? Except possibly to scramble her brain. Dull her edge. Soften her determination.

Did he think any number of presents, of whatever value, would persuade her to throw the race?

Did he hope that she'd give up her dream?

"Try it on, ma'am," Gillie urged, romantic stars dancing in her eyes.

Julia pushed herself up, stood in her chemise, and watched. Gillie shook out the folds of the magnificent garment, then held it out for her. Piece by piece, Julia layered it on, buckskin breeches, weighted overskirts, and jacket of superfine.

"Oh, la, ma'am! It fits like a second skin."

Julia walked over to the glass beside her wardrobe to admire it, feeling tall and proud. But both waistbands were a little tight. "You'll have time before tomorrow, Gillie, to set these buttons over just a bit. I suppose men don't make the best modistes," she added disparagingly. But inside she felt light and loved. What a stupendous present. What if none of her niggling suspicions was true? What if Henry simply wanted his marchioness dressed in style for a change?

Gillie giggled. "Begging your pardon, ma'am, but you can hardly expect a man to guess a thing like that."

"Guess what?"

"That you're increasing."

Julia's head whipped around, rather like one of Isabeau's mechanical dolls. "I beg your pardon."

Gillie's face fell. "Oh, ma'am, didn't you know? You're tired and tearful and grumpy and . . . pink. That's it. You look so rosy. You have that glow."

"I always glow, Gillie. I spend half my days outside on a horse," Julia snapped. But a fine trembling had started in her legs, and her stomach went queasy with dread.

"Snappish, too," Gillie said bravely. "It's nothing to get upset over, ma'am. It's a natural course in a woman. But so quick! He must be some kind of a lov—" She clapped her hand over her mouth, then went on. "Everyone will be thrilled."

Everyone but her. And Henry.

"Of course," Julia said numbly. "Thrilled."

"I was just a bit worried, though, about tomorrow's race. You won't be riding now, ma'am, will you?"

Julia plopped down on the upholstered bench beside her wardrobe, the full force of her predicament settling in.

263

"Gillie, we don't know for sure that I'm increasing." But saying the word made it feel real.

"You've had no cycles, ma'am. I would know. I'm the one as minds your cloths. Of course," she added discreetly, "perhaps you're not as, ahem, regular as some."

"Perhaps . . ." Julia answered. She was regular as the tides, as predictable as her best broodmare's cycles. Tugging off her too-snug habit, she thought feverishly back through every dangerous encounter she had had with Henry over the last crazy weeks. She'd not come to him ignorant: She knew it took a lot more than kissing to get pregnant. And she knew it was too soon to know whether the sheaths had failed.

They had had that amazing afternoon in the hayloft soon after she'd arrived. He'd pulled out, and she'd been so reassured when he'd said nothing of it afterwards. But as potent a man as Henry was . . .

"It's hardly possible so soon, Gillie," she said, knowing the reverse was true. She couldn't afford for anyone to know. She and Henry had played with fire. Heaven help her, it had burned them both.

"But just in case, ma'am, you won't be racing him tomorrow, will you?"

Julia put on the brightest tone that she could manage. "A little ride this early couldn't hurt."

Gillie's mouth dropped in disbelief. "I never heard of such with ladies."

"With *ladies*—precisely. Lucy the scullery maid is going on six months. No one helps her carry bucketloads of water up the stairs to fill my bath."

"But ma'am—"

"And think of our tenants who toil in the fields. No one makes them sit knitting by the fire before they're sure."

"But ma'am—"

"In fact, I've known women to have their first pangs harvesting the hay. I'm no less able than they to go on with my work just because I married your marquis."

Gillie visibly drew a breath of courage. "About the master, ma'am. What would Lord Rayne say?"

"What indeed?" Julia answered, feeling for one moment indisputably in the right. She exchanged the new habit for her comfortable old one, only to realize that its waistbands, too, were a trifle snug.

Lord Rayne would never know. Of course when he did find out that she was pregnant, she'd be in for a royal dressing down. But she could manage that. Because she would be fine tomorrow. What was harder to manage, she realized with a surge of unexpected pleasure, was Henry's gifts. They touched her heart, the jewels and this new riding habit. They also touched a nerve. She knew now what she hoped for with her husband. Not gifts, but the love behind the gifts.

"Don't worry, Gillie. I've ridden every day this week not knowing, and nothing happened. I'll be fine. And if there is a baby, so will she."

"Or he," Gillie amended, her face crimping with concern and disapproval.

Oh, right. The Heir.

Guaranteed to recommend her to her husband, she thought glumly.

"You're late," Henry said at the castle's round turret, designated starting point for the match race.

She was, but not too late and not too sick to notice the fine figure of a man he cut upon his very handsome stallion. Beneath him, Hazard pranced, churning the rain-soaked ground to mud. It had rained in the morning, and threatened to do so again. Beneath her, Minx was a quivering mass of anxiety, just as she'd feared.

"Only by moments, my lord. I wanted to give you a head start. To even the odds," she said flippantly.

"Full of ourselves this morning," Henry shot back, amused and . . . Blast! she couldn't tell what else he might be feeling. Already victorious, perhaps.

A footman offered brandy in a silver cup. Henry knocked his back, but Julia declined. Nerves had had her heaving since the crack of dawn. Nerves, or her condition. Gillie's dry bread crusts and a nip of ginger beer had settled her stomach. But she held her breath when alcoholic fumes wafted near.

Henry raised a brow at her omission, but said only, "Shall we race, my sweet?"

"Yes. And may the best man win," she shot back, trying not to let his rare endearment please her. Or distract her from her fretful filly, who hunched her back and bucked each time Julia spoke. She couldn't soothe her with her voice or correct her with a crop. She'd never started a race at such a disadvantage.

"Cousin, kindly give us a start," he instructed Erskine Pelham, the tallest in the small uninvited crowd gathered to cheer them on.

Cousin Erskine? What was he doing here?

Why not have Uncle Bertie start the race?

And why the crowd? Who'd tipped them off to come? Her match race with Henry wasn't exactly a state secret, but *she'd* told no one. Until yesterday, she'd not been sure if Aunt Augusta and Uncle Bertie knew. Today, here were the grooms and stable lads, and Grayson, cook, and Gillie, and that host of giggling scullery maids. Oh lord, had Gillie told anyone that she was pregnant? Surely, she would not.

Worse yet, there sat the rector and the magistrate on their sturdy cobs. Squire Purvis and his sons, mounted on their strapping hunters, looked primed for a rousing race. Exactly who, Julia wondered, was rooting for whom?

"Best of luck to both of you, and safe riding to all!" Erskine's booming ministerial voice muffled in the damp. "Ready . . ." His handkerchief of fine embroidered lawn fluttered against the leaden sky, then dropped to his side like a wounded dove. "Go."

Swallowing back a rise of nausea, Julia gave Minx her head. Henry's stallion and Julia's filly bolted on the same stride, on the same lead. Hazard quickly reached the great, ground-covering stride she recognized from their gallop on the shore.

Minx matched it easily, and Julia put her mind to the race. Henry had set them a difficult course. Julia was more pleased than worried. It meant he respected her. It might even mean he feared she was his equal.

News for him! She was. A couple of days ago, he'd shown her the three-mile course, trotting leisurely around it, him on his bay hack and her on Galleon. It looked deceptively easy at a trot. At speed, it would challenge both human and equine skills. A dozen obstacles— gates, hedgerows, and streams—spread across Pelham's rolling downs, and the cliffs down to the sea and back up.

It was as difficult as any course she'd ever run. More difficult than she'd yet tested Minx on.

After the start, Minx effortlessly cleared the wooden gate into the mares and foals' west pasture and pounded up the slope of a high down. Just over its rounded peak, there was a deep copse of woods. Minx fearlessly charged into the trees and zigzagged through the twisting, narrow path carved out by generations of pastured horses.

Henry followed, galloping his horse easily, clearly confident of winning. She clutched the reins, palms sweating and hands stiff, the worst possible way to ride any horse, especially a high-strung one. Henry had every advantage, on top of the obvious one that he was a man, and not pregnant.

He'd raced hundreds of times. She'd raced a few dozen.

He'd ridden his own lands since boyhood. She'd ridden the course but once.

He had to know hidden dips and deceptive turns and slippery landings, any of which could dump her on the ground.

Julia's knees went rubbery against her filly's sides.

Would Henry have set her up to fail?

Breathe. She told herself through a daze of nausea she'd been fighting since dawn. Soften your legs, your hands, your back, and give Minx no resistance, nothing to impede her as she galloped joyfully in front, twisting through the narrow path. Nothing to let Henry think they were anything less than flat out.

The dark, canopied woods grew lighter. Just beyond, soft in the midday mist, a massive hedgerow loomed. Two days ago, she'd dared Henry to include it. She focused on her spot, low with level ground before and after, and urged Minx forward. Ears keenly pricked, the filly loped to the obstacle, vaulted into the air, and skimmed it with a fluid leap. Julia's heart soared.

See that, Henry Pelham! You cannot keep two good females down!

Henry and Hazard cleared it handily, too, and at the exact same spot.

Bah! Julia thought, he should pick his own spots. But she forced her mind ahead to the double-gated oxer, made of sturdy oak. They hurdled over it, then over two more jumps. At last she could see the sea, its pewter gray stretching south to the edge of the leaden sky.

Henry pulled even and shouted something she couldn't hear. Two days ago, he'd insisted on the easy path, the one Isabeau had conquered. "Safer," he'd said. "I didn't think you chicken-hearted, Henry," she'd responded, but agreed to that path for the race.

Safe was a sop for solicitous lords and their timid daughters. Riding down it several times with Isabeau, she'd studied its twists and turns, and planned a shorter path. She gathered up the reins, and pointed her filly off the track.

Harsh masculine curses were lost in the bite of the wind, and Julia's pulse rose with the prospect of a thrill. Balanced over her horse's center, she trotted her mare straight down. Through no effort of Julia's, the filly was agile and fearless. She'd been born with a wild daring. Half galloping, half plummeting, they fell, and Julia experienced a pure physical joy she had only known with . . .

Henry. In his bed. Horse apples! This was no time to think of him, and certainly not that way. What had loving Henry got her? Restrictions and entanglements. Worse yet, he was plunging straight down, too. Chalk pebbles pelted her fancy new habit and plumed, cocked hat. The steel of Minx's new shoes rang out when they hit stone. And a furious masculine shout thundered out over the waves.

Slow down, damn you! . . . No good . . . dead!

Or some such injunctions. Julia laughed, intoxicated by her filly's power, and her own. They made it down to the jagged outcropping of rocks that rose up in front of the cave, and Minx daintily trotted through them, ears pricked with interest and hooves placed with care.

Julia glanced back. Henry and Hazard were worryingly near, relentlessly at her fetlocks. The devil that would not go away. Her heart sank. She rarely lost, but this was what losing felt like. Never mind that she was no longer quite sure what she was fighting for. She fought off doubts, turned all her mind and energy to every race she had ever won.

Minx coveted the lead. Falling behind enraged her, and leading fired her up. And she loved a flat out gallop—Julia could feel it through the saddle and the reins. As they cleared the rocks and neared the open sand, Julia touched her filly's neck and softened her hold on the reins.

Minx exploded. Julia had no time to gasp or catch a breath or think. She bent low over the crest of the filly's neck and exulted in her power and her speed. She barely heard the sucking of her hooves in the wet sand or the crash of nearby waves.

So Henry's roar of, "Are you mad?" caught her by surprise.

His hand on Minx's bridle made her see red. With the horses' heaving flanks bumping against each other, Henry slowed them to a nervous trot, then a prancing, edgy walk.

The Mad Marquis

"What the devil do you think you're doing?" Julia burst out.

"Saving your life," he shouted, a sharp breeze whipping his words away.

"I can save my own life, thank you very much. You have no right to interfere with how I run this race."

"You went off course," he ground out. "That, alone, invalidates your win."

"You came straight down, too, and a much faster route it is."

"A much more reckless route, hazardous to horse and rider. You could have killed yourself."

She snorted, and Minx arched her elegant neck. "Do we look even remotely hurt?"

"You look irresistible," he blurted with the oddest mix of anger and desire. "But you are utterly out of control. I have no choice but to win this race by any means I can."

He pivoted Hazard on his hocks and spurred him up the cliff.

Yelling a battle cry, Julia wheeled Minx and lunged up after him. Pebbles spit down on her face like insults, as her filly threw her body upwards.

At the top raucous cheers and applause greeted them. Minx bucked in protest at the noise. Caught off balance, Julia dropped a rein. She bent to retrieve it and kicked Minx forward past the blur of spectators. Purvis and sons? Erskine? Jem? Wat Nance? She wasn't sure. She wasn't sure why. They had to know the risk of frightening the horses.

Each of next three jumps seemed harder than the last, a gate, a hedgerow, and a double gate for the bull. Minx cleared them handily, but Julia was growing tired. Blast her condition! She yearned to curl up on her bed and sleep. Not so for Minx. The filly stretched out her neck in hot pursuit of Hazard, her competitive nature aflame. She gained on Henry and his stallion, and passed them with an extra kick of speed.

For the next-to-last obstacle, Julia laced her fingers through the filly's mane. The river wound through the Pelham lands with steep, muddy banks and icy water, belly deep.

Minx skidded down the bank, hooves sucking in the mud, and splashed into the churning water, undaunted by its cold and flow. She lunged through the deepest part, soaking the hem of Julia's heavy skirts, and Julia urged her to the opposite side to home. To a win. To independence.

Chapter Twenty-seven

> Ever since you last saw me inclined to faint, I have felt some
> gentle twitches, which make me begin to think that I am nour-
> ishing a creature who will soon be sensible of my care. This
> thought has not only produced an overflowing of tenderness to
> you, but made me very attentive to calm my mind and take
> exercise, lest I should destroy an object in whom we are to have
> a mutual interest . . .
> —Mary Wollstonecraft, from a letter to Gibert Imlay

Julia plunged her mare into the river at breakneck speed. Henry
swore violently. His wife was reckless and daring and very, very
good—qualities he admired—and she was obviously having the time
of her life. But had she lost all judgment? Since she'd thundered past
him on the turf, he'd held Hazard back, hoping she would think she
was winning and ease up. She hadn't. But whether she slowed or
held the course, he had not the slightest doubt that he could catch
her.

Henry kneed Hazard into the stream, and Hazard charged through
the rushing water, gaining on the mare.

Julia's filly lunged across the belly-deep stream and struggled up the bank. Henry watched in alarm as her hindquarters sank beneath the water. Her head went down. She thrashed violently to right herself.

"Julia!" Henry cried, her name torn from his throat.

If the filly could only find her footing, he assured himself, Julia's balance was excellent. She would pull herself out. But his heart hammered violently.

He pulled beside Julia, but kept Hazard well in hand to give them space. The filly clambered up the slippery bank, her hooves sinking in deep mud. On solid ground, she flagged her tail and raced away, horse and rider safe. Relief swept him, but then his anger flared. He'd been a madman to race his foolhardy wife. He should have known she'd court danger. He could have bet she'd risk her life.

Snorting his displeasure at being second, Hazard bunched beneath Henry and cleared the bank in a single bound. Henry glanced down at the sucking mire beneath him. Gleaming dully on the bank, he spied two twisted horseshoes. Minx's shoes. The mud had pulled them off.

Damnable luck! Henry cursed himself for routing them through the stream. There was a perfectly sound bridge a furlong east. His bride was racing toward the final obstacle with no traction for taking off or landing. Worse yet, knowing she would spurn an easy course, he'd picked a nasty downhill gate for last.

No hope for it but to head her off. He laid his crop on Hazard's shoulder, and his stallion collected himself and stretched out his long legs. Large and strong and fiercely competitive, Hazard gained steadily on Julia's filly. Still, Henry was surprised. The filly showed no sign of flagging.

He pulled almost even, but they were too close to the gate for him to pull Julia over safely. Ahead of him, the filly lifted like a bird and cleared the massive five-foot gate, knees and hocks tightly tucked up out of the way. Julia sat her flawlessly, such a beautiful picture of harmony and balance that Henry almost set aside his fears.

The crash, when they landed on the other side, seemed to take forever. Each separate harrowing movement burned onto Henry's brain. Minx's right fore hit the ground and slipped sideways. Her hind legs skidded out. Half down, she bucked for balance. Julia—and the bridle—catapulted across the turf. All his life he'd seen men take falls and usually get up and walk away. But this was not a man.

271

This was Julia, his lover and his wife. Her jaunty hat with its bedraggled plume sailed off, alighting in the hedge. The bridle snaked across the ground. Her heavy skirts flew up, and she crumpled on the ground.

Horrified, Henry gaped at his wife's body. His stallion pawed, furious to jump the fence and follow the filly. Henry was furious, too, but he checked the horse, checked himself. He wouldn't jump until he could land clear of her. Her skirts settled slowly, like a peahen nesting for the night. She wasn't getting up.

Raw and savage fear assailed him. He aimed Hazard at the far end of the gate, but his stallion's mind was on the filly and he came in too close. A wild look in her eye, a riderless Minx bounded across the field toward home, her bridle gone and saddle twisted sideways. Its stirrups banged her flanks. Frantic, she kicked and bucked.

Hazard pranced in place, trumpeting after her. Crop in hand, Henry popped the stallion's haunches. From a near standstill, Hazard leapt the gate and landed. Henry vaulted off and raced to the still form of his wife, tugging his distracted stallion to keep up. Henry wasn't about to let the blighter go—he'd need him to ride for help.

Hazard, never one to take indignity lightly, blew out his objections in a snort, then trumpeted louder for his filly.

At the sound of a distressed horse, Julia's eyes cracked open, wandering from the stallion to him. "Henry," she mumbled sweetly, "you were right behind me." Her eyes widened, narrowed. "Blast it all! We were winning. We'd have beaten you if we hadn't slipped."

"Slipped! Minx went down like a rock. She could have crushed you." He was yelling with a desperation he rarely felt. If his wife could think only of winning at a moment such as this, she was the maddest of them all. But God, did she have nerve and courage.

And he loved her for it. Almost as much as he hated the fear that ripped through him, the lack of control that mocked him. He fought it back. Julia Westfall Pelham, marchioness of Rayne, was not his father. Not drunk, not despondent, not welcoming death with open arms. But she was reckless, careless.

"You might have won if you'd shod your filly properly," he pointed out.

She lifted her eyes to the leaden sky. "Anyone can take a fall in this dreadful weather—you as easily as me."

272

"My horse is properly shod," he said brutally. "Yours lost two shoes in the mud at the bank."

Her green eyes narrowed. "That explains it," she said mysteriously. "Explains what?"

But she was ignoring him, wobbling to her feet. He offered a hand, and she refused it. Then he noticed the bridle in her grip.

"Why the devil are you hanging onto that?"

Swiping her feathered hat up off the ground, she jammed it on her frizzed auburn curls and gathered up her heavy skirts. "To catch my filly, obviously."

Over his dead body. "I have men for that," he grated. He'd had it with her pluck and grit and independence. She could have been *killed*. To stop her—to reclaim her—he took her in his arms. "I have men for everything but this."

She felt damp and limp and vulnerable. But more, she seemed to welcome his embrace. And for the first time, driven by his fears and his admiration, Henry Pelham kissed his wife with all the hope and tenderness and yearning he'd denied for weeks. From her, and from himself. Her face was wet, her mouth was cold, but her tongue was hot when he delved past her teeth.

For sweet moments, his country wench answered his kiss whole-heartedly. Then she slumped into his body and fainted dead away.

He fell to his knees beside her on the close-cropped turf, a desperate dread cloaking him. Had she been kicked? He'd heard of this. A man could take a terrible fall, stand up, walk off, and drop down a few minutes later dead as a shot duck. He chafed her face with his cold hands. He couldn't bear to lose her. These last weeks she'd brought conflict and confusion and adventure to his plodding, controlled existence.

"Julia, my brave girl," he pled. "Julia, are you all right? Julia, my love."

Her eyes fluttered open, and his blood pumped through his veins again. Thickheaded lout that he was, he'd never noticed her dense long lashes, her irises green as the grass around them and the trees.

"I'm all right," she said, but her voice was faint.

A fine anger possessed him. "You might be. But I may never recover. Your racing days are over."

That threat roused her. She lurched up and shook her finger in his face. "I'll have you know, Henry Pelham, I am perfectly capable

273

of racing my horse come rain or shine, over any course you care to set us. Carrying your child didn't even slow me down."

Henry rocked back on his heels, stunned. *"My what?"* His wife was pregnant, and hadn't told him?

Pregnant, and still she had risked herself and his child on a ridiculous dare?

An iron rage pulsed through him. He hoisted her in his arms to carry her home, oblivious to her not-inconsiderable weight. Two strides later, the men from the top of the cliff galloped up. They looked crushed to find that the race ended on a fall—and vastly curious to take in the domestic mêlée unfolding before their eyes. Only Cousin Erskine showed Henry any sympathy.

"Put me down. I can walk as well as you," Julia insisted, beating on Henry's shoulder with a fist and kicking his leg with her muddy boots. Which made her hip bump into his belly and one breast jiggle against his chest. Which reminded him of the bountiful temptations that had driven him to tup her in the first place. Which should have been the last thought on his mind just now. But it wasn't.

Simmering with anger and desire, Henry stalked across the pasture past the mounted spectators. Ignoring them, he strode up and over a stile, and crossed the lawn with Julia well in hand. Except for the pointy elbow relentlessly jabbing his ribs.

"People are watching! Put me down now!" she hissed.

"I may lock you up," he ground out. "But I will not put you down."

Kick. Kick. Kick. She was nothing if not strong. "I am not hurt. I just lost consciousness momentarily. Haven't you ever fallen off a horse?"

"Not when I was pregnant," he said, through gritted teeth. "When exactly were you going to tell me?"

"I only just found out yesterday," she countered.

"And you should have called off the race today."

"Why? What difference could one day possibly make? I have ridden practically every day since the child was conceived, and no harm done."

"You don't know that everything is all right."

"You don't know that anything is wrong. Henry, I am not a hothouse flower, and all your worry cannot turn me into one."

They were hissing whispers at each other to keep their fight private. The spectators had caught up. "Therese was in bed for months."

And Julia was glaring now. "Don't you dare think you can make an invalid out of me. I'm not sick, I'm pregnant. Having The Heir is not a disease like smallpox or gout. You should be pleased. After all, you are the first to know."

"That's a comfort," he said acidly.

But he was having to work to stay as angry as he thought he ought to be. As angry as she deserved. He didn't want another sickly wife. And he did want Julia. Her body, safe and kicking and carrying new life, felt so damn good against him. And her fighting spirit spoke volumes to his own.

Henry crunched across the gravel drive in front of the household staff. Mouths agape, they stood in military rows and stepped smartly back as he passed. No one dared to breach their lord's black humor. Not even the loquacious Raj ventured an opinion.

But his bride didn't hesitate. "If you paid attention to my courses like an ordinary husband, you would have already noticed."

Fighting words. He couldn't be and not be a husband at the same time. "Oh, no! You're not blaming this on me. You're the one withholding information." Henry pushed through the castle's heavy doors, fuming. She was twisting matters to her own ends.

"And you're the one who never wanted another child, my lord. But you are not turning away from one."

"Just try to keep me from it," he said, stomping up the winding stairs.

"Even if it's mad?" Her words and an elbow prodded him.

"Depend upon it, Julia. This child may be the maddest Pelham of us all. But if it survives its reckless mother to the day it's born, I'll stand by it through thick and thin."

Which he had known he would do, hadn't he? He liked knowing it now. It wasn't that he could never love another child. He doted on the one he had. He had just meant to spare another child the pain of fighting against its nature. He was carrying that child at this very minute, inside his provokingly stubborn wife. Touched by the realization, he laid his pregnant bride gently on their bed, and started stripping off her muddy clothes.

"I'm quite capable of undressing, too," she protested, but she was weakening.

"Shhh," he said, and scavenged about in her wardrobe for something warm and dry. Then he bundled her in her warmest shift and

275

gown, glad she was young and strong and healthy and about to become the mother of the next Pelham baby. "Now, my lady," he said, brushing her lips with the quietest kiss, "give my child some rest."

A nap didn't seem to Julia such a bad idea, especially as he ordered it so nicely. She was feeling just a little tired, a trifle sore and bruised. "Henry," she pressed him, "please find out what happened with Minx. Her hooves are hard as flint. She never threw a shoe till we came here."

Scowling, he pulled the covers up to her chin. But she thought he said, "I'll see to it," just as she snuggled her battered body down between crisp, damask sheets. She drifted, images of each thrilling jump racing through her mind. She almost nodded off. Then her mind would flash on images of Henry, proud and strong, effortlessly carrying her—oh, it must have been a furlong—from that last gate to home.

She couldn't sleep. Her back and shoulder ached, and one thigh throbbed where she'd landed on a stone. An hour later, she was still gingerly trying to find a comfortable position. But her body hurt, and her heart. She was so confused about her husband. So attracted to him. So rejected by him. He hadn't wanted a child with Therese, and had positively refused to have a child with her. Now he vowed eternal loyalty to any child of hers, whether it was mad or no.

Loyalty to the child. Not to her, his lover and the mother of that child. She would not cry, she would not even fret. She was made of sterner stuff.

Still, how was she to deal with carrying Henry Pelham's child? After giving Henry her virginity, this pregnancy was the most indisputably female milestone in her life. Shocking as it had been to find out she was pregnant, she was already warming up to the idea.

She wouldn't be such a terrible mother, not if effort and good intentions counted. Look how well she'd done with Isabeau. She'd come to care for the girl in ways she'd never imagined. She took pleasure daily in seeing her grow stronger, and she prided herself on adding to her joys and happiness.

The hard part was Henry. Here she was, trying to prepare herself for the single greatest change—the ultimate miracle—of a woman's life, and Henry clung to his old fears. He'd already decided that she carried The Heir, and The Heir would be quite mad. A momentary qualm seized her. Horsefeathers! she told herself stoutly. Its father might be thickheaded, and its mother horse-mad, but this child would be as sane as any of the Pelhams.

She drifted off to sleep, comforted by the thought. Both she and the baby deserved a little rest. In the late afternoon she awoke to a crackling fire, and to Henry, keeping vigil by her bed. She propped up on an elbow, too aware that he had gowned her in thick flannels that killed any possibility of desire.

"What did you find out about my filly's shoes?"

"Nothing you didn't already know. Guthrie explained what happened and how you handled it." He took her hand in his strong one, and gently chided, "You should have told me about that, as well."

His tender reproach made her feel terrible. How had she even remotely suspected him of trying to throw the race? "We haven't exactly confided in one another."

He turned her hand over and made thoughtful circles in her palm with the pad of his thumb. "Time we started, don't you think?"

Very well. She could make a start. "Yes. Thank you for getting me out of a tight spot this afternoon."

His brow clouded. Wrong start. "That wasn't a tight spot. That was a brush with death. You will drive me mad, Julia, taking such risks as that."

"I did not take a single risk I have not taken before. I'm an excellent rider, Henry. Smart. Experienced."

The fire cast harsh shadows on the chiseled planes of his face. "Plunging down that chalk cliff was smart?"

"You followed right behind me."

"Yes, but I'm even more experienced than you."

"But not indomitable. Face it, Henry. If my filly hadn't lost her footing on that landing, we'd have won."

He moved in closer, his gray eyes black with anger. Or was it angry concern? She wasn't sure, but couldn't help a rise of hope that Henry cared for her safety. No such luck. "I was holding back, hoping to slow you down. Hoping to prevent exactly the kind of bone-head accident you caused for yourself."

"I caused?"

"You know the risk of racing a horse with hooves that bad."

"We both took risks. I'm not dead yet, you know. Or should I say—" she patted her stomach to remind him "—we're not dead."

Fiona Carr

He scowled. "There shouldn't be a we."

Despite every warning, disappointment pinched her. "Yes. So you've told me. Again and again. Which makes this baby even more of a miracle."

He groaned. "A miracle? Perhaps. Perhaps you don't know what you've gotten us into."

"I didn't make this baby by myself. As I recall, you did your part—and did it, I might add, as well as any stud in your stables."

"Damn it, Julia. This is not a joking matter. The damage is done."

"I refuse to think of our future son or daughter as damage."

"Obsessed, then. What if the child's obsessed?" Her husband buried his head in his hands, defeat in the lines of his shoulders. "I've told you about my father. I've told you how hard I've fought my own obsessions."

"Don't forget your uncle's."

"His, too," Henry said gloomily.

"Look at me, Henry." She stripped his hands away from his face. "If I told you you were wrong about your uncle, would you consider that you might be wrong about the rest?"

"I *know* Uncle Bertie has spells."

"You know he bars his door. I went in, and he is, indeed, very ill when he locks you out, but it's not melancholia."

Henry scowled in disbelief.

"He had malaria in India. He promised me his episodes are getting fewer and milder. But he guesses if you think him well, you'll expect him to bear The Heir."

Henry arched a brow in disbelief. "If that's not mad, what is?"

Julia threw up her hands. "If he's not, you're not. If you could just think of them as passions. You have a passion for the things you love—your horses, your daughter, Pelham. So does Uncle Bertie for his menagerie. You're no more mad than me."

He searched her gaze, almost hopefully, but the doubt in his eyes was real. "That's some comfort," he said ironically.

"I am not now and never have been mad," she persisted. "I am different, perhaps, from other women, and I take risks."

"Not with our children. Isabeau is more risk than I ever wanted. Thank God, she cannot inherit. The burdens of the title would destroy her, and she, in turn, would destroy the marquisate," he said darkly, and stalked over to poke the fire and nurse his fixed beliefs.

The Mad Marquis

Julia lost all patience. Henry refused to credit her hard work and his daughter's amazing improvements. "I guarantee this child won't turn out to have her fears and limitations," she said hotly.

Outside the bedchamber door, she heard a gasp. A latch snicked shut, and the lightest footsteps raced down the hall. She swung her aching legs over the edge of the bed and stood. Too fast. She swayed and grabbed for the great, carved bedpost, but Henry was on her in an instant, supporting her with his strong arms and lean hard body. "Julia, my sweet, if you would just take care."

She straightened, and stood on her own. "Not that your concern doesn't please me—" it pleased her to her *toes* "—but who could that have been?"

"Who where?"

"At the door, listening to our spat," she said impatiently. "Grayson or Gillie have better training, better sense."

"Of course they do," he said indulgently.

It flashed across her mind that he might indulge her so for months, a benefit of pregnancy she had not imagined. "Eavesdropping would jeopardize their positions."

"Of course it would. And they know that." Henry dutifully checked the door, looked up and down the hall. "Nothing. No one. You're overwrought, you're tired. Perhaps you should have dinner here."

But just then, Aunt Augusta's gong rang out, its heavy brass *ka-thong* reverberating through the castle's twisting halls. Julia turned to her husband, inspired by his support. "Mustn't disappoint the family." Then she smiled up at him, hoping to inspire him in return. "But you'll have to help me into my dress."

Henry escorted his pregnant bride to the dining room through Pelham's twisting halls without another word. He was so befogged that he didn't notice anything different—except himself. Despite his shock and doubt and anger in the afternoon, the oddest, most welcome chords of pride and hope and joy now churned in his chest. They were too new, too precious to examine.

He was going to have a son, a chance to begin again.

Well, perhaps not a son, but a second chance to have a family, without a doubt. Because what if Julia was right, and what he called his mad obsessions were merely passions? Even his obsession with her. Good God, he'd been a sluggard and a dolt, slow to learn and clumsy in the way he'd treated her.

Was it possible for a man to love again? Possible for him to love grander, bolder, and more freely a woman who was more like him than not, a woman who would match him dare for dare, risk for risk, and stand up to him in a fight? He'd never wanted any woman the way he wanted Julia. Her company, not just her consort. When they were together, far from seeming mad, it seemed so right.

That rightness, not the madness, was what scared him now. Because it meant he would have to change. He'd have to kiss his iron control goodbye. He'd have to lean a little, give a little, even—heaven help him—let her sometimes take the lead.

In the dining room, Henry found his aunt in deep discussions with his cousin, who had decided to stay the night. Uncle Bertie hurried in with Raj on his shoulder, murmuring apologies for being late. "Where is that child?" Augusta asked, heading for her gong.

"That won't be necessary, Aunt," said Bertie in formal gentlemanly tones. "I am solemnly sworn to tell you that Lady Isabeau feels rather too tired tonight to join her elders. She prefers taking supper in her chambers."

"Surely, she's not ill," Augusta said.

"She was fine before the race," Henry said.

"Is she feverish?" Julia asked, all of them talking worriedly at once.

Bertie looked from one to the other, a quizzical expression on his face. "Not ill at all, just rather pettish."

"My girls go pettish, too," Erskine interjected sympathetically.

No one minded him. No one minded Isabeau's absence, least of all Henry, who was still trying to balance the discoveries of his day and rather relieved to know his daughter was upstairs safe. But by the time dessert was done, when it was time to join his uncle and his cousin in the library for port, he missed her fiercely.

He wanted to hug the child he had and think about the child to come. Evidently, Julia did, too. She crossed her silverware on her plate. "I'll just nip up and tuck Isabeau in."

"Uncle, Erskine," he said, "no port for me tonight. I'll join my wife."

"Excellent idea," said Bertie. "Tell Lady Isabeau good night for me, and zebra rides tomorrow."

Henry bristled. "Zebra rides?"

The Mad Marquis

"Just bamming you, nevvy," he said. Then he cuffed Henry on the arm and wished all a sound goodnight.

Henry guided Julia out of the room, his hand at the small of her back. Actually he wanted his hands all over her. A sudden notion, as bold as it was outrageous, shot from his brain to his loins. His wife was pregnant, the deed was done. He had no reason not to tup her until dawn. Unless, of course, she proved to be too bruised and tired. Then he would defer. But hadn't she taken a nap in the afternoon? Hope sprang in his heart, and a more carnal anticipation lower down.

He bustled her through the castle's eccentric old halls, keen to see his daughter, but urgent to complete his paternal duty and take his bride to bed.

Nurse met them at the door, twisting the lappets of her mobcap into knots. "I was just coming for 'e, my lord, my lady. I looked everywhere, and she's nowhere I could think of, your rooms, your aunt's, the gallery, the courtyard, the chapel, the kitchen. I searched them all. Lady Isabeau, I greatly fear, has fled the castle."

Chapter Twenty-eight

> To be a good mother, a woman must have sense, and that in-
> dependence of mind which few women possess who are taught
> to depend entirely on their husbands.
> —Mary Wollstonecraft, *Vindication of the Rights of Woman*

Julia joined Henry, his aunt, his uncle, Grayson, Gillie, Rutledge, Mrs. Lafferty and their various underlings to search the farthest corners of the castle. Dashing up and down every crooked staircase and twisting hallway, they inspected each room on its different level and spread out to climb the half-dozen mismatched turrets.

It cost them precious hours to confirm nurse's worst fears.

And Julia's first one. Isabeau had run away.

"She was the one outside the door," Julia whispered to Henry. Already distracted, he looked mystified. "Before dinner, the eavesdropper," she explained.

His face darkened. "Damnation. How much do you suppose she heard?"

"Perhaps not much. But she had to hear my stupid remark about her fears and her limitations."

"No worse than my cruel blunder. I said she would destroy the marquisate." Henry said harshly, obviously furious with himself.

Henry sent Rutledge to assemble all the castle men and nearby tenants for a night search. Then he pulled on his great caped coat, and gave Julia a worried kiss. "Don't worry, we'll find her."

"I'll be down in a minute."

He frowned. "You?"

"Of course." She tried not to be affronted. "She is in my charge."

After all the sweetness that had just passed between them, Julia should have been touched to see him bank his anger so respectfully. "I could have lost you in the afternoon. It is not conceivable I would let you risk your life tonight."

She was too offended to notice. "I'm the one who taught her to ride all over the grounds."

"And you went where? The menagerie, the maze, the orangery, the shore? Did you ride the pleasure grounds?"

She nodded, exasperated. "We went everywhere. That's why I should—"

"Trust me, Julia. I know where to look. I've lived here all my life." Then his voice firmed into the most tender of commands. "You have had a grueling day, my sweet. You will stay here and rest, for both your sakes."

Tender, but implacable. Heart sinking, Julia managed a small smile. "I cannot fight your logic."

A relieved smile, a quick kiss, and he was gone.

She managed to restrain herself for half an hour, her nose pressed to the mullioned windows of their bedchamber to watch the search. Henry she picked out instantly on the obscure black shape of his stallion. His caped coat flared about him as he galloped from group to group, no doubt urging his men to look harder, faster.

Under his direction, clumps of searchers fanned out toward each location, torches streaking crazily against the night. She quickly made out who was walking, who was young enough to run, and who was on a horse. Five men headed toward the maze, three to the orangery. Another group's torches flickered behind the trees of the pleasure ground.

Suddenly she heard muffled shouts. Every torch turned back to the stables, and she could stand no more. She might be pregnant, but she wasn't sick or faint of heart or cowardly. She was young and strong, and Isabeau might need her. Probably needed her. Henry might never forgive her for taking another risk today, but if she sat idly by and something happened to his daughter, she would never forgive herself.

She threw on her boots and threadbare riding habit faster than ever in her life and raced through Pelham's labyrinthine halls to the stable. Men packed into the yard. She pressed past sleepy-eyed stable lads and rough-clad tenants. She was jostled, and she jostled back. "Beg pardon, my lady," and "Very sorry, ma'am," followed in her wake.

She was tall enough to see a small circle cleared. Henry and Uncle Bertie dismounted as she pushed through. Cousin Erskine sat on one of Henry's hunters looking grim. In the center, Jem Guthrie held Fidget, saddled and bridled and blowing hard.

Wat Nance, arriving late, pushed in to see. "What's this?"

"Isabeau's pony," Julia bit off, racked with remorse. It was true. Using everything thing she'd taught her, Isabeau had run away. Then she'd fallen off, and was lying somewhere in a ditch, as the chill night settled in. Fears mounting, she patted Fidget's neck, then inspected the little fellow for any sign of anything whatever. The bridle was intact. The saddle hadn't failed.

"She must have taken a spill."

Henry had gone inscrutable again. "Evidently, my lady."

"Seemed a very steady pony when I saw her ride," Henry's uncle said sympathetically.

"He is, day or night," Julia defended her old friend.

"Not this night," Henry said acidly, then turned grim. "God knows where he's been. And it's too damnably dark to track him back."

"The gamekeeper works at night, my lord," Wat Nance opined.

Irreverent laughter splattered around the stableyard. " 'Im and 'i' jug o' ale couldn't catch old poacher Cray," came from the restless crowd.

"Enough," Henry said coldly. Sober silence reigned. "We won't know until we try. Look for the pony's tracks near the stable. Check every door, every path and lane. Find which direction he went out or came back. My daughter's life is in your hands."

His tone was ice. The men stood paralyzed.

"Move!" Henry roared. "Don't come back without a clue."

Lifting their torches high, they rushed out in all directions.

The Mad Marquis

Albert Pelham, patient and versed in the ways of animals, sank to the cobbled yard and ran his hands down the pony's legs. He lifted a hoof and cleaned it with a pick. Standing, he called Henry back. "His legs are wet, nephew, and there's sand packed in the recesses of his hooves."

"Sand is everywhere on this estate," Julia said with dread. "And streams and puddles, too."

Nance dismissed her with a look. "Sand is nearer the cliffs than here."

Henry's face went white, and Julia clasped his hand. "Isabeau would not go that far. She barely knows the way. It could be a puddle, Henry. Fidget's like a duck in water. He'll walk through anything."

Bertie touched his tongue to his damp hand and shook his head. "It's saltwater, m'dear. This pony's been to the shore."

Henry swore the foulest oath Julia had ever heard.

"It was too dark for her to find her way," she said. Isabeau did not have the knowledge or the daring to go so far alone at night.

Wat Nance stepped up. "It's a straight road, my lady. And a near-full moon, save for a few clouds." His condescending tone set Julia's nerves on end.

Jem Guthrie returned, solemn as a stone. "One of the boys found tracks to the south, my lord, and tracks back. Naught else."

"Pony tracks?" Julia couldn't believe it, not in the daytime, and certainly not at night.

"Shod, too, mum. Fidget's the only shod pony in the stables," Jem said.

She exploded. "Where was everyone? Wasn't anyone watching?"

"The match race set us off our schedule, my lady," Nance said, not bothering to mask disapproval. "We put up early tonight."

"She learned her lessons in secrecy too well," Henry said grimly.

Julia's heart cramped in her chest. "Oh God, you're right. I sowed the seeds. It was just that you—that I—that she—"

His eyes filled with despair, his voice with self-contempt. "I was too careful. You were too bold. She is too young to understand. I will bring her back, and you will be here for her. She will need you."

He meant for Julia to stay. He meant she could not go. Shame flooded her. She'd failed Isabeau, and him. Double failure, double misery. "I know you know your way, my love. Godspeed."

Every man with a horse mounted. Torches aloft and the odd lantern here and there, Henry and Wat Nance led them out at a cracking gallop. Jem Guthrie brought up the rear.

Feeling useless, Julia drifted over to old Galleon. He placidly munched sweet-smelling summer hay. In the privacy of his stall, she sank her head on his powerful shoulder, and wept for Isabeau and Henry. He'd meant to do right by protecting his daughter. Julia had meant well, too, by challenging her to face her fears. Where his protection had strangled her, Julia's challenges had set her up to take the gravest risk of her young life. Julia had given her the tools to run away: She'd taught her to ride, introduced her to the shore, trained her not to fear the cliffs, enticed her with stories of the ancient cave.

Good God. The cave. She'd never told Henry about their visits. He couldn't know how it excited Isabeau's imagination. He couldn't know to go there. Oh, but he would be furious if she went now. His fury at her for taking a modest risk now would be nothing to his grief if he lost Isabeau, Julia reasoned. She could take Galleon. She'd ridden him along the exact path she would take tonight; he'd been steady as a rock. Henry could entrust her and The Heir to the noble old campaigner.

Even faster than she had dressed herself, she saddled Galleon. In the harness room, she found a traveling lantern, lit it, and mounted. Once outside, Galleon's ears pricked up as he launched into his rhythmic gallop. For a while, she could see the torches of the searchers in the distance near the shore. One by one, the lights blinked out. The men must have gone down the cliff.

Heaven help them think of the cave, she prayed, and heaven help her hurry.

Galleon picked his way down the cliff, surefooted in the moonlight. On the shore, Julia saw torches and lanterns gleaming to the east, away from the cave. Why had they gone that way? They couldn't be tracking the pony. Any tracks would have been washed out by the rising tide.

Julia turned Galleon west, her heart thudding with dread. She had to check out the cave herself. Galleon stumbled at the rocky outcropping, and Isabeau's full danger struck fear in Julia's heart. The incoming tide smashed against the rocks, obscuring smaller ones beneath its relentless force. Navigating the outcroppings couldn't be trickier, more hazardous. Had Fidget stumbled? Had Isabeau fallen and been swept out to sea?

No, Julia refused to consider that. Isabeau was here and needed her. She thought of the child inside her, thought of how strong she felt, thought of those women having their first pangs laboring in the fields. She knew her strength. She knew it was a risk. But Isabeau's danger was a certainty. And she was the only person around.

Holding up the lantern, she pushed the gelding toward the cave's black mouth. At low tide in broad daylight, the cave had seemed romantic. In the dark, the rapidly rising water terrified even her.

Suddenly cold seawater swirled up to Julia's thighs. She gasped at the shock, but Galleon valiantly plowed ahead. So would she, she thought, summoning courage. Above the crash of waves, she heard a high, thin cry, like the peacocks' song that had haunted her for weeks.

This cry was human.

The lantern cast the dimmest light upon the damp, vaulted ceiling and the surging waters, barely enough to see.

"Isabeau?" she cried, kneeing Galleon on in. "Isabeau! It's Julia, come to take you home."

The haunting cry echoed again under the cave's high dome. Slowly Julia swung the lantern, praying for a glimpse of the child. "Where are you, *mignon*? I need to hear your voice."

"Giants' table, we're over here," Isabeau wailed, her hiccupping panic striking terror into Julia's heart. The tide had immersed the great flat rock. But she roughly remembered its location. There, to the right, halfway to the cave's back wall. Julia lifted her lantern, and pointed Galleon toward the spot.

Isabeau stood atop the storied stone, clinging desperately to the barnacled wet walls. And to her imaginary friend. Julia shuddered. The water had reached Isabeau's thighs, and it was rising.

But the child was only a dozen paces away. Julia kneed Galleon closer. His chest thumped into the table's edge. Blast and damn, her new daughter would have to come to her.

"Isabeau, Galley's here to take us out. We need you to walk across the table."

"Marie Claire's 'fraid . . ." she sobbed across the surging tide.

"Tell her to be brave!" Julia urged. She couldn't get off the horse, she had no way to secure him. But they needed him for a safe escape.

So Isabeau had to walk to them through the roiling water. "Galley's strong. He can carry us out. All of us."

Isabeau stepped tentatively away from the safety of her wall, and buckled, swept off her feet by the outrushing water. Damn again. What hadn't bothered her strong horse was disaster for a little girl.

She disappeared beneath the tide. Julia's heart dropped to her stomach, and her stomach to her toes. In seconds, Isabeau popped up, drenched and screaming, and scrambled back to the wall.

"We tried, we can't," she sputtered, hysterical. "We tried, we really can't."

Julia thought frantically. Was the tide still coming in? Or was it going out? She swept her lantern high. It was coming in. The barnacles lining the cave's walls showed how much higher the tide would rise. They were over Isabeau's head. She could not possibly survive that depth of water.

Julia had no choice but to wade across the table and protect Isabeau until help came. She wished she could just carry Isabeau back and get on the horse and go home, but not even Galleon would wait, untied in dark, strange waters, for her to fetch the child. She would have to let him go. Which left one question. How long could she stand there with Isabeau's added weight?

"Julia! Marie Claire is *freezing*."

"You hold on, both of you. Hold tight," Julia called out, grateful for once for Isabeau's little friend. Julia ripped off her habit's heavy jacket and knotted its sleeves around Galleon's neck. If he would just run off and find the other horses, the jacket would tell Henry she was alive. But how to tell him where? she wondered frantically. If only she could mark the cave. But how? Her blouse was white, if she could find someplace to tie it. It wasn't as if it would help her against the frigid water.

"Isabeau, I'm going out to put a sign up for your father," she cried.

"Nooo." Isabeau's fresh wails pierced her heart.

"I'll be right back, I promise," Julia yelled, turning her horse to the sea.

"Don't leave me. It's so cold and I'm so scared."

"I'm not leaving you. I'll never leave you, precious, just hold on."

Panicky hiccupping sobs echoed off the walls, but Julia hardened her heart against them. Outside, the wind cut through her wet habit. By lantern light, she looked for crevasses, an outcropping, a wayward shrub growing out of the chalk cliff. There. One rock jutted out above the tide's highest line. She stripped off her blouse and gasped. The cold damp air hit bare skin. She stood in her stirrups and knotted the sleeves around the rock. A sharp breeze fanned the shirttail, and it flapped in the breeze.

They couldn't miss it. If only they would come.

Galleon couldn't miss it either. He sidled beneath her, his rock-solid disposition tested to the hilt. Back in the cave, she called out to Isabeau, "Isabeau, hold tight, I'm back, I'm coming."

A heart-rending whimper floated over the splash and surge of the sea.

Holding the lantern well above the water, she swung off her horse and stepped into water to her thighs. Confused, Galleon stood for a moment, then blasted out the whinny of a lost horse and wheeled away to freedom.

Thigh-deep in the water, Julia pushed against the tide. How had she presumed, even for a moment, that Isabeau could stand up to its powerful surges? And why were they so powerful? Then she remembered. Toward the back, the cave got deep and narrow, making its currents twice as strong as in the ocean.

At the wall, she swept up the shivering child and clasped her to her breasts. She was thin and fragile, and she babbled as she sobbed. "I should have listened. She told me not to come."

Julia locked her knees, braced her back against the wall, and stroked the back of Isabeau's wet head. "Who, precious?" It couldn't have been her aunt, she thought, or her nurse, or the cook. They would have stopped her.

"Marie Claire." Isabeau was hiccupping again. "She told me it was wrong, wrong, wrong. But I made my father fight with you, and I am going to ruin Pelham, too, and so I ran away."

"You didn't make us fight, and you are Pelham's brightest diamond," Julia assured her.

"You're going to get a boy, and nobody will want me then."

Julia was shushing her and rocking her and talking all at once. "We will always need you and want you and take care of you," she crooned. "And do you want to know a secret?"

"I s'pose," Isabeau sobbed, for she was still heartbroken.

"It might not be a boy. You might get a baby sister."

The sobs eased, but did not stop. Julia, growing colder by the minute, settled in for a miserable wait. The lantern burned brightly, so she turned down its wick, hoping to make it last. Even if Galleon galloped straight to Henry and his men at the far end of the shore, they couldn't get back for half an hour. But she had Isabeau in her arms, and they shared each other's warmth.

Such as it was. Julia lost track of time, but not degrees of pain. And Henry didn't come. Entirely too quickly, she could not feel her feet. Isabeau, warming, offered to teach Julia a round in French. Julia struggled to distract herself with the song's cheerful intricacies. Her arm ached from holding the lantern above the rising water line. The water reached her hips, every surge colder and more powerful than the last. Or was she growing weaker? She had already had a strenuous day.

"Again," she said stubbornly, when they'd gotten through the round one more endless time.

Henry hadn't come. Her calves began to cramp. Singing, her voice quavered. Isabeau shivered constantly in her wet clothes, but they clung to each other. Julia wondered how much longer could she last. Not much longer, she feared. She stepped up and down the walls to ease the cramps. She felt among the barnacles for better handholds.

"Sing, Julia," Isabeau begged, when Julia forgot to.

"Can't you get Marie Claire to sing?" Julia said sharply. The barnacles tore at her fingers and broke her nails, but here and there she found a grip. And one spot higher up was almost wide enough for Isabeau to sit on.

Of course. A ledge. If she could just find a ledge for Isabeau.

Isabeau had stopped singing. Julia shouldn't have asked her to sing with Marie Claire. These days, she came and went on her own terms. "I just thought she might like to sing."

"Marie Claire is gone," Isabeau said despondently.

"Gone?" Julia was trying not to shiver, trying to find a ledge.

"She promised she'd stay here with me until my mother came."

Julia's heart pinched with the sweetness of that thought. And she had come for Isabeau. And that justified everything. "It was very brave of her to keep you company. Where is she now?"

"She said when you came, I wouldn't need her anymore."

"Oh, precious," Julia said, her throat tightening with emotion. With a bright and glowing love. She had to find a safer place for her brave little girl.

The Mad Marquis

"So we have to sing together." They began the round again, and Julia sang and searched for ledges. The cave's walls were so uneven, its chalk so brittle, and its barnacles so rough. She could punch her arm into some holes up to her elbow, some ledges would hold a fat barn cat. Julia even thought of hacking out a place, but she'd left her only blade in her saddlebag. Then her fingers found a deeper hole, a wider shelf, a higher canopy than she had felt before.

Finally. Her arms trembling, she lifted Isabeau up, set the sputtering lantern beside her, and almost collapsed with relief. Isabeau was safe from the rising tide. Now she could concentrate on saving herself and Henry's unborn child. Resting her forehead against the wall, Julia stretched up her aching arms, grabbed onto barnacles, and sang.

Chapter Twenty-nine

. . . vice skulks, with all its native deformity, from close investigation . . .
  —Mary Wollstonecraft, *Vindication of the Rights of Woman*

Henry heard sweet voices first, then saw a feeble flickering light.

"Uncle, cousin, there, on the right. Come! They must have climbed up on the giant's table."

They. He could only hope. He hadn't had a glimmer of hope in hours. Then he'd seen that white shirt flapping at the entrance to the cave. Hope faded fast. The cave was cold and murky, and the icy ocean tides roared in and rumbled out. Julia's lantern was too dim and far away to show him anything, even her. If he hadn't heard the singing, he'd have thought the lantern the sole survivor.

He barked another order. "Nance, Guthrie, bring light. And quit your bickering."

Henry had yelled urgent orders at his men for hours, and was desperately hoarse. He'd been afraid for Isabeau until Galleon galloped up, Julia's hacking jacket tied around his neck. Terror for his daughter and his wife savaged his senses. Isabeau was the light of his life. And Julia—he could see this now—was his inspiration. She dared him to be the man he'd sacrificed to sanity and duty. If he lost them now, madness would be a blessing.

"Julia? Julia!" he strained for a reply. Surely that had been her voice.

His small army swarmed the cave, their torches and lanterns casting macabre shadows on the vaulted ceilings and the wall. "Steady on, Julia! We're coming. Do you have Isabeau? Is she with you?"

He couldn't make out Julia's response, and his stomach clenched with dread. The water rose to the horses' flanks. Another half hour, and they'd have to swim out of the cave. His strapping bay hunter plowed to the giants' table where he and Erskine had played the heroic childhood games. The bay bumped up against it. One by one the others bumped up, too.

"Shouldn't we get help, my lord, and fetch a doctor to the castle?" Nance's teeth were chattering. "I could bring back ropes, blankets, a cart to carry them home."

"Right," Erskine said, his booming ministerial voice pinched with cold. "You get the doctor and I'll come back with the cart."

"Excellent, go, both of you," Henry said impatiently. Action was paramount, and he was glad enough to rely on Erskine's judgment and be rid of Nance. His head man's worrying deliberation had slowed the search by costly minutes, perhaps hours. "And be quick about it."

They surged out on the tide, and Henry focused everything he had on Julia and Isabeau, please God, if it was not too late. "Hold my horse, Uncle. I'm going after them."

Bertie brushed him away. "Rubbish, nevvy. I'm as strong as you and fresher."

But Henry flung himself off his horse, too primed by fear for his wife and daughter to feel anything but the urgency of the moment. He pressed his reins into Bertie's hands. "Take these, damn it, and be ready when I return. Guthrie, gather round. I need you to help mount them on the horses." He said *them* desperately; refusing to believe his daughter was anywhere but over there, in Julia's arms, and alive.

Fixing his gaze on the one dark form he took to represent them both, he waded through the water. His boots filled. His thick buckskin breeches grew heavier with every step. In its relentless ebb and flow, the tide seemed thick as mud, as tricky as quicksand. His lungs ached, and his mind swirled with the maddest tumult he had ever felt.

None of that mattered. He reached the barnacled wall, and there was Julia, drenched, wearing nothing but a chemise and the lower half of some old riding habit. She fell against his arms, rigid with cold. He gathered her to him, her eyes black caverns in her face, her poor nipples taut beneath her pitifully thin chemise, her cold arms stiff, and empty.

Anguish cleaved his heart. He chafed her hunched shoulders, to rouse her. "Julia! Isabeau?"

Julia had just enough strength to lift her head from his chest and look upwards. "Sing for your papa, precious," she eked out, her voice thin and raspy. "Show him where you are."

The words of a French children's carol drifted down, a high angelic voice wreathed in faint lantern light. He stepped back to see her, stumbling from a sucking outrush of the tide, and relief flooded him. "Isabeau!" he called out.

But nothing.

Julia sagged into him. "She's cold and terrified. You have to take her now."

"Yes. At once."

But how could he leave Julia, her skin pasty white, her body hunched, deadly water swirling at her waist, and rising. When they said women and children first, they never mentioned such a dilemma.

"You're the one who's freezing in the water."

"She's the one who's terrified." Her voice scraped with the effort to speak. "I'm stronger."

He pressed up to her, trying to impart warmth. "I don't see how."

"What if the wall gave way? Take her, Henry. Hurry."

He hesitated, torn. He wanted both of them safe, he wanted them safe now.

"Henry, take her! The cold will stop you faster than you can imagine."

Isabeau's song faded. Entreating Julia to hold on, he propped her against the wall and reached for his daughter. She slid into his clasp. Her skinny arms were bands of ice, her thin legs clamped around his hips. Her bones felt brittle, like kindling under snow.

"Cold, Papa," she said, taking a chokehold on his neck. And summing up her need and trust in two simple words.

His heart opened. He had to protect her as he had never done. "It's all right, *ma petite,* you're safe now. We'll go home, and cook will make hot chocolate, and nurse will pile up blankets toasty warm, and you can go to sleep."

Her head drooped into the curve of his neck and she murmured, "I went under the water. Mama came and saved me."

Her mama. What new madness was this? "Your mama?"

"Marie Claire said be brave. She said my mama would come for me. And then she went away." Harry slogged through the battering tide, struggling to hold his daughter above the icy water. That wretched imaginary friend was a terribly trivial matter up against saving his daughter's life.

"Mama said you would come, too. We waited and waited and waited and sang and sang and sang. And here you are."

Henry's skin prickled with a brand new joy. She meant Julia. Julia was her mother now, and they trusted him unconditionally to save their lives. He said, his throat tight, "I came as fast as I found out."

Isabeau grew heavier, bulkier, and the tide more relentless. Julia was right about the freezing water: It only worsened. By the time he got to Jem and Bertie, he could not feel his feet. How much more miserable for Julia, who'd been here God knew how long. He had to get back to her, but Isabeau clung to his neck like his uncle's monkey. He peeled her icy little fingers off his cape and tried to hand her off. "Here, baby. Let Uncle Bertie take you."

Her face puckered to resist him, so he said, as Julia had, "Be brave, *mignon.* I have to save your mother, too."

Bertie Pelham swept the whimpering little girl into his arms. Henry slogged back through the miserable water for Julia, his uncle's steady patter of nonsense the only note of cheer in the somber menacing dark.

At the wall, Julia still clung to the barnacles, paler if possible than before. And weaker, all her amazing vitality seeping from her limbs. Summoning a strength never tested, he folded her stiff body over his shoulder. He loved her large and strong, but her very size made her dead weight a greater burden. Buffeted by the unrelenting tides, he slid and stumbled with her to his horse.

When they reached the top of the cliff, there were no blankets and no cart. Henry's benumbed brain dully registered something very much awry, but they had more pressing worries. Guthrie and his uncle had sacrificed dry jackets to his wife and daughter. Sharp ocean winds cut through their thin shirts. Now everyone was seriously chilled, none worse than Julia. Great tremors sometimes shook her. Then she went appallingly still.

Sending Guthrie on ahead to alert the castle, Henry tightened his exhausted arms around his wife and grimly headed home. He kept his courage up by talking to her: She was brave, and she was clever thinking of the cave, and she'd be feeling better soon. She never answered, not one word.

Aunt Augusta met them on the doorstep and bustled Henry aside. "Nothing for you to do until the doctor comes. You'll just be in the way."

A battalion of maids and footmen swept Julia and Isabeau upstairs. Chilled to the bone in his damp clothes, Henry tagged along. He'd never felt more useless in his life, but he could not let go. He burst through the nursery door onto a barricade of maids undressing his daughter, piling blankets on her bed, and stoking fires. He smelled hot chocolate and broth.

"Out!" said nurse. "She needs her mother, and her mother's taken to her bed, to die or Lord knows what!"

Summarily ejected, he charged down to his bedchamber. Julia couldn't die! He wouldn't let her.

His aunt had commandeered his private lair. He pushed in to a chorus of eeks and squawks. "Absolutely, positively no admittance," his aunt said in her most autocratic Pelham manner. "Gillie's a simple country girl, and she won't stand for you watching her undress her mistress."

Who was marquis in this establishment? he almost roared.

In truth, he did not know what to do. He paced the halls, changed his wet boots, and tried to warm himself with a flagon of his best brandy. He stomped upstairs; he banged on doors. His wife's and daughter's rooms were barred to his every inquiry. He was not the doctor.

Bugger all, he swore to the portraits on the walls. His haughty, mad ancestors looked down with bland indifference. He'd be more appreciated in his stables.

They were deserted. Either no one was back, or everyone had

come and gone. He had no idea; he'd lost all sense of time. Julia's devoted Jem was rugging up a steaming Galleon, still damp from the cave's high waters. Erskine's town trap had been rolled out of the carriage house. And . . . and . . .

Henry thought he heard an angry rumble from the harness room. He walked softly toward it, almost unconsciously arming himself with a pitchfork and a lash.

"It isn't about money," said a muffled, possibly familiar voice.

"It was always about money," answered one in a higher tone.

Strange, Henry thought. Disgust snaked down his spine, and a sudden creepy certainty. He cracked the door wider. He knew the voices, but he had to be sure.

"You were supposed to sow the seeds of discord, not try to murder them."

Erskine. Henry's world tilted.

"Nobody's dead. But I worked my tail off to keep them at odds, and I want more money."

Wat Nance. It instantly seemed obvious. The hints, the fuss, the worry had all been a front for their nefarious scheme—a clever dodge, even if Henry had been the victim of the cleverness.

"I can't see that you did anything that actually worked."

"The spoke would have worked."

Henry stifled a tiger-sized growl of mounting rage. And checked a furious parrot's squawk of disbelief. What an idiot he'd been, cosseting and consorting with the would-be agents of his family's destruction.

"It wouldn't have worked, you fool." Erskine said again. Henry struggled with incredulity.

"It takes two to make an heir. We only needed to get rid of one of them," Nance observed with chilling zeal.

"Foul play involving a marquis or marchioness would have been investigated. A damn good thing it didn't work. Besides, we had both of them worried over that," Erskine said with even more chilling ennui.

"I went to a lot of trouble to ruin that filly for the race. That wasn't in our agreement. But that is not the point. I need more money."

In a threatening voice Henry could barely hear, his cousin said, "There is no more money until I am marquis."

Henry dropped the lash, tightened his hold on the pitchfork, and pushed into the room. "Disabuse yourself of the notion, Erskine. You will never be marquis. The line of descent is recently settled. I owe you my abject apology, however, for raising your hopes these last years."

If Henry hadn't been so angry and appalled, he would have enjoyed watching Nance slither away between the hames and harnesses and Erskine skate around his announcement. But Henry's control was thin. He hung onto it fiercely.

"This isn't what you think, Henry," Erskine said, putting on his mask of urbanity. His false face, the one Henry had believed for years.

"By all means, explain," Henry said.

"I asked Nance to watch out for you. The way I used to do."

Nance sputtered, but no words came out.

"For pay," Henry prodded.

"For his trouble," Erskine corrected. "For keeping me informed that you were well. I always took care of you."

Henry smoothed his brow, and thought. They had been friends. Erskine, a little older. Henry, a lot more daring. He'd gotten them into scrapes. Erskine had gotten them off the hook a time or two. Or four or five. Was Henry forgetting something?

"I grew up some years ago," he said dryly.

"And you grew into the marquisate," Erskine said with that ministerial compassion Henry had turned to over the years. When he married. When his daughter was born. When his first wife died. When he took another. *I understand. I sympathize. Anything I can do to help?* A chill crawled down Henry's spine. Erskine continued, "Making you a . . . target for—"

"Liars, thieves, and would-be murderers?" Henry cut him off, without emotion. But he resented all of this, and resented it here, in his favorite retreat of fine oiled leather, polished bits and stirrups. In his safe home.

Erskine laughed, a forced laugh, Henry thought. "Gamblers, horse traders, unscrupulous women. Jealous husbands, for all I knew."

Henry tensed. He couldn't help it.

Erskine raised a hand before his face, at once defensive and derisive. "No offense. Jealous husbands never were your problem. But women were, and are. Some women would do anything for your title, to get the one thing you did not want—another child."

Erskine could not know Julia was pregnant. And he could not

298

poison the prospect of this next child. "My wife is my responsibility. You do not protect me by endangering her. The spoke, the race——"

"Quite right, an unpardonable mistake. I admit I had reservations about your marrying Julia Westfall. I erred in telling Nance."

"You erred in noticing."

Erskine waved off his remark. "Nance mistook my meaning. It got out of hand from there. You shouldn't have brought in Julia's head man, Henry. He threatened to replace him. That put Nance's nose out of joint. Still and all, you must admit, no harm was done."

No harm? His cousin's and his groom's machinations had cultivated distrust in his marriage, had set up his wife for a life-threatening fall, and . . .

Henry remembered what he'd come for—to discover what had happened to the promised cart and blankets. That is, Erskine and Nance's *failure* to come back to the cliffs with the needed cart and blankets.

And their skillful retreat from the cave.

And the way Nance had led them east to begin with, away from the cave.

Away from Isabeau.

Sense deserted Henry. Clutching the pitchfork like a cudgel, he lunged, knocking both men to the brick floor. He grabbed Nance's throat, jammed his fingers into his hair, and slammed his head against the brick. Nance slumped, but Erskine stirred. Henry, moving on instincts honed by training horses, swiftly shifted his body and pinned him to the floor.

"You sabotaged . . . my daughter's . . . rescue." He punctuated each phrase with a fist to Erskine's face.

Desperate, and not so citified as he pretended, Erskine snaked his arms free and clawed at Henry's face. Henry pounded back.

Erskine grunted apologias. "I was—ummph—stopping him—rrmph—he was acting on his own—urrff—"

All Henry knew was the burning satisfaction of smacking flesh and cracking bone. Erskine and Nance had set his daughter up, then hampered her rescue. Henry wouldn't stop until his cousin's face was a bloody pulp. "You snake. You lying, crawling, sneaking snake."

A pistol fired above them. Henry paused, too charged to feel alarm. But Erskine quavered.

"Pit viper's the more accurate classification, nevvy, I rather think."

Fiona Carr

Henry twisted round to see. Uncle Bertie lazily waved a smoking pistol, its ornate design suggesting Indian descent. "I'd like a nice viper for the menagerie, Henry. But this one is not worth the mice."

A surprisingly strong hand grasped Henry's collar. "Up, lad," Bertie said with a tenderness Henry had never heard. "We may be mad, but we're not murderers. Your family does not want to see you hang."

Not murderers, but not mad either, Henry thought, pushing himself to his feet. "Erskine—"

"I heard. Guthrie fetched me. The magistrate is on his way."

"I can pin the deeds on Nance, but Erskine was in London."

Uncle Bertie looked a little lost. Or perhaps he just did not have his parrot on his shoulder. Damn, Henry thought. He'd have to pin his cousin on his own.

Erskine pushed himself up—a broken nose, split lips, steely Pelham eyes slitting and turning purple. Henry was not displeased to see the damage he had wrought. But he had to finish right. Erskine had been family, and the best companion of Henry's lonely childhood.

"The marquisate was never mine to give away, cousin, not even to you."

Erskine propped himself on a saddle rack. "You fooled the bloody hell out of me."

"You fooled me, too. We can't go back, and you can't stay."

Erskine's broken mouth twisted, not into a smile. "I have no desire to stay at Pelham."

"I mean, in this country."

Erskine uttered an oath clergymen were not supposed to know. "You blighter. I'm going back to London, broke. And beaten. To an expensive position, an expensive wife, and expensive children whose prospects I must purchase. Are you satisfied, Lord Rayne?"

It could not satisfy Henry to exile his childhood friend. But his most pressing concern was his family's safety. "I want you out of the country. I want you never to come back. If you stay, I will leave no stone unturned to uncover anything you did to anyone, children born, unborn, or yet to be conceived. I will see you jailed, or hung."

Erskine gave a supercilious smile, one Henry had never seen. One that came from an inner evil, hidden all these years. "I am an archdeacon of the church of England. I married you, both times."

Henry thought of Isabeau's mother, innocent and gentle. And Julia, the mother of more daughters or his heir, virginal, vital, strong.

Erskine's blessings had been sacrilege. Henry's vows stood true.

Even if it had taken him weeks to see his way to Julia.

"I won't have a problem reporting your secular schemes to your bishop or your archbishop. And you can bet, or rather I will, that Nance will sing for me to save his neck. I will make you a simple offer—you have four children?"

"Four and another on the way. Two girls and two boys, so far."

"Make them my wards. I will place your sons to their advantage and marry your daughters honorably in England or wherever they may choose to reside."

"In writing?"

"Fine. I want you gone by Christmas."

Christmas, before his child would be born, before he gathered his family round in peace, before he decided that beating his cousin's face to a pulp was a paltry punishment for what he'd done.

Erskine gave a jerky nod, and limped out to the yard. Bertie was waiting there. Guthrie had trussed Nance in their best ropes and leathers and harnessed Erskine's team. Erskine climbed into his elegant town trap, and Bertie handed him his reins. He yanked at his wheel horse's mouth and popped the leader with his whip, the first time Henry had ever seen his cousin's horsemanship fall short. They trotted off, staccato hoofbeats on the gravel drive fading in the night.

Exhausted, Henry headed home to the security of his castle. The only two things he wanted in the world were to make sure his daughter was safe and sound, then fall asleep with his arms around his wife.

Chapter Thirty

> . . . I began to think that there was something in the assertion
> of man and wife being one . . .
> —Mary Wollstonescraft, from a letter to Gibert Imlay

Through the night and the morning and into the afternoon, Henry
tore himself away from Julia's bed and made brief visits to his daughter in the nursery. To his great relief, she was recovering fast. To his
great worry, Julia was not.

He hovered over her bed, watching for signs that she had not
ruined her health. In the middle of the night, the doctor had arrived
and strictly enjoined him from disturbing her. Against the pillow,
her fiery curls had been restored to life, but she slept the deep—and
please, God, healing—sleep of exhaustion.

Damned interfering doctor. Henry needed to touch her, needed
the assurance that her skin was warm again, her pulse pumping all
that energy to her strong limbs and stronger heart. She had saved
his daughter, had risked her life without a second thought. He hadn't
bargained to marry a warrior-woman. Now if she would only wake
and rise to fight again. Fight him. Him, most of all.

On their bed, she moaned and flinched, dreaming, he imagined, of the dangers she had faced. She curled up and whimpered, like a small, lost child. He couldn't bear the separation. He stripped down to his small clothes, slipped between the sheets, and carefully arranged himself around her bruised and battered body. He circled an arm around her breasts, melded his chest and belly to her back, tucked his knees into the bend of her legs.

Her body had warmed, but she was too damned still. As close as he was, her breathing seemed ragged, her pulse too weak, her color ashen. He made himself lie quietly, willed his breath to steady hers, sent his heat and strength to help her heal. He drifted with her. Slept. Woke when she stirred and turned to face him. The fire had gone out and his vast bedchamber cooled. From the slant of light through the mullioned windows, it looked like the middle of the afternoon. He'd rested for hours. He'd needed rest.

Her emerald eyes fluttered open, bright again. At the sight of him, they widened with dismay. "Oh, Henry . . . what happened to you?"

"Sorry. I feel asleep," he said drowsily.

"No, I mean this." Her battered fingers traced odd patterns on his face. "You've been clawed."

He'd forgotten his cousin's desperate fingernails. "It was nothing."

"It doesn't look like nothing." She propped up on an elbow for a better look. Her breasts jiggled beneath her nightrail. She looked rumpled, ravaged, edible. "What happened?"

"Nothing you need to worry about." She'd trusted Erskine. He couldn't tell her. She was not yet strong enough to know. "The doctor wants you to rest."

"Oh, no, you don't," she said, a shadow of her saucy self returning. "Don't start with me on that delicate-pregnant-woman-needs-her-sleep bit."

"You slept all day long," he said. "The doctor wasn't even sure you'd recover."

"I am recovering. But . . . Isabeau. Is she . . . ?"

"You took better care of her than you did of yourself."

"I feel fine." In her thin night rail, with her frazzled hair, she looked more than fine to him, like his country wench, come from a tumble in the hay, with her neat breasts and long legs and hot, quick passion. "But . . . Isabeau?

"She's in the schoolroom, teaching Uncle Bertie's monkey how to dance."

Julia worried her lips with her teeth. "And . . . Marie Claire?"

He wanted to kiss the worry away, not talk about his daughter's non-existent friend. "In hiding, as usual, when I'm around."

"Not hiding, Henry." She moistened her lips as if the cold had chapped them. "I think it's permanent, this time."

His lusty thoughts had fogged his brain. "Permanent?"

"Marie Claire is gone. She kept Isabeau company in the cave until I came. Henry, she told Isabeau I would come. Which is to say, Isabeau trusted I would come." Julia's voice quavered. He saw tears, heard pride.

She had his attention. "Of course she trusted you."

"Then Marie Claire told Isabeau that she was going away, that I would take care of her now." Julia pressed her face into his chest, her thick auburn hair silky against his shirt. Silky. Thick. Sensuous.

But he managed to say, "I'm proud of you," his voice clotting with tenderness. And hunger. It ate at his loins, gnawed at the root of his manhood, his need for this brave woman. Who was talking, not quite well enough, or experienced enough, to grasp his sweet suffering. He made himself listen to her.

"I'm proud of Isabeau. She was so scared, so brave. And to give up her imaginary friend . . ."

"She's getting you in her place." He lifted her chin with fingertips and gazed into her eyes, showing her the depth of his desire. "We're getting you."

Then he kissed her forehead gingerly. He couldn't hurt her there, could he? Damn the doctor's orders. He wanted her to be well enough to make mad, passionate love, here, in the middle of the afternoon.

She pulled away, scowling. "I am not an invalid."

And with that fearless adventuring spirit that aroused him to his bones, she proceeded to give him the very kiss he craved, not a proper sickbed kiss of comfort and well wishes, but a robust kiss, a kiss that told him she was well enough to tup . . . and ready, too. Ravening lust fired his loins. He banked it valiantly and waited for her lead. Her hot tongue rimmed his lips, explored the edges of his teeth, hunted the tip of his tongue.

He was in heaven. He cupped her buttocks with his hands and tugged her to him. "Uhhh," she groaned against his mouth. "Fell there." But she returned to her kiss, hands angling his jaws for kissing. "Ouch," he muttered. "The scratches." "Ummph," she said, and took the back of his head instead.

She seemed to want a long kiss, a deep kiss, a breath-stealing kiss that knew no ending, and he relaxed his jaw and let her have her way.

"I think you're going to be all right," he muttered when they came up for air.

"Why ever would you think not?" she asked, a little indignant, and a whole lot mussed. "I always sleep after I take a hard fall. Hours extra." Her color had returned, and the sharp planes of her face—how had he thought it mannish?—had softened with desire.

"And after standing in cold water for God knows how many hours?"

She lifted her chin. "Actually, I never tried that. And I'm not planning to again, not until our next wild offspring needs rescuing."

He put his hand on her still flat, still muscled belly. Despite his fears, nothing there seemed fragile. "And how is our next wild offspring?"

Her brow furrowed. "Fine, I think. No, I'm sure. Except for some stiffness here and there and the bruises you found, I feel fine." She sat up, pulling the sheets with her. "You still haven't told me who scratched your face."

He really did not want to talk about his cousin with his hot, recovering wife at his fingertips. On the other hand, when they next kissed, he wanted her full attention. With a groan he rolled over on his back. Stretching out one leg, he drew up the other, tenting the covers over his true aim and intention. Quickly, he told her what he'd learned and what he'd done and what a fool he felt at being so deceived.

"My uncle warned me," he concluded. "I didn't listen."

"I didn't either. We are well rid of your cousin. But don't blame yourself. Family loyalty—" she traced the outline of his lips for emphasis "—is not foolish. It's a positive virtue. Family loyalty . . . and love."

If family loyalty made Julia so bold, he thought, he would elevate his aunt and uncle, crown his princess daughter, and make his new son king. And if Julia was bold enough for this, he would let her set the pace for their afternoon dalliance.

Would they make love once or twice? he wondered idly, watching her green eyes darken as she figured out exactly how it was that a woman mounted a man. He exploded up into her, thinking, as she rode him to their finish, she had never run so glorious a race.

He had hopes for twice. Afterward, he spooned himself around her curvy bottom, extraordinarily content. His horse-mad bride was bent on transforming his world, on making it very nearly perfect.

Or so he thought, until she sighed. "Not a bad bargain we struck for a marriage of convenience."

He was still puzzling over what she'd said when Aunt Augusta's gong summoned them to dinner. They nipped upstairs for Isabeau, and he piggybacked her down. She giggled as she ordered him to turn or trot or halt. By the time they reached the dining room, Henry and his daughter were both a little silly. Henry found he couldn't keep his arm from around his wife, who, for all the giggles, seemed a little sad.

"Look at the table!" Isabeau cried. "It got squashed."

Harry scowled. The table hadn't changed its position or its length in his lifetime, and now it had been foreshortened into seating for no more than six.

"Aunt Augusta's handiwork?" Julia suggested.

"The carpenters for your new bedchamber probably needed something else to do," he prodded deliberately.

Julia set her hands on her hips, quite convincingly put out—and back to her well self, Henry was pleased to note. "About my separate quarters . . ."

He arched a brow. "Anytime you wish, my sweet—"

"There will be no separate quarters," she began, launching a new tirade. "It was a bad idea to begin with, and it's an even worse one—"

Henry couldn't stop himself. He cut her off with a crushing kiss, her lips already swollen from the pleasures of their afternoon. When he was done, she looked up with a glare. "If you think that you can control me with those kisses for the rest of our—"

With a smile, he repeated slowly, "Anytime you wish, my sweet, you can call off the carpenters."

"Oh," she said, flummoxed at first, then recovering. "I will call them off tomorrow."

Which would have been the perfect answer, but she seemed a little sad. Isabeau was tugging at them to pick seats at the new table.

The Mad Marquis

"I'm sure Aunt Augusta has a plan," Henry was saying when Uncle Bertie finally arrived, pet parrot and monkey on his shoulders.

Isabeau rushed over to them. "Do you know where Aunt Augusta is?"

"My lips are sealed." Uncle Bertie pressed his lips together as if he held state secrets. Then he set his monkey down and handed it its little drumsticks. At his silent signal, it began to beat the drum.

Enter, Augusta Pelham, a shy smile playing about her mouth.

Whatever Julia had been sad about, she hid it and gave a girlish squeal. "Aunt! Fancy you!" she cried out, rushing to embrace her. Then she held her at arm's length and looked her up and down. "Oooh, I should have bet you'd come through. I'd be raking in guineas by the buckets."

Henry blinked, amazed. His aunt was sporting a new dress. A modern dress. No belled hoops, no crackling starch, no threadbare silk or grim dark bombazine. Blushing like an ingénue, Augusta Pelham made a stately turn to display her fashionable attire. The fabric swept straight down from her bosom and showed off her slender dignity.

"I told you you'd look fabulous in crimson," Julia babbled on, more nearly feminine than he'd ever heard her. "And, oh, this figured silk—it's rich."

"It's Polly Le Brun who's rich," Augusta Pelham huffed, trying to look severe but failing because she looked so pleased. "How can such a skimpy bit of cloth cost so much?"

Henry strolled up and bowed over his aunt's hand. "Worth every guinea, Aunt, if you are hap—"

Meanwhile, Uncle Bertie, taking in the historic change, gave a long low whistle of appreciation. Raj mimicked it beautifully, and the monkey banged its little drum.

"She'll break hearts now," Bertie said lightly, as if confiding in the parrot, but loud enough for everyone to hear. *Break hearts, break hearts,* Raj seconded the notion. Bertie offered his aunt a congratulatory kiss on her cheek.

Smiling broadly, Augusta batted him away. "Shame on you, Albert Pelham, lying to an old lady. " 'Twas never about broken hearts."

Henry *had* always wondered . . .

"What was it about, then, Aunt?" Julia echoed his thought.

The smile slipped off Augusta Pelham's face, and old regret

showed through its handsome wrinkles. "I wanted never to forget the price I paid for not following my dreams."

A shiver of recognition caped Henry's shoulders.

Julia turned and gave him a speaking look. "This family needs more dreams," she said softly. "Even . . . miracles."

"Miracles, yes." The miracle was his bride, who made him question his old life. The miracle was the new life she carried. The miracle was that she'd provoked him into seeing himself anew. He'd always thought that mad marquises who fought for sanity couldn't afford dreams. Except perhaps with his horses, he'd denied every last dream he'd ever had—and his heart, and his passions, and his desire. All in the name of saving Pelham from its past.

He glanced at Julia. Would she forgive what a slowtop he had been? Perhaps. His heart warmed with hope. For she simply watched him, quietly, as if she believed he would figure it out. Suddenly, he did. Her dreams had always been enormous, and she'd fought to secure them tooth and nail.

He hadn't. He'd fought his family's ghosts, his ancestors' reputation, but he'd never fought for dreams.

His gaze locked hers. Her lips curved, but a shadow haunted her eyes.

"Time for dinner," Aunt Augusta announced, clapping her hands and ordering everyone about. Henry and Julia sat side by side, and close, with Isabeau between Julia and his aunt.

A bit irregular, Henry thought, but with the rest of his world turned upside down, this adjustment would be minor. And pleasurable. He imagined Julia stretching a barefoot toe to stroke his ankle, and envisioned long winter evenings ahead, when perhaps she didn't look so distracted when she thought no one was looking.

By the time Farley and the servants marched in with salvers and covered dishes of duck and roast and greens, he was starving. Well into the second remove, Isabeau chirped in her little girl's best grown-up manners, "I was just wondering, if I may ask, Papa. Since you and Mama didn't finish your race, who won it?"

"He did."

"She did."

Julia and Henry said in unison.

Rare laughter ricocheted round the dinner table. His, and their uncle's, and their aunt's, and even a little from his sad wife.

Bertie Pelham offered Raj a bit of cabbage and looked up. "When do you race again?"

"Each other?" Julia slanted a glance at Henry.

"Never," he said.

She pokered up. "If you think I'm giving up my privileges . . ."

"I think your privileges have just become . . . negotiable."

"I'd rather win them fair and square."

"You did win in the realm of spectacular falls," Henry said, hoping to tease away that lingering sadness.

"And down the cliff and across the stream and over every obstacle," she added, racing the race all over again. "Don't forget. I was winning when Minx fell. If we never race again, you must take that into account."

"You cannot say you won every leg of the race," he said, testing her.

"Correct," she conceded. "You had a head start to beat me up the cliff. And you won in the matter of hauling heavy objects across the lawn and up the stairs."

"Not as heavy as you will be—" he weighed his words, aware three pairs of eyes were watching him—five if he counted the monkey and the parrot—

"Henry, no! It's still our secret."

"Too late, my dear," said Aunt Augusta. "Last night he had to tell the doctor."

Julia glowered at his aunt. "He told you?"

Aunt Augusta shrugged, a little smug. "I did learn in the line of duty."

"Zebra's spots! I should have guessed," said Uncle Bertie, smacking the heel of his hand against his forehead—and beaming. "Extraordinarily fine performance, my dear boy, and not a moment too soon." Isabeau bounced in her chair between Henry's bride and aunt. Uncle Bertie slid a glance at her. "Best not for little pitchers yet, eh?"

Isabeau's lower lip, not seen in weeks, popped out. "I just hate secrets."

"She needs to know sometime," Julia advocated.

Henry blanched. Too formal, too real if his only daughter knew.

"You tell," she said, almost shy.

"We're going to have a baby, *ma petite,*" he said aloud. It was the first time, and his throat closed on a powerful surge of pride.

Isabeau brightened. "A sister!" Then drooped. "A brother."

Julia put her arm around her. "It could be either one, precious."

Isabeau shook her head, dejected. "You won't need me anymore."

"Because you might have a little brother? That's not the way it works. We'll always need you. What matters is that we love each other. Which we do. Don't we, Henry?"

"Of course we love you, Isabeau."

Isabeau gave a tentative smile. But Julia's look was challenging, and his aunt and uncle positively glared. What had he said wrong? They all loved Isabeau. That was never in doubt.

What matters is that we love each other. Which we do.

Which Julia did. It startled him like a starter's gun. How had he missed that? "Are you saying that you love me?"

"Of course she does, you nodcock," Aunt Augusta chimed in. "That's been obvious to us for weeks."

Julia drew herself up, comfortable before his relatives. "I did tell you, Henry."

"Yes, but we were—" he stopped. A man did not discuss such things, even in the bosom of his family. Especially in the bosom of his family.

Augusta Pelham pushed back her seat and stood, less bulky, more stately than before. "My dear nephew, a man may say he loves you in the heat of his desire, but a woman says 'I love you' from her heart."

Bertie seated his monkey on his shoulder opposite his parrot, and awarded Henry a mighty glare. "So it's time you got off your high-horse, nevvy, and admitted that you love her back."

Julia sat silent, uncertainty furrowing her brow. Where was her boldness now? Henry wondered. And then he knew. No wonder she was sad. Her boldness and her heart were in his hands, entrusted to the most thickheaded, reluctant man she could have agreed to marry.

Reluctant no more. He bucked himself up. "Well, then, yes, I do."

"Not good enough, old chap," his uncle said heartily. "Take it from one who knows. You have to say the words."

"Not that it's any of your affair," Henry sputtered, unused to condescending treatment in anything, least of all in matters of the heart.

"Zebras' spots," said Bertie. "The Heir is all of our affair, the future of our family. And by the by, Henry, don't sit staring at your plate when you tell your bride you love her. Stand up properly and say it like a man."

The Mad Marquis

Bertie Pelham snapped his fingers, and like magic, his dapper little monkey performed a drum roll.

To Henry's surprise, his mouth went dry and his heart thudded in his chest. He loved his wife. He hadn't planned to. And he hadn't told her. Telling her was the boldest dare, the greatest risk he'd ever taken.

So why not tell her here, for them to hear? His mad family had witnessed the most hazardous challenges of his life.

He stood, gave a formal bow, and helped her to her feet, a smile tugging at the corners of his mouth. She seemed a little stiff, but to his relief, the sadness slid off her face, and acceptance softened it. He never imagined loving anyone the way he loved Julia, and he certainly never imagined declaring himself before the world.

He took her hand and kissed its palm and gazed into her green eyes. They glittered with hope and . . . invitation. "I love you, my reckless, horse-mad bride," he said, and took her in his arms before his daughter and his aunt and uncle, and the monkey, and the parrot. "The sun and moon and stars are yours."

Julia pulled back. "And the horses?"

"We settled that."

She looked alarmed. "I didn't finish the race."

Sometimes it was very good to be marquis and have the final say. "You finished the race that counted."

She scowled, not yet trusting him enough. "The race that counted?"

"The race to win my allegiance and my heart."

"You're saying yes."

"Yes, to training, breeding, and even racing again some—"

She didn't wait for him to finish. She flung her arms around him and rewarded him with a kiss. Julia had gotten very good at public kissing, Henry mused as he welcomed her lips on his. He prolonged their latest demonstration for the family, taking full advantage of all he'd learned about her to slow the kiss and not go so deep, but plant some tasty promises for later on tonight.

Their daughter cheered.

His aunt and uncle clapped.

Raj chanted on about *the mad marquis,* and the monkey made an awful clatter as he banged on Aunt Augusta's gong. Madness. Merry madness.

If Julia's love was madness, he'd protect it for a lifetime.

311